SURE BETS

Thorne's boss in the Bureau told him the Chicago operation was a cinch. A computer would pick the winners in every sport, and the bookies being squeezed would start singing. No problem.

Greco's boss in the mob told him getting a lock on the spring football betting was a cinch to make the big money pour in. No way to lose.

Greco's pal, Pizza Sal, told him that one coke shipment from his buddy in Florida was a cinch to cure his cash-flow difficulties. No sweat.

But in a world full of rogue cops, double-crossing hoods, and women looking out for number one, the cinch was trouble. . . .

"Sharp dialogue . . . the curious alliance between lawmen and outlaws . . . a raw, no-fat shot of the Chicago crime scene, straight up."
—*Kirkus Reviews*

"The staccato pacing of George V. Higgins . . . the no-frills realism of Elmore Leonard . . . Richard Martins is a significant new voice in fiction."
—*Booklist*

COPS AND KILLERS

THE CINCH

Richard Martins

AN ONYX BOOK

NEW AMERICAN LIBRARY

PUBLISHER'S NOTE

This novel is a work of fiction. Names, characters, places, and incidents either are the product of the author's imagination or are used fictitiously, and any resemblance to actual persons, living or dead, events, or locales is entirely coincidental.

NAL BOOKS ARE AVAILABLE AT QUANTITY DISCOUNTS WHEN USED TO PROMOTE PRODUCTS OR SERVICES. FOR INFORMATION PLEASE WRITE TO PREMIUM MARKETING DIVISION, NEW AMERICAN LIBRARY, 1633 BROADWAY, NEW YORK, NEW YORK 10019

Published by arrangement with Villard Books. The hardcover edition was published simultaneously in Canada by Random House of Canada Limited, Toronto.

Onyx is a trademark of NAL PENGUIN INC.

SIGNET, SIGNET CLASSIC, MENTOR, ONYX, PLUME, MERIDIAN and NAL BOOKS are published by NAL PENGUIN INC., 1633 Broadway, New York, New York 10019

First Signet Printing, June, 1987

1 2 3 4 5 6 7 8 9

PRINTED IN THE UNITED STATES OF AMERICA

For Ellen Soeteber

Anybody's stupid,
they don't bet the dog at home.

—S. J. CATANIA

1

SONNY GRECO was stuck in the longest, toughest, absolute worst losing streak of his life. Just when he figured things had to get better, that nobody can lose forever, he picked up the call from J. J. O'Connor.

Pizza Sal had gone and got himself cracked.

"We have problems," the lawyer announced.

"You couldn't get down in time," Greco guessed. He knew the scam from way back: O'Connor claiming he was locked up all day in court, trying to save the vig with Greco's phone men by calling in after hours, placing his action head to head, even up.

"So who do you want?"

"Let's try Salvatore Joseph Catania," O'Connor said. "Tells me he belongs to you."

"Now what?"

"If that's yes, I'm ahead for the year."

"He's mine," Greco admitted.

O'Connor rustling through papers: sound effects.

"Area Eight Vice hit his house at seven-thirty. Mister Catania, they assert, was closing out an illegal sports book at the time. So the officers closed him."

"They got a case," Greco said. It wasn't a question.

"Sure looks like it. I'll have the particulars for you

later. I just wanted to get a green light before moving ahead."

Greco stared at the flashing buttons on his other phones, seeing each one as a debit, another negative number. What a goddamn week it had been. Monday the house got stuck thirty thousand when the Blaze opened at Soldier Field. No one in town thought they could cover six points; no one except Greco, who decided his customers were too down on local teams. So he went against the flow; didn't lay off a cent. Sure enough, the Blaze managed to gain sixteen yards total passing and woke up 35–7 losers to an expansion team of rookies even the computer hadn't heard of. Making it worse, Greco held back ten dimes on his own. It would take that much, more or less, to get Sally off and he still had to confront Johnny Roses with the Blaze move. Any way you'd slice it, whatever Greco tried was guaranteed to go straight south.

"Well, what do you say?" O'Connor asked impatiently.

"Where do they have him?"

"Eleventh and State. There's bond court later tonight. I imagine it'll take two dimes, maybe twenty-five hundred to bail him out. I can cover it, you say so. Or let him sit until morning. Whichever you want."

"Felony bust," Greco guessed from the number. Not since his baccarat move in Vegas had Sally beaten anyone for anything.

"Class two," O'Connor verified. "Seems the arrest team came in fast and hard through the back door. Some of Mister Catania's customers were still calling in while they were on the scene. But the biggest problem is they found him with all his paperwork intact."

"They got his sheets!"

"And about thirty-eight hundred cash."

Greco fumed silently about Sally's failure to observe rule number one: Never let them get your sheets. No matter what. Why the hell did they invent flash paper anyway?

"The fucker should rot in jail!"

"Then I'll wait until the arraignment," O'Connor said.

Greco took a deep breath and tried to calm himself.

"No," he conceded. "Get him sprung tonight. Sal may not be the best and brightest, but he stands up as straight as anybody. No sense letting him sweat the night with all them shines in the lock-up."

"There's a four-hour swing for processing, prints, warrant checks, all that," O'Connor said. "I'll try to speed things up a little, but I doubt Mister Catania will be freed before midnight. One or two, make it."

Greco stopped thinking about how to handle Sally's accounts and punched O'Connor's number into the keyboard.

"You're stuck seventeen hundred from last week," he said. "I'm taking fifteen off now. Consider it a retainer."

"Put a nickel of it back on the Pacers," O'Connor said. "They're a cinch to cover at home, and it's always easier playing with the house's money."

Think like that and some day I'll own *your* house, Greco sneered inwardly as he entered O'Connor's five-hundred-dollar bet.

"Pacers plus three and a half, counselor. You got it."

"Who do your people need?"

"I think the same side," Greco said. "Do me a favor, will you?"

"If I can."

"Tell Sal to meet me at Dead Dom's when he gets out."

"*Where?*"

"He'll know," Greco said, hoping Diane would see him after her shift.

"You got it," O'Connor said, mimicking Greco's clipped voice.

Comedian, Greco thought.

It took five tries to get through to Berwyn Bobby. Greco got right to the point, telling him to pick up the rest of the clear-outs. Bobby, as always en route to the track, started bitching about the sure thing he needed in the fourth race at Sportsman's.

"Pizza Sal got cracked," Greco interrupted.

"Damn," Bobby said, adding as an afterthought, "Hey, you know he won't talk to nobody."

"Least of my worries."

"Okay, I'll close for you. Who we need most?"

"Pacers, for one."

"That all?"

"If I knew the numbers, I wouldn't need you to clear out," Greco snapped. "That make sense?"

"Yeah, right," Bobby realized.

"Get on it. I'll call you later for the totals."

"Yeah, right."

If Bobby wasn't the boss's nephew, Greco knew, he'd be overextended stacking tomatoes at the Jewel. "Disorganized crime," he muttered into the dead phone.

Greco wound down his computer and changed programs. The way the family had set it up—probably sent someone to school for it—anyone searching for his book would first have to beat half a Martian Invaders game, then come up with a four-digit access code. He slipped the cartridge on the bookshelf between the twins' language lessons and walked into the dark kitchen. Mork and Mindy flew to the attack instantly, whining and yapping in alternate cadence when Greco popped the refrigerator door. For all he cared, the Yorkies could starve. But the twins cherished them and Camille swore it was healthy for them to do so. Besides, he realized, when Camille got back from Lauderdale, there'd be enough hell to pay for things he'd truly forgotten or never knew he'd done.

Greco threw the gray cold cuts back into the keeper and settled for a Heineken. The Yorkies held fast at his heels while he rummaged through the cabinets for dog food. When he came up empty, they got a full can of Mary Kitchen corned beef hash. Mork sniffed at it curiously; Mindy, the one with the pink collar ribbon, needed only a glimpse before whimpering back to her position on the sofa.

"Look, I eat this stuff," Greco scolded Mork, who took a tenuous lick at his bowl before he, too, retreated to the living room.

"Hell with you!" Greco hollered after him. If the hash was still untouched by morning, he'd try them on some scrambled eggs. And when Pizza Sal got back on the street, *he'd* have to feed and walk the damned things until the twins got home. The first step of his being punished, the first of many running through Greco's mind.

He went upstairs and dressed in corduroy trousers, V-necked sweater, loafers: very neat and off-hours executive, he thought, parting his sand-colored hair high, brushing it straight back. He looked down at the princess phone, but decided to call Florida in the morning. Better time to talk with the twins and, the way things were going, remind Camille not to empty out every boutique between Miami and West Palm.

"I'm only buying what we need," she'd assure him. But not until the AmEx bill came could Greco be certain how Camille defined her terms.

He finished the beer, collected his things from the dresser top: wallet, Piaget watch, the gold Tiffany dime-holder his phone men had given him for Christmas, just a month before Illinois Bell took its pay phone mutuals up to twenty-five cents a shot. Another stroke of fortune.

The March night was clear, damp, cold. Still-frozen trees creaked in the wind. Potholes buffeted the blue Mark VI as Greco headed eastward into the city.

Recalling Diane's refusal to fix breakfast and the empty ice box at home, Greco treated himself to an Italian beef sandwich at a stand on North Avenue. He ate standing by a counter near the frosty window, a cup of lemonade cutting the bite of hot peppers. In case Diane gave him a replay, he ordered a pepper-and-egg to travel, tucked it securely under the armrest as he turned north to Armitage and north again through the Latino neighborhood on Milwaukee, swerving around the double-parked clunkers that made the strip a slalom. Why worry about parking tickets, he thought, when you don't even have a green card?

Two miles on he saw the red, white, and blue OLD STYLE sign swaying precariously above the door of the Friendly Northside Tap. That's what the phone book called it. The only ID on the sign said *Package Goods*. Greco laughed as he slid into the parking lot. If people only knew what kind of packages were passed over the bar, what Dead Dom used to call "the goods" . . .

His kid was working the bar. Greco threw him a wave and headed for the last stool by the beer cooler.

"Your old lady still soaking up that Florida sunshine?" Dom Junior asked.

"Nickel-a-day's worth," Greco said. "I get any fan mail?"

"One guy dropped off a couple hundred. I think it was D-23. But I had to pay off too. So it's a push."

"Terrific."

"Diane's coming in at ten," Dom volunteered. "She had to drop the kid off at her mother's first."

"Do me a favor: mind your own business."

"Hey, sorry." Dom started down the boards but Greco called him back. He brought a vodka-soda with him. "Here, try this."

"Forget it," Greco said. "Little on edge tonight."

"How come?"

"Pizza Sal."

"Yeah. Couple a guys were in here looking for him last night. Sure looked like the muscle to me."

"They can't touch him now," Greco said, wondering who Sally had gotten into this time. "He's sitting down at Eleventh and State with a felony bookmaking rap to keep him company. That's for openers."

"We just *had* an election," Dom said. He reached back without looking and instinctively found the bottle of Jack black. "What the hell happened?"

Greco relayed what O'Connor had told him.

"He should be out tonight, for a couple of dimes deposit."

"Just what you need," Dom commiserated. "Any idea how they turned him?"

"Not yet," Greco said. "Could be somebody swapped his number for a free ride. Or they're running phone screens again. Or Sally didn't pay off."

Dom drank a quick shooter and refilled his glass.

"You gonna close down for a while? Wait until the heat's off?"

Greco shook his head, said not a chance.

"I may move some offices around," he said. "Maybe put all of them in a district where we've got some protection going. That's unless the feds start sticking their noses in too."

Dom stepped up and offered the studio apartment he kept on the side for card games and other sporting events his old lady wouldn't approve of.

"You could use my play room for a couple of weeks," he said. "Got a phony name on the lease. Set up an office there until things quiet down."

"It's a thought. Thanks."

"No problem," Dom said. "Family tradition."

"That's for sure," Greco agreed. "I can't believe Sally screwing up like that. Lawyer tells me the cops grabbed all his sheets. Everything."

"He should know better," Dom said. "If he was straight at the time."

Right on the money, Greco thought. Who else but Pizza Sal would do lines *in* the hospital, day after catching an attack of angina?

"We'll go over the figures later," Greco said, seeing the bar action heat up.

"Like I said, Diane's here at ten."

Greco sipped his drink and watched young Dom run the boards. He was built thick-necked, ox-like; except for the beard the image of his late father who, besides running the Friendly Northside Tap, had handled one of the largest horse books in town before his liver finally shut down. Dom Venuti, now Dead Dom to all who knew him, had become an area folk hero for the night in Sixty-eight when a U.N. team tried to stick up his joint. Three of them came in wearing ski masks—a black, a Cuban, some hillbilly from downstate. Dom sized up their Saturday Night Specials, figured maybe one of them might fire. Still, he fell on his knees before a dozen stunned patrons and started begging, pleading for mercy.

The banditos couldn't believe their eyes as the big man went down sobbing. They screamed at him to get up, open the register. Dom got back on his feet all right, with the fourteen-shot Browning Hi-Power he kept stashed under the bar.

It came up all cherries for the bad guys. Dom shot the first two without regard for race, creed, or national origin. Only the black dude survived, his wounds too grim for even the old Hearst *American* to report in detail. Something to do with his ability to sustain a relationship. Greco remembered it vividly. It happened right after he'd married Camille and started making mozzarella all day at her father's cheese factory. But instead of the night MBA program he had promised her, Greco began working as a runner for Johnny Roses, stopping at Dom's place twice a week. Christ, a lifetime ago . . .

"Later," Greco said.

He drove over to Clark Street, left some cash at another drop joint, fought the traffic hard to make it back by nine-thirty so he could catch Diane before she started her shift.

The place was full when he returned. Half the patrons were Greco's customers, via Dom's phone; some occasional, some compulsive. He knew he had to sit down and drink with them. Buy a few rounds, accept a few more. It was business. Dom's players were mostly blue-collar guys: not big, but steady. They paid every Thursday when they lost. Not like the flashy downtown crowd Greco dealt with at Fairweather's, the ones who tried to square accounts with markers and stock tips. Still, after a session with the crew at the Friendly Northside, Greco usually found himself thinking it was time to take a straight job.

Airlines Al was the first to hit him up. He came down the length of the bar, ear guards dangling from his work belt, a stack of pilfered flight coupons in his left hand.

"These are good for Florida," he said. "Just don't use them round trip. One way at a time, at the gate. I'll show you how to fill them out."

"Wish I could do it," Greco said.

"You got a month on them, at least."

"No, thanks anyway."

"Some other time," Al said. "Maybe we can do Vegas together."

"Sounds great."

Greco decided to wait it out in Dom's back office, but Fat Georgie was already next to him offering a drink.

"Gimme a Rhine wine and soda. And back up Sonny," he insisted.

"You drinking Rhine wine?" Greco asked.

"On a diet," Georgie explained.

"Listen to this one," Dom said as he poured the drinks. "Go ahead. Tell the man."

"It's the best diet of all time. Really works," Georgie began. "I lost sixteen pounds in four days. Swear to God, I did. What you do is start off in the morning with a quart of prune juice . . ."

"Can you believe it?" Dom asked.

Greco shook his head.

"It's not so bad," Georgie insisted. "The rest of the day you drink a gallon of apple juice. Get all the vitamins and minerals you need with that. You do this a week before you get back to solids."

"Wheeff," Greco gagged.

"But you're not supposed to get fucked up either," Dom prodded. "Like the other night, Georgie comes in and has a glass of rosé to treat himself. What the hell, light, he lost sixteen pounds. Then he has another with Airlines Al, another with Vinny, another here and there, and like that all night. Next thing I know he's downed a gallon of Carlo Rossi instead of apple juice, and he's moving in on Michelle the dyke."

"Bull-Mich?"

"I didn't know," Georgie protested. "She looked straight."

"You couldn't read her tattoos?" Greco asked.

Dom kept laughing. " 'Cause he got so wasted I found his eyeglasses in the urinal when I'm closing up. Musta fell right off his face."

"No more of that rosé stuff," Georgie pledged.

Diane walked in just as Dom bought them a back-up. She came straight over to Greco, gave him a light kiss on the cheek, and turned him down flat.

"I can't," she said. "Donny's coming back early. He called me this afternoon from New York."

"No big deal," Greco lied.

"I didn't think so. Anyway, you know the rules."

"Do what you have to do," Greco said.

"My loss," Diane replied icily.

Greco watched Diane slip off her jacket, tuck the thin lavender polo shirt inside her Sergio's. Her movements were slow, feline, sensual. He could understand why the dean of that college up in Wisconsin had gone bonkers over her when Diane worked the Cairo Club. Christ, before the auditors got him, he'd embezzled fifty thousand dollars of bursar's funds to tip Diane and the other girls for nothing more than some rub-downs and bubble baths. At least that's all Diane claimed he got, and Greco wanted to believe her.

"I'll catch you later," he said.

She came over and took his hand, a different, softer person inside a minute.

"Look, I'm not working tomorrow night," she said. "And Donny doesn't have to know it. Maybe we could do something. Go somewhere and talk."

"Sounds goods. I'll throw in dinner."

"As long as we talk," she said.

Greco watched Airlines Al look longingly at Diane as she shook up her first Margarita of the night, her breasts bouncing to the rhythm of rattling ice. How the hell did she end up at Dead Dom's? Then, too, how did he?

"I'll be in the office," Greco said. "When Pizza Sal gets here, tell him to come back."

True to form, Pizza Sal never showed up.

Instead, he rolled by Greco's place the next morn-ing, dragging himself up the long walk to the brick ranch house that filled a double corner lot on the better edge of Franklin Park. Greco, awakened by the anxious Yorkies, knew at once that Sally had never been to sleep, had probably tried working out his anguish by taking home a couple of ladies from the Cairo Club. He looked like death.

"Cops broke my fucking door down!" Sal bellowed when he got inside. "Kicked the living shit out of it. I had to go home and move some furniture around to prop it up."

"They're the enemy. What'd you think?"

"Yeah? Well they would've been responsible, some-body breaks in. I could sue the bastards."

"You have enough court time coming up," Greco said. "You let them get your sheets."

"Lookit, Sonny, they were on me in a second. I just ran out of flash paper that afternoon, had to use an old notepad I had laying around. Should have taken the cover off, I guess. Maybe I could've tried lighting it."

Greco gave him a wave that said "bullshit."

"Come on," Sal said. "What'd you want me to do? Tell my people they can't play because I ran out of flash?"

"Guess not," Greco conceded. "One-in-a-thousand shot you're gonna get cracked."

"Well I didn't cover it."

"You'll get off," Greco said. "But it's going to cost us."

Sal followed him into the kitchen and sat at the marble-topped Florentine table, rubbing its surface affectionately like it was his first time in the house.

"This is perfect."

Greco watched mute as Sal took a Ziploc bag from his pocket.

"Good thing they didn't find this." He laid out two six-inch lines, maybe a half-gram total, crushing the rock with an AT&T credit card. He did them both.

Greco said, "The feds would've been a lot more thorough. You're just lucky they were locals."

"They were douche bags," Sal proclaimed. "One of them turns on my speaker phone while the other guys are tossing my desk. B-16 calls in late trying to make a play. 'Give me the Knicks for three dollars,' he says. The cop gets real tough-like. 'This is Sergeant Bostic, Bastock, something like that. Chicago Police Depart-ment,' he says. So B-16 yells back at him, 'Look, I don't give a fuck who you are. I'm down on the Knicks for three hundred!' and hangs up on him."

Greco covered his eyes and moaned.

"Who the hell is B-16?"

"I don't know him to recognize," Sal replied. "He's been playing with us six months, maybe. Jeez, I thought that cop was going to shit."

"If only they didn't get your paperwork," Greco said.

"At least B-16 owes us three-thirty. Cops told me later the Knicks went south."

"Knock it off!" Greco barked, a losing battle once Sally's coke kicked in. "We got a real mess to figure out."

"I had most of it on back-up notes," Sal said proudly. "Coded so nobody could read them. Still got them home, too. Bigger problem is I didn't have time to lay anything off. Lots of late action came in against the Pacers, and they got pounded pretty good."

"I know," Greco said, thinking that at least J. J. O'Connor lost again. "We got crushed all over."

"Nothing I could do, Sonny. Swear to God!"

"Too late to worry about it. I should have dumped some Pacer action myself. So we both screwed up." Greco watched Sal fidget with the food bag. "How did they miss your stash?"

"Connie was there," Sal explained. "You know, from the club. She was in the shower getting ready for work when the cops hit. Kicked in my fucking door, right? Anyway, she hears the whole thing going down—guys screaming at me, reading me my rights."

"So?"

"So I tell them my lady's in the toilet. I guess they don't want to blow the bust on some technicality, like crashing in and catching her on the crapper. So Connie just stays in there flushing the bowl every two minutes, just to piss them off. Finally the cops get so frustrated they haul her ass out. By then, I guess they're figuring if we had anything, it was flushed

down the tube. So they don't even bother making a
full search. Like I said, douche bags."

"You live with angels. A charmed life," Greco said.

"That so? How come the cops got all my cash and
I've gotta pay out two dimes tonight? Or else."

"The guys from Dead Dom's," Greco recalled. "So
you *are* in trouble."

"Nothing major," Sally said, because to him, nothing ever was. "Not enough they're gonna start taking
fingernails. Not yet, anyway."

"I'll cover the payment for you," Greco said. "You
were there for me when I needed help."

Greco felt it un-American to carry less than twenty-
five hundred cash in his pocket, although lately his
sense of patriotism was getting tougher and tougher to
sustain. He counted out the hundreds and handed
them to Sally.

"Hey, thanks a lot."

"Cops pocket what they took off you?" Greco asked.

"Naw, can you believe it? They turned it in for
evidence. That mick lawyer you sent down tells me I'll
even get it all back. But he had to put up the bond
himself. Three dimes worth."

"He probably wants five percent a week on it,"
Greco said. "A lot of people going to wait to get paid
off."

"Goes around, comes around, Sonny. You've carried them enough when they came up short. Let 'em
wait."

Greco gave a shrug as Sally laid out another pair of
lines. He did one and offered Greco a crisp, tightly
rolled C-note that a minute ago was his.

"The family finds out you're fooling around with
stuff again, they'll be the ones taking fingernails for
souvenirs," Greco said.

"Yeah? What've they done for me lately? Go ahead."

"What the hell," Greco shrugged. He did a single
line and rubbed the numbing residue across his gums.

Sally said, "Where do we go from here?"

"We're meeting the boss tonight. Dinner," Greco replied.

"Tonight?"

"You be ready on time," Greco said. "And don't be so goddamn cavalier about losing your sheets. You know the way he gets."

"Jeez, tonight?"

"Why not?"

"I was gonna meet somebody and pick up . . ." Sally began.

Greco's searing look told him he'd better forget the whole thing.

2

ASSISTANT U.S. Attorney General James Jonathan Bidwell said they were going to use a billion bytes of computer power to beat the mob at its own game, going to break the bank of syndicate gambling and hang its bosses out to dry. That's why they were coding it Operation Clothesline.

Bidwell proclaimed, "What we have here, to use the vernacular, is a lead-pipe cinch."

Doc Hermann warned them that everything was security level five from now on in. All joint operations with local authorities were on hold; information sharing was to be kept minimal.

"No one outside the strike force is to have access to the data we're presenting today," he said. "If any of you talk in your sleep, move it over to the guest room for the next ninety days."

The requisite chuckles.

AAG Bidwell underscored the point. He spoke about leaks that had blown past operations, about compartmentalization and linear structure, and why they were doing it the way they were: corporate style, he said, with centralized management controls.

"It's not democratic, but effective as hell," Bidwell concluded.

Then he broke the region down into tactical groups, city by city, and made his pairings.

Frank Thorne couldn't believe it when Agent Mary-Agnes McCaskey of the Rockford office was assigned to manage his cover company.

"I'm only saying yes because we'll be working together," she told Thorne after AAG Bidwell moved on to the Milwaukee group. "An early dinner so we can talk things through."

"Strictly business," Thorne said. "You know me well enough."

"Yes, I do."

Thorne watched Bidwell ferret over to the Kansas City team, shaking hands as he went. Federal law banned smoking in the meeting room; Thorne tapped his PaperMate vicariously, like a Lucky Strike with rigor mortis.

Bidwell shook more hands and climbed back to the podium.

"You have your team assignments and operational law guides," he said. "Take the guides at their word. I don't want to see anyone blowing a case on a point of law."

Unlike Doc Hermann, a large fleshy man who reminded Thorne of a defensive line coach, Bidwell was compact, almost delicate. But he moved in a wiry, ready-to-pounce way seemingly modeled after Bobby Kennedy. His accent, Thorne knew from his Navy days in Norfolk, was Carolina Piedmont, probably refined at Charlottesville.

"Each strike team will report on a weekly basis directly to me," Bidwell said, adding as a conciliatory afterthought, "keeping Director Hermann fully apprised, naturally."

Whatever emotions the regional Director of the Organized Crime section (hence the acronym "Doc")

had about surrendering his command to some smart-
assed AAG from Washington were concealed under a
jowly smile. Thorne appreciated the gesture: classy.

Bidwell moved across the room, suit coat opened,
hands tucked inside his narrow waistband.

"Questions?"

Ted Jaeger, the brown-noser from Des Moines, asked
about operations in other regions. Bidwell told him
proudly that the central region was the spearhead,
that they would set the standards for the time when
Clothesline was rolled out elsewhere—New York, Philly,
the Coast.

"You are the vanguard," Bidwell said. "The shock
troops. Anything else?"

No one moved.

Thorne decided to sneak a cigarette. MaryAgnes
McCaskey frowned as he lighted up and smoked
nightwatch-style, hand cupped around the burning tip.

Bidwell launched into his summation:

"First we have to hurt them. Then, you all play it
right, we'll move our own people into the syndicate's
top echelons."

His delivery reminded Thorne of the sales pitch
Patsie once did for Mary Kay Cosmetics: short, punchy,
always asking for the order.

"This time we have the edge," Bidwell orated forcefully, waving his arms. "The taxpayers are going to get
what they expect from the Bureau—what they're paying
us for. We're cutting our way right to the heart of the
mob. The scalpel is in our hands.

"Let's go out and use it!"

Doc Hermann trailed along as Bidwell made a final
swing through the audience. Thorne guessed the room
had been stealthily borrowed from some IRS auditors:
gray metal desks arranged in tidy rows across the
charcoal carpet, walls of pallid, eye-soothing green.
Bidwell shook the remaining hands—Jaeger's, Olson's,
a few others, before pausing at Thorne's desk.

"Chicago is the key," he said. "I want the old man and the whole family wrapped up for the Fourth of July. I know you can do it for me, Frank."

"Yessir." Thorne dropped his cigarette to take Bidwell's hand. "The whole outfit."

"That's the spirit."

"Talk with you later," Doc Hermann grinned.

"He's kidding," McCaskey said as Bidwell left the room. "Isn't he?"

"Make no small plans," Thorne said. "Old Chicago motto."

"We think a little smaller up in Rockford," McCaskey said.

"Time to scale up, play the big time."

"Who do you think dreamed this one up?" Vic Olson leaned over to ask.

Olson was Thorne's counterpart in Milwaukee, a small, stocky man whose build and dark complexion belied his Nordic surname. "Somewhere along the way, a bitch got over the fence," Olson would say. Thorne liked him.

"Bidwell himself?" Olson asked. "Or did those computer whiz kids at 935 Penn sell him a bill of goods.

Thorne and McCaskey shrugged in tandem.

"I thought they were calling me in for a budget cut," Ted Jaeger said. "Not for something like *this*."

"Doc Hermann wouldn't waste the travel expense to cut your budget," Olson said. "You get a piece of paper from GAO, just like I did."

"Yeah, but Jesus, what an operation."

"You could always try private practice," McCaskey quipped to Thorne's delight. "Only a quarter-million lawyers working the street."

Jaeger saw Thorne's smirk and reached for the gauntlet.

"How's Pamela?" he asked.

"It's Patricia. And she's fine."

Thorne turned to MaryAgnes, said he'd meet her in ten minutes. "You bring a bag?"

"It's checked at reception," she said. "I wasn't sure about getting back home tonight."

"Ah-ha!" Jaeger bellowed.

Thorne said, "See you down at reception."

"Say hello to Patricia for me," Jaeger called after him.

Olson, good man, cut the bastard off at the pass. "I'll walk along with you," he said, taking McCaskey's arm. "We have some overlapping territory to figure out."

Thorne went upstairs to his cubicle. He followed procedure and cleared his desk of papers, locking them away unstacked and unsorted.

"I'll be in at noon tomorrow," he told Alice, his quarter-of-a-secretary. "Anything comes up, you can reach me at home."

"Home until noon," Alice read back her notation.

"Right."

Thorne put on his Burberry knock-off raincoat with the dingy winter lining still buttoned inside it. He was almost to the elevators before remembering to call Patsie over at Sears Tower.

"Again?" she asked wearily, when Thorne gave her the news.

"Afraid so," he said.

"It's getting to be a habit, isn't it?"

"The whole central region's in town," he explained. "Staff conference. I'd forgotten all about it."

Thorne hoped that would buy him clemency. Patsie knew how he hated staff meetings, especially after the long and fruitless days he spent battling administrative services over expense sheets and staff overtime. Thorne, who considered himself a street cop first and foremost, had problems with things like that. It was duly noted on his last performance evaluation.

"Something important?" Patsie asked.

"Not really. Just another meeting."

"I see," Patsie said coolly, distracted.

Thorne wondered if she were deciding to resume last night's argument where they'd left off, or take it to another plateau. More likely, she'd be thinking about old wounds he thought had healed. One thing about Patricia Becker-Thorne: she never forgot a grievance and would recall them with computer-like precision from her emotional floppy disc.

"Look, Pats," Thorne said honestly, "this has nothing to do with last night. I'm sorry we fought; I'd like to be home with you. But it's important I meet some people for dinner. I'll call back if I'm going to be late."

"Make it by ten," she said. "I have a ton of invoices to go over. Then I'm washing my hair and going to bed. By ten, either way, Frank."

"By then," he promised.

Thorne met Agent McCaskey in the lobby of the Everett McKinley Dirksen Federal Building. Her medium-length hair looked as ebony black as the granite column she stood against while talking with Vic Olson. In contrast, save for the random freckle, her skin was milk glass. Good looking lady. Damn, she was.

Olson pointed outside. A sudden, lake-effect snow squall was sweeping over the city, tying up Loop traffic, blackening the sky.

"I'd better try to make a run north," Olson said. "See you guys soon. Best of luck."

"Take care," McCaskey said.

"See you."

Ted Jaeger caught them before they could step outside and lose themselves on South Dearborn. He wasn't about to quit.

"What are we doing?"

"Why don't *you* get the fuck back to Iowa," Thorne

snapped. It had nothing to do with MaryAgnes Mc-Caskey. He just hated the prick.

"Come on, Frank. Don't get thin-skinned on me," Jaeger said. "I thought we might make it a threesome for dinner. Or four, if the wife's coming along."

McCaskey beat Thorne to it.

"We have work to discuss," she said. "Tonight's threesome will be me, Frank, and the Bureau. Maybe we can all go out and celebrate together three months from now."

"You really think so? I see a lot of problems with this. Legal, operational, the works. Don't you two?"

Jaeger waited for a reply, got none. "Good hunting anyway."

"Pain in the ass," Thorne grumbled.

"He's harmless," McCaskey said. "But he *is* a pain in the ass."

Thorne looked at the blowing snow and frozen traffic. "I hope you booked a room."

"Palmer House. It's the closest I could think of."

"You drove down?"

McCaskey nodded.

"Better we let your car sit and try for a cab," Thorne said.

"To where?"

"A place you should know about. Where I think we might get a start on all this."

"Strictly business, then."

"Just like I said."

MaryAgnes gave him the first warm look of the day.

"Lead on," she said. "If you can find a cab in this weather, you can do anything."

Thorne shielded her from the wet snow as they pushed through the crowd. He knew a bar on Adams with a good early hours crowd arriving from all over the Loop. They got a taxi in minutes. Thorne gave the driver a Rush Street address.

"I'm assuming you wouldn't mind a drink first," he said.

McCaskey turned from the snow-stuck window, said not at all. "Tell me the truth, Frank. Why do you think Bidwell teamed us together? I'm strictly administrative. Hell, the two men who report to me are better field agents than I'll ever be."

"Mister Inside and Mister Outside," Thorne said.

"Football?"

"Exactly. Blanchard and Davis, back in the Forties when Army was a powerhouse. Blanchard was the big fullback, handled the inside plays. Davis was fast and ran the ends, a great open field man. Same thing with us. We need a good cover business that's managed right."

"Me?"

"You," Thorne replied. "With all the players and money we'll be handling, your background will be an advantage. Dealing with the cruds on the street, setting up the accounts, that's my end."

"Mister Outside," she said. "I'm not sure I like the metaphor, but I suppose it's appropriate."

The cabbie skidded through the Wacker light, nearly broadsiding a CTA bus. Thorne heard him obliviously singing in Farsi and repeated their destination address. The driver nodded and sang them across the Chicago River.

"I'm not sure I like being stuck in an office," McCaskey said. "But combining territories does maximize manpower."

Thorne said, "Look at the demographics. Most of the family's front line men—phone men, office managers, collection specialists . . ."

"Who?"

"The muscle boys. Legbreakers."

"God!"

"They're all in my district," Thorne went on. "South and West Sides, the near suburbs. The old man too, though he's supposed to be semiretired. Bidwell wants something on him for publicity's sake. Why the hell not, I guess. Nobody's managed to put him away before. But me, I want the guys they call the nephews. They're the family's senior managers. They run the gambling and vice operations and keep the money lines open to Las Vegas."

"And they're all competing for the old man's chair."

"You bet they are," Thorne said. "So far they've been surprisingly patient and peaceful waiting for it. Maybe now we can shake things up a little."

McCaskey said, "I still don't see how it ties in with my district. Compared with the Chicago family, our people are like minnows in a shark pool."

"You have to follow the money trail. The cash that vice generates," Thorne explained. "A lot of that is going northwest, like as far as Rockford. It's a different organization now. Not just the old time city boys— Italians, Jews, Irish doing street stuff. Today it's second and third generation, guys out of business school. They do shopping centers, commercial developments, real estate deals tied to pension funds. That's the trail we want to follow—where and how and with whom the revenues end up."

"Ambitious, if you think it's do-able."

"What counts is Bidwell thinks so," Thorne said. "Your agents will be important when we get organized."

"They're good men," McCaskey said.

"Doc Hermann says so too," Thorne said, a compliment.

The cab drove past Fairweather's. Thorne rapped on the Plexiglas safety shield, interrupting the driver's Caspian Sea chanty.

"You say what street?"

"We're here," Thorne hollered.

"Okay, boss."

Thorne gave him five for a three-fifty fare. Olson, whose cousin had been a hostage in Teheran, would have stiffed him completely had he been along. Not the penny but the principle.

"I'll get the one going back," McCaskey said. "Partners, right?"

"Partners."

Thorne had been cultivating Fairweather's for months. Its clientele was mainly past and present jocks, lawyers, stockbrokers, advertising and media types, traders of every commodity known to Western man and, like mung beans and copra, some that weren't. What they had in common was gambling. They loved the action and had the cash to play it. The electronic scoreboard that hung over the bar, updating games minute by minute, score by score, made three-fifty a beer more than equitable.

The bartender who greeted them was a likable South Side kid named Val. Thorne knew he fronted for the outside book, handled pick-ups and drops which, at Fairweather's, had to mean big money. But Val was straight with everyone, always ready to get it done for you. Whatever happens, Thorne already decided, the kid gets himself a pass.

Val said, "How's the bond market, Frank?"

"Flat as this bar."

"Too bad."

Thorne reached over and shook the damp hand. McCaskey stepped up and, already in character, clung hard to him.

"I want you to meet Mary," Thorne said. "Good friend of mine."

"A pleasure."

"Mine, too," she said.

Val looked at McCaskey with trained eyes. "First time here, right?"

"I'm new in town," she said.

"Just moved in," Thorne corroborated.

Val said, "The city's looking up. Welcome to Fairweather's. Anything you need, just ask for Val, you got it. And watch out for this guy."

"I intend to," McCaskey smiled back.

Thorne ordered a Dewar's and soda; McCaskey a chablis, up.

"Who is it tonight?" Val asked Thorne.

"It's the Knicks. We couldn't win a road game with this team if we played eight men at once and threw in the Luv-a-Bulls for back-court pressure."

"Knicks may be too many points," Val reflected.

"Lay them. Trust me."

"We'll see."

When they found a table, McCaskey said, "Maybe Jaeger's right, you know. I see a lot of problems our bright young AAG glossed over this afternoon."

"You talking operations or legalities?" Thorne asked.

"Operations, for now," she said. "Especially how we set up the network."

"It's finding the right bankers," Thorne said. "And getting our people cleared for the numbers we need to hurt the family in their pocketbook."

"I suppose you know some people we can do business with."

"I have some in mind," Thorne said.

"I thought you might."

"We can use eight men up front," Thorne calculated. "We switch them around with each betting office, that gives us ninety-six accounts in all. We can do a lot of damage with ninety-six big winners. Especially if we use the cash surplus to work a way inside the family."

McCaskey continued to doubt it.

"Besides being dangerous, we're putting a lot of trust in Bidwell's whoopsy-whee computer system."

"If they can figure out how to drop a rocket in your coffee cup from ten thousand miles away, I think they'll be able to pick us a few winners," Thorne said.

"I imagine so," McCaskey said weakly.

They stayed at Fairweather's long enough for Thorne to down four Scotches and finish the day's first pack of red dots. McCaskey was only on her second chablis when they decided to walk next door for dinner.

Thorne left a five-spot on the bar for Val and reassured him that the Knicks were a cinch. Outside, the squall had passed speedily to the southeast and, after picking up tons of moisture from the warm waters of Lake Michigan, was gearing up to dump two feet of snow on hapless South Bend.

Thorne held the door open as McCaskey stepped into the pine-paneled seafood house. The headwaiter recognized Thorne and scurried forth from his station by the lobster tank. He led them to a table and explained that the evening's specials were grouper and pompano, both flown in from the Gulf that very afternoon. Thorne decided on another round of drinks.

"There's one thing I'd better tell you before we go any farther," Thorne said.

"What's that?"

"I'm not really an agent."

"You're not?"

"Investigator is all," he explained. "I wear an agent's stripes on my sleeve, but they're only pinned on."

"No law degree?" McCaskey asked.

"Did a year at Northwestern," Thorne said. "Couldn't hack it at all. Torts, property, all that stuff. Don't know how you people do it." He took a long pull on Scotch number five, lit a fresh Lucky. "Anyway, I picked up on my NROTC commission. Somehow, probably right, the Navy figured I'd be better off in criminal investigation than driving ships. The Bureau found me there when my second hitch was up and I got tired of saluting."

He looked over to see McCaskey laughing into her hands. "What's so funny?"

"I'm affirmative action myself," she laughed. "I never even *applied* to law school."

"CPA, then?"

McCaskey shook her head. "Sociology degree and a Master's in criminology. I planned to go into penal reform, until the Bureau decided my gender was right for a job offer. I thought I might get a chance to do field work, so I joined up. That's it."

"Some crime fighters, us," Thorne said, starting to laugh himself.

"At least we're doing it."

"I guess."

"You sound like you're not sure."

"I'm just a cop," Thorne said. "I get paid to do cop work, not decide what's crime and what isn't."

She said, "None of us are. But I get the feeling that's what you're doing—you've decided that betting on a ballgame isn't a crime."

"Maybe I think this whole operation is grandstanding," Thorne said. "Showing off the Bureau's muscle, spending a fortune here to shut down what's perfectly legal in Nevada, Atlantic City, Puerto Rico. Fighting organized crime is one thing, cracking down on bookies is another. Hell, the *Tribune* runs an American flag on page one every day, then prints the early betting line in Sports so gamblers get a head start figuring out their plays. We even have a state lottery that pays out half as much as the policy runners, and the taxman is right there to take half of that when you win."

McCaskey said, "For someone who does cop work, you're putting yourself above the law. Or at least deciding which laws you like and which you don't."

"I've met bookmakers I like and cops I don't," Thorne said. "You can understand that."

"Yes I can, but your argument is still full of holes," McCaskey countered. "The lottery funds schools and libraries, not whorehouses and some gangster's yacht. It's apples and oranges to compare them."

Thorne shrugged. "Only thing matters to me is that one's a felony I get paid to stop. Personally, I'd take the mob's nine hundred fifty to one pay-out over the state's five hundred."

McCaskey ran her fingers along the stem of her glass and tilted her head.

"Frank, are you testing me for some reason?"

"Maybe you. Maybe myself," Thorne replied.

"Then I'll put my other arguments on hold until you're sure," she said. "Right now, I'd better think about getting a place to stay down here. And I don't mean the Palmer House."

"We'll find you something Near North," Thorne said. "Furnished, safe street, et cetera. Doc Hermann can't bitch about funding that."

"He'd better not."

Thorne's question came out of left field, first surprising him, then making him feel stupid.

"You have a boyfriend?"

"Does it matter?"

"No. Not really," he backed off.

"Good, then I'll tell you, partner to partner," McCaskey said, thankfully taking him off the hook. "I know you're only asking because I'll be here for so long, because of the problems that might cause a relationship."

"That *is* why I asked," Thorne said. It sounded right.

"No current boyfriend," McCaskey said. "Live-in or otherwise. Not now, anyway.

"I see," he nodded feebly.

"I am divorced, though. Which isn't easy when you try living a single woman's life in Rockford. It's a lot farther from Chicago than ninety miles on the tollway." She paused as if thinking over her next statement, and continued without any prodding from Thorne.

"My marriage lasted three years. A terrible mistake, hopefully the worst I'll ever make. I almost hate to tell you this . . ."

"Tell me what?"

"With all this talk about sports . . ."

"I like sports," Thorne said.

"He was a baseball player," McCaskey said, shaking her head in a half-smile. "He made it as far as Triple A ball and sixteen games in the majors. He was a pitcher, in case you're interested. Played in the Cardinals organization. So at least you know I can read a box score."

Thorne followed the game closely and was trying to recall a pitcher named McCaskey.

"Lefty or righty?" he asked.

MaryAgnes read his mind.

"McCaskey's *my* name," she said.

"Bad luck."

"Well, no visible scars," she said cheerfully. "Just so you know I'm neither especially vulnerable nor trying to live up to my namesakes."

"Mary?"

"And Agnes. The patron saint of virgins. Did you ever read the poem?" she asked. " 'Young virgins on St. Agnes Eve, with visions of delight, dream soft adorings of their loves, in the middle of the night.' It's by Keats."

"All St. Agnes Eve ever meant in my house was it's supposed to be the coldest night of the year," Thorne said.

"Thanks a lot!" McCaskey barked in false anger.

"You have to admit there's a connection," Thorne teased her again.

"I can, believe me." She pored over the menu for a discreet length of time, then said, "What about you, Frank? Besides the fact that you're happily married, I don't know much else about you. You're always the silent one at staff dinners."

"You know the high points already," Thorne began. He went through the details of his life dispassionately: growing up in the Episcopalian north suburbs, then away to college, the Navy. He told her about Patsie and her rising career in merchandising for Sears; case goods, he said, which meant furniture with no cushions. They lived in Evanston, had no children. He liked to sail.

"Not the stuff of tragedy," he wound up.

"That red hair and you're *Ulster* Irish," McCaskey said incredulously.

"Only half," Thorne said. "The other's Scotch-English."

"God," McCaskey sighed. "Are we going to have a partnership or a civil war?"

Thorne studied her smile as the waiter began their dinner service. When he remembered about calling Patsie, it was long past ten o'clock.

3

SALVATORE Joseph Catania officially became "Pizza Sal" in autumn, 1981, when he parlayed a chain of Chicago-style deep-dish pizza restaurants to beat Las Vegas for a sixty-thousand-dollar line of credit.

Sally knew the business, of course. He was even on a first-name basis with the three Sarkis cousins who owned it.

It was the summer, a year before he hit Vegas, that Sally dropped out of sheet metal school and hired on as a delivery man for Goomba's Best Pizza. It was destined to be short-term employment, Greco remembered as he drove in to get him, what with Sally running around the West Side for dollar tips and yelling at the Greeks all night to at least *try* and get the street names written down right.

When he finally had it with greasy boxes and decided to walk out of their Grand Avenue outlet for good, Sally said *adios* by sticking Nicky Sarkis for the cash equivalent of seventy-three large pies, most of them extra sausage.

That, and the few hundred he'd stashed at his mother's place, got Sally to Vegas. How he managed the rest nobody knows for sure, but a trio of casino credit managers bought the idea that the famous Goomba's chain was *his* operation. His markers were good everywhere. Mister Catania. Mister Salvatore. Pizza Sal.

The man lives with angels.

Naturally, he scored big on his maiden voyage. Greco remembered him flying back first class, the pockets of his leisure suit bulging with crisp hundreds. That's how he made the down payment on the bungalow and financed his first major acquisition of blow, most of which he ended up doing himself or giving away to friends and the girls at the Cairo Club.

The next time out, Greco tossed ten dimes into the kitty, tagged along for the ride and the opulence of Sally's complimentary suite on the Strip. Their first day was low and slow. Greco hit the tables for a few hours, doing himself neither damage nor good, and ducked out for a shower and snooze. Somehow he slept past midnight. Panic struck when he realized Sally was still downstairs playing, Greco's cash in his pocket.

Greco ran down to the casino, shirttails dangling from his trousers. He was at the baccarat table now—Sally, two shill broads who'd dropped out of play and were watching him with true fascination, a Saudi shiek and his affectionate French companion, a Japanese shipbuilder, and some blond guy named Lance who sold sand for half a million an acre out by Palm Springs.

Sally, puffing his way through a huge H. Upmann panatella, had the house so buffaloed the pit-boss asked *his* permission to let the underdressed Greco come to the table. Sal threw him a magnanimous nod of approval.

"What the fuck are you doing?" Greco yelled in his ear when he saw five thousand sitting on "Bank."

"Hey, relax," Sal said calmly. "I want you to meet my friends here. This is Lance, Yoshiro, Shiek Ben-Ali and, of course, Nicole."

Greco stood dumbstruck, two security men beside him in case Mister Salvatore changed his mind.

Sally kept the shoe, doubled up twice, and pulled four natural nines in a row. He walked out with that forty thousand, another eighteen he'd picked up in spurts at the crap table, and the phone numbers of both shill broads—Annette and the nameless blond Greco turned down at dinner later that night. On the plane back, Sonny got his ten thousand repaid, plus the twenty he needed to get out of the deep hole he'd dug himself with Johnny Roses. Sal settled with the juice loan boys who were searching for him everywhere, and still had enough cash left to buy himself a Corvette and an ounce, fittingly enough, of pure Colombian flake.

It was the third trip that he stuck the house for sixty dimes worth of bad paper.

"Pulled one monkey after another," he bitched, turning out his pockets, the ultimate sign of defeat. "Sonny, you wouldn't have believed it. Ice-fucking-cold!"

Thing was, Greco reminded himself as he turned into Sally's driveway, despite his disappearing act, the Vegas people never came after him. Anybody else gets the heavy muscle. All Sally ever got were occasional letters saying, "Surely a man of your position will remit ten thousand dollars towards his balance . . ." And like that.

Six months later even the letters stopped. Sally headed off to Atlantic City backed with a new business affiliation for collateral—Wellington Institute, the sheet metal school he'd attended for two weeks.

"How was it?" Greco inquired when Sally got back and paid up what he owed from betting hoops.

"Atlantic City?"

"What else we talking about?" Greco said.

"It was green."

"Was what?"

"All I saw was the felt on the tables, what the hell else you think?" Sally shrugged. "I did hear some people talking about this beach they got there."

"You win, lose, what?" Greco persisted.

Sally revealed he'd netted eight dimes but wasn't going back.

"The place ain't Vegas," he said. "In Vegas you can watch them sink the *Titanic* right during the show at MGM. Honest to God, right on the stage."

"Terrific," Greco said.

"And you don't get my kind of credit in A.C. either."

"Good thing."

"The rooms are all right," he went on. "Food's okay. Go to dinner with Mickey Mantle, if you want. But the broads are real weak, come down from them insurance companies in Newark. Down the shore, they call it. I'm talking about gum-chewers here, Sonny. Even the hookers in A.C. chew gum."

After that excursion, Sally decided to invest the remainder of his bankroll in betting baseball, five hundred a unit. Twenty-cent line, who cares? He ended up stuck fifteen thousand by the All-Star break and Johnny Roses was fuming over it. So Greco put him on the phones for a nickel a week off his figure. After all, Sally had come through when he needed him, Greco recalled as he hit the horn.

They were a team ever since.

Sally came out on the third blast, climbed into the Lincoln, unzipped the Izod windbreaker that stretched tight across his belly.

"Where to?"

"Padrino's."

"Don't know it. They got good food?"

"You're not along to play restaurant critic," Greco said. "You came to answer any questions Mister Ross has about you getting busted. You speak when spoken to. Got it?"

"Okay, okay." Sally sulked against the car door and lit a Pall Mall.

Greco drove to the near West Side, Chicago's Little Italy before Mayor Daley had half of it razed to build Circle Campus.

"I talked to O'Connor again," Sally said. They were on South Halsted, heading through Greektown. "He says it's no sweat I'll walk. We wait for the right judge, then he sinks the whole thing on probable cause, bad evidence, whatever."

"Even after they got your sheets?"

"Proves nothing," Sally said. "Could be anything, you try and read that. I get a pass on the phone calls too. They had no warrant to tap or intercept calls."

Greco said, "Tell all that to the boss. He'll want to hear about your special code, why you don't need flash paper, water paper, nothing."

"Consider it done."

He took a drag on his cigarette and wrinkled his nose as he inhaled. "Hey, Sonny! What the hell you been running around with now Camille's on vacation. This car stinks!"

"Toss that," Greco said, finally remembering the pepper-and-egg sandwich under the armrest.

"Eecchh," Sally gagged. He flipped the greasy torpedo at some wino at the West Madison corner. "And you talk about my habits. Jeez."

They stood under an arbor of plastic grapes in Padrino's foyer until the hostess came by. Greco duked her a ten and got a large booth in the rear of the dining room. He ordered a vodka; Sally, keeping calm on Valium, wanted only club soda with lime.

"Don't go getting air-headed on those pills."

"Valium Lite," Sally said. "Only shuts down half a lobe."

Greco decided on the veal special and a side of macaroni. Sally wanted a T-bone the size of a toilet seat, dancing with death after his bout of angina.

"Hold up till our friend gets here," Sally told the waiter like he was throwing the party.

Johnny Roses arrived ten minutes later: always on time, always in a hurry, checking the Cartier watch he wore upside-down on his left wrist before sliding into the booth and pointing at Sal.

"What's he doing here?"

"I thought you'd want to hear what happened with the cops," Greco said.

"What happened is your worry. Go take a walk," he told Sal. "We got business to talk."

"Consider it done. I'll wait at the bar."

Even Sally knew Johnny Roses was not to be pissed off summarily. Though small, slight, on the nervous side, he was one tough mother. Probably had pushed a button or two in the early days; would again, given cause. Still, Greco thought . . .

"Hold it," he said. "Sal and I go back a long ways. He's helped me out and he's in the business. No sense he can't stay and eat his steak."

"I know what business he's in," Johnny said. "Still doing that stuff, ain't you?"

"Not a chance!" Sally replied, his voice pained. "I got heart problems, you know. No way I touch that stuff anymore."

Johnny Roses slid farther into the booth and checked his watch again.

"Sit still and shut up," he said.

Greco put in their order and added on a bottle of Corvo red.

"I'm not here to eat macaroni," Johnny growled. "I want to know what's going on, how we're doing. For your sake, it's got to be better. People upstairs are getting hot."

Bad timing. But Greco had to tell him about the Blaze move. All of it.

"Monday night was a killer," he said. "Blaze cost us

thirty dimes alone. I called around to lay off, but everybody else was holding too. I guess it's the new league. Nobody's sure how to play them."

The boss tapped his knife impatiently.

"We weren't the only ones got hurt there," he said. "But we sure were the worst. Next time you get those kind of numbers, find me and *I'll* see they get laid off."

Greco went on with the rest of it.

"I held back another ten dimes, went against the flow—"

"You did what?"

"It looked like a good move, with all—"

Johnny Roses cut him off again.

"I don't want to hear things like that. It's your problem, Sonny. You're gonna eat this one yourself."

"Throw it against my commission," Greco said. "We'll balance out the basketball and see what the difference is. If I have to start up baseball ten dimes light, I'll do it that way."

Sally decided to back him up.

"Anything I have coming from the phones goes against Sonny's figure," he said. "This happens in the best of families."

"Shut up and listen," Johnny Roses barked. "Maybe you learn once and for all, if you didn't have the right cousins around you'd be walking with two canes strapped to your wrists."

Sally held up his hands. "Sorry."

Greco prayed he'd keep his mouth buttoned until the boss calmed down.

"I'll put your ten thousand on hold," Johnny Roses told Greco. "We got other business to talk over."

"I'm listening."

"I met with Sid Paris and the other nephews last night," Johnny Roses said. "They told me how they want things, which is how they'll be. Three things you need to know. One, we shut down college basketball right now. Too many games, nothing but problems adjusting the lines, all the services giving out two, three winners a night. It's too damn much, and I'm taking heat for ever putting it on the board. So, starting tomorrow, it's off."

"TV games too?" Greco asked.

"Everything."

"But we got the NCAAs coming up," Greco said. "We don't handle the tournament, we lose a lot of accounts."

"Let them play with the renegades. Way everybody's been getting hit, they'll never get paid. They'll all be back in the fall."

"You say so."

Sally knew enough to keep silent.

"The family says so. You're the college man, Sonny. You got a certain amount of cash to invest, right? Where you gonna put it? Where you make five percent, and lately not even that? I want that kind of return, I'll go buy some laundromats and have you two clowns out delivering soap."

The waiter came by with an armful of platters. Greco said to keep them on hold. No sense breaking in when the boss was on a roll.

"Number two. We're gonna push this spring football league. That's the move I sold the nephews. New teams, new players, not too much information on the street. A lot of players over there are on their last legs, careers almost over. So, maybe one or two, here and there, can give us a little edge with the points."

Greco said, "But look at last Monday. We got crushed."

"That'll happen once in a while. But overall, we'll come out ahead by a big margin. I figured it from every angle. It's the best thing I can put on the P & L sheet, it's the edge I got over everybody else trying to move up now the old man's not well. So that's it—we go with spring football and drop everything else until September."

"Sid Paris bought the idea?" Greco asked.

"For now. But nothing's forever in this business. He remains to be convinced, so we need results."

Greco and Sally nodded.

"You heard none of this," Johnny Roses barked at Pizza Sal.

"Hey, nothing," Sal assured him.

"We'll handle pro hoops through the end of the season," Johnny Roses said. "That's been okay so far. No real damage."

"We'd be dead without it," Greco said, skipping over the beating they'd taken on the Pacers the night Sally got cracked.

"We got some pluses with the pros," Johnny Roses said. "We know who's heavy into blow, who's got some white chick on the side his old lady don't know about, all that. You can move the points around how you want, only don't touch the over-and-under. But watch yourself. Move it half, one point tops. We don't want to be everybody's middle."

Greco went along with that. He'd tried working the middles a year before, him and Sally betting them together. Find one line at, say, a point-and-a-half spread; find another at two-and-a-half. You bet both teams: the underdog with the higher line, the favorite with the lower. You can't lose more than the ten percent vigorish, and the final score falls on two points flat, you win both bets. It worked fine until the night Pizza Sal got high and forgot to call in the second side. It took Greco three months to square up with a nervous small-time book in Milwaukee.

"Like it or not, that's how it is," Johnny Roses said.

The waiter came by again. Greco gave him the high sign. He brought the pasta first, a mound of *arrabbiata* served in a skillet.

"How do you eat like that?" Johnny Roses asked.

Greco had never once seen his boss enjoy a meal. "I ordered for three," he explained.

"Once a day is all I eat." Sal tried to cop out when his mammoth T-bone arrived.

"How old are you?" the boss asked in disgust.

"Thirty-four."

"You look fifty. You say you got a heart condition and eat like that?"

"Just a little angina," Sally insisted.

If the boss had only seen him in the hospital, Greco thought. Laying out lines before his stress test.

"The last thing," Johnny Roses said. "We don't handle baseball this year. Not worth the time or money, even with the twenty percent line. Day in, day out, it's too much for too little."

That one hit Greco hard. He wanted the action, needed it. Besides keeping his people on the phones, hanging on to his clients, there was the house in Lake Zurich, riding lessons for the twins . . .

"You don't look so happy."

Greco said, "Suppose I wanted to handle baseball myself. And finish up the college hoops too. Could you get me a blessing?"

"You trying to become a self-made man, Sonny? Go your own way?"

"I'm trying to survive," Greco said. "My customers can't go a day without betting something."

"Your customers suck," Johnny Roses said. "You got more late payers on the books than all the other managers put together. And you never tighten up on them. All this Mister Nice Guy shit means nothing. They might love you on Rush Street, but you're better off being respected by our side."

"I do what I have to do," Greco said. "No reason to get tough. I know I got people late, but they're all good. Sometimes, the more cash you're worth, the less you have liquid."

"You're jerking yourself off, but that's *your* problem. Like holding back ten dimes on the Blaze. Jesus."

"What do you think? I get a blessing to handle baseball?"

"You want it, probably. You know how the old man feels about you. You get what you want, within reason."

"I need it," Greco said.

The boss leaned forward and spoke in a whisper.

"I'm telling you this, Sonny. Get yourself into any more trouble and it's your ass on the line. Don't even think of coming back to me for help. I'll hold the ten dimes from the Blaze, but that's it."

"That's history," Greco said.

Johnny Roses checked his watch again and climbed out of the booth. He glowered down at Pizza Sal.

"How the hell *did* you get nailed?"

"Don't know. But I'm sure going to find out," Sally boasted.

"You do nothing without my saying so. And you keep the hell off the phones."

"Absolutely."

"Who's on his case?" Johnny Roses asked Greco.

"J. J. O'Connor. He says Sal will walk on probable cause. When the right judge comes along."

"You take O'Connor's fee off the house account. We don't let nobody go to court unprotected. Not even this shithead."

"He's in a great mood," Sally said when the boss moved to another table and sat down with some local merchants who weren't in the family but wanted people to think they were.

"You should see him when he's mad," Greco said.

"Hey, we got the action you wanted. College hoops, baseball, we're right there on the cutting edge."

"Yeah, and maybe we'll come up losers one more time."

The look Sally gave him, Greco knew the thought never crossed his mind.

Diane rolled on her side and pushed against Greco's shoulder, nudging him awake.

"I didn't mind your standing me up for dinner," she said. "But we were supposed to talk."

"We did."

"You know what I mean."

"I do?" Greco said, yawning.

"Not this time, Sonny. You can't cop out whenever you don't feel like facing facts."

Greco decided to face one.

"I was wondering what happened to Donny," he said. "You never mentioned it, why he's not here."

"That's out of bounds, damn it. Just like Camille."

"You're the one said there were rules."

"What in God's name do you want from me?" Diane cried, pushing away from him. "Your wife's out of town, you come over here and screw me whenever you feel like. What else, Sonny? Want to beat me up a little? That make you feel better?"

"No, you're liable to like it."

A murmur of laughter rose in Greco's throat. Diane came back against him.

"Sonny . . ."

"Let it drop," he said. "Everything bugging me has to do with business. Not with us, you."

"It's more than that. Talk to me," she persisted.

Greco said, "I feel like a six-foot man in a four-foot bottle. Everything's pushing in on me. Pizza Sal gets cracked before he can lay off some big bets, the boss wants me to sit down until . . ."

"It'll get better. You know it will."

Greco raised his arm to see Diane's face. The eyeliner smudged across her damp cheek was somehow exciting, erotic.

"I don't think I can handle it much longer," he said. "I used to love making all the moves, watching the whole board, see who covers or not. No more, babe. Just clearing out my offices is a royal pain, let alone hitting the bars, seeing customers, picking up tabs so they pay me a few hundred on account."

"Then get out of it. You don't have to hustle for Johnny Roses or anyone else."

"You should talk about hustling," he said cruelly, wanting sympathy, not counsel.

"You can be really rotten," Diane shot back. "What I have to do to support my kid is none of your damn business. Okay, I worked the Cairo Club. But I didn't trick!"

"I know. I'm sorry."

"I was stupid at nineteen," she went on. "I'll give you that. Running with some Hell's Henchmen biker who couldn't do anything but get me pregnant and hit the clutch when I told him. But what about you, Sonny? You doing any better for yourself at thirty-six?"

"You got any suggestions?"

"Do more."

"More than what?"

"Than what you're doing now. You're smart, educated. You can do whatever you put your mind to, if only you believed it."

"I see a lot of college men pushing cabs around town," Greco said.

"Another cop-out."

Greco reached for his glass and took a sip of watered-down vodka.

"Is it?" he said. "Well I didn't plan on making book like you didn't plan on giving out bubble baths at the Cairo Club. At least the family took us in, gave us something to do, make a living. Sure, I worked my ass off getting through DePaul nights. All it got me was a year in Nam humping a ruck through the jungle."

"What does that have to do with now?"

"You wanted to talk—I'm telling you. I was still a little goofy when I got home. Went right ahead, got married. What the hell. Camille had been waiting for me almost two years. But the wedding dress ain't even back from the cleaners when she tells me she's pregnant. Nine months after the wedding to the goddamn day, the twins are here. That's great, but she and me are still strangers. You don't get to know somebody with two screaming babies in the next room."

"Tell me about it," Diane said.

"Best job I could get was selling cheese for Camille's old man. Stuck it out four years, making shit wages, him hating me all the time for screwing his precious daughter. If some of his restaurant accounts weren't connected with the family and introduced me to Johnny Roses . . ."

Diane took his glass and wet her lips. Greco's eyes fixed on her breasts as she sat up. He hated whoever had tattooed the tiny heart on the left one.

"So we both had it tough," Diane said. "But life's not all extremes. There's a lot of ground between making cheese and making book."

"I'm still open for suggestions."

"Study up and take a broker's exam. Get into real estate, you'd be good at it. Or buy a seat on the Exchange, do some trading. Commodities, options, currency."

"I can't see it."

"Then what?" she asked, glaring at him. "You say you want out of the family, but there's nothing you'd leave for. That make any sense?"

"If I got some cash together, maybe open a restaurant . . ."

"You'd be more of a slave than still working for your father-in-law. You see yourself down at the Haymarket, five o'clock in the morning, haggling over tomato and chicken prices? You're bored talking with customers now. How about smiling at people all night who only stop by to bitch about their food?"

Greco couldn't help grinning.

"Great! Now we know all the things I can't do."

"I still say you should think about the Exchange. That's where it is, these days. Action, money."

"You going to borrow me the hundred thousand to get started?"

"You can get it. I've met people who make that much taking a weekend trip to Miami. Or New Orleans. Which is where the business is now."

"You can't be serious," Greco said. "Or you've started listening to Pizza Sal."

"My point is," Diane said, "you can find a way to get whatever you need for a fresh start. Beg, borrow, or steal, as long as you want it bad enough."

"That'd make you happy," Greco said. "Have some nice respectable man in the house. Someone like Donny. Wears a coat and tie, wingtips. La Salle Street type who flies you to New York and L.A. on the good old expense account."

"I told you before, what's between me and Donny is out of bounds."

"I know, you got rules. Like when he gets back to town and we're not supposed to know each other. When he comes into Dead Dom's to pick you up."

"When you go *home*!" Diane snapped.

Greco stiffened, took a deep breath. Diane was doing all she could to avoid another fight. She pressed back against him beneath the coverlet, throwing her leg across his.

"Let it go for tonight," she said.

"What I said before," Greco reminded her.

"I know you're under lots of pressure. Talking about Donny won't help. I wanted to be with you tonight. Isn't that enough?"

"It's good to hear."

"That's all there is then."

Greco pulled the coverlet across his back as he moved over her in a soft, rocking motion.

"Damn," Diane whispered, pushing up to accept him. "Nobody plays by the rules anymore."

4

THORNE was ahead of schedule.

In four working days he had established Assets Management Partners, Ltd., a bona fide Illinois corporation serving investors in options, commodities, money market instruments. An AMP, Ltd. logo he'd designed was embossed on five hundred business cards: Frank T. Becker, President. The Exchange, with some of its floor traders recently indicted on drug trafficking charges, cooperated fully: Thorne's dummy file went into its central data bank while Exchange Properties, Inc., a real estate subsidiary, supplied La Salle Street office space complete with furniture, library, listings on all lobby directories. The doors open, Bidwell's tech people came through with terminals and recording equipment. Only the telephone company balked at Thorne's ambitious timetable, but visiting a friend in the Illinois Bell security office unfroze the gears.

Thorne went on line.

He sat at his mahogany desk puffing on a Lucky, surveying his setup: AMP looked successful, professional, certainly six years old. He knew he could sell it. All that was left was finding the right buyer.

Agent McCaskey arrived at two-thirty. She wore

high brown boots that climbed under a long russet skirt of thick tweed. Her black hair was tied back, neat and glistening.

"I found an apartment on Astor Street," she said, handing Thorne a slip of pink note paper monogrammed *MAMcC*: address, phone number printed out carefully in upper and lower capitals.

"The agent calls it a two-and-a-half room furnished efficiency. But I'm still looking for that half-room. Unless it's the bedroom."

"Astor's fine. Right where you should be."

"It's also nine-fifty a month, plus utilities and security deposit. I wonder what Doc Hermann will say about that."

Thorne replied, "He can handle it. We're going to break the bank, remember?"

"I'm glad you're starting to believe it."

She began emptying the contents of a canvas tote bag into her desk; it looked haphazard until she arranged each drawer's contents precisely.

Thorne said, "I'll write a company check for your expenses." He showed her the checkbook, business cards, letterhead.

She said, "That makes sense, if we're supposed to be hot and heavy together. Could be fun, being a kept woman. For a while, anyway." She looked at the materials carefully. "Yes, these look good."

Thorne handed her a sheet of paper.

"I made up a list of items we should have in-house," he said. "Could you pull them together for me?"

McCaskey ran through the list quickly: magazines, *Wall Street Journal,* coffee maker, bar setup.

"You want *sherry*?"

Thorne said, "Respectable investment counselors may drink straight gin, but they always keep the sherry in plain sight and offer it first."

"Sounds devious. Where did you hear that?"

"My father," Thorne said. "When he was down

here, he kept bourbon in the sherry decanter. No one knew for years he was downing a fifth of Old Crow every day."

He pulled a ring of keys from his pocket and divided them into sets.

"There's a manila jacket in the lock file," he said. "I started a list of agents we can use to establish accounts. Four from the strike force, plus a few inside people who are underemployed and won't ask questions. Look it over, add the people you want from your office. I'm heading out for a while."

"Where to?" McCaskey asked, marrying the office keys with her own.

"Have to meet my contact with CPD, get that buttoned down. Then I think I'll head north, see about getting business underway."

"Fairweather's?"

"Could be," Thorne said evasively. Dodging questions about his field work was a hard habit to break.

McCaskey got the message.

"See you tomorrow."

"Why don't we meet for dinner?" Thorne offered in apology. "Say eight, eight-thirty? Somewhere near your apartment?"

"I have all my unpacking to do. I'd better use the free time to get organized."

"You still have to eat," Thorne said.

"But I don't need an escort, do I?"

"I thought I'd show you around the neighborhood. Where the stores are, laundromat, decent Chinese take-out . . ."

McCaskey's response was cool and dry.

"I think we'll spend enough time together on the job. Let's not trip all over each other after hours."

Thorne said coolly, "AMP Limited opens for business on Monday. Tomorrow we'll find out how Bidwell's program is running, iron out any bugs. Over the weekend we take a break. It might be our last one for a while."

"I'll be here at eight in the morning."

She went on organizing her desk, didn't look up or say a word as Thorne walked out the door.

Thorne had said he'd meet Lieutenant Jack Corrigan at Bernie's Luncheonette in the south Loop, where the corned beef was supposedly lean, top shelf. Besides, Corrigan once cautioned him, we get together anywhere near Eleventh and State, too many people start asking questions, too many eyes giving us the once over. Thorne had said back that Corrigan just worried his captain would find out he depended on the Bureau for all his leads. Corrigan laughed at that and picked up their first tab at Bernie's. Thorne believed they were friends.

He ducked into the storefront as an elevated train screamed around the Van Buren turn on worn track and rattling trestle. As a boy, Thorne had always worried a Lake Street express would come crashing down on him. Then, a few years back, as he came out of an office on Wacker, one nearly did—the motorman, flying high on fresh-dried Hawaiian, took the Lake-Wabash turn in tempo with the James Brown tune on his Walkman and dropped four cars down onto the street, forty feet below and twenty from where Thorne stood gaping.

He saw Jack Corrigan sitting at a corner table: a muscular ex-Marine gunny with a Fifties crew-cut of graying hair. The man next to him was equally large, with darker, harder eyes.

"Pull up a chair," Corrigan motioned. "You haven't met Tom Massey yet."

"Not yet."

"He just transferred into the section. We're working together for a while. See if it pleases him."

Thorne shook the meaty hand.

"Good to meet you."

"Same here, Red."

"Frank will do fine, detective."

Thorne hated all allusions to his hair color. Ted Jaeger used to get off calling him Agent Orange until Thorne said, one more time, he'd punch his lights out in front of the entire regional staff conference.

"Whatever you say," Massey smirked.

Thorne grabbed a metal chair, vinyl seat-top held down with strips of gray duct tape. He decided to put his cover story on the back burner, what with the new man sitting in. Corrigan deserved to get some answers: he was a good, honest cop who'd stand up when you needed him. But Tom Massey bothered the hell out of Thorne already.

Thorne said, "It's been a while, Jack. You working on something big or just busting retirees playing bingo up on Sheridan Road?"

Corrigan, who never smiled, simply shook his head.

"Been so slow I took a bunch of time-due," he said. "Massey here was sitting at my desk when I got back. So I figured, just in case I'm getting bumped over to crowd control, I'd better bring him along to make sure you still get your tickets fixed."

"He's kidding about the desk," Massey said.

"I hope so," Thorne said.

"We made a few scores last week," Corrigan said. "Mostly small potatoes stuff—some runners, a couple of bars."

"That's what they pay us for," Thorne said.

"Got one thing that looks promising," Corrigan said. "Guy named Catania, phone man for the outfit, probably belongs to John Ross, Sid Paris, that part of the family."

Thorne searched his memory and came up empty.

"Don't know the name," he said.

"Salvatore Joseph," Massey added.

Thorne shook his head.

Corrigan said, "Cal Bostic nailed him with his handle still on paper. We're working over his system now. Man has a lot of players, looks like pretty big action. We're spinning the phone numbers around, see if we come up with seven digits that somebody big will answer."

"If he's family," Thorne said, "I'm surprised you ever got his paperwork. They don't make mistakes like that."

Massey said, "Everybody screws up, some time or other. We got lucky."

"Or he's not connected at all," Thorne said.

"I don't think Catania goes high up the ladder," Corrigan said. "But I'm sure as hell he can tell us who does. We're gonna try and turn him."

"Which means you want help."

"Run him through your machine for us, Frank. The one we poor local cops need a warrant to get at. I'll take anything that'll flesh out his package—income taxes, withholding forms, service record, whatever's in there. You know the drill."

Massey said, "This way, we get something worthwhile out of him, we can split the proceeds."

"That's not how it works," Thorne said. "Usually, after one of your judicial geniuses fumbles the ball and the guy walks out of court, I'm left trying to piece together enough evidence for a conspiracy or tax bust."

"They're not *our* judges, pal," Massey snapped back.

Corrigan stepped in like a referee, ordered apple pie and coffee times three. What the hell, Thorne figured, Massey was one of Jack's own.

"I'd be happy to let Catania walk if he gives us anything," Corrigan said. "Could be what's in your machine will help us flip him. Get me enough for a warrant to screen his phones, I may turn up an interstate connection for you."

"He's kidding again," Thorne told Massey. "Knows better."

The waitress slid three plates across the table and sloshed coffee into their cups. Massey mumbled a profanity.

Thorne didn't like it, but he had to tell Corrigan after all. Massey must be there for a reason. Maybe he *was* stepping into Jack's shoes. With all the political back-stabbing going on in the department, the third chief in three years shaking up the troops, anything was possible. And Thorne's first priority was to get himself some running room.

"Jack, I'll have to get you another contact agent at the Bureau," he said flatly.

"You quitting, Frank?"

"No such luck."

"Am I, without knowing it yet?"

"Not that I've heard."

"Then what?"

Thorne said, "I've been yanked off the strike force. Benched, you could call it. Management's grumbling about productivity, cost efficiencies, all that OMB crap. They want manpower applied in other areas. So they're pulling me inside, off the street. All I know so far is my new thing involves securities fraud, trading violations, the Exchange. Sounds like a lot of paper pushing, but I go where they send me. Thing is, it's nothing we can work a split on."

"Well I'll be . . ." Corrigan said. "Just like that."

"I only found out yesterday. You know how these things go."

"Securities," Corrigan ruminated.

"I'll get you whatever we have on Catania, Salvatore Joseph," Thorne said. "Give me his ticket."

Massey reached inside his coat and handed Thorne the arrest report. "Here you go, pal."

Thorne said, "Couple of weeks, I'll have someone in place to work with you. All low-key, off-the-record, like it's been with us."

"How long you on the sidelines?" Corrigan asked.

"I'm supposed to look at it as greener pastures," Thorne said. "I make it about three months."

"Three months. Here I thought those big securities cases always took years to build." Corrigan shook his head. "I'll be damned."

Thorne knew already Corrigan was too smart to buy his spiel. But if that's how Bidwell and Doc Hermann wanted it, he'd give it one more push and get the hell out.

"All I know is what I hear from the District," he said. "Looks like most of the deep digging was done in New York. I'm just finishing up some legwork out here, getting the ribbon Justice needs to tie up their package. Right now, I don't know any more to tell you."

"If it's good for you, I'm all for it." Corrigan cut into his pie and speared an apple slice. "Tell me this, Frank. Who do I call in the meantime? You sure don't want me going to Doc Hermann."

"Until things shake down, you still come to me," Thorne said, against his better judgment. "I'll front it myself, work your stuff on overtime, whatever. Let's see what happens."

"Whatever you say. For a while."

Thorne knew he had to fall back on friendship.

"Look, I'm only trying to be up front with you guys, tell you face to face what's going on. But you have to remember, as far as CPD is concerned, I'm in the investment business, not on the strike force. That's official."

"It stays between us," Corrigan assured him.

Thorne looked at Massey.

"The three of us?"

"I go with the lieutenant. All the way," Massey said.

"Bank on it," Corrigan promised.

Thorne rose from the table, belted his raincoat in a half-knot. Time to let things settle down.

"Today's Thursday. I'll have Catania's file to you by Monday," he said. "Wish me luck?"

"Nothing but the best," Corrigan said. "See you around."

Massey poured the coffee from his saucer back into the cup.

"What was that all about?"

"Beats the shit out of me," Corrigan said.

"You don't buy his act either."

"Thorne's a good man," Corrigan said. "We're together a long time and he's always been straight with me."

"That's history. What about now?"

"Now I think he's lying through his teeth," Corrigan said. "No way the Bureau would pull their top field agent off the strike force to make the SEC, some lawyers in Washington look good. Not a chance."

"Then what? He get himself in some kinda trouble?"

"I'm a lieutenant, not a psychic," Corrigan said. "But I sure as hell plan to find out. Too bad he's seen you, Tom. I wouldn't mind keeping an eye on Thorne for a while, see who he's hanging around with these days."

"You want me to follow a *fed?*" Massey asked incredulously.

"They do it to us all the time."

"Ex officio, like?"

"If you're trying to say we don't tell the captain, the answer is yes."

"Might be fun," Massey said. "Don't worry about him spotting me. I've tailed people three months who couldn't recognize me at breakfast."

"You that good?"

"Over in Narcotics, you're either good or you don't last long," Massey said. "So when do I start?"

Corrigan thought it over while finishing his pie.

"Monday's fine," he said. "Right after you find

Salvatore Joseph Catania and drag his dago ass downtown. I'll give you the rest of what I'm looking for then."

Fairweather's doorman took Greco's Lincoln to a loading zone on Oak Street that cost twenty a night for Traffic Control to forget about. Greco watched him peel away and went through the revolving doors. Val, soon as he saw him, built a tall Smirnoff-soda with lime.

"Good thing you stopped by," Val said. "There's business we should talk about. My relief's here in fifteen minutes."

"I'll be around."

Val drew a circled "X" on the back of Sonny's tab, marking it "house."

Greco moved through the crowd. Thursdays, always, were big nights on the strip. Fridays, people have to get home on time, see their families, start the weekend. But Thursdays are good nights to catch up on work, maybe see the client for a cocktail, things like that. Fairweather's was packed with dark suits, skirts and sweaters with pearls.

"Hey, Sonny!"

Greco turned slowly. Maurice wasn't hard to spot, being one of just three blacks in the place. He was a curious mix of Ivy League-dapper: pin-striped Brittany suit with a too large, too wide foulard tie. Most people figured Maurice for a Leo Burnett creative type. Greco knew he ran a good stable of ladies and a large South Side numbers book, a little *bolita* thrown in to keep the Latins happy.

"What's shakin', Maurice?"

"Hanging in there, Sonny. You?"

"About the same."

Maurice came closer and bumped glasses with Greco.

"You look a little naked," Greco said.

"Look what?"

"Tyrell," Greco said, wondering about Maurice's ever-present bodyguard/chauffeur. "Don't tell me you gave him a vacation?"

"Naw. The fuzz give Tyrell his vacation," Maurice said, trying to speak softly and still be heard above the din. "Dumb mothafucker goes out and boosts himself a new Caddy over near Lincoln Park. Big blue Coupe deVille. Tyrell's all duded up, got his Super-Fly hat and all, gonna head West and party for a time with his new wheels. He ain't five blocks gone, the fuzz pull him over and throw him across the hood. Fuckers start laughing at him too. 'How'd you know?' Tyrell's yellin'. 'How'd you get me so fast?' Cops drag him around back the car. There's this big red sticker on the bumper. *Save Soviet Jews!* Cops say Tyrell don't look like no rabbi, no dentist. One peek at that sticker, and Tyrell's behind the wheel, they got no choice but to grab his dumb ass."

Greco, choking, spilled half his drink over Maurice's Italian loafers.

"That's gospel, baby. Lookit, you know anybody that's good, you send him over to see me. Need a replacement, dig? Maybe this time I'll hire some Chuck."

Greco said, "Pizza Sal may be looking for work."

"You kidding me? Shit!"

Greco moved farther down the bar. Three, four players grabbed him to check their figures, promised him cash tomorrow. A few others asked him about the DePaul game. The ones he liked, Greco told straight: Blue Demons would cover six points at home no matter who they played, Chicago Bulls included.

When all three night bartenders were in place, Val stripped off his red waistcoat and came over.

"How'd we do?" Greco asked.

Val shook his head. "Lost."

"Jimmy's coming by later with some cash. Anybody's anxious, tell them to wait it out."

"It's not that," Val said. "There's a guy here I think you should talk to. Over at that table."

Greco took a surreptitious look. "The redhead?"

"That's the one. Tall, thin guy."

"Where do you know him from?"

"Here. Been coming in for months now." Val thought back. "He's in some kind of investment business. Bonds, I think. Has an office at the Exchange."

"But he hasn't been playing."

"Not with us. We just talk a lot, you know. He's on top of it, Sonny. I can tell you that."

"So are the cops," Greco said.

"I doubt it. No way."

"You have the good eye."

"It tells me he's straight," Val said confidently. "And it never fails."

"Never once turned up a cop. Just players who can't seem to pay." Greco absent-mindedly handed Val his empty glass.

"Guess I'd better see what he wants."

Thorne had watched Val walk around the bar and buttonhole the brown-haired man in the cashmere sweater. The man had tried shooting Thorne a concealed glance, then started toward the table. Thorne made him mid-thirties, a little more; average build, good looking, with soft, almost gentle blue eyes.

"My name's Sonny."

"I'm Frank Becker. Take a seat and I'll get a round."

"Sounds good to me."

Greco sat on Thorne's right and tried looking inside his coat for a badge, holster, wire, anything. Thorne caught his gaze and appreciated the effort. He flipped his coat wide open to pull a package of Luckies from his shirt pocket.

Greco refused his offer. "You go ahead. I may have a cigar later."

They spent several minutes on preliminaries, talking

about Fairweather's, the action, what a good man Val was.

"Speaking of Val," Greco finally said, "he tells me you have a little business you'd like to discuss."

Thorne said, "Only if you're *in* the business. That's what I'm looking for." He handed Greco an Assets Management Partners business card.

Greco held it a moment, recalling Diane's counsel that he get a seat on the Exchange, make some big, clean money. He said, "Tough business, options, commodities, all that."

"I'm also interested in sports futures."

"I like that, sports futures," Greco smiled openly. "You play, Frank?"

"Middle of the roader," Thorne shrugged. "Point is, I'm in the market for a new source to handle a good-sized piece of action."

"Why's that?"

Thorne made a point of looking to Val for a go-ahead sign, figuring Greco would welcome the caution.

Greco did. "You can talk to me," he said.

"It's more than wanting to play myself," Thorne began. "I have a lot of accounts—my clients, actually—who know I like to bet a few games and who want some action for themselves. They call me, I do them the favor of putting their plays on my number. That was okay with me, for a while; good public relations with my investors."

"Sure," Greco nodded.

"Trouble is," Thorne continued, "now I'm getting more calls than I want. I'm in a position where I can't say no, but it's becoming a hassle all the time, trying to get everybody down. It's too big, too unwieldy for me to handle."

"So you end up holding some plays," Greco understood.

"Only by default. Bookmaking's not my business."

"It's tough to get caught in the middle all the time."

"You got that right."

"So, turn it all over to the guy you're dealing with. Why wouldn't he want your people to play directly with him? Good enough for you should be good enough for him."

"He'd love it," Thorne said. "But he's a one-man shop. Runs everything out of his back pocket, I think. He has enough of one game, or he wants to get out early, he just closes down. That's when I end up holding plays I don't want to make. Even, say, I come out ahead, it's action I'd rather not have. I take enough risks on the Exchange every day. I don't need any more after closing."

Greco said, "I see your point."

He ordered a second round on his tab when the waitress flitted by. "This bookmaker you have, mind if I ask who he is?"

Thorne had it laid out, waiting.

"I got his number from a friend three years ago," he said. "But I've never seen him once all the time I've been playing. We talk twice a day like old friends, but I could run him over on Michigan Avenue and not know who he was. A messenger comes by my office on Thursdays for the pay-out or pick-up. All the main man ever gave me was a lot of bad advice."

Greco knew it wasn't one of his people. Still, no sense competing with anyone who works for the family.

"Why don't you give me that number?"

"Would you want to do business with me if I did?"

"Absolutely not," Greco admitted. He liked the guy already and, in his business, instincts were great references. Besides, he'd check him out thoroughly before doing a damned thing. Johnny Roses wasn't much on instinct.

"The same rule holds if we get together," Greco said.

"Absolutely yes," Thorne assured him. "It's the only way I'd want it."

"Good."

Their fresh drinks appeared. Greco decided it was time to back off a little, lighten things up and see where Frank was coming from. They turned to the risks and rewards of trading options, the furor of the commodities pits, the Cubs' lingering need for a lefty reliever. When the waitress brought a third round, Greco rolled his eyes at her tightly leotarded figure.

"That's a nine, at least," he said.

"I give her a four."

"A *four*?"

"That's the Budweiser system," Thorne grinned. "It would take four Clydesdales to pull her off my face."

"I'll drink to that!"

Hope he's not trying to cover up being gay, Greco thought. All his gay players wanted to do was bet hockey for even money and no goals. No, he decided, stick with the instincts.

Thorne figured enough time had passed, enough small talk. "So look," he said. "Here's the proposition I have for you."

"Go on."

"I have twelve, maybe fifteen players I could bring you. A few of them are two, three dollar bettors. Most bet nickels and dimes. Some want five thousand a day; one guy plays ten dimes a game. And these people are into parlays, round robins, all that stuff."

"That's action," Greco said.

"More than my man can handle. Val says not for you, and my people want to play."

"Lots of people do," Greco said. "But they don't want to pay when they lose."

"That's why I have a crutch to offer you," Thorne said. "I stand behind each of my players personally for the first few weeks, or however long you think it takes to prove they're square. Let's say up to ten thousand per man, in case anyone goes south. I'm sure it won't happen, but I can understand your concern."

Greco looked at him incredulously. "If I ever start investing in the market, you're the man I'm coming to, you do that much for your clients!" he said, thinking: Jesus, I hope Frank isn't that stupid.

Thorne said, "I might have some incentive in this, too."

Thank God, Greco almost blurted out loud.

"A *fair* incentive," Thorne added.

"You mean commission?"

"Call it whatever you want. Let's say I bring you fifteen accounts. I stand behind them until you're satisfied. The payments and collections, either way, are handled through my office in the Loop. I'm used to brokering."

"And you charge both sides for the service. Me and them." This guy Frank was starting to surprise him.

"Not at all," Thorne replied. "I have to front the book because my clients are all name people, people who'd never want it known they get their rocks off putting a thousand dollars on ten kids from the projects chasing a basketball. I'm talking about bankers, politicians, even some judges who invest with me and like to bet a little on the side."

Greco said, "I have a judge that plays, too. He's always late."

"I think it's worth ten percent of your net to eliminate the worry," Thorne declared.

"That's standard. But I have two questions."

"Shoot."

"Why did you come to me?"

"And?"

"You own this big investment business, have all these important clients on your roster. Why do you want to get involved with booking for a few extra dimes?"

"Good questions, easy answers," Thorne said. "I came to you because word had it Sonny Greco's one of the best. You have the connections to handle my business. You keep your mouth shut, and you always pay off."

"Okay. Go on."

"Also, I can't keep holding all this action myself. Besides tying up my afternoons, most of my cash is committed minute-to-minute on the Exchange floor."

"And my commission is going to be your pocket money."

"No way," Thorne shook his head. "I don't need the cash we're talking about. It's simply that I've reached the point with my clients where I can't refuse them. But I don't want to end up holding onto ten, twenty dimes a week either. Win *or* lose."

Greco knew more was coming, but sat silently until Frank told him the rest.

"The other half is, I love the action. Right now, I play a game or two a day, not getting rich, not getting killed. Kind of an entertainment tax. Now, you take on my players, put me on commission for what we win, all of a sudden I have an interest in every game, every day. It's degenerate as hell, but it sure sounds like fun. Can you understand that? It's like betting the board."

"You don't get enough action trading on the Exchange?"

"As W. C. Fields once said: 'Not the way I play it!' "

Greco watched the waitress pass by. "She sure is something," he said, buying time to think things through. At least Frank wasn't looking to become some kind of mob groupie. He'd met enough of those already.

"That she is," Thorne agreed, watching her pass by. She had eyes the color of McCaskey's.

"It might work out," Greco said. *"Maybe."*

"The thing is," Thorne reiterated, "you get no names and no faces. To you and your people, they're nothing but numbers and balances. All I'll need to get things started is an office they can call for lines and plays. As we say in my business, I'll interface with the customers."

Thorne lighted another red dot and let things sink in. "What do you say?"

"I say I'll have to think it over," Greco replied.

"You should."

"I know."

"But not forever. I'd like an answer by next week. The earlier the better. Just tell me yes or no."

Greco shook his hand and gave Thorne his patented response.

"You got it!"

5

WE COULD play tennis," Patricia Becker-Thorne said as she came into the living room.

Thorne was stretched across the sofa wearing an old terry bathrobe, going through a clipboard of notes and memoranda on Operation Clothesline. He felt elated, exhausted, both at once. Beyond setting up the AMP cover company and getting Sonny Greco three-quarters on the line, Thorne had managed on Friday to establish betting accounts with Sandy Lowenstein and Tony Scarpo, who handled the family's gambling operations on the far North and far South Sides respectively. Knowing Thorne for a while, they took his action in a flash, not even pausing as Greco had to think it over and run the appropriate background checks—checks Thorne knew would come up clean thanks to Doc Hermann's team of paper placers, the cooperative management of the Exchange, and his well-meaning contacts on the street.

Even McCaskey's office got off to a flying start, lining up accounts with the head of the Rockford outfit: a small-time liquor distributor named Bagley, who figured he'd have no downside risk, what with the Chicago people standing behind him.

In all, assuming Sonny Greco came through, Thorne's strike team would open the week with sixty-six active betting accounts—enough to meet AAG Bidwell's well-delineated criteria and, if Justice's computers did their anticipated job, hit it right, more than sufficient to make the Chicago family scream in pain when they lost the Bureau's first five-star play.

Thorne flipped through the papers again, read a second advisory from Bidwell directing team leaders, if possible, to wager on sports other than football. Don't frighten off any bookmakers by concentrating too soon or too heavily on the spring league, it said. What Bidwell really meant, Thorne knew, was that he wanted the strike force to lose a little on the side. He just didn't have the balls to put it in writing on Department of Justice letterhead.

"I said, we could play tennis," Patsie repeated. "Don't I even merit a response?"

"It's twenty degrees outside."

Thorne laid the clipboard on his stomach. Patsie stood over him in gold lounging pajamas: from his angle the high cheekbones and flat forehead that photographed so well gave her face a hard, hawkish look.

"It's still March, Pats."

"They're *indoor* courts, Frank. Remember the club we joined last year, the one you never have time to visit? Tennis courts, jogging track, pool. All of them are inside."

Thorne tore Bidwell's advisory into shreds.

"I just feel like hanging around the house today. Being lazy."

Patsie said, "No wonder. You've hardly been home at all this week. You care to tell me how much longer it will go on like this?"

"For a while," Thorne said. "Couple of months."

"Shit," Patsie hissed.

"When it's over, I think I'll come home with a promotion in hand."

"More extra work than extra money."

"It's important, Pats."

"I know. To you."

Thorne recognized the mood and should have changed course. Instead he asked, "How come your career is so damn important and mine is only bothersome and inconvenient? Explain that to me."

"I only asked you to play tennis," Patsie said, green eyes flashing.

"That's not the problem. And you know it."

Patsie sat in a wing chair and leaned forward, forearms on her thighs.

"At least I share my job with you, Frank. Good and bad, but *all* of it. You tell me nothing, not even obliquely, about the days and nights you're gone. I understand there are things you can't talk about, things you'd rather not bring home. But even working for the Bureau can't be ultrasecret all the time. I think you just use that as a way of shutting me out."

"That's not true," Thorne argued. "I told you from the day we got engaged how it might be, that there'd be weeks like this when I'm tied up in knots trying to be someone I'm not, seeing people I don't want to see, to do things I don't want to do."

He watched Patsie brooding and wondered if he'd oversold her and, perhaps, even himself.

"You told me," Patsie admitted finally. "And maybe I thought it was romantic. Then."

"But not now."

She threw her head back into the chair. "What's romantic about a husband who spends half his nights bouncing around North Side bars so he can send a few gamblers to jail?"

Thorne got up and freshened his Bloody Mary at the bar cart, a gilded extravagance Patsie insisted on buying the last time she decorated the house. "What the hell do you expect from me?" he asked. "A single-handed defense of liberty and the American way? I'm just a cop, for Christ's sake."

"I expected a marriage," Patsie shot back. "More of one than we have now."

Thorne said, "You have your tough weeks too. Meetings, traveling to suppliers, making those presentations day after day. It's not only me who's wrapped up in work."

"Perhaps that's the trouble. It's both of us."

Thorne drained his glass, sat on the arm of Patsie's chair.

"I know things haven't been great between us lately," he said. "Could be that's the one thing we're *not* working at."

"You make marriage sound like a second job."

"Things can slip away, even in a good marriage. And we have one, Pats. You know it as well as I do."

"I suppose," she conceded.

"Tell you what," Thorne said, touching her face softly. "We have a whole weekend together. Let's use it to get closer, stop coming at each other."

"That's what I want too."

"I know how we can start."

Thorne began their lovemaking on the chair, leaning over to kiss and stroke her. Patsie slid out of her pajamas and onto the Berber rug she'd uncovered in a Tangiers bazaar, Thorne following her down. At the last minute she mounted him, digging her knees tightly into his ribs as she came with a startling, out-of-character scream.

Later, still on the rug, halfway through a cigarette, Thorne said, "Tennis, anyone?"

"I don't think so."

"Feel better?"

"Much."

"Me too."

He found his cast-aside robe and covered them both.

"Looks like the early part of next week is pretty

open for me. We could meet after work, have an early supper and catch a show, come home for a repeat performance."

Patsie stared at the ceiling, silent.

"Well? How 'bout it?"

"Wish I could," she said. "But I have to run over to Grand Rapids for a few days, look at some new designs. Everything's all arranged."

"No problem."

"I'd postpone it if I could. Only, if I can find the dining room line we need, get an exclusive at the right price, I may not be the only one around here that's up for promotion."

"I hope you find it."

"We still have all weekend," Patsie said.

"Sure we do."

Thorne slipped his arm under Patsie's shoulder, but his mind slipped back to Fairweather's, weighing his chances of going in as partners with Sonny Greco.

Frank Thorne's opening Monday at Assets Management Partners, Ltd. went like this:

•The United States Department of Justice, Federal Bureau of Investigation, decreed that the Tampa Bay Bandits, two-point underdogs on their home field, were the betting lock of the week.

•Sonny Greco agreed to take all of Thorne's action, less ten percent of net winnings, and thus became the federal government's number one bookmaker with the Chicago mob.

Greco phoned that day at two o'clock sharp.

"AMP Limited," Agent McCaskey answered formally. "One moment, please." She pressed the hold button and pointed the receiver at Thorne. "Call for you, Mister *Becker*."

Thorne looked at her anxiously.

"It's him," she said, unprompted. "Greco."

Thorne punched his right fist soundly into his left palm. "Come on, Sonny! Say yes! Say yes!"

McCaskey released the hold button. "Mister Becker will be right with you, sir.

Thorne took a deep breath and hit the *record* switch concealed beneath his desk top. He and Greco exchanged greetings, pleasantries. Thorne complained about losing a nonexistent wager on the Sixers; Greco said he had liked them as well.

"I thought I could stop by your office," Greco said. "Better we talk business face to face."

"That mean we're doing business?"

"When I get there," Greco stalled.

Thorne stopped himself from telling Sonny to make it fast, the sooner the better. Easy does it: don't push him.

"I'm caught up in one helluva day," he said. "Lots of late action building on the floor, and my backside's overexposed on some short contracts. Better make it after the close of market."

"See you at four-thirty," Greco said.

Thorne hit the playback switch to make sure the machine was tracking.

"Today you get to meet Sonny Greco. He's coming by to eyeball the company. We're in like Flynn."

McCaskey listened to the tape carefully. Greco's voice came through clear and staticless.

"He sounds like a man who doesn't take chances," she said. "I'm sure he'll want to know more about Assets Management Partners than the color of our carpet."

"He knows what he needs to know if he's coming here at all," Thorne said. "My guess is he's had the family's lawyers checking us out for days—papers of incorporation, annual reports, Exchange membership, all of it. We must have passed the preliminaries. Now it's on to the main event."

"Everything's moved so quickly . . ." McCaskey wondered.

"A gold star for Doc Hermann," Thorne said. "He's the one personally put the papers in place. Even the company credit cards are back-dated to 1978."

McCaskey nodded, still thinking. "Someone as careful as Sonny Greco might bring a microwave scanner in here, check out the office for microphones. It's simple enough. The ones I saw at Quantico looked like pocket calculators."

"I hadn't thought of it," Thorne admitted, glad she had.

"Greco might."

"Here's what you do while he's here," Thorne said. "Run the afternoon market reports through the computer, get print-outs of everything. Keep your typewriter going too. All that juice in the air should override any detector Greco might have."

"As long as you get him to speak up."

Thorne came out of his chair and punched his palm again.

"Greco's the key," he exclaimed. "The one man in this operation who can get us inside the family."

McCaskey gave him a quizzical look.

"I must be missing something," she said. "My files say that Lowenstein and Scarpo run operations just as large as his. We've even targeted them to assume greater losses. I realize Greco handles the downtown crowd, but I can't see why you're hanging so much on him."

"You have to look beyond the numbers to understand it," Thorne said. "Which is how I spent my weekend once I got through all the bullshit advisories from Bidwell."

"Finding out what?"

"I had Washington run every scrap of data they had on the old man—friends, associates, everyone he's been seen or photographed with for thirty years. What

I found out is, Greco's not just an employee. He's *part* of the family."

"Related to the old man?"

"Eighteen cousins removed," Thorne said. "Not close enough to matter."

"Then it's his wife," McCaskey guessed.

"His father. He and the old man grew up together on the South Side, played on the same semi-pro baseball team back in the Thirties. When Greco's father died—Sonny was barely a teenager—the old man started watching out for him. He made sure the rent got paid, picked up Greco's tuition at Holy Name Academy, took care of whatever Sonny needed."

"And got him a job with the syndicate," she guessed again.

"No. It looks like Sonny did that on his own, but with the old man's approval, of course," Thorne said. "Point is, he's closer to the old man than Scarpo, Lowenstein, anybody else we've got on the list. He can walk into the mansion whenever he feels like, and maybe bring a friend along. That's why Greco comes first. I want to be that friend."

McCaskey sat by Thorne's desk, crossing her legs elegantly, her nylons causing only the slightest hiss of friction.

"Even if you do cultivate a friendship with Greco," she said, "it doesn't follow you'll be invited to Easter dinner with all the bosses, the old—"

The soft chiming of the *receive* bell on her terminal interrupted McCaskey's challenge. She entered their access code, hooked up the secure modem, and spoke to Thorne over the whirring sound of the printer.

"Here we go," she said. "The Attorney General's sports handicapping service is officially open for business."

Thorne leaned over her shoulder as the data came in from Washington.

"According to the best computer minds in the U.S.

Department of Justice, the steam team of the week is Tampa Bay. Not warranteed. Guaranteed."

"There's more," McCaskey said. She waited until the machine clicked down and tore off the green-striped print-out. "Here."

"Bidwell put up two other games, probably to test his program," Thorne read. "But the five-star move is tonight at Tampa Bay. They're two-point underdogs at home. Bidwell's version of the billion-dollar brain says they'll win straight up, four points or more. Now we wait and see if the Vegas oddsmakers catch on and adjust the spread."

"Why would they change it?" McCaskey asked.

"Too much money bet on one side. Or their computers say the same thing as ours. That's one thing our actuarial wizards forgot to account for—last minute adjustments to balance out the action."

McCaskey checked her watch and gathered a pile of notes.

"I'm scheduled to talk with the strike team at three o'clock," she said. "That's when I give them the teams and amounts to bet."

Thorne read the print-out another time and made his decision.

"Tell them they're on their own tonight," he said. "It's every man for himself."

"On their own?"

"That's right. Have each agent make one thousand-dollar play, two others for five hundred or less. And they bet whoever they want, no help from us."

"The thousand dollars goes on Tampa Bay," she said, confused.

"Don't even mention that Tampa Bay is the move. Just give them the spreads and turn them loose. Bidwell's right about one thing: we pound football too heavily at first and the house is liable to take it off the board completely. Fact is, I hope we lose a few thousand," Thorne considered. "Like John Carradine playing poker in those old Westerns. Lose first, then up the ante like we're struggling to get even."

"Why don't we just bet *against* Tampa Bay if you want to lose?"

"I don't want to establish a pattern this early on, make it look like all our people are dancing to the same band," Thorne said. "So tell everyone to roll their own dice and see if they can win anything without IBM in their corner."

"What do I tell Washington?" McCaskey asked. "How do I say, 'The hell with you, Mister Attorney General'?"

"Tell Bidwell we want a chance to test *our* system, see if our agents know a damned thing about what they're doing."

McCaskey said, "I'll phrase it differently, but he'll get the message."

Thorne sat back, lifted his feet onto the desk blotter. He watched McCaskey activate the conference net, deal with the collective force of twenty-two government agents who were engaged in the task of betting on football games with the Chicago mob. Some fucked-up way to be a cop, he told himself, already thinking about what might happen to Sonny Greco when Bidwell and the Bureau got what they wanted.

Greco arrived at four-thirty and change. He wore gray trousers, camel's hair blazer, striped Sulka shirt opened at the collar, J & M penny loafers. He introduced himself to McCaskey, who sat waiting in the reception area, and followed as she led him breezily into Thorne's office.

"Nice quarters. Impressive," he said.

"A little small," Thorne said. "But I don't need much space up here. My action's on the trading floor. With all these computers and stuff, I even get by with a combination secretary–office manager."

"That's nice too."

"Yes, she is."

Greco finished surveying the room and took a seat. "I've thought about your proposition, talked it over with my people."

"And no doubt checked me out."

"Like you did me."

"True." Thorne nodded. "Did I pass muster?"

"So far so good," Greco said. "Your business looks solid and you don't owe any money around town. That's best of all."

"That's good to hear."

Thorne leaned over his desk, got the tape recorder going as McCaskey came back inside and started running the market finals. Thorne apologized for the noise and explained about the position he'd taken on some soybean contracts.

"So are we in business?" he asked Greco matter-of-factly.

"I'll take your action," Greco said. "Let's hope it's a good move for both of us."

"We're a cinch."

Greco took Thorne's business card from his wallet and pushed it across the blotter.

"The office your players call is written on the back. It's open five to seven every night; eleven to one on weekends. When baseball starts and the Cubs are home, he'll be there an hour before game time. Any other day games you can bet the night before; but if the scheduled pitchers change, all bets are off."

Thorne read the phone number aloud to get it on tape. "Where's this exchange?" he asked.

"South suburbs," Greco said. "A couple of direct mail houses operate down there, got people calling in all hours to place orders. That makes it harder for the cops to run phone screens. We hope."

"Live and learn," said Thorne, wondering if Corrigan's squad had figured out that one and neglected to tell him.

Greco went on, "You assign each player a number from one to twenty. Make sure they use the prefix letter 'F' when they call in. It's F-1, F-2, whatever. That breaks them out from the pack, makes it easier to keep their figures straight."

"What else?"

"We have everything up," Greco said. "All basketball is eleven to ten—bet a hundred, win a hundred or lose one-ten. Same for football, a ten-cent line."

"The same for baseball?" Thorne asked.

"We start doing baseball, the price goes to twenty cents," Greco replied. "You bet a seven and a half to five favorite, you win a hundred or lose one-fifty. The underdog pays one-thirty to win, a hundred to lose."

"Expensive."

"Not if you bet the dogs."

"Easy for you to say," Thorne laughed.

"We all read the same pitching form," Greco smiled back.

Thorne decided to take a break. He poured himself a Scotch and made Greco a vodka and soda.

"You mentioned parlays and round-robins," Greco recalled after a short sip on his drink. "A two-team parlay, both winners, pays thirteen to five. A three-team robin pays seven-eighty a hundred. Anybody wants to do multiple-team robins, the way to figure the number of parlays involved is to subtract the highest number and add up the rest. With a five-team robin, you subtract the five, add up four-three-two-one, you get ten separate parlays hooked together. The phone man has all that in front of him. He can tell your people how much they'll win or lose, depending on the prices and how many of their teams cover."

Thorne did his math on the blotter.

"So anybody betting a five-team hundred-dollar robin," he calculated, "loses five hundred if no teams cover, or picks up twenty-six hundred if all bets win."

"That's the way your side sees it," Greco laughed. "I see robin-players financing me a condo in Maui."

"Sure, even when they win they're paying vigorish," Thorne said, putting down his pen. "So what kind of limits are we talking about?"

"You're the one standing behind it for a month. Make it easy on yourself."

"I still need to know your ceiling."

"I'll take up to ten thousand a play," Greco said casually. "Football I can go higher—twenty-five dimes, you got somebody that long on green. But start moving those kind of numbers and the big boys get involved right away. Make sure your customers know that. These people can be rough with slow pays. I say slow because, with them, there's no such thing as a no-pay. It's just when, not if."

Thorne tried not to flinch. Greco must have cleared him all the way to the top to get that level of action. Operation Clothesline was on the way.

"Clear enough," he said.

"Just so you know up front. No one wants any misunderstandings, any reason to get upset."

"My people least of all," Thorne said.

"The week runs from Tuesday through the Monday night football games. You and I can balance out on Thursdays. Let's keep it informal, meet somewhere fun, grab a drink. We can start tonight," Greco said. "I have to meet someone at the Trader's Pub. Come on down when you're through here. My round."

Trader's Pub was the last place Thorne wanted to drink in. If he supposedly was prominent in the business, how come no one there knew him from Adam? Take a pass.

"Give me a rain check," he said. "I have a lot of calls to make and," he nodded toward McCaskey, "there's an office matter that needs some attention."

"As hard as she works, you'd better keep her happy," Greco said. "I'll catch you at Fairweather's, say tomorrow or Wednesday. Nobody says it has to be *all* business."

"Nobody at all," Thorne agreed.

Thorne and McCaskey went through the Greco tape a second time, debriefing, planning their next moves. Thorne knew this: Money was the key. McCaskey's records had to be airtight, every play and every payment accounted for precisely, or the family's arsenal of lawyers would get the case thrown out of court like a misdated parking ticket.

Most important, he knew as well, was to get Greco and his bosses passing the cash on camera.

"Jurors can't follow a money trail that's buried in computer tape and six-column ledgers," he said. It was after dark, the Exchange Building silent, empty. "They don't hear the words, see the pass-along, they don't believe it. Sometimes, even then . . ."

"Too dangerous," McCaskey argued. "I may not have much field experience, but I don't think you're going to get these people anywhere we can set up video. And a wire is the first thing they'll look for."

Not if Sonny Greco wears it, Thorne thought, getting far ahead of himself. He said, "There are ways. Tech services has a warehouse full of stuff—tooth implants, filament mikes that blend into the hair, all that."

"And the other side knows all about them," McCaskey persisted. "They probably buy from the same vendors we do. Let's stay with the phone taps, what we get on tape here. For now, anyway."

"You may be right."

"I *am.*"

Thorne heard the edge in her voice: tension, fatigue, both. She closed her file jacket and rubbed her eyes with balled fists.

"Go home, get some rest," he said. "I'll stick around

and see how we do without Bidwell's brain behind us."

Thorne pulled off his tie and started going over the roster of agents, checking the codes he'd assigned them as bettors with Greco, Scarpo, Lowenstein. McCaskey took the computer off line; she stood and smoothed her skirt gracefully.

"Sonny Greco's an interesting man," she said. "Good looking, well mannered, articulate. I'd never make him for a syndicate bookie."

"They don't all look like Frank Nitti," Thorne said. "Sanford Lowenstein could be a corporate attorney for Standard Oil, you ever saw him. Now Scarpo—Tony Shoes, they call him—he's a different story altogether."

"Taken in by looks again," McCaskey laughed. "Still, I can tell you two get along, even like each other."

"Just business, is all."

McCaskey had her coat on when she came back to Thorne's desk. "You needn't hang around here. Everything will keep till tomorrow."

"It's okay," Thorne said. "Patsie's away on business. Went to Michigan to look at some dining rooms."

"Then how about that dinner you offered me last week? I'm starved."

"You're not too tired?"

McCaskey shook her head.

"You're the one who said I have to eat anyway. Give me an hour's head start to go home and freshen up. Come by and see the flat you're paying nine-fifty for. I'll fix drinks, or we can run over to Fairweather's."

"I didn't think you liked the place," Thorne said.

"I'm only thinking about your street cover. Big gamblers always keep girlfriends on the side, and bosses sleep with their secretaries. Your inference was pretty strong on the Greco tape."

"Nothing personal. I just wanted to quell Sonny's ardor."

"Something less than ardor. A compliment, I'd call it."

"I'm protective by nature."

"I hate that in men," McCaskey said, breaking into a bright smile. "After being desk-bound all these years, I might as well use the opportunity to live it up like you field people do. Burn up the expense budget."

"Dinner on Doc Hermann," Thorne smiled back. "See you in an hour."

"I saw a Creole place near my apartment. Looks interesting, if you like that kind of food."

"The Breaux Bridge?"

"That's the one."

"It's terrific," Thorne said. "I did time in New Orleans back in my Navy days. This place is as close as you can get."

"*Laissez le bon temps rouler!*" McCaskey beamed back. "Let the good times roll!"

6

SONNY GRECO was tired of throwing the party. Maybe taking on some new action would turn things around, change his luck. Like going down on a black broad, whatever else was supposed to work.

He'd felt that way—upbeat, ready to go on a roll—since Johnny Roses had bought his proposal over the weekend, agreeing to handle Frank Becker's action, throw him ten percent of the net for commission. A good omen. They called the boss "Johnny Roses" because that's what he always came up smelling like, no matter how much shit he'd stepped in.

That was Saturday. They were practicing short putts on the circle of plastic green in Johnny's basement. "Go ahead, you think they're worth something," Johnny Roses said. "But watch yourself. You're carrying enough deadbeats already."

"The money's there," Greco said, assertive, reassuring.

"What we're talking here is people we don't know. Brought to us by somebody we don't know either. Keep that in mind."

"A better way to do business," Greco said. "Nobody

claiming he's somebody else's cousin. And we got Becker standing behind them for the first ten dimes they owe."

He watched the boss stroke a six-footer that died a few inches from the cup. Greco thought he'd snap the Ping in half.

"We don't know this guy can stand behind a fifty-dollar bar tab. The first thing you do is find out."

Johnny Roses then gave him the number of an attorney near the Daley Center; not J. J. O'Connor, another Irishman named Boyle who was wired into City Hall. Boyle kept a private cop on his payroll, the boss said. The kind who could tell them fast what they needed to know about Frank Becker and Assets Management Partners, Ltd.

"Call Boyle tonight. Get him moving before you do. It will cost us," he said grimly. "The action better be there."

"It is," Greco said.

Johnny Roses went one-for-five on the six-foot putts. Greco sank four in a row. Definitely on a roll.

"Enough of this!" Johnny bellowed, staring fire-eyed at the contoured shaft of his Ping. He walked to the bar, poured two Buds and lit a Macanudo. Greco aimed his fifth putt wide-right to keep him calmed down.

"We'll do a practice round soon as the weather breaks," he said. "No Nassau, no press, nothing."

The boss had already switched back to business.

"I asked about your picking up the rest of college buckets," he said.

"And baseball," Greco reminded him.

"That too. You got the green light, Sonny. Use the regular offices, just make goddamn sure the figures are kept separate. Don't even think about moving cash back and forth. You got some people worried about that before you even start."

"Nobody has to worry," Greco said, wondering who went to bat for him. Johnny Roses told him.

"There's no street tax either. The old man himself said so. 'Sonny's a good kid,' he says. 'Let him have it.' Till then there were objections. Some people were looking for twenty percent of the bottom line."

"Sid Paris?"

"For one. There were others."

"What did you say?"

"It's what I say now that matters. And it's like this—you take a beating, it's your headache. I don't want to hear one fucking word you end up stuck fifty, sixty dimes on those damned college games. Remember, people all over are working them kids, a few points off for a few ounces of nose candy."

Not a chance, Greco thought. The old man was behind him. Another good omen.

"It's a winner," he said. "I feel it in my bones."

Johnny Roses said, "Everybody feels like that. Right before they take a royal bath."

Greco drove out of the Loop, past traffic court on La Salle and west on Chicago Avenue. Sure, there was always the risk he'd lose on college hoops. But if he played it smart, moved the lines around, he felt he could clear at least enough to pay Johnny Roses what he owed from the brilliant move he'd made holding back on the Blaze. And baseball, with that twenty-cent line, had never failed him once.

Absolutely. Sonny Greco is back in business, firing away. Go to the window.

He decided to skip his meeting at Trader's Pub, bypass Rush Street and the Near North joints, head up to Dead Dom's, see what Pizza Sal wanted, maybe catch the West Coast games on the satellite. Get home early, he figured. Scramble up some eggs for himself and the doggies, make it a quiet night. Camille and the twins were due home soon. He'd straighten up the house, get someone over in the morning to do dishes, laundry. Sure, unless Diane had something else in mind.

He took his usual seat at the end of the bar, ordered a greenie. Dom flipped a rug under the bottle of Heineken.

"Diane's staying home tonight," he said. "Wants you to call her. Pizza Sal's back in my office, probably doing shit. He's been flapping around all night like a ruptured rooster. Must have had his cage rattled good and hard."

"Doesn't take much these days," Greco said. "Let him sit a while. Hand me the bar phone."

He called Berwyn Bobby, who bitched about needing a raise for the extra work until Greco told him to shut up and read out the figures. Sixteen F players had called in, Bobby said. All of them came out swinging: dimes, nickels, a couple of parlays. Bobby made it six good-sized losers, seven more stuck about a nickel each, two guys pushed. The only winner was plus four dollars. It *was* turning around, Greco thought. So far, so good.

"What about Tampa Bay?" he asked. That game worried him most.

"They're up twenty-seven-ten with five minutes left. Pittsburgh was laying them two points."

"Who the hell came up with a line like that?" Greco fumed. "Tampa was a cinch and they *get* points!"

"Same price all over," Bobby said. "I called half a dozen places just to be sure. Two points came right out of Vegas, and nobody wanted to fuck with it."

"Give me the damage report."

"Most everybody went to the bank on Tampa. The only players didn't cream it were the new ones. That's the good news. The bad is, I think we're stuck about twenty dimes."

"The boss is gonna love that," Greco moaned. Maybe Johnny Roses had sold spring football too hard; two weeks into the season and they hadn't come up with one plus figure on it. The family must be getting nervous.

"I wonder why these F players mostly laid off the game," Bobby said.

"Maybe they talk to each other. Or the guy handling them gave out some free advice, told them to take a pass. Smart if he did, in the long run. Tampa was so obvious it looked like a trap."

"It was for us," Bobby said. "At least we're above water with the college hoops."

"Any big moves?"

"Georgetown, but they didn't cover."

"They'll still be there," Greco said.

"Not tonight. Even your pals at Dead Dom's dropped thirty-six hundred on them. Got beat by Seton Hall at *home.*"

Greco looked down the bar and understood why Dom was pouring himself a double shooter of Jack. He said, "Clear out the other offices and call me tomorrow with the totals. I'll be home all day."

"Don't forget to walk the puppies," Bobby wisecracked.

Greco envisioned his smirk and suggested he perform a physically impossible act. Dom walked over after he'd hung up.

"Bad night in football," Greco said.

"A lot of my guys had Tampa Bay," Dom said.

"Yeah, and Georgetown too."

"I can't believe that one."

"It happens."

"Where the hell *is* Seton Hall anyway?" Dom pondered. "You ought to send them a scholarship or something, winning like that in overtime."

"You don't know?" Greco said in disbelief. "You guys put over three dimes on a game and you don't even know what state the school's in?"

"What school's that?" Airlines Al jumped in. Thanks to employee privileges, he was the best traveled of Dom's regulars, making it to the Derby each May, Vegas twice in winter.

"Where's Seton Hall at?" Dom asked.

"Philly," Al said, confidently. "Them, Villanova, and I think St. Joe's, John's, somethin' like that."

"Sounds right," Dom agreed.

"Yeah, down the street from the Citadel, Temple, something like that," Greco said, throwing up his hands.

He found Pizza Sal back in the office, Kleenex pushed against his face, a rolled-up hundred sitting on the desk.

"Kid Shaleen. The man with the iron nose."

Sally wiped at his nostrils. "Great stuff. You want a whack?"

Greco turned him down, said he was trying for an early night.

"I'll never sleep anyway," Sally said.

"You never do."

"Not from this. It's them fuckin' cops. They had me all afternoon."

"Had you where?"

"Where the hell do you think? The Athletic Club? I was at police headquarters, is where. Some lieutenant named Corrigan wanted to talk a little business. You know the script: first they make you sweat, then turn real sweet and say all your troubles are over if you speak up."

"What about O'Connor?" Greco said, nervous, knowing Sally needed all the help he could get in stress situations. "He had to be there or they turn you loose."

"In court all day," Sally shook his head. "I got a hold of him later. He was real pissed off at first, wanted to make a stink downtown about them leaning on me without counsel in the room. I told him forget it. Cops were just taking a stab."

"Do we know this guy Corrigan?"

"O'Connor does. Says he's a real Boy Scout. Been around Vice for a while, but nobody we know ever's got to him."

"The way your luck's running, nobody ever will," Greco said. "So what'd he want, this Corrigan?"

"He wanted me to roll over and play rat. Says he's got an okay from the state's attorney to drop charges if I play ball. 'What kind of ball?' I ask him. That's when his partner steps in, a real big prick, name of Massey. The two of them start doin' a good cop–bad cop number on me—Massey talking about hard time in Stateville, getting rectal expansion therapy from some horny buck spade. Like that."

"He probably lost a sawbuck to his own bookie," Greco said. "What else?"

"Then this lieutenant, Corrigan, he brings out all my rap sheets. Jeez, they even had my service record, knew all about the auto parts business I got nailed for when I was in the motor pool out at Leonard Wood."

"Means they talked to the feds."

"Musta, 'cause they start asking why I don't pay no taxes either. Corrigan's trying to be nice now. 'You don't want us to call in the IRS. We're sweethearts next to them,' he says. I tell him back he can call in the fuckin' Marines for all I care. But it was tough, Sonny. They had me sweating three hours."

Greco said, "Somebody must be putting the squeeze on. Cops sound like they're sweating too. Which means they don't have shit going for themselves."

"They got some balls asking me to give up my players, other offices, everything, just to beat a chicken shit rap O'Connor says won't stand up anyway." Sally rubbed his hands together nervously, staring at Greco.

"You think O'Connor's right about my getting off?"

"For what he gets paid, he'd better not make promises he can't keep," Greco said. "Relax. You'll be fine."

"Sure. No sweat."

He sat back in Dom's chair trying to appear calm and collected. Greco saw the perspiration beading on his forehead. You relax too, he told himself. No reason to worry about Sally giving up anybody, anything, ever. He had his habits, sure, but disloyalty wasn't one of them. Even Johnny Roses knew that much.

The real worry was a possible offensive by Chicago Vice. Usually they just cracked a few phone men around Super Bowl time; make a point, get some press. This year, Greco recalled, hardly anybody got nailed. Johnny Roses attributed their free ride to all the changes inside the CPD: cops getting bounced around thanks to the novice pols in City Hall. Whatever was happening, Greco knew someone higher up than Lieutenant Corrigan was calling the shots. It was Johnny Roses' job to tell the family, theirs to find out who and how much it would take to defuse him.

"Where do you sit with O'Connor?"

Sally said, "Preliminary hearing's a week from Tuesday. That's where this probable cause thing comes in. O'Connor says they had no right to bust in my goddamn door, so they can't use anything they got inside. Now he's working on a judge. Guy named Twitchell's his first choice. He and J. J. are like this," he said, entwining his index and middle fingers. "We need a few continuances to get him, but O'Connor says it's worth the wait."

"What I say is, you'd better lay low for a while. Stay off the phones, don't go near the offices. And keep away from the blow. You know how you get when you start partying."

Sally showed him the Ziploc was almost empty.

"I just did a little 'cause I get nervous hanging around jails. Maybe I'll move down south with Berwyn Bobby," he suggested. "Run in some new lines."

"Don't you ever listen?" Greco erupted. "I just said you're off the phones."

"You mean nothing?"

"Not for a while. O'Connor comes through like he says, you get a pass, we'll figure something out. But you know the boss's rules—you're out of action at least three months after a bust."

"That's bullshit!" Sally raged. "No reason I can't work the phones. It's my ass, I get cracked again."

Greco looked at him dispassionately. Pizza Sal was the consummate phone freak, calling everyone he knew twice a day just to verify nothing was going on. The day of his brief second marriage, Sal worked the phones up to an hour before the ceremony. That night, supposed to be blissed out in Miami Beach, he'd told Greco deadpan, Sally rolled over at midnight and started dialing. His bride first thought he was calling room service, ordering more champagne. Instead he called Sports Phone to get the West Coast finals, see how the house was doing.

"C'mon, Sonny. I can still work the phones."

"I can't let you. No way."

"I've gotta do something for cash."

"You sit tight," Greco said. "I'll carry you for a while. But you have to come up clean before you go back to work."

"Lookit," Sally said, his jaw rattling, "I owe some people around town. I can't keep stalling them until O'Connor finds the right judge or Johnny Roses says it's okay to work again. I've been making my payments, Sonny. But now, these people can get nasty."

"Tell me who it is," Greco said. "Maybe I can talk to them. After all, you've been taking heat for the family."

"That's not it," Sally stalled.

"Who is it?"

"Chuckie Franco."

"You went and picked the best," Greco said. "That bastard *likes* breaking legs."

"That's what I'm telling you."

Greco dreaded his next question. "How much you into Franco for?"

"Eighteen."

"Eighteen what? Hundred?"

"Thousand," Sally said, almost whimpering.

"You been free basing?" Greco roared. "You get into Franco for that much, there's no way . . ."

"I had no choice. You think I wanted to go see Franco at all? But some other people were involved, so if it wasn't him . . ."

"The ponies," Greco knew. "You started with the track again. What'd you do, take Berwyn Bobby's sure picks for a dime a pop?"

"I had my own winners," Sally protested.

"You ain't had a winning horse since Ernie Banks was a rookie!"

"There's also this guy from down south. I took his merchandise on consignment, twenty percent down. Kind of a balloon loan," Sally went on. "But him I can stall a while. The guy's great. If I had the cash, I could pick up a key or two below wholesale. Stuff so good nobody believes it. We could duff it up, double our money in a week, with a little left over to . . ."

This time Greco lost control and unleashed a barrage of insults at Sally's impaired thought processes.

"You know how the family feels about us going near that stuff. Johnny Roses, the old man, they go crazy just hearing somebody does a line, let alone deals. We got warned once. That's all the grace we get."

"I'll handle it," Sally said. "No one could put you within ten miles of anything. All I need to get rolling is twenty-five dimes buy money."

"You get nothing," Greco said flatly, his tone leaving no room for speculation. "Even if it wasn't for the old man, you know how business is going."

"And you know how Chuckie Franco feels about waiting for his money. You want to see me in a hospital with sandbags hanging off the bed?"

"I'll talk to Franco," Greco promised. "We'll work out something."

"Hey, you'd better." Sally fumbled in his pockets to find a Pall Mall. He kept thinking, dreaming out loud. "This deal could be *sooo* sweet . . ."

"Knock it off!" Greco yelled. "You go making any moves like that, swear to God I'll deliver you to Franco myself."

"I'll do nothing," Sally gave in. "Just get Franco to sit still a few more weeks. I'll figure out something."

"You got it," Greco said, then added realistically, "at least I can try."

7

SONNY GRECO'S turn-around never happened: he spent the next month getting crushed from every conceivable angle; whatever his players did was blessed by the angels.

Like the semi-final game of the NCAA tournament, Georgetown versus Kentucky on a neutral court. Greco believed to his bones that Georgetown was a lock, so he moved the line favoring them from 2 to 3½ points. No way the smart money would give away that much. After all, Georgetown had lost to Seton Hall at home and barely gotten by a trio of dink teams in the early rounds of the tournament. Kentucky's twin towers, he figured, made them look like a five-star play, a cinch.

The trap was set.

No one bit.

Every big money player in his book loaded up on Georgetown, points and all. Greco thought he had a chance at halftime—Kentucky leading 29–22 and the Hoyas shooting the worst twenty minutes of basketball he'd ever seen in a high school game, let alone the NCAAs. Maybe, just maybe, he had a winner in spite of himself.

Not a chance.

Kentucky came out in the second half and hit three of thirty-three shots from the floor, their first bucket coming after an eleven-minute, sixteen-shot drought. Even the Hoyas looked stunned as brick after brick bounced off the Kentucky rim.

Final score: Georgetown, 53–40.

Final figure: Greco stuck twenty-six thousand.

The championship game didn't help much either. Despite a big spread—Georgetown giving 6 to 8 points, depending on the source—the entire Western world took the Hoyas again. Greco laid off all he could, but ended up eating another ten dimes as Georgetown buried the outgunned Houston Cougars, 84–75.

Baseball opened that same week and didn't treat Greco much better. He felt confident when the early money started pouring in on the Cubs, who'd had the worst spring training record in both leagues, losing eleven straight out in Mesa. Ah, Chicago fans, Greco thought. They'll never ever learn.

He and Johnny Roses went to an icy, windblown Wrigley Field for the home opener. The Cubbies won handily, 9–1, beating a rookie Mets pitcher named Dwight Gooden. They also won ten of their next twelve games and ended up in first place of the National League East.

Scratch the rest of Greco's bank. He'd start to work from savings and, when he could get the key, whatever was stashed in Camille's safety deposit box. Which still wasn't enough.

Johnny Roses' bank, which meant the family's, was equally deep in a hole. That spring football league was killing them. Frank Becker's players were killing them most of all. Whoever these guys were, they never lost.

"Maybe we should take football off the board, close down for a while," Greco said after the boss erupted about their losses.

"We stick with it," Johnny Roses said intractably. "Nobody can keep winning at this pace."

"Unless the fix is in."

"That's *our* business."

"Whatever you say."

The only good news Greco heard that entire month was that Pizza Sal got off.

He was talking with Camille long distance when O'Connor called on the office phone. Camille was saying she wanted to ride out April in Florida, wanted her mother to visit there a few weeks, wanted twenty-five hundred cash wired to her by the weekend. School was no problem, she insisted. What with the Easter recess upcoming and a Montessori-certified tutor in every day, the twins weren't falling behind a bit. And their tans . . .

"Fine, that's what you want," Greco consented.

Camille said that he should come down too, there was plenty of room in the house.

"My other phone's ringing. We'll talk tomorrow when the twins are around."

Greco switched lines before Camille could extract any more promises from him. J. J. O'Connor made his announcement boastfully.

"Mister Catania will not have to face the burden of a trial," he said. "The charges against him were dismissed."

"He's off?"

"That he is. If you spring for dinner, I'll be happy to tell you how we did it."

With Diane working the bar at Dead Dom's and Frank seeing his accounts, Greco figured he could use some company. O'Connor barely filled the bill, but he had gotten Sally off.

"Why not? You know Padrino's, down on Taylor Street?" he said.

"Sure. Great veal."

"Meet you there in an hour. You make any plays tonight?"

"Haven't had a chance to look," O'Connor replied. "My defense of Mister Catania took precedence. I might take a late game with you, head to head."

Nothing changes, Greco thought. Least of all his luck. "Padrino's in an hour."

Greco dug a sports jacket from the hall closet, wrapped a blue cashmere muffler around his neck. As he stepped outside, Mork and Mindy scampered in and ran whining to their bowls. Greco decided he'd better feed them, and might as well check in with Berwyn Bobby. It was another football night and Johnny Roses was squirming.

"Who is it?" Greco asked as he flipped the Yorkies a can of tuna.

"L.A.'s the move," Bobby reported. "The F players jumped all over it. Hard. You want the totals?"

"Just give me the line."

"Los Angeles laying three and a hook at home."

"That *smells*!"

"Three and a half is everywhere," Bobby said. "I can try to lay some off, you want. What the hell, maybe we'd be smart to take a position ourselves. I have some open account numbers."

"The boss says we don't lay off. Hold everything you got."

"How about I throw down a few dimes for us? Why should we be the only ones missing the party?"

"Leave me out," Greco said. "Way things are going, I'd probably lose on a last-second earthquake."

He checked his watch, allowed four hours for road time, dinner with O'Connor, a quick stop at Fairweather's. "Call me when you get back from the track," he said. "I'll be at Dead Dom's by midnight."

"Better run a tab," Bobby said. "That's how bad it looks."

Greco took the Eisenhower downtown, passed the

time by bouncing back and forth between the five baseball games his power-boosted car radio could receive—Sox and Brewers at home, Cubs and Cardinals away, Seattle already destroying the Yankees. When he reached Padrino's, O'Connor was well into the stand-up martinis.

"We lost the motion to dismiss for lack of probable cause," he began. "You were right about someone tipping the police about Mister Catania's book. Not only did they get his phone number, they also ran a screen, saw the blip during betting hours. With a hundred plus incoming calls between five and seven every night, the judge had to grant them cause."

"You couldn't get to Twitchell?"

"The good Judge Twitchell had his hands full today," O'Connor said. "The two brothers who shot a cop in the projects last week . . ."

"I remember. They didn't have a city sticker on their car."

"They were in the courtroom as well, along with a large assemblage of press covering them. The judge had to be careful, discreet."

"Pizza Sal in court with two cop killers. Great," Greco shook his head.

"It *was* a felony charge," O'Connor reminded him. "But I found a way through the minefield that is law."

Greco had never seen anyone strut like a rooster while sitting on a bar stool.

"The state's attorney decided to strike twice, thinking his iron was still hot, and entered Mister Catania's betting records into evidence. If they stand, Salvatore goes to trial, Judge Twitchell or no. So I move to suppress on the basis they were merely personal documents, household materials, maintained with no criminal purpose or intent."

"They were in *code*," Greco said.

"Everyone has a system, a kind of personal shorthand," O'Connor went on. "No matter. It all went perfectly. You see, Mister Catania had the foresight to inform me that, in the absence of flash paper, he'd written his tallies in a bound notebook that also contained the gin rummy scores he kept with his lady friend, the one in the bathroom."

"I remember," Greco said.

"I pointed these scores out to the bench. Judge Twitchell looks over the notebook, sees the boxes as well as all these numbers. He reminds the prosecutor that playing gin rummy at home does not constitute felony gambling in the state of Illinois."

"But all the plays he took," Greco said, perplexed.

"Exactly the response by the young man from the state's attorney's office. Judge Twitchell inquired of them too."

O'Connor ordered a back-up martini, relishing his moment.

"I reply these numbers only refer to the score of Mister Catania's ongoing gin game. 'And what were the stakes of this supposed game?' the prosecutor asks. A fatal mistake."

O'Connor swirled the olive around in his glass. "I conferred with Mister Catania to determine exactly what stakes he and the lady were playing for. 'For sex,' he says bluntly. 'Body rubs, blow jobs, things like that. She'll testify to it, you want her to.'"

"Unbelievable," Greco gulped.

"Inspired, actually," O'Connor contradicted. "And very well represented. So I approach the bench and make a motion to dismiss. Our boy prosecutor is stunned. Twitchell is worried about the basis of my motion—he wants to grant it if at all possible, but remember, all these reporters are hanging around waiting for the cop shooters to come up.

"But I tell the judge in a whisper that Mister Catania's notes refer to the specific sexual favors he would give or receive depending upon the outcome of his gin rummy match. These favors were recorded in code in an understandable attempt at discretion. Judge Hiram A. Twitchell freezes for a moment, envisioning such testimony at a trial. Then he looks down at the notebook and begins laughing in a most unjudicial manner.

" 'Apparently, Mister Ryan,' he tells the state's attorney, 'your case against Salvatore Catania has just been Schneidered. Motion for dismissal is granted for lack of evidence.' "

"Sally's been touched by God," Greco sighed. "He beats a bookmaking rap for getting his knob polished! I don't believe it."

"Neither did the prosecutor," O'Connor said, grinning. "If the press hadn't been on the scene, I think he would have started bawling his eyes out.

O'Connor rolled the stem glass between his stubby fingers, presavoring another taste of English gin.

"We still have the matter of fee to discuss," he said.

"No worry. You know who's standing behind it."

"John Ross, is it?" he whispered.

Greco nodded.

"Then my fee shall be only five thousand. My fee, that is. There were other expenses incurred, you understand."

"Just give me the total."

"Sixty-five hundred. A bargain, really, when you consider all . . ."

"You'll have it inside a week," Greco said.

O'Connor nodded his acceptance of terms. "Before we proceed to the veal, might you take something on tonight's Los Angeles–New Jersey game?"

"It's gone," Greco said, tired of thinking about it. "The pregame show ended when I walked in."

"What's the difference? I haven't been away from the bar. The score's still zero-zero for all I know."

"Okay, fire away."

The lawyer took a gold Cross pen from his pocket. Greco told him to put it away, said he'd remember.

"Who do you want?"

"L.A., naturally. Say a thousand, laying three points."

"Three and a half," Greco corrected him. Maybe Bobby was right, he thought. Should have played the damn thing himself. Why let everyone else keep winning. He turned to O'Connor, who wore a puckish Beefeater grin.

"You got it."

Detective Tom Massey found his boss in a dark, noisy cop bar on the north edge of Dearborn Park. He skirted the two guys who wore shoulder holsters while playing a money game of nine-ball, grabbed a used glass and poured himself a beer from Jack Corrigan's pitcher.

"That fucking creep Catania got off."

"So I heard," Corrigan said. "J. J. O'Connor may be a drunk, a crook, whatever. But he knows his way around a courtroom."

"And the right judge," Massey carped.

"No use sweating it. Life's too short."

"It still sucks," Massey said between gulps of Old Style. "The mob gets the top shyster in town. Our side gets some punk state's attorney two years out of law school. You don't sweat that, lieutenant?"

"That's how it is."

Massey shook his head, wondered why Corrigan looked so defeated. He said, "I'm sticking close to Frank Thorne. Not a real tight tail. Like you said, here and there, when time permits. I'm not sure everything he told us fits."

Corrigan looked him in the eye for the first time. "Say what you mean, Tom."

"Maybe Thorne was telling us the truth about being into a securities thing for the Bureau," Massey said. "He's spending his days at an office in the Exchange Building. Assets Management Partners, it's called. Which makes sense."

"It does to me," Corrigan said. "We could run a check on the company, but if Frank's gone under-cover, I don't want to screw up anything he's got going."

"It's his night moves I'm wondering about," Massey said. "He's been burning up Rush Street, Near North lately. I'm talking three, four nights a week here. Throwing a lot of cash around too, more than Uncle Sam ever paid him. And he's got this broad with him a lot. Dark hair, Irish eyes, a real looker. They've been hanging out at Fairweather's, both of them."

"Good place to run a smoke screen," Corrigan said. "Where all the brokers, traders go after work."

"A lot of gamblers hang there too."

"So?"

Massey said, "You remember the guy Cal Bostic brought in, the one who tipped him off to Sal Catania's book. Well that guy thought for sure Catania's banker was a guy named Greco."

"I know Sonny Greco. He runs one of the family's top books in town. I've been wanting to nail him for years, but he always comes up clean, nothing sticks."

"Looks like Frank Thorne knows him too," Massey said. "That's who he's been playing pals with when that broad isn't hanging on his arm. I'm telling you, him and Greco are as thick as thieves."

"Thorne and Greco," Corrigan said, slamming his glass, coming out of his slouch. "So either Sonny Greco's gone into the investment business, which I kinda doubt, or Thorne was giving us a long line of bullshit about getting pulled off the street."

"Or maybe he's playing footsie with the mob, on his own time," Massey said, hoping.

"That I don't buy," Corrigan said.

"You saying you don't want to know either?"

"Lookit," Corrigan barked. "I'm the one put you on this. Don't ever tell me what I don't want to know. Don't even think it."

"Hey, sorry," Massey backed off. The guy was steel-spined.

Corrigan sloshed his glass with beer, watched the head spill over and form a puddle on the table.

"You stay with Thorne," he said. "As much time as you need to. Be careful, don't blow anything he might have working. But I want to know everything that goes on between him and Sonny Greco—where they meet, who they meet, *everything*. You tell me all this face to face, nothing goes on paper. Far as the captain thinks, you're on special detail and that's it."

"I'm not sure I like the rules," Massey said, thinking: who the hell is Corrigan anyway, ordering me to follow a G-man without an okay from the brass? "My ass is on the line, anyone finds out."

"I thought you were so good nobody ever found out," Corrigan said. He mopped up the spilt beer with a napkin, thinking it through carefully.

"I can't get you a green light on this," he admitted. "The Bureau can follow us all over creation, but no one'll let us play turn-around. But you do the legwork, I'll cover your tracks inside. Any problem, I take the heat."

"Nothing on paper," Massey consented. "We talk private."

"Stay on his ass," Corrigan said.

"That broad's too, with any luck."

Corrigan gave Massey an icy stare. Colleague or not, he couldn't help disliking him.

"Since I don't think either Thorne or Greco will drop in here for a drink," he said, "I suggest you get moving."

Massey left with his glass still full.

Thorne led MaryAgnes McCaskey to the table farthest from the jukebox, then hit the bar.

"Sonny Greco been around?"

The hulking bartender gave him a long look.

"I'll take it, you got something to leave for him."

"The other way 'round."

"Yeah, everybody," the bartender shrugged. "He'll be in a little later."

"I'm a friend of his. Name's Frank."

"Dominic. Dom."

Thorne shook his huge mitt, ordered Scotch for himself, the usual white wine for McCaskey. He saw Dom checking out the projection TV while pouring their round.

"What's the L.A. score?" he asked.

"Jersey's up ten–zip, almost the half."

"I thought L.A. was a lock."

"Not the way they're playing."

"See what you mean," Thorne said, watching the L.A. fullback run out the clock by colliding with his pulling guard. He flipped Dom a deuce tip, carried the drinks to the table. McCaskey was looking over the Friendly Northside Tap, amazement in her eyes.

"A long way from Rush Street," Thorne said.

"This is what I call a real tavern," she said. "Not without a certain charm, if you don't mind the smell of stale beer."

"One of Greco's drop points," Thorne said. "The bar runs a local book for him, handles collections and payments. For a cut of the action, naturally. One thing I've found out, nobody does a thing for Greco without taking a cut."

"Just like us," McCaskey said. "I went through our totals this afternoon."

"How much are we up?"

Having broken her lifelong habit of making and carrying notes, McCaskey paused to think.

"We've turned two hundred thousand over to Doc Hermann," she said. "There's another twenty-five or so in the company account, and we have fifteen more due this week already. Greco owes us thirty-five thousand and change."

Thorne saw the first-half statistics roll across the TV screen. "Sonny may be getting some back tonight. I think AAG Bidwell is about to lose his first five-star pick."

McCaskey sounded as if the possibility never occurred to her. "Really?"

"It may be better in the long run," Thorne said. "If we keep on clubbing the book, the family's liable to shut down before we can line ourselves up with someone important. Greco's only a starting point, right?"

McCaskey nodded. "Bidwell's due in town on Wednesday. I have to set up a strike team conference, have a status report ready."

"Bidwell wants more out of us than a report," Thorne knew. "What good is the cash we're winning if we aren't getting higher up the family tree? I'm going to make my move tonight. Greco's got to be hurting. I think it's time for the full-court press."

"Remember the entrapment guidelines. If we've created the circumstances that entice him into an illegal arrangement . . ."

"It's not Greco I'm after," Thorne repeated.

"Shhh, he just walked in."

Greco looked surprised to see them. He paused to talk with Dom, kiss the young, attractive woman who'd taken his place behind the bar. In the neon backlight, her head of tight blond curls looked like a gold football helmet.

"Everybody loves Sonny," McCaskey noted.

"Looks like she has reason."

"What are you two doing here?" Greco asked when he reached their table.

"We were at Fairweather's until it got too packed," Thorne said. "Val told us you come here a lot. We thought we'd try it out."

"Fairweather's this ain't," Greco said, rolling his eyes.

"Mary thinks it has charm. You remember Mary, from my office?"

"Absolutely."

"A *certain* charm is what I said." She and Greco shook hands politely.

"Have a drink with us," Thorne said.

"My treat."

Greco called out the name Diane, ordered a round on his tab. He asked Thorne about the game, sighed in relief hearing L.A. was down ten points. The half-point was starting to look large, he added. Maybe they could win one for a change.

"Frank and Mary. Friends of mine," he said when the blond brought their drinks. "This is Diane."

"And these are on the house," Diane said. "It's my last week working here. Time to get a little even with Dom."

"What's this last week stuff?" Greco asked.

"I'll tell you later," Diane said.

The way she said it, Thorne guessed, their date was unbreakable.

"She's lovely," McCaskey remarked as Diane went back behind the bar.

Greco seemed embarrassed. "Nice kid. Known her for years," he said. "She's been watching out for me while my wife and twins are in Florida."

Thorne knew from the Bureau's reams of intelligence that the old man took a dim view of adultery, and rarely condoned divorce. He came to Greco's defense, saying, "The last time my wife got back from a trip, she hit me with separation papers. I hope you fare better."

McCaskey swallowed hard and reached for one of Thorne's cigarettes. "If I'm going to break training, I might as well go all the way."

Thorne cursed himself silently. Nice way to break the news, dumb ass. He should have told McCaskey sooner, in private. Why had he kept it bottled up inside himself for a month? Why did he always hold back like that?

"They're on the board!" Dom bellowed. Thorne and Greco turned to see the replay: L.A. capping an eight-minute drive, squeezing into the Jersey end zone on straight-ahead blocking. But the Generals had gotten a touchdown themselves, making it 17-7 over the favored home team Express.

"I need this one bad," Greco said. "Your players have been killing me on football. Fact is, everybody's been killing me. Just that your people are infallible."

Thorne leaned forward on his forearms, spoke softly.

"I didn't come to talk business, Sonny. But since you brought it up, I've got people getting anxious for their cash. They paid on time when they lost. Now they want it back."

McCaskey discreetly excused herself for the Ladies.

"One fucking night they lost," Greco said.

"Still . . ."

"Come with me. See what I can do."

Thorne followed him into Dom's office. Greco unlocked the desk drawer, retrieved two envelopes. He tossed the glassine one to Thorne while he ripped open the larger manila.

"Go ahead, you use that stuff."

"Occasionally," Thorne said.

"Don't know anybody in your business that doesn't. Occasionally," Greco laughed.

Thorne put out a short, modest line. He inhaled it slowly, not wanting to pull a Woody Allen and sneeze cocaine all over the dingy office.

Greco divided the cash into three piles. "There's fifteen dimes there," he said. "Go on and count it, five a stack."

"No need," Thorne said. He watched Greco pocket what was left over—two, three thousand tops.

Greco said, "I'm light about twenty. I'll get the exact figures tomorrow, call you at the office."

"This should keep them quiet," Thorne said. "How long for the rest?"

"End of the week. Tomorrow starts a new balance."

"Maybe we'll get some back, Jersey stays on top."

"Christ, I hope so," Greco said. "I had a long session with my boss today. He's more than a little pissed off, the way football's going. Everybody's getting hit hard. Not just me, all over."

And they're all *my* people, Thorne said to himself, thinking of what the strike force had done to Scarpo, Lowenstein, the guy up in Rockford. Bidwell's computer had so far been unerring. At least until tonight. Or had he purposefully given out a loser to keep the book open, hoping?

"It's uncanny," Greco said.

"I can't believe my players are this good. Never were before," Thorne said.

Greco said, "Better than good. For people you say don't even know each other, it sure looks like they talk."

"What do you mean?"

"I mean there's always one game especially they cream me with. All of them load up."

"I'm not touting them," Thorne said. "You look at my sheet, you see I haven't made a penny since we started together."

"Yeah, I wish they *would* talk to you," Greco conceded.

"Suppose they stop playing? Decide to pocket what they've won and sit down?" Thorne asked, a preemptive question.

"I never knew a winner who did. That's the one plus we got going, the one my boss is counting on. He says it can't keep up like this."

Thorne knew the time was right to step out, see if Greco would take the bait and starting moving him closer to his bosses, the nephews, the money men. Get up that high and every front business the family held could be traced, audited, broken under the statutes of RICO—the Racketeering Influenced and Corrupt Organization Act.

"If things are going that bad," Thorne said, "maybe I could help you out."

"Like how?"

"A little short-term cash."

"I thought your money's tied up on the Exchange."

Greco's voice was edgy, on guard. Thorne considered pulling back, but knew he had to have something more than net winnings to give AAG Bidwell.

"Mine is," he said. "But I have lots of clients looking for high returns. Venture capital, call it."

Greco seemed to relax. "Go on."

"A lot of this money is looking for a short-term home, people stashing it somewhere between other deals. Now, if what they earned on it was tax-free, no one would bother asking questions about how I placed it." Thorne felt the coke kicking his speech into overdrive. He forced himself to slow down, make it sound like he was merely thinking out loud. "Like your boss says, it has to turn around soon."

Greco said, "All the years I've been in business, I've never seen a month like this."

"So maybe I can see you through it," Thorne said.

"Interesting idea. How much you talking about?"

"We put the right terms together, I'd say a quarter million for openers. Double that if it works out right."

"That's really 'sports futures,'" Greco recalled, playing with Thorne's cash while he thought. "Nice idea, but the people who bank us—do I have to elaborate?"

"Not at all. I always figured you were part of the big picture."

"So, these people can afford to hold the action themselves, wait for things to swing back their way. Not that they like losing, but no one's anxious to see outside money coming in. These people lend, not borrow."

"Look, I'm not trying to stick my nose where it doesn't belong," Thorne said. "I just thought if I could help take the pressure off . . ."

"For a few points."

"Nothing out of line," Thorne said. "There's a downside risk involved too."

"You keep all your bases covered. I'll give you that."

"Look, Sonny, you're my friend. And I like to help friends any way I can. But with a half million of my clients' cash, there has to be something in it for me."

Greco pushed the money across the desk. "Your lady's waiting alone out there," he said. "And we got a big game to bring in."

The subject was closed. But somehow, Thorne knew, Greco's denial was temporary.

He saw McCaskey sitting on a bar stool talking furiously with Diane. "They're getting on."

"Yeah, broads," Greco shrugged.

They joined Dom at the foot of the screen.

"L.A. scored again," he reported. "Took the one-point conversion. It's seventeen–fourteen, one minute to go, and Jersey's got the ball."

"We're home," Thorne exclaimed.

Greco said, "Never go to the window while your horse is still running."

"Like we could have overtime here," Dom added.

The Jersey team, however, managed to preclude the possibility. Backed up inside their ten-yard line, they decided to take a two-point safety instead of punting from deep in their end zone against a hard-rushing L.A. defense. Their free kick sailed out past midfield, where Los Angeles, now down 17–16, took possession with twenty-eight seconds on the clock.

"Looking good now," Greco said. "They'll try a few

short passes, go for the field goal. But they still can't cover three and a half points. And overtime's history."

"My round," Thorne called to Diane. As Greco calmly lighted a cigar, Thorne found himself actually pulling for Sonny to win. He wondered if he were crossing the worst line an agent could: getting too close to your target.

"Here we go," Dom said.

Los Angeles hit two quick passes for nine yards. Short of the first down, almost out of time, they lined up to attempt the game-winning forty-eight-yard field goal.

"You're right on," Thorne said. "We cover either way."

"That's it," Dom agreed.

Greco said nothing.

What happened next defied every bit of football logic. As the L.A. coaching staff would try explaining in the *Sporting News*, their place kicker was worthless beyond forty-five yards. So instead of a low percentage attempt, they decided to sneak for the first down, stop the clock. The one more pass they had time for, even a four-, five-yarder, would get them close enough to give their kicker a decent shot at the posts.

Jersey, intent on blocking the attempt, saving the win, sent eleven players against the kicker. When L.A. snapped the ball to their blocking back and not the holder, there was no one to touch him.

The ball carrier slid off tackle, found himself suddenly and surprisingly free in the Jersey secondary, lumbering unimpeded towards the goal line. A speedy defensive back with a good tackling angle almost reached him at the five, Thorne cheering for him loudly, a trio of zeros on the time clock. But the winded L.A. runner managed a final sprint and dove into the end zone, too exhausted to even try spiking the ball.

Final score: Los Angeles, 23–17.

Final cost to Greco and Johnny Roses' bank: a cool hundred thousand dollars.

Thorne ripped apart his pack of cigarettes and threw the shreds over the bar. Dom cursed everyone, black, white, or yellow, who'd ever put on shoulder pads.

Greco sat silently, emotionless. His first words were to order another round of drinks, telling Diane to put them on his tab. Thorne was amazed: no curses, no breast-beating. The man had class.

"Forget the commission this week," Dom moaned.

Thorne said he still couldn't believe what'd happened.

"Never go to the window . . ." Greco said again. He spun a quarter turn to face Thorne squarely. "Might not be a bad idea, you and my boss getting together to talk. Just don't tell him your name up front. After what your players won tonight, he's liable to put a bullet in your head."

Thorne drove MaryAgnes back to Near North, went through the proposition he'd given Greco, explained that after the beating the outfit took on Los Angeles, he had a real chance to deal with some bosses, maybe even a nephew.

"Now we've got something to give Bidwell," he said.

McCaskey sat leaning against the passenger door. "He'll be pleased," she said flatly.

"Aren't you?"

"Of course."

She kept silent through a quartet of stoplights and the congestion at State and Division. Finally, as Thorne neared her apartment, she asked, "What's this about you and your wife separating? Was that just for Greco's benefit?"

"Trial separation," Thorne said. "I should have told you sooner."

McCaskey turned quiet again. Thorne watched a black Chevy four-door follow him around the corner

and accelerate quickly past them as he pulled in front
of MaryAgnes' building.

"When did all this happen?" she asked.

"The problems or the paperwork?"

"If you'd rather not talk, Frank . . ."

"Sorry," Thorne apologized. He shut down the en-
gine, lighted a Lucky and began to wonder himself.

"I guess it came to a head when she got back from
Michigan," he began. "I was always gone and . . ."

"I understand," McCaskey said.

"I should have told you when it happened, but
somehow it didn't seem real. And I thought a trial
separation meant a week or so. But Patsie doesn't like
incomplete thoughts. She went to our lawyer, had
papers drawn up. We're to stay apart for six months,
minimal contact, nothing social, which I take to mean
conjugal."

"I'm sorry, Frank. I really am," she said softly.

"Me too. At least I think so. The thing is, I can't
understand why I was surprised, the way things have
been for the past year. Maybe I just didn't think it
could happen."

"The sense of failure," MaryAgnes said. "Sometimes it's more painful, more numbing than the sense
of loss. The toughest thing to handle is guilt."

"I should be used to it," Thorne said. "How many
nights can you phone in apologies?"

"Don't get down on yourself. That's absolutely the
worst thing you can do. I know from experience."

"I hear you. Besides, she was away as much . . ."
Thorne's voice trailed off. What was the use?

"Put the time to advantage," MaryAgnes said. "Everyone needs to find out exactly how deep the feelings
are."

"Or aren't."

"That too," she agreed. "That's the risk both of you
take. I'm sure your wife isn't feeling much better
about it."

"Probably not."

They sat quietly for several minutes. "Where are you living?" MaryAgnes finally asked.

"At home. Evanston. Patsie wanted a place in town, be closer to her office, save the commuting. It's probably right around here somewhere. She's to tell me her address when she's settled in, for administrative purposes only."

"Damn, I am sorry," MaryAgnes said again.

"You needn't be." Thorne suddenly realized his comment sounded cruel. Before he could correct it, MaryAgnes opened her door.

"Good night, Frank;" she said icily.

Thorne wanted to call her back, explain what he'd intended. Let it go, he decided. Enough for tonight.

"I'll be in early tomorrow," he said. "Help you get organized for Bidwell."

"Fine."

Thorne watched her safely inside. Only when he turned back to the wheel did he see the black Chevy again flying past him, its speed denying any search for a parking spot. Thorne hit the lights, tried to read the plate number. The Chevy trucked a fast right onto inner Lake Shore Drive. When Thorne reached the corner the light was red, he couldn't squeeze out fast enough into the oncoming traffic. When he did, the Chevy had disappeared into the downtown flow, lost in the jumble of red taillights that filled Michigan Avenue.

Thorne made his U-turn by cutting through the Ritz-Carlton driveway. By the time he got back on the Drive, heading north along the lakefront, he'd reached a decision—if he ever saw that Chevy tail him again, it was time to start wearing his gun.

8

PIZZA SAL'S ability to keep dodging bullets fell apart the morning Greco walked into Chuckie Franco's candy warehouse. Just hearing Sally's name sent Franco into orbit.

"That little fuck-knuckle is into me for eighteen dimes, plus interest," Franco snarled. "I'm gonna get back every penny coming to me, or I turn him into *braciole.*"

Greco followed him around a stack of wooden pallets into the long, dank, tin-roofed building. Franco's short legs seemed to bow under his bulk.

Franco had started out with the family as a bodyguard and collector, back in the early days when the old man believed muscle was a sure cure for default. Though he was still tight with the nephews, Sid Paris in particular, Franco was pretty much on his own now; distributing candy and gum to family-owned newsstands and vending machines, running a good-sized juice loan operation with the nephews' blessings. Franco's terms were simple: five percent a week on the unpaid balance. Pay him back in two, three weeks, it was cheaper and cleaner than screwing around with a bank, let alone the Shylocks at a finance company.

Take any longer and you took your chances. Real ones.

Sally couldn't be grounded to the water pipe and get that deep into someone like Chuckie Franco, Greco thought. Not when he has to come up with nine hundred a week juice just to keep walking without a limp.

"Listen," Greco tried bargaining when Franco paused to inventory a load of Baby Ruth and Mounds cartons, "you know Sally got himself busted doing family business. He stood right up to the cops too. They tried to flip him, he said to screw off."

"That's good," Franco mumbled. "But it's worth nothing to me."

"The family's behind him," Greco said.

Franco was unswayed. "Stop pullin' my chain, Sonny. The family hates his fucking guts. You know it and I know it, so don't hand me crap about his connections. His own people are tired of putting up with him."

Greco watched him rip open a box of Mounds bars, pull out two. He tossed one to Greco, devoured the other in a giant double gulp.

"All right, Sally's no prize catch. I'll give you that. But he's my friend."

Franco swallowed hard and cleared his throat.

"Sonny, you're okay," he said. "Everybody around likes you, even the old man. You never cause nobody no problems, and you're always right there. So take my advice—don't go stickin' your neck out for that little scumbag. Sleep with dogs, you get fleas. *Capisce*?"

"All I'm asking is you give Sal a little more time to get things squared away. You'll get your cash. All of it."

"This I'm sure of, Sonny."

"Maybe you could hold up on the weekly mutuals in the meantime, at least until . . ."

"What the fuck you think I'm doing here? My business *is* the weekly mutuals. I hold up on nothing, least of all for him."

Greco made his final offer.

"The eighteen Sally owes you will pay back twenty if you can wait a few weeks. That's all I'm asking. I'd pay it myself if I had the cash handy. But he got cracked before he could lay off, the house is getting killed all over, business is bad."

"So word has it," Franco said.

"Then you know what it's been like."

"It's like a lot of people are upset," Franco said. "And that means the squeeze is on. Which includes Charles Franco." He stepped toward Greco and put a meaty hand on his shoulder. "I got obligations myself, understand? Just like any business, any bank, I got backers who want their dividends paid on time. I've gotta get my cash when it's due, or I gotta do what I gotta do."

"I'll put up my own marker for the twenty dimes," Greco said. "Thirty-day call."

Franco straightened his brow. "You know what you're doing here?"

"I go back with Sally a long way," Greco said. "He helped me out when I got in truble. I can't stand around, see his legs get broke for eighteen dimes."

"Twenty," Franco corrected him.

"You'll take the marker?"

"From you, I'll take it." Franco's face came as close to smiling as his jowls permitted. "I'll need two thousand up front. That takes care of his interest from before, what's already on the books and don't get erased. You settle up inside a month, it's twenty dimes flat."

"Don't break your heart."

"Not for him. You don't want it my way, you take a walk. Just remember I'm giving out eighteen dimes for two, and you get a month to handle it. That's cut-rate, pal."

"It's a deal," Greco nodded. He dug into his pocket, came out with what remained from the envelope he had picked up the night before at Dead Dom's. As for Camille's twenty-five hundred . . .

"Here's your two thousand."

Franco counted it carefully, tucked the roll into his shirt. "For your sake, Sonny, make sure the rest gets squared on time. Lotta heat coming down all over. Nobody gets a bye, not even you."

"Like the old days." Greco took a pen and paper from his coat but Franco waved him off.

"I need nothin' on paper," he said. "You say you owe me, that's good enough." Franco reached in for another candy bar.

"Besides, I know where you live."

It was afternoon when Greco made it to Pizza Sal's bungalow. Two extra cars sat in the driveway: a white Mustang with red pinstriping, a platinum Cutlass Supreme that looked vaguely familiar. Greco parked on the street, had to wait a long three minutes before Sally got around to opening the door.

"Yeah, hey . . . Sonny." He was muttering again.

Sally wore a maroon bathrobe, a pair of fruity white mules. Greco could see he hadn't slept all night and was still wired. Then he placed the Cutlass from the Cairo Club and understood it all.

"Party still going?"

"No . . . well . . ." Still muttering.

"Well, can I come in?" Greco barked.

"Yeah, sure." Sally rubbed his eyes hard and opened up. "It's okay," he yelled back into the house.

"How many guests you got?"

"Few people came by from the club."

"Which you closed, right? Five A.M.?"

Sally shrugged, nervous.

"Terrific."

Greco walked through the empty living room, into the kitchen. The house reeked of stale grass; the counters were strewn with glasses, melting ice, the remnants of a liter bottle of Stoly, some empty splits of Cordon Rouge.

"You go first cabin," Greco said.

"Fix you something?"

"It's not even one o'clock," Greco snapped. "You been partying all night, all day, while I'm out taking care of business. Your business, asshole."

"C'mon, lighten up. Nobody says I can't relax a little, all the stress I'm under."

Greco felt his fist clench automatically, but fought off the urge to pop Sally one. He wore his best con-man smile, probably the same one he used to beat the hard guys in Vegas. Greco could only laugh at him.

"What the hell."

"Yeah, what the hell," Sally beamed. "At least have a beer."

Greco walked into the TV room while Sal rummaged through the icebox. Two young ladies wearing only floral bikini underpants were engrossed in the continuing drama of "The Young and The Restless."

The one with the larger breasts giggled, "Hi."

"You're Sonny, right?" the other said.

"How's the bubble bath business?" Greco asked. An insult.

"*Hard* work," the big-breasted one teased Greco back, rubbing her nipples.

"But Sally gets you the stuff to make it easy."

"It's always the best. And he's there just when you need him most."

"For you, maybe," Greco sneered.

He went back to the kitchen, hating to think about Diane's tour of duty at the Cairo. Sal handed him a bottle of Old Style and sniffed at a quart of milk like a wary alley cat.

"Think this is off?"

Greco dumped it immediately. "Not as bad as you'll be when Chuckie Franco gets through with you."

"Jeez, you saw him?"

"This morning," Greco nodded.

"And?"

"Get rid of the creamettes and we'll talk."

"Sure, no problem."

"Then do it." Greco took a pull of cold beer. Breakfast.

"Upstairs too?"

"Upstairs what?"

"You know Toby, works the bar out there?"

"The Cutlass," Greco replied.

"He's upstairs in the sack with Kathy. The little redhead who . . ."

Greco thumbed toward the TV room. "So you had those two all to yourself."

"Yeah, double-bubble," Sally grinned. "They're great and, what the hell, while you're young . . ."

Greco grabbed Sally's robe and pulled him close, this time ready to crack him one.

"You got ten minutes to clear out this house," he ordered. "Toby, Kathy, the two twinkies in there, and anybody else you got stashed away. Ten minutes, or your youth ends here and now."

"That's clear."

It took twenty minutes to empty the place, but Greco let it slide. The two girls downstairs wanted to keep the party rolling; Greco turned them down flat. Pizza Sal had trouble getting Toby and Kathy from their Morphean bed. Greco watched them clump out the door sullenly.

Greco said, "I'm out trying to save your dumb ass. You're at the Cairo Club giving away blow to every scar in the joint."

"It's the stress," Sally claimed again.

"You catch another angina attack, or maybe this time get the big one, all I inherit is an evening with Franco's muscle."

"So what happened?"

"You're covered for a month. One month. Only."

"Don't worry, I'll come up with it."

"I had to put up two dimes for the juice you owed. And Franco's got my note for twenty."

Sally seemed relieved. "That's okay. I got something going now that's guaranteed."

"Don't let me hear any shit about your good buddy in Miami," Greco said.

"What kinda choices you think I got?"

Greco couldn't think of anything except armed robbery. But knowing Pizza Sal, he'd probably shoot himself in the foot.

"Get a job," he said inanely.

"One that clears me twenty dimes in a month? You got something like that, I'll take it."

"I told you before how the family feels about anybody dealing that stuff."

"Screw 'em all," Sally yelled. "You tell me I'm out of a job—off the phones, can't work for anybody else. So what I do from now on is my business. Nobody helped me out with Chuckie Franco."

"I did!" Greco shouted back.

Sally slumped into a chair, breathing hard. "It's my only shot getting healthy," he said. "No way it'll come back to you. I've got this . . ."

"Don't even tell me."

"You know, if you ever need . . ."

"Can it," Greco said. "I remember when you stood up for me."

"I'll have it again. Whatever you want."

"I want you to do me two things," Greco said.

"Name them."

"Tell me you understand that, if you ever go near somebody like Franco again, I'm gonna cut off your nose. Then hand me the phone. I've got to tell Johnny Roses how bad we got hit last night."

Outside the nights he and Frank did the Rush–Division scene together, Greco managed to keep the booze in check. But going over his losses with Berwyn Bobby and the other phone men, waiting for Diane to complete her penultimate shift at Dead Dom's, he'd kept the doubles coming. Back in her apartment, trying to lift himself off the low sofa, he watched helplessly as the glass of vodka slipped from his hand and shattered in slow-motion across the dull parquet floor.

"Damn it," Diane hissed. "I just got Stacy back to sleep."

"I'll get it."

"You sit still."

Diane gathered the shards of glass carefully, wiped up with paper towel. Then she brought out instant coffee. The cup's decaled message: *Smile.*

She said, "If things are that bad, it's time for you to quit. Tell Johnny Roses tomorrow. He'll understand."

"You think it's that easy, I give two weeks notice and walk out? Besides, how do I clear the book upstairs when I'm stuck over sixty dimes on my own?"

"I didn't dream it was that much," Diane said.

"Maybe more. The week isn't over yet."

Diane stared back at him, thinking. "Your friend Frank, the one who's on the Exchange. Couldn't he line up something to help get you even?"

"No problem," Greco said. "I'll just go down there, hand him my Visa card for escrow. First thing tomorrow, before they take it back for nonpayment. That's what I'll do—short everything, trade a hundred contracts a day, no sweat."

"You've got to do something more than get drunk!"

"A bank heist might do it. Only nobody keeps that much cash in the drawer."

"Cut it out!" Diane snapped.

Greco struggled to sit erect, drink some coffee. He managed two large sips before realizing he'd scalded his tongue. Diane fought to cover up her laughter.

"At least Sally's case was dropped," she said, trying to cheer him up. "Not everything's going bad."

"That's the cheapest part of knowing him," Greco said. "Pizza Sal, the rancher."

"What are you talking about?"

"He's been investing in horse flesh again. Usually with a saddle, sometimes a sulky. Sportsman's Park, Hawthorne, like that. Good thing Arlington burned down or he'd be stuck double."

"He bought a race horse."

"Just backed a few," Greco said. "Mostly with money he didn't have. So he goes and gets himself into the juice for eighteen thousand. Now he's short, and these people don't like waiting. They're not Household Finance, Di, garnishing somebody's paycheck, forty bucks a week."

"So that's it," Diane exclaimed.

"That's what?"

"Why he came over here and wanted . . ." Diane's face looked as if she'd just figured out the ending to an Agatha Christie plot.

"Wanted what?"

"It's not important."

"Tell me," Greco insisted.

"Just that I know now why he's seemed off balance lately. More so than usual." Diane leaned over and took a sip of Greco's coffee. "Do you think he can get out of it?"

Greco said, "He's out but I'm in. I went to the money man this morning and covered him. A few thousand up front, my marker for twenty more."

"Sonny, no!"

"It was that or see him in a wheelchair the rest of his life. The boss took him off the phones, won't let him work for months, if ever." Greco sank back into the cushions and looked at the ceiling. "But Sally's always got an answer. This time it's getting into the cola business. Says he can pick up a key or two of pure Colombian for thirty-five dimes per. Great stuff, and he should know."

"He told you that?"

"Sure he did. He's looking for a partner."

Diane made her calculations readily. "Stuff that good would bring back a hundred per key," she said. "Maybe a little less if he sells ounces, but that cuts his time and risk. At thirty-five ounces per kilo . . ."

"How come you know so much?" Greco wondered. "You take a course in metrics?"

Diane lit a cigarette and glared back at him.

"I've been around the block. You know what Stacy's father used to do."

"Ride motorcycles and beat up fags," Greco said.

"What do you think the Henchmen did for cash? They didn't wash cars, Sonny."

"You in the business with them?"

"Does it matter now?" she asked back.

"No," Greco lied, remembering the girls in Sally's crib, thinking about the Cairo Club. Around the block, she called it. How many times around?

"Past is past," he said, mostly to himself.

Diane said, "Sally's no fool. Forget his problems with gambling and he's really pretty sharp, especially about stuff like that. With a good partner to keep him under control, he'd make it work."

"I may be half in the bag, but I hear a message coming," Greco said.

"You're looking for a bankroll to go in with Frank on the Exchange, well . . ." She paused to gauge his reaction, got none, and went on. "Put together a deal or two with Pizza Sal, you could maybe make a few hundred thousand."

"Forget it!" Greco erupted, not thinking about Stacy. Diane quieted him and spoke softly.

"I don't like the idea either, but you're the one saying you need cash. And why not? You have contacts, know people who use that stuff like bath powder. I'm not saying you stand on a corner selling grams. It's big money contracts or nothing."

Greco said the first thing that came to mind.

"My boss would have my nuts on a platter for messing with that. I don't even want to think about the old man. I'm cleared to run a sports book. I go fucking around with some Cubans, I'm history."

"It's not a career," Diane said. "One or two times and you're out of it. Who'll know?"

Greco replied, "You wouldn't dream what they know. You think nobody polices that action? They got a pact made with the Latins, a mutual hands-off society. Don't forget the real cops either. I don't want to think about doing a dozen in Joliet."

"You could land there for what you're doing now," Diane said. "Ever think about that?"

"All the time," Greco said. "But at least I have the family behind me—good lawyers, connections downtown. Anything happens, the twins get taken care of. I do that kind of deal, who's going to back me up? Pizza Sal?"

"I guess you're right," Diane conceded, exhaling a thin wisp of smoke. "It doesn't make sense for you."

"No way to save a car company either," Greco said. "You do what you do."

Diane stood and offered her hand. "I have a surprise to show you. In the bedroom."

Greco followed her unsteadily. The bed was neatly made, the coverlet folded back, beckoning. Diane stopped him from lying down.

"Look in the closet," she said.

Greco slid the hangers back and forth, kicked at the neat row of shoes on the floor. "What am I looking for?"

"Can't you see what's not there?"

Greco turned back to the clothing. "No."

"Any shirts, neckties, like that?"

"Donny," he realized.

"The absence thereof," Diane said. "I told you there were rules I play by. I broke it off with him."

"You sure you know what you're doing?"

"Don't worry, I'm not asking you for anything. It was time for *me* to get my life together. No more trying to feel something for Donny, no more wasting time at Dom's place."

Greco watched her slip out of her clothes, climb into bed.

"You sure about this?" he said.

"Sonny, why don't you just shut up and come here. For surprise number two."

9

JOHNNY ROSES rolled his hips slowly, dropped his left shoulder, and shanked the bright orange ball into a low gray sky. Greco saw it reappear over the right rough. It hit and died in the wet grass about eighty, ninety yards behind his fairway lie.

"Everything's soaked out here," Johnny Roses bitched, flipping his club upside down, rubbing the persimmon face. "The damn thing slipped right off."

Greco said, "They got a gin game going back in the clubhouse. Let's throw it in, what do you say?"

"I say you want to sit around playing ten cents a point with some fat old men, you go in. I need to loosen up, get the air."

"We'll try for nine," Greco gave in, knowing his boss would not. "You still want a Nassau?"

"Scotch game. Prox, low total, double for birdie. Twenty-five bucks a crack."

"Throw in longest drive."

Johnny Roses aimed his club down the fairway, then sighted over to his short lie in the rough.

"Too late now."

Greco knew he could spot Johnny five strokes a side, swing one handed, and still win. But seeing his grim mood, he decided to play him to a push, save all the grief.

"Press on the last hole," he suggested as a compromise. "Loser can double up."

Johnny Roses mumbled an okay and tossed his driver to the caddy. "Move out," he ordered. "We're walking and talking."

The caddy, a sullen, acne-scarred kid in jeans and a hooded sweatshirt, slumped off under the weight of two bags, Johnny's touring pro model large enough for the entire Ohio State golf team. Greco guessed his boss had probably slipped the caddy an extra twenty to move his ball around, fluff up his lie, whatever he could manage. The last time Greco had taken his phone men out, Berwyn Bobby caught Johnny Roses' caddy dropping ball number three just beyond a tricky dog-leg bunker.

"I don't mind the money," Berwyn Bobby had railed. "Just tell me how many fucking balls he's playing out here."

Johnny Roses kicked the mud off his shoes as they strode off the tee. "How'd you end up with the college hoops?"

"Not good," Greco said. "The tournament hurt a lot."

"Did I tell you? Too much information on the street, all them services putting out winners for a fifty-buck fee."

"I'm doing okay in baseball," Greco lied. "So far, anyway."

Johnny Roses walked on slowly, silently, his head down as though moving through a minefield. Greco cut his step in half to stay alongside.

"I'm in trouble, Sonny. Real trouble."

"I know, banking all this football."

"What'd you hear?" he asked anxiously, freezing in his tracks.

"It's nothing I heard, just that I can add. When my

offices are taking a six-figure bath, I've gotta believe there's problems."

"Some people are real upset," Johnny Roses said. "I tried telling the nephews it's not just here. Milwaukee, K.C.—everybody's taking it on the chin. I hear some places are closing down, gonna wait for the NFL. Some people may be down forever."

"It's got to swing back our way, sooner or later," Greco said.

"Who the fuck says so?"

"You do. Or did."

"That's why I got troubles."

"Maybe we should close down too," Greco said.

"Too late for that."

Johnny Roses saw the caddy waving and began angling toward his ball.

"So far the old man's been calm," he went on. "But the nephews aren't so patient. All they think about is negative cash flow. All they get is more pissed off at me."

"They're pushing on everybody," Greco said. "Even the juice guys are bitching."

"Screw 'em," Johnny barked. "That's a cinch business—low risk, zero overhead, all you need's muscle. Those guys would puke, they had my problems. I'm the one who sold the family on handling this goddamn football season. I go back now, say we close down, all I've done is cost them a very large piece of change. That's not appreciated, Sonny. Not when they all got perfect hindsight."

"The old man himself gave you the green light," Greco said, searching for optimism. "Who's gonna go against *him*? Besides, we're not the only ones getting beat, so you're not the only one who's made a mistake. The old man's had losing seasons before."

The caddy kicked Johnny Roses' ball from the tree line, giving it a clear approach. Johnny circled it like a cat. But instead of hitting a seven-iron to loft it out of the rough, he tried to press for extra distance and cracked it with a five. The ball died as it labored through the wet grass. Only Johnny's wiry strength got it to the fairway, about twenty yards ahead of Greco's tee shot.

"Nice out," Greco said.

"Good thing I missed them trees."

"See, your luck's changing."

"You may be in the business, but you don't understand what's going on," Johnny Roses said as they began walking. "So I'll tell you—the old man is still in his chair, makes all the big decisions, gets the respect he deserves. But his mind's thinking national, global. It's the nephews who run operations, day to day, dollar for dollar."

"And they're all competing," Greco said. "Duking it out for the top slot."

"Truth is, the old man ain't crazy about any of them. I hear he's closer to some of the out-of-town families than these guys. Which puts more competition on the track. So the nephews got to face up to two things—keeping the old man happy for as long as he's got, and keeping the out-of-town bosses impressed with how they're running things, how much cash they're making. Just in case they get acquired."

They played their balls in turn: Greco hit a four-iron to the front edge of the green; his boss rolled a five-wood into the left trap. Let's see him kick that one out, Greco thought.

"You got as many people on your ass as me, you couldn't hit a green either," Johnny Roses moaned. "Not everybody inside the family is as easygoing as me."

Greco said, "So you have to make your move."

"I don't know how much more they'll listen to. Especially Sid Paris. You'd think I was stealing food from his kid's mouth."

"Sid Paris may be a tough prick, but on his best days he couldn't wash the old man's jock."

"Lookit, Sonny, you think because the old man likes you, you're part of a family? Well get this straight—none of that matters. There's no family anymore, not like it used to be. No honor, nobody's close to nobody, no mortar holding up the bricks. It's a goddamn corporation. And the guys we got for executives would as soon have your liver on ice as have you over to the house for dinner."

"So what do you do? Keep open and keep praying we start to win?"

"You got a better idea? Like I buy everybody a round at Padrino's, tell them I was wrong about the business they pay me to run? Hey, I ate up all that cash. Now I'm sorry. That your answer?"

Greco had only one idea, and thought he'd back his way into offering it.

"My new players aren't helping us much. I don't understand how they keep winning."

"We got new action all over," the boss said. "All of it's winning. I think people crawled out of the woodwork to jump on the bandwagon."

"From where? I know players get bored between baskets and bases. They'll bet anything. But I've never seen action like we're getting on the spring football. I can't figure it."

"I can."

"How's that?"

"A lot of independents, the renegades, they closed up after getting beat so bad on the hoops. Either they were smart enough not to open back up for football, or too poor to try. So we made our move, took everything we could get."

"You mean *held* everything," Greco said. Stupid.

Johnny Roses spun around and glowered at him.

"You're talking like Sid Paris now," he said. "Only Sid forgets he was the one pushing me to get the independents out of action. Either we get a street tax or we start breaking bones, he says. I tell him and the old man we don't want to fight it that way—things get rough again and maybe the feds step in. What we do, I tell them, is take all the players we can, new accounts that will stay with us all year long. You're in a service business, that's marketing."

"And the old man bought it," Greco said.

"Sure he did. You know he doesn't like trouble on the street. He saw enough of that in the Fifties, guys getting hit all over town, ending up in car trunks."

"So you've got no problems. Your ass is covered."

"For as long as *he* lives. Which I pray is a hundred at least."

Greco looked down into the trap. Johnny Roses' ball was half-buried in sand that looked like unset concrete. The caddy delivered a wedge, Johnny shooed him away.

"We're still talking here," he snapped. The caddy sulked back behind the green and sat on Johnny's oversized bag.

Greco said, "I think I've got a way to take off some of the heat Sid Paris is giving you, how we can refinance our bank without going back to the family for more cash. This guy Frank Becker, the one who—"

"Don't get me fucking aggravated," Johnny Roses fumed. "What he cost us already . . ."

"It's not him," Greco countered. "Just that his players are on a streak."

"Who isn't?"

Johnny Roses jumped into the trap and dug in. As he lined up his shot, Greco said how he'd checked Frank out, got Boyle on it, and everything came up kosher. Johnny silenced him as he went into his backswing, came down strongly enough to compensate for the wet sand. Only he didn't catch enough of it. The ball sailed to the far side of the green, barely holding it.

"You're still putting for par," Greco consoled him.

"Yeah, forty feet worth."

Greco walked across the soft, spongy grass. The boss told their caddy to leave the putters, wait on the second tee.

"So what about this guy?"

"He's got a business proposition in mind," Greco said.

"I'm listening."

"Frank tells me the other night he's got access to big money—you know, investment capital from clients who can afford a few risks and are always looking for ways to beat the IRS. Frank says he can put a package together to cover our losses, bank us short term."

"This guy wants to borrow us a bank?"

"Beats going back to the nephews for it," Greco said. "We get a good rate because his people don't have to declare any interest. He gets a point or two for himself, and we've got a cushion so we can stay open, wait out a turnaround."

"It's horse shit," Johnny Roses said flatly. "You think Sid Paris wants to start screwing with the IRS, or let somebody from outside get involved in family business?"

"Frank's involved with us, not him."

"The same thing."

Greco said, "Even the old man won't stay patient forever. If your tit's in a wringer, a fresh bankroll might get it unstuck. All it costs the family is a few points they ain't gonna miss."

"Why the hell you pushing this, Sonny? You getting a few points for yourself?"

"I'm trying to stay alive. Just like you," Greco said. "The buckets took all my cash, and I haven't seen a dollar's commission in months. Not to mention what I owe you and . . ." He hesitated, deciding to skip the Pizza Sal–Chuckie Franco horror story. "And some other people. I'm in the same boat you are, Johnny.

I've got to stay open and ride out the streaks. If not, I'm on a Greyhound out of here."

"Jesus," Johnny shook his head. He gave his putting line a quick eye, locked his knees tightly, and laid up six feet from the pin. "That's better," he said.

"At least it's worth talking to Frank," Greco said. "Maybe you could work something out. He's good, this guy."

"That's what you think, huh?"

"What do you have to lose?" Greco asked back.

"More than you realize. Still, it's something to keep in mind."

Greco squatted behind his ball and figured the break. Screw playing Johnny Roses to a push, the hard-headed son-of-a-bitch.

"What does it cost to talk?" he said, lining up.

"Nobody's gonna do any talking yet," Johnny said. "We see how it goes for another few weeks. I got a hunch we won't need to call up any reserves."

"The same feeling I had when I took over college basketball," Greco reminded him.

Johnny Roses seemed to get the point.

"Tomorrow I meet with the old man, Sid Paris, the other nephews," he said. "They tell me to close down and eat the losses, then that's it. But I'm gonna argue we stay open, tough it out. What the hell, it's a million bucks we walk away."

"How much?" Greco jumped.

"You think I'm in trouble over a few dimes?"

Greco stepped away from his ball as Johnny Roses paced nervously around him.

"So let's see what happens at the meeting. If the timing's right, I might mention this guy's proposition. Sid Paris has always been drooling over the Exchange. He might see this as a way to get the family an insider, maybe use him to wash out some cash. But you say nothing to him unless I tell you to. Got it?"

"I got it."

"Then putt out."

For the first time ever, Greco felt a little sorry for Johnny Roses. Without a second alignment, he instinctively stroked his ball high left. It caught the break perfectly and slid downhill into the cup.

"Goddamn!" Johnny Roses hollered.

The gray sky began to collapse over the course, dumping a mushy mixture of rain and spring snow. "C'mon," he said, "we're bailing out of here."

Greco didn't bother picking up his ball. He waved to the caddy and followed his boss back up the fairway, into the clubhouse.

"You know," Johnny Roses said wearily as they stood at the bar, "after all these centuries, now the Church says there's no such thing as purgatory. You got heaven or hell, take your shot. You can't play the middles, try to buy yourself some time off. Just like here, Sonny. Try and play the middles, you get fucked every time."

10

IN THE La Salle street offices of Assets Management Partners, Ltd., Agents Thorne and McCaskey rowed against the currents of technology, transferring the computer-generated records of their operation into the thick, black-and-red-bound ledgers the good citizens of a federal grand jury could hopefully comprehend.

McCaskey worked at a hard, steady pace—professional, impersonal, not once mentioning Thorne's confused marital status or the troglodytic manner by which he'd informed her of it.

Thorne pushed away his fifth cup of afternoon coffee, crushed out his twentieth Lucky Strike, closed the contact report he'd been working on for the imminent review of Assistant Attorney General James Jonathan Bidwell. His concentration was slipping; gone, in fact. Once again he found himself with nothing to do but wait for Sonny Greco to make his move.

Thorne said, "It's after six in Washington. Bidwell's probably having a snort. I think I will." He opened the bookcase bar, poured a long Scotch and short soda.

"You've been awfully antsy today," McCaskey said.

Thorne wanted to assure her the problem was strictly business.

"It's Greco," he said. "He was going to take my offer to his boss. I thought I'd have heard back by now."

"Bureaucracy everywhere. Give it time." McCaskey began running a fresh tape. "The last one," she said. "Everything we have on Bagley and the Rockford operation."

"I want the family, the old man," Thorne said. "Not some branch manager from the sticks. Greco's got to come through for me."

"Give it time," McCaskey repeated, peeved.

"I'm going to head north, see if I can find him."

She turned back to the lines of data flashing across the green terminal screen. Thorne put on his tie, jacket, raincoat.

"Wish me luck?"

"Luck."

Thorne left the office telling himself the woman was made of ice.

He took a rumbling gypsy cab to Fairweather's. It was six-thirty when he arrived, already dark and bleak. The rain had turned to sleet, then to snow—the Chicago version of April showers. Everywhere else Thorne had been stationed with the Navy, the Bureau, people complained about having too short a spring, too wet a spring, something. Here there was no spring at all. Two weeks from the last snowfall, you could bank on it hitting ninety.

Thorne was barely settled at the bar, Val pouring him a tall one, when Maurice sauntered over, his black three-piece suit set off by a bright pink necktie. Since Thorne had become a regular, hanging at Fairweather's with Greco, he'd gotten to like Maurice. Good thing AAG Bidwell didn't give a crap about numbers and *bolita*. Having to bust Maurice would take a lot of heart out of the joint.

"Hey, Frank."

"What's new, Maurice?"

They slapped palms softly, Thorne pondering the value of Maurice's watch and rings.

"You ever find that back-up man you were looking for to replace Tyrell?"

Maurice jerked his head sideways. "Over there by the door."

The man was built like the black chopper pilot on "Magnum," definitely capable of turning Fairweather's into a lumber yard if the mood struck him. Moving his gaze up from the chest and biceps, Thorne realized he was white.

"Not a brother, Maurice?"

"Shit no, man. Not after Tyrell got himself taken down for GTA. I need dependability, Frank. This time I hired myself a See-cilian. One tough dude, Carmine."

"He can dance with my girl any time he wants," Thorne said.

Maurice leaned over close. "I think you got a problem, baby."

"Like what?"

"Like you've grown yourself a tail."

"Black Chevy four-door," Thorne knew.

"You picked him up too. Right on."

"How did you spot him?"

Maurice said, "I was schmoozin' with some folks across the road when you pulled up. I saw him laying back behind your cab, checkin' his watch when you got out, writin' things down in his little black pig notebook. Ugly mick face. Gotta be some cop."

No, Thorne told himself, that didn't make sense. Or did it?

"Where's he now?"

"Parked on his ass around the corner, probably waitin' on you," Maurice said. "Lookit, you want to shake him, we get you out through the back door. Val take care of it, man."

Thorne took a long pull on his drink. "You carrying, Maurice?"

"Me? No way. Maurice don't mess with drugs."

Thorne squinted at him. "You got a piece with you?"

"A piece? Shit, I wouldn't know how to point it right. I'm a lover, not a fighter."

"Too bad you're not both," Thorne shook his head. Investment counselor or not, he wished he had his S & W Model 19 stuck under his coat.

"But my man over there," Maurice volunteered. "Say you want some help and Carmine'll get it done."

"I want his piece."

Maurice lifted his lanky frame off the stool. "I give you the nod, come and get it."

Thorne saw Carmine grimace, protest. But Maurice must have said something about a bonus, Thorne guessed, because Carmine suddenly turned docile and followed his boss into the john. He came out seconds later and motioned to Thorne.

"You be careful now, baby. Hear?" Maurice said when Thorne stepped inside the stall. He handed over a Heckler & Koch P9S automatic and looked on amazed as Thorne expertly cleared the breech, checked the magazine, snapped a 9-mm parabellum round in the chamber.

"My goodness gracious!" Maurice exclaimed.

"Nobody has to know about this," Thorne said. "It's private business."

"Some business, my man."

"The guy outside's no cop," Thorne tried explaining. "He's a private investigator one of my ex-partners put on me. A little business venture we were in together went sour, and this guy wants to bring a suit against me. He's trying to prove malfeasance on my part."

"Mal-what?"

"That I fucked up. The guy in the Chevy is looking to get some bad character shit against me, make me look bad in court. Bar habits, broads, bad associations, like that."

"Like me," Maurice grinned.

"Like anybody who doesn't wear his collar turned around. You, you're the best. But I especially don't want to get Sonny Greco involved in all this."

"I hear you, Frankie. I know nothin'."

Thorne said, "I'm just going to scare him off, let him know he's been spotted and I don't appreciate it. Maybe he'll figure whatever he's getting paid isn't worth the hassle."

"That thing should do it," Maurice said.

"Tell Carmine he gets it back inside the hour."

"No problem. He's cool."

"How much did you have to pay him?" Thorne asked, reaching in his pocket for the Bureau's roll of cash.

"Paid him nothing, man," Maurice said, declining the money. "Carmy's gonna get himself some first quality head tonight. My treat, dig?"

Thorne slapped him a low five and stepped from the stall. "I might take some of that myself, she's got a friend."

"More than you'd believe," Maurice laughed. "So make it any time, whenever you feel the urge."

Val asked no questions and led Thorne back through the kitchen. "You come out on State," he said.

"I owe you one," Thorne said.

"Forget it, the winners you've been giving me," Val said. "But I'd sure stop fooling around with married ladies."

Thorne walked two blocks south, crossed Rush Street to the east, followed an alley that brought him out fifteen feet behind the parked Chevy. Maurice was right on: without a doubt the car was unmarked Chicago cop, might as well have gumballs on the roof and WE SERVE AND PROTECT stenciled on the doors.

Thorne crouched low, moved behind the deck to the passenger side. If the door was locked, he figured one look at the H & K would get it opened fast. A break: he saw the latch button sticking up.

One, two, deep breath . . .

Thorne popped the door, the automatic went inside ahead of him.

"What the . . .?"

Thorne jabbed the muzzle hard into Detective Tom Massey's ribcage. Massey let out a pained groan and a rush of foul breath.

"Start driving!" Thorne ordered.

"Whaaag," Massey tried saying before his wind came back.

"Drive, or I'll blow your nuts off right here."

Massey looked down with wet eyes at Thorne's aiming point. When Thorne jacked the cocking lever, Massey nodded and hit the ignition.

Thorne directed him to the parking lot at North Avenue beach. It was full of snow-route towaways unclaimed from winter and the carnage of countless fender benders on Lake Shore Drive. Massey, as told, kept his mouth shut all the way there.

Thorne leaned against the door, lighted a cigarette, the H & K still pointed at Massey's scrotum.

"Now," he exhaled, "tell me what the hell you're doing on my case."

"Ask Jack Corrigan," Massey said. "When you told us you were being pulled off the strike force, he got to wondering. I'm supposed to keep a check on you, see what you're working, if it's something you should share with us."

"You've been on me since then?" Thorne asked, angry at himself for missing it, trying to figure how much of his ticket Massey had punched.

"Not all the time. Not at first," Massey said, surprisingly cooperative. "But Corrigan got all worked up when I started placing you with Sonny Greco. That really lit his burners, you and Greco doing the Rush Street thing together, hanging out with all the big money players at Fairweather's. That wasn't too discreet, pal."

"Jack's got some pair of balls having a federal agent followed. Or he's gotten approval from the department. Which is it?"

Massey shrugged. "All Corrigan's got is a hunch. Whether it's that you're trying to sneak something past us or, perish the thought, you might be playing ball with the other side, he's not saying just yet. So why don't you tell me?"

"I'm asking what you think."

"Me? I'm just trying to make a living." Massey reached inside his coat slowly. "Just a cigarette," he said. "Besides, even if you've gone on the family's payroll, and that's why your own people yanked you inside, you're not stupid enough to blow up a cop. So get that Kraut automatic out of my face."

"I ought to take you outside and kick your ass!"

"Now that I'd like you to try," Massey said as he stuck a cigarette between his lips. "Maybe you're that good, maybe you're not. Say the word and we'll find out."

Thorne stared back into Massey's hard, unyielding eyes and decided the point wasn't worth proving. Yet. He threw Massey his cigarette lighter and stuck the H & K in his belt.

"Where do we go from here?" Massey said through a cloud of smoke.

"That depends what you're after."

"Like I said, making a living."

"For Corrigan too?"

"Screw Corrigan. I've been working Vice with him only a couple of months. I owe him nothing."

"You still haven't told me what you think I'm doing."

Massey said, "I don't get paid to think. I get paid to deliver. Now, if you're asking me how much I know, that's a different story." He took another deep drag; relaxed, confident. "I know you're fronting some securities business on La Salle Street. Which is what you told me and the lieutenant. I also know you're spending a lot of time with people in the rackets. People like Sonny Greco, that little nigger Maurice, even the late great Dom Venuti's kid. Maybe one's part of the other. Maybe not."

"Suppose not," Thorne said, already seeing where the son-of-a-bitch was headed.

"Then I'd say you're making extra cash by keeping the family's book out of trouble while you're out chasing some wheat thieves from the Exchange. Maybe you're selling Greco the idea that he's getting special consideration, which would be a great con if you're not even working his case anymore."

"You've got one helluva imagination," Thorne said.

"That so?" Massey said, his face tightening into a thin smile. "Well here's the point I'm making. Your fucking wheat thieves are federal action. But whatever you got going with Greco and the outfit falls on my turf."

"And Corrigan's, don't forget."

"All he knows is what I tell him. See, he wants none of this on paper. I talk to him face to face when I have something. Like tonight. Maybe."

Thorne took the maybe seriously.

"Let's say I'm working on something private, nothing to do with the Bureau or the family's book. Sort of a special placement thing that's got lucrative potential, but not exactly what I'd like to see kicked around at Eleventh and State. So maybe, just to buy some silent running, keep the department's nose out of my business, I could see my way clear—"

"How much we talking about?" Massey interrupted.

"You don't want to know more about it?"

"I don't want to know shit. You want me off your ass, want me to stall Corrigan and forget about the company you keep, that's one thing. The rest is your business. All I need to hear is a figure."

"Five hundred."

"Fuck you."

"A week," Thorne countered. "I'll need two, three weeks more to wrap things up. You keep Corrigan in check that long, you get to go home early and you pocket a dime, fifteen hundred."

"You're the one said the business was lucrative, pal. All you're offering me is chump change. Bump it up to twenty-five hundred flat and I'll let you ride free for a while."

Thorne started thinking it through, but not how Massey might have figured. He had more than enough cash to cover the payments and still keep it off McCaskey's books, away from Bidwell. Then, when he made the move with Greco's bosses, he would give Massey's ass to Jack Corrigan as a peace offering. One or two photos of the cash changing hands would do it. Corrigan would be hot, but getting a kinky cop off the streets would make him feel better.

"You've got a deal," Thorne said. "Twenty-five hundred for telling Corrigan nothing I don't clear first. For staying as far away from me as you can."

"For the time being," Massey added. "Which don't mean forever."

"Don't push for more than you're worth."

Massey gave Thorne another shrug. "I'll need a down payment."

"Five hundred is what I've got."

"Good for earnest money. I'll take a thousand next week, and the week after. Anything else you want, any extras, we adjust then."

You sleazy bastard, Thorne said to himself as he peeled off the money and watched Massey grab for it. The next time we do this I'll have your ugly face in the cross-hairs of a 500-mm lens.

"Beats dealing with pushers and junkies all the time," Massey said as he stuffed the bills in his pocket.

"That where you come from? Narcotics?"

"How'd you guess?" Massey sneered.

"And you got transferred out for taking . . ."

"They transfer everybody out, sooner or later. That spreads the action around, keeps people happy. It cost me plenty, moving over to Vice."

"I'll bet it did," Thorne said.

"Past tense. The future's looking brighter."

"Don't get greedy on me," Thorne warned him. "Or even think about trying to cut yourself in on my business."

"Don't get so uptight, pal. There's room in this world for everybody."

Massey rolled down the window, flipped his butt into the snow. The ride back to Fairweather's was as silent as the one over. Massey pulled up a half-block short of the bar.

"You've made the smart move," Thorne said, opening his door.

"Except for one thing."

"What's that?"

Massey rubbed his bruised ribcage in an exaggerated motion.

"Except that, you ever put a hand on me again, I'll personally break both your fucking arms. You got that straight?"

"Then don't . . ." Thorne began, but Massey hit the gas and fishtailed away in the slush.

Thorne pointlessly stirred the cup of black coffee, thinking over his cast of characters.

Detective Tom Massey. A surprise intrusion, a potential liability, sure. But also a great piece of video waiting to be made. Anyone walks around with his hand stuck out that far was bound to screw up. Thorne would be there when he did.

AAG James Jonathan Bidwell. Thorne ran a quick inventory of what he had for their impending review. He would lead with Anthony (Tony Shoes) Scarpo and Sanford (Sandy the Panda) Lowenstein, both of whom were sufficiently wrapped up in McCaskey's computer and phone tapes to provide for a decade or so of counting crows on the Route 63 power lines outside the federal penitentiary in Terre Haute. Throw in a dozen phone men and office managers, two wire rooms that were ready to fall, that should get Bidwell's attention. Odds were that somebody in the group would roll over and spill his guts to the Bureau. Not Scarpo or Lowenstein, certainly. They wanted their families looked after while they learned how to digest elbow macaroni and Velveeta casseroles. But someone with enough information to top off the gambling with rack-eteering and conspiracy indictments, maybe even give Bidwell the linkage he wanted with the top people in the family. Not bad, Thorne decided, for six weeks of sitting in a brokerage office on La Salle Street and running a major bar bill at Fairweather's.

Sonny Greco. Thorne's trump ace, if Bidwell would let him hold it until the final trick. Get to Greco's bosses, pump a few hundred thousand of government cash into their businesses, blaze open the money trail to syndicate-backed operations all over the state. Get that going and the old man himself might be within reach. Work with the tax boys, throw in RICO, and the Justice Department could end up seizing his damn golf clubs. A little time, patience, luck, it would all come together. Only . . .

Thorne pushed away his cup and plate, went for another Lucky. He never got past Sonny Greco. With all this good stuff going, what was it that kept gnawing at him, tightening his gut? Having to bust Sonny, when all he ever offered Thorne was friendship and a little side action? Hey, that's the breaks. Sonny knew the risks. Forget it. No way he could give Greco a pass; no way Sonny would finger anybody else to save his skin, hide down at Maxwell AFB with the rest of the snitch witnesses, all the creeps with permanent tics from looking over their shoulder twenty times an hour.

Which meant, bottom line, that when Bidwell and the other big bags at Justice raked in the chips, Greco would be the one who'd have to settle their tab.

Do it all right, Thorne knew, and Sonny Greco ends up a long time dead.

Thorne looked out the steamy window. Rain and sleet had filled the potholes out on Rush Street, turning them into deep, treacherous pools. A toney young woman struggling with a wind-caught umbrella and a green Marshall Field shopping bag misjudged one and stepped into a calf-deep sea of muck. Thorne saw her trembling lips swear at a disinterested divinity. Sonny Greco, crossing from Fairweather's, offered her an extricating hand. The woman gave him an extended middle finger before marching south toward Oak Street. Greco laughed and hopscotched his way into the coffee shop.

"Val told me you were here."

"I hung around for an hour. Nobody knew if you were going to show."

Greco brushed the droplets from his pigskin jacket, looked down and shuddered at Thorne's half-eaten mushroom burger and neoprene French fries.

"Forget that, will you? Let's take a ride."

"Where to?"

"Out west. Unless you're meeting your lady."

Thorne shook his head. "Hair-washing and leg-shaving night."

"So let's hit it."

They drove south to Ontario Street and onto the Kennedy ramp. Far as Thorne could make out, Tom Massey had settled for his down payment and taken the rest of the night off.

"You see Maurice?" he asked.

"He's around," Greco said. "Got himself a new pair of shoulders. White guy, this time. Carmine. He's a legend on the South Side, back from eighth grade when he was a crossing guard and beat up two beer-truck drivers for parking in his intersection.

So Maurice had kept his word and his mouth shut. Thorne owed him two now.

"What's with you and Maurice? Business or pleasure?"

Thorne said, "He asked me to check out some things on the Exchange. I think he's ready to try out the market."

"He could *buy* it," Greco said. "That shine's got more cash than Continental Bank, and it's better managed. Maurice don't borrow to no Brazils and Argentinas."

"If he did, he'd collect," Thorne said. He silently counted the days since he'd made his offer at Dead Dom's. Maybe Greco had taken his proposition upstairs, maybe tonight he was going to deliver. Wanting it to happen, Thorne said, "Better let me know if we're going somewhere to talk business. I haven't worked up any numbers yet, or gotten firm commitments."

Greco shook his head.

"What's that mean?"

"It means no sale."

"Who'd you talk to?"

Greco's voice turned sharp. "The man I'm supposed to talk to. Okay?"

"Sure." Thorne knew he had to back off. It rolled out naturally or not at all. "Your choice."

"Their choice," Greco said. Satisfied that the White Sox were sleeted out at Comiskey, he turned off the radio.

"Lookit, tonight we're just going to relax, have some fun. Like my friend Pizza Sal says, we've gotta cut back on the stress. But just so you know, my boss didn't slam the door on your offer. Consider it on hold. Everybody keeps winning, he may be interested. May be he even takes it upstairs. Understand?"

Thorne feigned a nervous sigh.

"That bother you?"

"I want to know who I'm doing business with," Thorne said. "I don't know anybody named 'upstairs.' "

"If it comes through, you'll know. You may not like who it is when it happens, but these people believe in close working arrangements."

"That sounds like a warning."

"A fact of life."

Thorne said, "Your call, Sonny. But my people are wondering when they'll get paid."

"I have a package coming later," Greco said. "Enough to cover most of the week. Everything but that fucking Los Angeles game. My calculator doesn't go up that high."

"High enough that the house might close?"

"If I knew I'd tell you," Greco said. "I don't even think they know for sure. But everybody'll get paid. Tell 'em."

"Maybe they'll give some back this weekend." Thorne decided on the spot they would. Not enough to kill his proposition, just enough to keep the house thinking the odds would swing back. A delicate balance: say twenty, twenty-five grand.

"If not, I may hit you for some cash myself."

"Name it."

Greco turned and smiled. "You would, too."

"You say when. As much as I've got."

"Some shit," Greco said as he turned into a graveled parking lot. "Guy I've known a couple of weeks is ready to bail me out of trouble. Guys I've known for years . . . aw, screw it!"

They were out by Mannheim, near the airport. A store across the street advertised peep shows and latex novelties. The neon sign that flashed weakly over the blockhouse Greco pulled up to said: THE CAIRO CLUB. STEAKS. SEAFOOD. DANCING.

"We going for a steak?"

"Not a chance," Greco laughed. "This place don't even have a stove that works. You get hungry, we order sausage and peppers from a takeout joint on Harlem."

"I'm becoming an honorary Italian," Thorne said.

Greco kept laughing. "Worse things could happen."

Thorne heard the music seeping through the black enameled doors before Greco swung them open.

"She's a ma-ni-ac, ma-ni-ac, I know . . .!"

Thorne and Greco walked around a fabric-covered partition, into the main lounge. To the right, past the bald man who threw Sonny a wave, was a curving oval bar. The two bartenders who worked it looked like they learned their trade at Stateville. Each of them handled a party of seven, eight conventioneers wearing "Hi!" badges from an RV show. Thorne watched them order tiny champagne cocktails, probably ten bucks a crack, for the girls working the stool side of the bar.

"This way," Greco said.

They cut across the empty dance floor, around a cluster of tables for two. Along the back wall three naked go-go dancers performed atop four-foot-high, glitter-covered cylinders. They were all amazingly alike in height, figure, Orphan Annie wigs, pubic hair shaved and dyed into Valentines.

"Ma-ni-ac! Ma-ni-ac!" they lip-synched to the cracked

speakers. *"And she's dancin' like she's never danced before!"*

Greco pointed Thorne toward an upholstered booth.

"My friend Sal Catania," he said. "Sally's okay except for two things. You don't loan him a nickel you ever want to see again, and you don't go partners with him on any deal, no matter how good he makes it sound."

"I got it."

"Remember it and you're doing yourself a favor. It just cost me two dimes and a lot of paper to keep him walking."

Sal Catania had a head of thick curls that looked too large for his slight, sloping shoulders. Seeing Greco, his eyes flashed a smile of welcome.

"Sonny! My man!" Sal grabbed the two girls he sat between by their napes, sliding them with him to the center of the booth. "Sit down here," he said, obviously flying. "I'll order over some extra company when they're finished dancing."

Greco said, "This is Frank. Good friend of mine."

"Hey," Pizza Sal said, looking Thorne over.

"He's okay," Greco added.

Thorne said hello, took the left side seat to give himself a full view of the club.

"I'm Marci. This is Carol."

"Hi," Carol chimed in.

"When Sonny says it's time to relax, he's not kidding," Thorne said.

"He learnt it from me," Sal boasted.

"He's right," Greco said, looking around the room. "Start a tab, order me a vodka-soda. I'll be back in five minutes."

Sal stuck an unlit panatela in his mouth and made a grand gesture toward the bar. Marci lowered her tube top slightly and placed a warm hand on Thorne's leg.

"What would you like?"

"Scotch," Thorne said.

"Get Johnny Walker Black," Marci whispered. "The boss drinks it. It's the only one not watered down or married with Clan McGregor."

"Thanks."

"For sure."

Thorne saw Greco cautiously approach a booth at the far corner of the room. He stood still half a minute, until getting the nod to join them from one of the three men sitting there. Thorne could only see the back of a thick neck and large head on the one seated closest to him; the one farthest away was smaller, darker, nervous looking. Between them, back to the wall like Thorne's so he could take in the entire club, was an old friend. Thorne had never met him personally, but for eight years had studied his surveillance photos in the Bureau's organized crime file. Sid Paris! Sonny Greco's strings were being pulled by Sid Paris, Thorne exploded in silence. Number one of the troika of nephews in line for the old man's chair. Sid Paris. Holy shit.

Sal Catania poked Thorne's bicep, bringing him back.

"Time for a pick-me-up. Whadda you say?"

He delivered an amber vial from his shirt pocket. Marci and Carol watched transfixed as he unscrewed the cap, extended the spoon.

"Just keep it down. People Sonny's talking to don't appreciate this stuff, who the fuck knows why."

Thorne watched the girls eagerly dip into the eighth-ounce bottle.

"Tell me that's not great shit," Sal winked.

"No speed in it," Marci sniffled. "Just fine."

"What about you?"

"Later, you say it's good," Thorne replied.

"Bet your sweet A it's good. You're a friend of Sonny's, you just let me know. I can get whatever you want, for fun or profit."

"I might take a little of both."

"Then sometime, you and me gotta talk in private."

"Tell me where and when," Marci giggled. "I can still do some shorthand."

"We don't write up no contracts, asshole," Pizza Sal laughed.

"We're not getting any drinks either," Thorne said. He stood half up and waved toward the bar. But his eyes were focused on the booth where Greco sat. Sid Paris was already gone.

"You're drunk," MaryAgnes McCaskey declared flatly.

"Should have called first. But I was in the neighborhood."

"It's four A.M., Frank. Call it a night, will you?"

Thorne saw her clutch at a golden sliver of quilting, all he could see of her robe through the barely cracked door.

"Let's talk."

"You *are* drunk, damn it. I'd say a first-class Fairweather's package."

"C'mon. Greco just dropped me off. You want to blow my cover as a keeper of beautiful women? Besides, the cocaine should kick in any minute now. I'll be fine."

"I don't think you're teasing," McCaskey said.

"I'm not."

Thorne heard her mumble something about a life full of little boys, saw the door open slowly.

"You get time enough for coffee."

"Coffee. Good."

Thorne followed her inside the apartment, the tightly belted robe defining the elegant contours of her backside.

"This is business," he said.

"You still need some coffee."

"Fine. It's four o'clock."

Thorne's jacket came off inside his raincoat. He was

barely settled in an armchair when McCaskey's electric kettle began to whistle. She fixed him a cup of instant, double strength.

"It's good."

"Thanks." McCaskey sat on the sofa, tucking her legs under her body in a way Thorne considered physically impossible. "Now what?"

"Is everything ready for Bidwell? All the books, tapes . . .?"

"All ready, Frank. Just like I told you this morning. Is that what you've come here to talk about?"

"No, because there's a lot more we have to do," Thorne said. "And we'll need it done tomorrow."

McCaskey leaned forward, starting to believe him. "You're serious, aren't you?"

"I'm not here to play midnight cowboy," Thorne grumbled. "I said right away we have matters to discuss."

"I've heard that one before."

"I'll bet you have. Only not from me."

"Touché."

Thorne let it ride.

"I know I'm half-wasted here, but it was all line-a-duty. I've got crooked cops, cokeheads, hookers . . . a guy I really like who's gonna end up getting killed . . ."

"Frank, what in heaven's name are you talking about?"

Thorne got down half the coffee, tried rubbing his eyes into focus. "Okay. You ready? Here goes . . .

"One. Place called the Cairo Club, out in Rosemont, off Mannheim. You know it?"

McCaskey shook her head. "It's a little out of my territory, and a *long* way out of my scene. But I know the area, that strip near O'Hare. After hours spots, clip joints, pros for the out-of-towners. Didn't some college dean buy himself a lot of trouble out there, with money that wasn't his?"

"Lucky guess," Thorne said.

"Not the way you look," McCaskey shot back.

"Tomorrow, run the Cairo Club through every check you can think of—owner's licenses, deeds, property tax records, staff payroll with names and addresses, all of it. Anything's leased, from the land to the glassware, I want to know the lessor and lessee. Code it all priority five, agent's eyes only. You get any bullshit from the BB stackers in records section, go see Doc Hermann. He's still the boss, last time I looked. Tell him what we want and how we want it, which is fast. Tell him BBC—Before Bidwell Comes."

McCaskey fell back into her habit of note-taking, scribbling a tight personal shorthand.

"And if Doc wants to know why?"

"You tell him Sid Paris. He who sitteth at the right hand of the old man himself. He's no customer of the Cairo Club, believe me. My guess—you forget about the bubble baths in the basement—my guess it's a family banking center: a laundromat, clearing house, where the nephews meet to talk business. Like that."

"Sounds lovely," McCaskey said. "To think I used to complain about Fairweather's."

"But you like Dead Dom's."

"What else?" she asked, losing patience.

"Sid Paris. Pull together every shred of paper and tape in the building. If IRS hands you any shit about clearance, head back to see Doc Hermann. He's got one of their district directors tied to a gay bar on Clark Street. One phone call about the gown he wore to Butchie's place, you'll get whatever you want."

"Thy will be done," McCaskey said.

"Now, two . . ."

"This makes three."

"Three. Six weeks back, when we first opened up, I pulled a package on one Salvatore Joseph Catania. It wasn't worth much, but as a favor I passed it on to Jack Corrigan, lieutenant, runs Chicago Vice down at Eleventh and State. Instead of pulling it all over again, save time and call Corrigan yourself. Give him some baloney about updating it. Tell him you're my secretary or something, say he'll get it back with additions."

McCaskey let the pencil slip from her fingers.

"Your damned secretary is what I'm starting to feel like."

"I've got no time for thin skins," Thorne said. "Anyway, it's not true."

"So you say. But I'm chained to a computer terminal all day while you're out tracking down bad guys like the Lone Ranger. I've got my instructions. Now I want to know what this is all about. Or have all your promises about teamwork and partnership gone out the window?"

"Mister Inside and Mister Outside, remember?"

"Only when you feel like it," McCaskey railed.

Thorne crumpled the empty pack he'd pulled from his pocket. "Come up with a cigarette while I get my thoughts together."

"You shit!"

She stomped into her bedroom and brought back an opened pack of cigarettes. "Two weeks old at least. Enjoy."

"You should cut down," Thorne said.

"I want to know what's going on, Frank," she persisted.

Thorne lighted a Virginia Slims menthol extra light, took one drag and crushed it out. "Okay, one . . ."

"Enough with the laundry list," McCaskey barked. "What happened tonight?"

"Greco's people turned down my offer. Sonny says it's on hold, but I don't think they're going to bite. Not if his major boss is Sid Paris. The thing is, the refusal puts Sonny and us in a box.

"I think you're trying for too much," McCaskey said. "We have everything Bidwell wanted from us. Scarpo, Lowenstein, Bagley, Greco, their whole operation . . ."

"Maybe Bidwell doesn't get Sonny Greco. How's that sound?"

"Like you're not making sense."

Thorne pulled himself up and grabbed his raincoat as McCaskey stared at him in bewilderment.

"Here's fifty thousand cash," he said. "It's supposed to come off Sonny Greco's figure. But it's not going to. Keep it in the office safe, unmarked, untagged. Greco's balance stays unchanged. I'll tell you why as soon as I'm sure myself, soon as I can call in some favors from our brethren over at DEA."

11

ASSISTANT ATTORNEY General James Jonathan Bidwell caught an early flight out of Washington National, arrived at Assets Management Partners soon after eleven, and immediately assumed eminent domain of Frank Thorne's desk.

"Smarter that we meet here," Bidwell said. "No sense taking the chance of someone spotting you two at the Dirksen Building. Besides, I wanted to see all the luxury the Bureau's paying for."

"We've paid our own way," Thorne said.

"That's what I'm here to find out."

"Director Hermann is due any minute now," McCaskey said.

"It's the three of us today," Bidwell said. "Senior *Agent* Hermann has other commitments. So let's get on with it, shall we?"

McCaskey handled the presentation expertly. First came a profile of each target, then the telephone taps and betting results, which led her naturally to the ledgers. She sat dutifully alongside AAG Bidwell as he ran his index finger down each page of summary, uncrossing and recrossing her legs, Thorne noticed, each time Bidwell circled a bottomline figure with his red felt-tipped marker.

"Right," Bidwell said finally.

Thorne checked his watch: Bidwell had been bean counting for an hour. McCaskey reversed her legs for the eleventh time.

Bidwell said, "I assume you've had these materials duplicated and secured."

"A back-up set has been transmitted to Washington," McCaskey answered quickly. "A third is secured in the A-level safe at the DOB. We're the only ones cleared for access."

"And Doc Hermann," Thorne added. He was still nursing his Cairo Club hangover and getting more fed up by the minute with the officious little prick in his chair. "Doc doesn't retire until February."

"Right," Bidwell said.

McCaskey shot Thorne a nervous glance.

"For added security," she said, "all we keep here are the active computer tapes. Besides our access code, we've installed a second cipher that has to be run through the main bank in Washington. Without both, they're gibberish."

Bidwell nodded approvingly and tapped a load of fresh tobacco into his white briar pipe. Thorne suddenly remembered what his carrier-pilot friends at Pensacola called pipes—Link-trainers for cocksuckers. Perfect.

"This page is a summary of cash-flow-to-date from each target," McCaskey said, sliding a twelve-column statement across the desk top. "Again, we've used a coded digital matrix—no names, no telephone or account numbers. The agents we're using as bettors are keyed on the left side. When we reach the evidence stage, I suggest this be translated at headquarters to bring it into parallel with the phone and voice tapes. That will give everyone a common lexicon."

"Very good."

"Thank you, sir."

"We've got more tapes here than Radio Shack," Thorne quipped.

Bidwell circled the bottom line without acknowledging him and slipped the document into his triple-locking Hartmann case.

"Not bad at all," he said.

"We're kicking the hell out of the mob," Thorne said. "I'd call it better than not bad."

Bidwell sat back in Thorne's chair, removed his reading glasses, pulled on his pipe. McCaskey nervously recrossed her legs.

"The dollar amounts are ahead of forecast," Bidwell said dryly. "To date, *in toto*, we've managed to beat the Midwestern crime families for about three million dollars. Three point one-two-eight, actually."

"One third of it from this office," Thorne reminded him.

"Indeed. A major contribution from *the* major crime center."

McCaskey sensed a confrontation and pulled her chair next to Thorne's. The look she gave Thorne told him to keep his mouth shut. She'd take it from there: Numbers are my ballgame, Frank. Stay out in the field where you belong. To Bidwell she said, "Let's not forget the assets the Department can seize under RICO. I'm preparing a separate dossier on that now. And, when we move into phase two and penetrate some of the family's business operations, I think we'll have an extraordinary package to take into court."

Bidwell nodded. "Don't worry. You'll both receive all the credit you deserve. All the way to the top. Thorne, you've done some fine work out there. I think even you've become a believer."

"I used to be a cop," Thorne said.

"And now?"

"I'm not sure."

McCaskey interrupted again. "At first, I thought

the money we'd win was secondary to penetrating the syndicate. But seven figures in seven weeks is amazing, especially when you include the games we lost on purpose. I still don't know how anyone can write a computer program around someone who's wide open dropping a pass in the end zone, or fumbling a yard short of the goal."

"Actually we *can*," Bidwell said smugly. "Not play by play, of course. But on a complete game basis we can forecast events to within probability tolerances that enable us to keep winning. Your point, for example. We factor in the number of times a particular pass receiver will be used in each game and in each yardage situation. We also can anticipate the type of pass pattern he will run, the team's play-calling profile . . ."

"The PCP," Thorne said.

"Exactly."

"Incredible," McCaskey said, concealing a grin.

"With all the variables accounted for," Bidwell went on, "we've been able to pinpoint negative scoring impact . . ."

"NSI," Thorne blurted again.

". . . to pinpoint dropped touchdowns, fumbles, missed kicks and the like," Bidwell went on, "to one point seven-seven-four points per game."

Thorne lit a cigarette and blew a cloud of smoke upwards. "Sonny's got no fucking chance," he said softly.

"Sorry?"

"Nothing."

McCaskey came in quickly: "Perhaps I've spent too much time in the audit section, but I know brokerage houses have sophisticated data banks too. And not one of them can guarantee you an eighth of a point per share on IBM, let alone one point whatever on who's going to fumble a football."

"Ah, well," Bidwell smiled, his first of the meeting. "But Merrill Lynch doesn't have the back-up we do.

In their case, the computer is providing a statistical forecast for a human being. For us, it's the reciprocal. We take the computer forecast and adjust the numbers in our favor. It's what your bookmaker friends would call the winning edge."

"You're really losing me now," McCaskey admitted. "And you, Thorne?"

Thorne watched Bidwell watching him, probably hoping he'd open his mouth and insert foot. Thorne picked up his cigarette . . . It fell into place in a flash. Goddamn, he should have figured it out before.

"The point spreads! You're working the point spreads too!" he erupted.

"Not working them, Thorne. Setting them."

"No wonder the book is getting killed. You've got someone on the inside. In Vegas."

"I'm surprised you didn't figure it out sooner," Bidwell said. "Let's hope your bookmakers will take a tad longer to put it together themselves."

"You're controlling what comes out of Las Vegas, what appears in the newspapers?" McCaskey asked.

"At this point I'll just say that, with some assistance from inside the Las Vegas handicapping network, we're adjusting the published betting lines to our advantage. Just enough to make certain our computer-selected teams win. The major television games are, of course, a priority. To take a lesson from Willie Sutton, that's where the money is."

"No wonder the man on the street has been cleaning up too," Thorne said. "When you lower the point spread enough to make the favorites cover . . ."

"Disinformation, n'est-cè pas?" Bidwell smirked.

"I still don't understand," McCaskey said.

"The majority of bettors usually play the favored team," Thorne explained. "In terms of dollars, bookmakers usually end up with fifty-two, fifty-three percent of their handle on the favorite. If it wins, the book comes out a little ahead because of their ten percent service charge for the losers—vigorish, juice, whatever you call it. If the favorite loses, doesn't cover the spread, better yet. The book is up fifteen percent."

"Exactly," Bidwell said.

"If any game is bet so strongly one way that these percentages are out of whack," Thorne went on, "then the bookmaker has two choices—either hold it and gamble himself, or find another house and lay it off. The ideal for every book in America is to have a million bucks on each team and pocket a cool hundred thousand no matter who wins. Now we enter the picture. If whoever we have in Vegas puts out a phony spread, one that makes the favorite so attractive that everybody loads up on it, the book has nowhere to lay off. He ends up holding the action and takes a royal screwing thanks to us."

"That's approximately correct," Bidwell said. "We have our underdogs too. The key factor is selecting which games give us the maximum advantage over the house."

"You're right," McCaskey whispered to Thorne. "Greco doesn't have a prayer."

"What I've found surprising," Bidwell continued, "is how close the Las Vegas betting lines come to ours. I know the syndicate has computers too, but I never thought they could come as close as they do. Tells you what we're up against, how sharp these people are. Which is why we've found it necessary to make our little adjustments."

"I thought you might have a few players on the string," Thorne said. "That would sure help your NSI."

"It has been discussed," Bidwell said. "Especially with key players that have been lax with the IRS. But so far, we haven't had to call in those chips."

"But our bookmakers adjust the point spreads up and down until game time," McCaskey said. "We're always having to compensate for last minute changes."

"That's why we've had some agents playing the middles," Thorne said. "We bet both teams and win both bets when the score lands in between two different point spreads."

"Amazing, isn't it?" Bidwell beamed. "And I rarely even watch football."

"With the computers and fixed spreads together, how many points are in our pocket before kick-off?" Thorne asked.

"How many is secondary to predictability," Bidwell said. "But our five-star selections approach a three-and-a-half-point advantage and are running about ninety-seven percent winners."

"I sure as hell wasted a lot of time watching bad games," Thorne said, "thinking the outcome was in doubt."

"We at least had to keep *you* honest, didn't we?"

Bidwell spun the locking cylinders on his case, came around Thorne's desk and rested his narrow ass on the overhang.

"My turn for questions," he said.

"Shoot."

"With very little field work involved," he began, "very little personal contact on your part, we've put together first-rate cases against Misters Scarpo, Lowenstein, that small operator from Rockford . . ."

"Bagley," McCaskey reminded him. "Daniel Bagley."

"My point is, all these cases were built with telephone taps, some video surveillance, using our agents . . ."

"What's your complaint?" Thorne asked.

"What I'm trying to understand is your strategy with the man you said would be our spearhead into the family. With all the time and effort you've spent working Mister Greco, we don't seem to be getting a fair return. Fact is, Thorne, anyone looking over our balance sheets and your memoranda might conclude that Greco is getting preferential treatment."

"I'm giving Greco extra rein for the very reason you

cited," Thorne countered. "He *can* get me inside the family, right up to the nephews, maybe the old man himself."

"Your record of collections doesn't support that premise. Greco is the slowest pay on our books."

"I'm working Sonny Greco my way," Thorne said as McCaskey winced. "Which isn't sitting behind some damn computer terminal and adding up winners."

Bidwell stiffened visibly, gripped the desk top with both hands until his fingertips turned white.

"Let me put it to you in a different, less delicate way," he said, nodding toward McCaskey. "We have Sonny Greco by the balls. I want to know why you're not squeezing them harder. What's going on out there, Thorne? What is it between you and Greco?"

Sonny Greco stopped counting long enough to watch Jeff Bridges bang Rachel Ward on Pizza Sal's pirate cassette of *Against All Odds*. Wonderful stuff: Everybody's into the outfit, the book is pulling all the strings—politicians, zoning boards; he even gets to Alex Karras, history repeating itself. Might be time to take a shot at the Coast, Greco fantasized. It sure as hell wasn't working out that way in Chicago.

Bridges, the injured wide-receiver, was licking perspiration from the team owner's daughter's neck when Greco hit the hold button. Diane had pulled a disappearing act on him, gone more than a week, God knows why. Camille, not that it mattered, was still tanning her shoulders in Florida, overtipping Cuban waiters while the twins learned how to use an abacus in some goddamned Montessori school. Greco fast-forwarded past Ward's writhing image: he was in no mood to watch other people screwing while he was taking one himself, which was what the numbers told him.

The cash Johnny Roses had sent over was stacked into four piles, twenty dimes each, partial payments for what each office had coming. Greco used an old number-three pencil and a sheet of rice paper to do his tallies, figuring he could punch them into the computer later, hoping that reverting to the old system would change his luck.

Something had to.

He rechecked the totals. Even after paying Frank the fifty large, he was still far short of the mark. The damage from college hoops, the NCAAs, was almost settled. But working it down had used up the entire bank he'd gotten from Johnny Roses, plus all his cash on hand. Camille had better return his call fast, pull her ass off the beach, tell him what was left in the safety deposit box and where she'd hidden the key.

The doorbell rang twice: fast, back-to-back chimes ordering him to move double time.

In case the feds were coming to call, Greco carried his sheets and a desk lighter to the window. He laughed at himself when he saw Pizza Sal standing on the stoop.

"What's going on?"

"Doing some paperwork," Greco said. "Watching your movie."

"I'm laying low too."

"Yeah? Last time I saw you you were heading for a motel with two broads and an eighth of blow. You call that low?"

"No more," Sal insisted. "I got those chest pains again, thought I was catching a heart attack."

"So give it up for a while."

"*Nada más,* really. But I think it's the nerves causing me the problems, all the pressure." He pulled a director's chair next to Greco's desk, looked longingly at the four stacks of hundreds.

"You were with the big people last night," he said. "What did they tell you?"

"About what?"

"Jesus Christ, Sonny. What do you think about what? About me squaring things with Chuckie Franco."

"Franco's got his down payment. He's going to wait for the rest. What else is there?"

"I thought maybe Sid Paris, Johnny Roses might put in a good word—"

"Come on!" Greco snapped. "These people got other problems than worrying about you. All they know is you're on a three-day roll with Marci and that other broad. It doesn't look to them like you're suffering any."

"I still thought that Johnny Roses—"

Greco cut him off once more.

"Johnny's so uptight you couldn't get a pencil up his ass with a jar of Vaseline. I think he's in real trouble with the nephews."

"He's in trouble? *I'm* in trouble!"

Sal came out of his chair, started pacing. "That's what you get for standing up to the cops."

"Roll over and see what you get," Greco shot back.

Pizza Sal fell back into his seat, told Greco he didn't understand all his problems, how much other trouble he was in.

"Look," Greco said. "Franco's sitting still for a month. And things are starting to turn around. Even Frank's players gave back twelve dimes last night. So, we get back on our feet, we'll get Franco taken care of. Enough, if not all."

"You want to take that chance, fine. I don't. Chuckie Franco would enjoy hitting me with a blow torch. Bet a thousand on a horse you could buy for five hundred?"

"What else you got in mind? You ready to try the track again?"

"Like I told you, if I can put together one good-size deal, we're both out of the woods. I talked with your buddy Frank at the club. I think he's interested, if you go in on it too."

Greco hated the temptation. But another check of the bottom line and his question came automatically.

"Who's your source?"

"This guy I met in Miami," Sal began. "Lived in Venezuela once, but went to school here. Not a grease-ball type, no accent, nothing like that. Name of Kerry Delgado. Kerry, can you believe it? Went to Princeton or something. No kidding."

"I'll bet. Only you could hook up with an Ivy League soda merchant."

"He's got the whole thing down to a science," Pizza Sal went on. "He takes a percentage up front for setting up the buy. He handles all the arrangements, getting the merchandise, sending it north to somebody here in town who gets paid the balance when we pick up the goods. I mean, Sonny, it's so sweet you wouldn't believe it. Some old black lady mules it up from Gulfport. Miami's only good for paperwork these days. Stuff comes through New Orleans and up from Mississippi. The old lady's a real grandmother type, brings it in shopping bags on a Greyhound, underneath the homemade pralines for her grandkids. Nothing fancy, which is why it works. Always."

"No such thing as always," Greco said. "Unless you're dead. Who's the contact here?"

Pizza Sal shook his head as he lit a smoke.

"I hate to say this, Sonny, but I can't tell you that. It's the one thing I swore to with Delgado. Nobody gets any names or we risk the whole thing going off."

Greco threw up his hands. "You saying I'm good enough to come up with the buy money, but not good enough to know who I'm dealing with? That's bullshit, Sal. I want a name, a face, somebody we can check out."

"You got me. Ain't that good enough?"

"Screw you."

"It'll work, Sonny. A cinch."

Pizza Sal froze when the telephone rang.

"Sit still," Greco told him. "I'll take it upstairs."

He got to the bedroom phone on the third ring.

"Damn it, Sonny," Camille shrieked. "You didn't wire me the money like you promised."

Greco fell across the bed and heard her out.

"I've been calling and calling. You're never home."

"I am now," Greco said. Neither are you is what he thought.

"My mother's been paying for everything. I'm so embarrassed."

"I couldn't find the key."

"What key?"

"To the strongbox."

"I have both of them with me," Camille said.

"Why's that? You the family banker all of a sudden?"

"Because what we have in there is for emergencies. Take what you need out of checking, the passbook account. But not . . ."

"This *is* an emergency," Greco argued back. "The other accounts are dry and I need to get at some cash. Can you understand that?"

"You're in trouble."

"I damn well will be," Greco said, listening to Camille's labored breathing.

"Please, Sonny, don't touch the jewelry," she pleaded.

"What can I touch without a key?"

"I'll send it to you tonight," Camille surrendered. "Special delivery, I guess. Or should I use Federal Express, something like that?"

Greco decided on the spot: he missed the twins terribly and, just maybe, Sally's friend Delgado was worth checking out. Maybe one good deal to get back on his feet . . .

"Sonny, what should I do?"

"I'll come down myself," Greco said. "Spend a few days with the twins, try and relax a little. Assuming that's okay."

"You know it is. And the twins would love to see you." She paused several seconds, then said, "You're in that much trouble?"

"I said I'd like to see you, all of you. If there's room?"

"There's my room."

Greco tried recalling the last time he and Camille had made love. He failed to come up with a date.

"Absolutely," he said.

"When can you get here?"

"Late tomorrow. Maybe the day after."

"Let me know which flight and I'll pick you up. Miami, Lauderdale, whichever is best for you."

"I'd better rent a car. It might be late."

"No matter," Camille said. "Call me when you're ready to leave. And . . . Sonny . . . I've missed you a lot."

"Yeah, me too."

Greco walked downstairs slowly, wondering how to tell Pizza Sal they'd be taking a trip to Miami without committing himself to anything more than a few days in the sun.

"I'm going to do a beer," he called in to Sal. "You want something?"

"Got coffee?"

"You take instant?"

"Milk and three sugars."

Hearing the refrigerator open, the Yorkies began yapping from their incarceration in the basement.

"What the hell's that?" Sal jumped.

"The dogs want out," Greco said.

"Fuck," Pizza Sal said. "Who doesn't?"

"You think he bought it?" asked Thorne.

"I'm too tired to think," McCaskey replied. "God, what a day."

"What a son-of-a-bitch, you mean." Thorne closed the door behind them.

"I don't suppose you can head up a strike force like ours without becoming one," McCaskey said.

She slipped off her coat, held out her arm for Thorne's. "The pressure gets to you sooner or later, everybody wanting everything at once. And all the politics."

"I know the feeling," Thorne said.

"Just be thankful Bidwell decided to fly back to Washington. If we had dinner together, I'm sure you'd have said something else you'd regret."

"You make a good referee."

For the first time he surveyed McCaskey's apartment, admired all the things she'd added to make it hers, envied her a little for having it. With him and Patsie holding on their collision course, Thorne decided he'd look for one like it: put up a wall of bookshelves, some old Navy pictures; buy a cord of real oak logs for the fireplace, not the gas burner Patsie had insisted on to obviate any chance invasion of insects, buy himself . . .

"I really think it went well," McCaskey said soothingly. "Good enough to earn us a drink at least. Scotch, right?"

"Over ice."

"I bought soda just in case."

"Soda, then. A tall one."

Thorne hit the armchair and kept going over the day. Maybe he should have given Bidwell some of what he'd worked out for Tom Massey, how he might handle the deal with Sal Catania and use it as a lever with Greco. But if Bidwell still thought he was letting himself get sidetracked, then the bastard could . . .

"Here you go."

McCaskey handed him a large tumbler. Thorne took a swallow and made the proportions half-and-half. "Cheers."

McCaskey looked down at her blazer and skirt.

"Give me a minute to get out of uniform and I'll join you for one."

"I thought we might have dinner."

"You have to be bored with restaurants and taverns," she said. "And I haven't cooked for anyone in . . . in a long time. So if you don't mind a jambalaya made with frozen shrimp, I thought I'd whip up one here."

"Don't think I could beat that."

"You could, but what the hell," McCaskey smiled.

Thorne asked, "How did a farmer's daughter like you get into New Orleans cooking? First the Breaux Bridge. Now jambalaya."

"I lived in Louisiana for a while," she replied. "When my husband was playing AA ball for the Shreveport Captains. I mean, after a life of burnt pot roast and Jell-O-mold salad, becoming a Creole food freak was easy. You should have seen the pounds I put on—all that gumbo, oyster pie, étouffée, nothing bland or boring."

"Except maybe him."

"You're out of line, Frank."

"Sorry. That was stupid."

McCaskey shrugged it off: forgotten.

"I'll change and get the pot started."

She ducked into the tiny bedroom, closed the door modestly. Thorne went back to his triple Scotch, Bidwell's admonitions still ringing in his ears. Sure, he had gotten a perfunctory nod to proceed the way he wanted with Greco. But Thorne also knew, deep down, that for whatever reason, Bidwell didn't really want to hear about his plan. Keep up the financial pressure, squeeze Greco hard and you'll work your way up the ladder, get to the high echelons of the family. That's what Clothesline was about, Bidwell said. But squeeze too hard, force Greco's bosses to close up, who's the one that screwed up? Bidwell? Fat chance.

"My finest at-home attire," McCaskey said. She

wore a loose cowl-necked sweater with its sleeves pushed up, a pair of straight-legged Levi's that were worn pale and soft. No designer's name on her butt, Thorne noted, none of those things Patsie called lounging pajamas.

"You look great."

"Liar, liar, pants on fire . . ."

"No, really."

McCaskey let the flattery bounce off her gracefully. She poured herself a half-glass of Soave and sat cross-legged on the sofa. She said, "Why are you so antagonistic with Bidwell? I know he's a little obnoxious, but he gave you the green light."

"That was covering his ass. If everything works out, Bidwell grabs the managerial credit. If it falls apart, there's nothing on paper to tie him to a bad decision. No," Thorne said, "when we should be taking a new tack, all Bidwell wants us to do is tighten the screws on Greco. How tight that should be, of course, he won't say."

McCaskey put down her glass. "I have an idea, something that's been on my mind lately."

"I'm listening."

"Don't get angry then. Take it in the spirit intended, that I'm only trying to help."

"You threw me a couple of lifelines today. Say what you want to say."

"I think you're letting yourself get too close to Sonny Greco. I think Bidwell senses it too, and that it's starting to worry him."

"I thought that was the idea of going undercover."

"I mean *personally* close."

"That's how it works," Thorne insisted. "I have to stay tight with him."

McCaskey shook her head in denial. Firmly.

"See it the way I do, Frank. You genuinely like Sonny Greco. You enjoy hanging out with him. And I think you like the action as much as he does—betting all the games, laying out lines, Dom's, Fairweather's, wherever else you two go. You looked disappointed when you heard that Bidwell had fixed the spreads so Greco would lose."

"That's nonsense!"

"I realize the way things are, that you have the time now . . ." She paused and took a reinforcing sip of wine. "Sorry, now I'm out of line. What I'm trying to say, what Bidwell picked up on too—you didn't have to go out and play every night with Scarpo and Lowenstein. You've got a case without—"

"I said from the beginning that Greco was the key. He's the one who talks right to the old man, who works for Sid Paris, number-one nephew."

"One question, Frank. Suppose you could make a case against Paris and not have to arrest Greco? How would that go?"

"Greco's my target, nothing more. But if I have to . . ."

"Then you've thought about it too."

"Look, maybe I'll have to give Greco a break to get what we want on his bosses. Maybe he gets immunity and, like Bidwell says, a spot in witness protection. That's fine with me as long as we get the big people, not because Sonny and I drink together."

"Two professionals, each doing what he has to do."

"Call it respectful adversaries. Greco probably would."

"You still aren't hearing me," McCaskey sighed, refilling her half-glass.

"I think you're the one confusing motives," Thorne said.

"I didn't bring this up to scold you," she persisted. "But see it from where I sit. Sonny Greco is a nice, likable guy. Maybe he should be selling commodities or real estate. But he's not, Frank. He may be fair and honest with you, but he hasn't exactly taken the high road either. His bosses kill people, for God's sake. And Greco knows they do."

"Thanks for the clarification," Thorne snapped. "Just remember who's been working the street all these years while you were playing bookkeeper in Rockford."

"And *you* remember who told me that bookmakers aren't criminals."

"I was talking about gambling," Thorne said. "And the little guy who makes a living giving people what they want, what they can get legally in another state."

"You call Sonny Greco a *little* guy?"

"Of course not. But he's no hit-man either."

McCaskey sat back, lowered her voice. "I don't want us to argue," she said. "But whether you believe it or not, you're causing problems with Bidwell. You try and get away with only the vaguest explanations of what you're doing. You avoid every direct question he asks you."

"I don't like lawyers."

"I don't either. But he's our boss, damn it," McCaskey shot back. "You have to tell him what you've got going. And you have to tell me, which is something else I'd like to talk over."

"Should I tell you the local cops have been on my tail since we started this?"

"Are you sure?"

"I'm sure," Thorne replied. "I bought one of them for twenty-five hundred of the Bureau's money."

"Not Lieutenant Corrigan," McCaskey said. "The one I spoke to about the Catania file."

"No way," Thorne said. "Jack Corrigan is as straight as they come, which is how the whole thing got started. Anyway, it's a new guy on his staff. Tom Massey, first-class creep."

"Why didn't you tell Bidwell?"

"Because he wouldn't have laid back and waited until I shake things out. The bastard would probably start up another strike force and go cop hunting on me, which is all I'd need to blow apart everything I've built up with my contacts on the street."

McCaskey stood and came toward Thorne. She reached down and took one of his cigarettes.

"I'm getting an ugly premonition that some people are going to get hurt before we've finished with this," she said sadly.

"No one's going to touch a fed," Thorne assured her. "I wish I could say the same for Sonny Greco. That's why I feel like I'm walking a high wire all the time, Bidwell pushing me one way, the outfit pulling me the other. If I don't do it my way, my speed, there's going to be a bloodbath in this town. And Greco's right in the crosshairs."

"Then set your sights a little lower. You can't always deliver as much as you want. Wrap up Greco now and we still have a nice package."

"Frank Thorne delivers what he promises." He reached up and took McCaskey's hand. "Someday I'd like to prove it."

"Maybe someday," McCaskey smiled, not moving to or from his touch. Thorne gently lowered her face to his, kissed her in a mild, almost sibling way. The response was still neutral.

"Never on an empty stomach, Frank. And I'm starving to death."

"And after dinner?"

"On a *full* stomach?" she laughed. "God, you want to see me throw up?"

"Hobson's choice," Thorne laughed with her. "I'd better fix myself another drink."

"And I'll deal with the rice and shrimp."

McCaskey took a step toward the kitchen and froze.

"I don't blame you for caring about what happens to Greco," she said.

"Conscience is a character flaw in this job," Thorne said.

"Caring isn't."

McCaskey pivoted in a sudden, surprising gesture, leaned down and returned Thorne's kiss. This time the neutrality was gone. She rolled her tongue across his teeth, bit softly into his lower lip. Thorne pulled her sideways across his lap, her legs dangling over the arm of the chair. He moved to kiss her again. She pulled back and fixed her eyes on his.

"I'll take now instead of someday," she whispered, her hands reaching around and tugging at Thorne's belt.

"Now's just fine," Thorne said.

Afterward, the two of them close in her three-quarter bed, she mentioned Sonny Greco's name another time before falling asleep on Thorne's shoulder.

"I think I finally understand what you want from Sonny Greco," she said.

"What's that?"

"You want him to forgive you."

12

SONNY GRECO threw an armful of Golden Bear golf shirts into his flight bag and began searching the dresser for swim trunks. When the telephone rang he automatically cursed Pizza Sal, who was already late and no doubt phoning in another lame excuse.

"What's your problem this time?"

"Who the hell are you suddenly?" Johnny Roses barked back. "That any way to answer a phone?"

Greco tried explaining about Pizza Sal.

"That asshole. No wonder," Johnny Roses said.

"Sorry. What's up?"

"We have a meeting."

"We do?"

"People I was with the other night went over all the numbers. They're steamed, Sonny. I didn't want to do it, but I figured mentioning that proposition of yours might take the heat off. They're interested, want to see your banker."

Johnny never liked using names on the phone. But this time, Greco knew, it sounded like real trouble.

"I thought we were starting to come back," Greco said.

"Yeah? Well you thought wrong. Maybe if you kept on top of the figures . . . The meeting's set for tonight."

"Can't it wait a few days? I'm on my way to O'Hare, going down to see Camille and the twins."

Johnny Roses was stone. "Your fuckin' vacation's what can wait."

"It's no vacation," Greco said. "I have to see about picking up some extra cash. I got nervous customers out there."

"You just got cash."

"Not enough. I've got my own tabs too."

"Goddamn basketball," Johnny Roses muttered.

"You got it."

"They waited this long, they can wait a few days more. We've been paying out enough to run Cook County. So tonight, you come see me and the boss. Bring along your friend from La Salle Street. I want it right from his mouth."

Greco knew it was useless to protest. "I'll try to catch him at his office."

"You better. I feel a blow torch heating up under my ass, and I want it turned off fast."

"Okay, okay." Greco pulled his shirts from the bag and flung them across the room. "Tell me where and when."

"We'll talk over dinner. Give us a chance to feel this guy out."

"Padrino's?"

Johnny Roses made a growling sound.

"Don't you ever read beyond the sports page? Padrino's got itself burned down last week."

"You're kidding. Who'd they piss off?"

"Naw. Word around says it was a friction fire. You rub the mortgage and insurance policy together, and sparks fly."

"I thought they were doing great."

"That's what you know. So meet me eight o'clock.

The Bella Sicilia. Eight sharp, Sonny. Remember who's gonna be there."

"I'll call Frank now."

"Do it."

Greco thought it over, knew he had no choice but to ask him.

"Can you get me a couple extra dimes until I make it to Florida?"

"You've got a big pair, you know that, Sonny? After everything I've been telling you, you want a few *extra* dimes."

"Look, I wouldn't ask unless . . ."

"Yeah, life or death."

"Almost," Greco said, thinking of Camille's charges and the airfares.

"All right," Johnny Roses relented. "You get it tonight. Just don't make this a habit. I told you once, keep a side book open and you got to cover it yourself."

"I'll square with you in a week," Greco said. All he heard back was the click of his boss hanging up.

Pizza Sal was standing in the kitchen when Greco came downstairs. He looked like a parody ad for Ralph Lauren—blue Polo jacket unzipped halfway down his bare chest, white trousers and Herb Tarlick loafers, amber sunglasses wrapped around his eyes.

"You ready?" he asked impatiently.

Greco shook his head. "Taking a rain check. I just got a call, have to meet some people for dinner. We'll probably go tomorrow, day after the latest."

"I got everything set up with Kerry Delgado!" Pizza Sal exploded. "I mean *everything*!"

"That's your problem, because I haven't decided to do anything yet," Greco said. "Delgado can wait a day or two. If he doesn't, then he's too damned anxious to be straight. Maybe you're too anxious too."

"Come on, Sonny. You forgetting what's due Chuckie Franco?"

"We'll take off as soon as we can," Greco said.

"I've got to make a few calls first, then you get hold of your friend in Miami and tell him to hang on. Just watch it on the phone, okay? We're talking interstate, anybody looks at the records."

"Then what?" Sal asked. "Where am I gonna go around here dressed like this?"

"You stay here and feed my dogs," Greco said. "Then put on my coat and take them for a walk. This way you'll stay out of trouble, give your heart a rest."

Greco found Frank Becker's business card and punched up the number for Assets Management Partners, Ltd. While he was holding, Greco thought he heard Pizza Sal say something about Diane.

Sonny dismissed it as mere babbling.

Johnny Roses swung his Seville into the darkened driveway and waited with the headlights off. He saw the side door open several inches and a hand come out of the house and signal him five minutes. He hated waiting for anyone, but for Sid Paris you waited with your mouth shut, then did as you were told.

He lit a Macanudo and tuned in the White Sox game. Luckily, with the weather in town what it was, they were playing the Twins in Minneapolis. The Sox were one-forty favorites, but Johnny had liked the Twinkies for a dime. Always take the domes at home, he figured. Houston, Seattle, Minny, all good underdogs on their home field.

By the time the door opened again, the Sox had hit back-to-back homers, Greg Walker's stuck somewhere in the roof. Johnny Roses got a start when he saw two men coming out of the house—Sid Paris and a shorter, heavier man whose backlit face he couldn't make out. Maybe Sid was bringing along his own banker, he thought, noticing the attaché case. Why waste time, right?

"How you been, Johnny?" Paris asked, sliding into the passenger seat.

"Could be better, you know."

"Always." Paris cracked his window and waved away the cigar smoke. "You know Chuckie Franco, right?"

"Yeah, sure. Couldn't see you under that hat. How you doing?"

"Menza-menz'."

"I thought we'll be talking cash, might as well have Chuckie sit in," Paris said. "You know how Chuckie looks at numbers."

"Good idea."

Franco grunted something unintelligible.

"Sonny will meet us at the Bella Sicilia," Johnny Roses said. He began to back down the drive; looking over his shoulder he saw Franco's round, sweaty face. Chuckie gave him a smile, said he was famished.

"Greco's bringing along his man from La Salle Street. This way," Johnny explained, "you want to do something, we can skip the middle man."

"Hey, I didn't ask for your fuckin' Mister La Salle Street," Franco growled. "We're just talking among ourselves here, in the family."

"I just thought . . ."

"It's okay," Sid Paris said. "We gotta meet this guy sooner or later."

"Yeah, why not," Franco agreed. "I just don't like people making these kinda decisions for me."

Johnny Roses said nothing.

They merged onto the southbound Kennedy, heading for the Harlem Avenue exit.

"My people are looking pretty good this week," Johnny Roses said. "No big moves came down against us. We got a little back."

"How little?" asked Sid Paris.

"Close to twenty-five grand," Johnny Roses exaggerated. "Like I been saying, it has to turn around. And, we pull off a good deal with Sonny's man, nobody has to be disturbed about draining cash from other businesses."

"About time you had good news," Paris said.

"No shit," Franco grumbled.

"I'm telling you, it's going to work out. End of the season, we'll be up a bundle. Believe me."

"I did," Paris said. He took Johnny's cigar from the ashtray and hurled it out the window.

"So anyway," he went on, "how your wife and kids doing? I ain't seen any of them since Rosalie's wedding, which was very well done, too."

"Everybody's fine," Johnny Roses said, cutting over to Harlem. "My old lady got herself in this aerobics class and dropped like twenty pounds. She looks terrific, you know, but there's never no food in the house. I'm talking total mind-fuck with this diet stuff. All I ever see is brown rice and steamed broccoli."

"So tonight you enjoy," Paris said. "The Bella's got good food."

"Calamari," Franco wheezed.

"There you go," Johnny Roses said. "Throw in some spaghetti *aglio-olio* with the anchovies and bread crumbs." He ran a yellow light and made his turn onto Grand. "You been on the course yet?"

"In this weather?" Paris asked incredulously.

"I tried it once with Sonny. It's still soaked."

"If we ever get some sun, we'll go out at my place," Paris offered. "You, me, Sonny, whoever. Chuckie's got no patience for the game."

"No patience, period," Franco agreed.

"Too bad the old man can't do it anymore."

Sid Paris said, "He still rides around some when the weather's good. And don't putt against him for money. That touch he ain't lost."

Johnny Roses slowed down as they passed an old movie theater, now some kind of warehouse.

"It's near here, right?"

"Take the next left," Franco directed. "There's never no room on the street here. Drop it in the lot behind the movie."

"Got it."

"Cut through the alley, you don't have to go around the block," Paris said.

Johnny Roses pulled into the empty lot, swerved around a pothole and parked under the fire escape.

"The Bella's right down the street," he assured himself.

"Over that way," Paris pointed.

"Okay, *mangiamo!*" He reached for the door handle but felt Sid Paris grab his arm.

"One more thing," Paris said.

"Sure. What?"

"I'm sorry it has to be this way. But you fucked me good with all your noise about us doing this football."

Johnny Roses gave him a quizzical look, then heard something that sounded like gum snapping. Before he could turn back to Franco, the muzzle of the automatic was pressed against his head. He heard the first of the three muffled explosions before his world went black.

"Let's move it!" Franco barked as he looked at Johnny Roses' bloody head slumped against the steering wheel. "C'mon!"

"Prints, you asshole!" Paris hollered back. "Wipe everything down good. Put that piece away clean."

Franco unscrewed the silencer and put it in the styrofoam compartment of his case. The .22-caliber High Standard had rubber tape around the grip and trigger, but he wiped it down anyway and put it next to the back-up piece. Franco wondered why they'd given him two guns, two silencers. What the fuck was this anyway? A Roy Rogers movie?

"Done," he said.

"Now we go," said Paris.

They climbed out of the Seville, walked hurriedly toward the alley. A nondescript Ford LTD came speeding up. Paris stopped suddenly.

"You'd better double check," he said. "Make sure Johnny's not breathing."

"Christ, I put three in the back of his head," Franco said. "Two right here," he touched his skull.

"Yeah, so you did."

Franco threw the attaché case in the back of the Ford, climbed in clumsily after it.

"You guys okay?" the driver said.

"Terrific," Paris replied.

In five minutes Paris and Franco were back on the expressway heading north. In ten more they were where friends would swear they had been all night—at a party watching the Sox game.

The only question that kept Chuckie Franco awake that night was why they'd put two pistols and two silencers in his case.

Thorne checked his watch while Greco poured another two glasses of red wine.

"It's almost nine o'clock."

"He probably got hung up," Greco said. "It happens."

"I'm in no hurry."

Thorne ate a piece of provolone to quiet the nervous rumbling in his stomach.

"Ross will come on like a real tough guy," Greco said. "But he's really okay. If Sid Paris shows up, then . . ."

Thorne feigned a perplexed look. "Who?"

"My boss's boss. He's probably the one who'll make the decision. Most people think he's first in line for the top job."

"You too?"

"Like I told you, I bank on nothing these days."

The restaurant's owner came to the table, nodded at Greco.

"We're still waiting for some people," Greco told

him. "But tell the kitchen to work up some hot antipasto for four."

"It's not that. Are you Mister Greco?"

Sonny nodded.

"There's a call for you on the pay phone. Out by the bar, turn left. Important, the man said."

The owner strolled to a nearby table and joined the two couples occupying it, pouring their wine munificently.

"Told you somebody got hung up."

"I'm not going anywhere," Thorne said. "Just getting hungry watching everybody else eat."

Greco walked briskly to the bar, picked up the dangling receiver. The voice was muffled but vaguely familiar.

"This Sonny Greco?"

"That's me."

"Tell me your wife's name before you got married."

"Who the hell is this?"

"Shut up and give me the name."

"Tough to do both," Greco said. Then he recognized the voice, told him, and listened silently.

"Now lookit, your meeting is off. You go home. You stay there. I mean you don't go outside to pick up the paper until you're told. Understand?"

"Yeah, but—"

"Listen to me. You forget about ever going to meet your boss. It's all clear with the restaurant. Nobody's ever seen you there. So you forget it too."

Greco had no option. "What about the guy with me?"

"What? You're not alone?"

"One of my customers is here. We had business with Johnny Roses."

After a pause, "The same goes for him. You tell him—no meeting, no names, nobody knows nothing. Now get the fuck out of there and go home."

"On the way."

Greco hurried back to the dining room. Thorne saw him whisper something to the owner before coming to their table.

"Let's go. We're out of here."

"We're what?" Thorne was confused, angry.

"Just shut up and I'll explain in the car. Come on. We're history."

Greco threw a fifty on the table, headed for the door. Thorne caught up with him on the sidewalk.

"What the hell's going on, Sonny?"

"I got a hunch Johnny Roses ain't gonna make any more meetings," Greco said.

Seeing the fear in his eyes, Thorne shut up.

Tim Ryan, the pharmacist at the Rexall drugstore on Grand Avenue, was counting the long minutes until his ten o'clock close. After eight, except for rare emergencies or when panicked mothers ran in for children's ampicillin or tetracycline, all he had to deal with were nervous dopers with forged prescriptions for Dalmane or Dex, depending on which way they were heading. Ryan swore at himself as he lost count of the anti-hypertension tabs he was filling for an early delivery. Wish I could do a few ups myself, he thought. Get through this bullshit night.

He saw the figure at the dispensing counter from the corner of his eye.

"Can I help you?"

"I . . . need . . ."

Ryan started to look up. "I said, can I . . .? Oh, Jesus Christ!"

"I . . ."

The voice trailed off as the man sagged against a Dr. Scholl's display rack. Ryan ran around the counter and eased him down to the floor. He was slight and wiry; beneath the blood that covered his head and face, the druggist guessed there was dark hair, dark skin.

"What happened? Somebody hit you?"

"I was . . ." the voice collapsed again.

"You been mugged? Who hit you?"

The man exhaled a labored breath and fell into unconsciousness.

Ryan got to the phone and punched 911. The police operator told him casually that ambulance calls were the Fire Department's turf. Unless a crime had been committed, the paramedics would . . .

"The guy's been mugged or something. Clubbed in the head," Ryan insisted. "He's bleeding all over the place and blacking out. I'll treat the shock, but get the cops and an ambulance here fast!"

The dispatcher made him repeat the address twice and promised a prowl car. "They'll call the ambulance, the meat wagon, whatever he needs." He hung up before Ryan could again say to hurry.

The man on the floor tried to speak as Ryan propped his head on a pillow of cotton balls.

"I want . . ."

"How did it happen? Were you robbed?"

The man's eyes rolled back, but he managed to tell him.

"Shot . . . they shot . . ."

Ryan remembered his medic training at Fort Sam Houston and cleared the airways. He lifted the still-bleeding man and gasped at the black holes that appeared to penetrate the skull just beneath the crown.

"Jesus, in the head!" he yelled.

"They shot . . ."

"The police are on the way. And an ambulance. You'll be all right."

"No . . . no police. I want . . ."

Ryan leaned over the body and listened to the faltering voice. "Here they are. Relax," he said, but the man was out again.

Two uniformed patrolmen came into the pharmacy, hiking up their pistol belts and holsters as they walked.

"Whatcha got here?"

"Somebody get their head slapped?" the other asked.

"He's been shot. I think there's bullets in his brain."

"Since when you been to medical school?"

The older officer bent down and moved his hand over the darkening wounds.

"Goddamn if he hasn't been shot. Better make the call," he told his partner.

"I still get a pulse," Ryan said. "Pretty strong too. I think he just passed out." He looked up at the hovering cop. "I can't believe this. He just walked in here like that. He gets shot in the head and *walks* in here."

"Did he tell you anything? Say what happened?"

"He wasn't connecting," Ryan answered. "I think he was trying to say he didn't want me to call the police."

The patrolman looked up haltingly. "What else?"

"Just before you got here, before he blacked out, he started asking for somebody called Gee. Yeah, I think it was Gee. Something else too," Ryan recollected. "It sounded like scumbag."

Thorne's cigarette smoke swirled in the weak amber street light that filtered through the gangway window. MaryAgnes was still close against him, asleep. He reached for the last of his drink; she made a murmuring, raspy sound.

"Can't you sleep?"

"Not yet."

She propped herself up on her elbows. "If something's bothering you, we should talk about it."

"I'm just thinking," Thorne said.

"And I'm listening."

"I can't get the pieces to fit right. Nothing's coming together the way it's supposed to. Confusion reigns."

"I thought I was the serious one," MaryAgnes said. "Don't think about it now, give it some time. We're both alone, attracted to each other. Let it go at that."

Thorne lifted his arm, allowing her to slip under it and snuggle against his chest.

"That's not what I'm thinking about," he said. "This is probably the only part of it that makes sense."

"Damn it, Frank!" MaryAgnes cried. "We're in bed together and you're still thinking about the job."

"Not until you fell asleep and I couldn't," Thorne said. "Before that my concentration was elsewhere."

Partially reassured, MaryAgnes kissed Thorne's chest.

"It's still Greco, isn't it?" she said.

"Our meeting tonight. Or whatever it was supposed to be. Maybe I should call him, find out what happened, what he knows."

"Let it rest, Frank. You're not going to make things happen faster by pressing him. There could be a thousand reasons Sid Paris decided not to show up. Don't assume it's because of you, because they found out something."

"You're forgetting about Tom Massey," Thorne said. "There's always the chance he's got connections with the family. He'd sell to anybody with a fistful of fifties. If he sold me to Paris or Johnny Ross, we end up with nothing but a second-rate bookmaking bust. The kind Sal Catania walked away from."

"Worse things could happen," MaryAgnes said.

"Sure. Except if the outfit's made me as a cop, Greco takes all the heat. Literally."

"Not again!" MaryAgnes was wide awake, angry. "You keep trying to wear two hats, you'll end up wearing a straitjacket instead of a badge. Let Greco worry about Greco. Dealing with the family is his business. Yours is getting him convicted and sent away. Listen to me, Frank. Sonny doesn't *need* you."

The telephone buried beneath a bolster pillow made a coughing noise, cutting off Thorne's protest. Mary-Agnes reached across his belly to grab it. He watched her lips tighten as she listened to the caller.

"Yes, sir. As a matter of fact he is here. Yes, sir."

"Who the hell . . . ?"

MaryAgnes covered the receiver with her hand. "The boss."

"Bidwell?"

"Doc Hermann. He wants to speak with *you.*"

"What's going on now?"

She pushed the phone into Thorne's hand. "Suppose you tell me."

Thorne said, "Good evening, Doc. Agent McCaskey and I were just going over—"

"Knock it off, Frank," Hermann barked. "I'm not checking up on your action. It's business."

"That's why I'm here," Thorne said feebly.

"Listen up, will you? There's been a blow-up on the West Side. You ever come across a guy named John Ross, Johnny Roses? He captains the family's gambling operation."

"I was supposed to meet him tonight," Thorne said. "My contact with the outfit tells me Ross has powerful friends."

"And powerful enemies. One of which put three slugs in the back of his head. God only knows how, but the lucky son-of-a-bitch is still alive."

"Johnny Roses has been shot," Thorne repeated for MaryAgnes.

"Three times," Hermann said, annoyed. "He walked into some drugstore and collapsed. The CPD tried to take over, but Ross won't talk to anyone but the Bureau. That means you, Frank."

"Where is he?"

"CPD moved him downtown to a protected room at Northwestern Memorial. Number 327, Prentice Pavilion."

"That's the women's wing," Thorne knew from past experience with Patsie.

"That's why we call it protected. The patient's name is Mrs. Robert Jones," Hermann said. "This may be the break we've been waiting for, if Ross decides to spill his guts."

"If he makes it."

"You'd best get over there and find out," Hermann said.

"Does Bidwell know?"

"I just hung up with him. He insisted that you deal with Ross face to face. I told him it was risky, that if Ross made you, the whole plan with Greco might wash out. No matter the logic, he wants you there, says if Ross wants to play ball with us, seeing you makes no difference. So can I assume you're putting on your pants and heading for the door?"

"They've been on all night. But I'm moving."

"Say good night to McCaskey for me, you lying son-of-a-bitch," Doc Hermann laughed.

Thorne gave MaryAgnes the details as he dressed.

"Ross was sitting with Greco and Sid Paris the night I was at the Cairo Club. Bidwell knows that, that Ross might recognize me."

"He must have a reason for ordering you to see him."

"Bidwell's been right on the money so far," Thorne admitted. "The family's starting to come apart under the money pressure." He picked up his jacket, opened the door bolt. "I'll call you when I have news. It may be late."

"It's late now. But who's going to sleep? Especially since my reputation is ruined."

"So get some coffee going. I'll need it when I get back."

"Wait!"

MaryAgnes retrieved Thorne's ID wallet and Model 19 from the nightstand. "You might need these. Just the ID, please God."

Thorne clipped the holster to his belt.

"If Massey went to the family about me and Greco, I'll blow his head off myself."

"No jumping to conclusions," she cautioned. "Worry about yourself, for a change."

Thorne kissed her abruptly and hit the street. He caught a Checker on the corner of State, gave the address for Northwestern Memorial.

"You could walk there in three minutes," the driver moaned.

"And I could pull your fucking license in *two*!" Thorne shoved his ID in the startled driver's face. "FBI emergency. Move it!"

The cab screeched off and ran the Division Street light. Thorne sat back feeling confused, anxious, but somehow content.

It was good to be a cop again.

The night nursing supervisor on the third floor of Prentice Pavilion looked at him hostilely.

"Mrs. Jones," Thorne said. "Room 327."

The nurse studied his ID, then motioned Thorne past the nursery, down the long green-carpeted corridor. "Last room on the right."

Thorne was halfway there when Jack Corrigan jumped out of a visitor's lounge like an expectant father. He grabbed Thorne's arm and held on hard.

"I thought you were doing stocks and bonds."

"Soybeans, pork bellies, anything for a buck."

"You're full of shit, Frank. Right up to your lying eyeballs."

"Afraid you're right," Thorne shrugged. "So what the hell happened to Johnny Ross?"

Corrigan let go of Thorne's sleeve.

"Johnny Roses came as close to catching his last bouquet as anybody on God's good earth," he said. "Right now he's all clammed up, won't talk to anybody but you people. 'I'm only talking to the Gee,' he says. So whatever you find out, be kind enough to fill an old friend in."

"Let's say we find out together."

Thorne gave him a half-shove toward Room 327. Stay with me, Jack, he thought. You'll get a fair cut from the middle of the deck. For old time's sake.

"It's okay," Corrigan told the supposed orderly, who looked absurd with a long-barreled Colt protruding from his white tunic.

"Is he conscious?" asked Thorne.

The guard shrugged his ignorance.

"He's drugged up pretty good," Corrigan said. "But I think so. Goddamnedest thing I ever saw. Three slugs literally bounced off his skull. Point-blank range, judging from the powder burns. Talk about hardheads."

"The family grows them tough," Thorne said. "What else you got?"

"Not much. The police surgeon is checking him out now. All Ross told us, he was just getting out of his car when somebody walks up behind him and *pop-pop*. That's complete bullshit, of course. Shots came from inside the car, probably a back-seat job. We have his wheels downtown, running it through the mill with some of your evidence technicians. Doc Hermann sent them over."

"Ross *was* denied his civil rights," Thorne tried joking.

"You could say that." The weak grin fell off Corrigan's face. "Frank, before we go in there, anything you want to tell me?"

"Like what?"

"Like why you've been screwing me around," Corrigan snarled. "The outfit starts blowing up people in my city, I'm not going to sit still for a bunch of federal bullshit, especially when you're feeding me a line of crap about commodities fraud."

The surgeon came out of Ross's room while Thorne struggled for a reply.

"Amazing," he said. "Absolutely amazing."

"How do you see it?" Corrigan asked.

"You get my best guess is all. Looks like three shots

from a silenced automatic—.22- or.25-caliber—fired either against or within an inch of Mister Ross's cranium."

"Then how?"

"Did he survive?" the doctor answered. "Could be, at such close range, the silencer suppressed enough gas so the bullets couldn't gain sufficient velocity to penetrate the skull. Or, another possibility, the silencer was defective—not tooled right or fitted to the gun properly. The lab will have to corroborate, Jack, but it's happened before. If the silencer is off-line a spec, the slugs can pick up a wobble. In this case, Ross can thank the god of his choice, they may have had just enough wobble to skid off his head."

"A ricochet from an inch away?" Thorne wondered.

"Very possible," the surgeon said. "Especially if the shooter used a hot cartridge. Then the combination of the silencer choking out a high-velocity load, or a bum silencer angling the slugs a millimeter or two . . . well, bullets can ricochet off something as hard as the human skull. In Ross's case, he's suffered three bad burns, some sheared off tissue, but that's all."

"Great hit-man," Corrigan said. "Could have done better with a bat."

"Absolutely," the doctor agreed. "Crushing head blows are the deadliest of all."

"Surprised his hair didn't catch fire," Thorne said. "All that flash."

A smile crept across the police surgeon's stolid face.

"But Mister Ross wears a very expensive hair replacement," he said, "fastened directly into the scalp tissue with sutures. Until this evening, that is. His piece is treated with some goo that makes it easier to groom and, thanks to the Consumer Product Safety Commission, happens to be fireproof. As I said, amazing."

He extended his hand to Thorne, then Jack Corrigan.

"Glad you called me in on this one," he said. "I can't wait to write it up for the convention next month."

"Save your byline until the case is wrapped," Thorne insisted.

"Of course," the doctor demurred. "By the way, I think they've found a slug imbedded in the dashboard. So if you locate the weapon, we can put this together nice and tight."

Thorne and Corrigan thanked him for coming out so late.

"I'd suggest you wait a few hours before talking to Ross. The sedation is peaking now, he may not make a lot of sense. Tomorrow morning would be better, even though he's going to have one helluva headache. Good night."

The police surgeon started down the corridor. Thorne and Corrigan shot each other long looks until, like children, they broke into simultaneous and uncontrolled laughter.

"Did you hear?" Pizza Sal screamed over the phone. "Jesus, you hear about it?"

Greco had it figured already, but followed instructions.

"Hear what? I've been home all night."

"It's the boss. They say he's been shot," Sal reported. "It was on the news."

Greco poured himself another blast of Remy.

"In some lot over by Grand," Sal went on. "No word whether he's dead or alive, even where they took him."

"Who took him?"

"The cops, the feds, who the hell knows. There was this bulletin after the late sports, and that's all."

"Where are you?" asked Greco.

"Up at Dead Dom's. You better get here fast, Sonny. We got some talking to do."

Greco knew he couldn't overrule the ominous phone voice.

"No, you come here. Park a block away, walk around back. Anybody spots you, get lost fast and call me later."

Pizza Sal sounded puzzled. "You okay?"

"A-one," Greco said. "Why not?"

"I'm leaving now."

"Pick up a suitcase on the way," Greco said. "You're going to take a little trip, do some business for us. You understand?"

"It's still packed in my trunk. See you in twenty."

Greco dropped the receiver, drank his cognac in a gulp. No way it could be tied to Frank, he told himself. Frank didn't even know who they were meeting until Greco told him at the table. Then the phone call, Greco thought back. That's what really began to frighten him.

13

THORNE got back to the hospital at six in the morning. He found Jack Corrigan hunched over a table in the cafeteria's artificial daylight. The staff was working its way through a shift change: those coming off duty sucked on yogurt bars or drank cartons of milk to bring themselves down; those going on fought to get awake with pints of coffee drawn from a bank of stainless steel urns. Corrigan looked worse than either side: suit rumpled and slept-in, necktie a greasy rope hanging down his chest, eyes red and impatient.

"Grab two coffees and sit," he said.

"Later. Security says Ross is awake and making all kinds of noise. I'd think we'd better get up there fast."

"Now it's we?"

"From here on in," Thorne said. "If you can get your nose back into joint."

Corrigan pulled himself up and walked with Thorne to the elevators.

"Ross is one tough little monkey," he said. "Even last night, before the doc shot him up, I could see he was ready to explode, go back out after whoever popped him. I think we put the pressure on, light that fuse again . . ."

Thorne saw it a different way.

"Let's take the easy road first," he said. "We're here to pay Johnny a condolence call—Sorry you got into trouble. What can we do to help you?"

"You want to stop for flowers?"

"I want you to lighten up," Thorne shot back. "Johnny Ross isn't some second-string punk we can scare into talking. So let's find out where he's coming from. Besides, we don't even know for sure that the family ordered the hit, if it was a hit."

"Come off it, Frank. It wasn't a gut-check, for Christ's sake. Call me old-fashioned, but I figure when somebody tries to waste you with headshots, you've got reason to talk."

"Or get revenge. There's a difference."

"So what is it you want?"

"Ask me on the way back down," Thorne said, stepping into the empty car.

Corrigan said, "Look, maybe I'm too tired or too much in the dark to see all the angles you're working. But make no mistake, I want whoever pushed the button on Ross and everything I can get to put his ass in Stateville. This is my turf, Frank. And you're the one cutting across it."

"You bury the hatchet with me, you'll get that and more," Thorne promised.

The elevator climbed in slow, jerking movements to the third floor. "Here to see Mrs. Jones," Thorne said as they strode past the nursing station. No response.

"I don't think they appreciate us," Corrigan said.

"You want to see babies and bedpans in your squad room? Same thing."

Corrigan motioned the two CPD guards to step away from the door. "Ready?"

"Let's do it."

Johnny Ross was sitting up in bed, looking like an irate sultan with his head wrapped in a turban of white bandages.

"Hey, more cops. That's great."

"You sound chipper this morning," Corrigan said.

"You think so, lieutenant? Then let me tell you what. I got a headache that won't quit, not to mention how the burns feel. The one thing I don't have is an earache. So where's my telephone?"

"No way, Johnny. No calls for a while. In or out."

"Cut the shit," Ross barked. "I'm the victim here, remember? You stick me away in some broad's room with daisies on the wall—no radio, no telephone. I'm telling you, I have a constitutional right to talk with my family."

"They're being kept posted on your condition," Thorne interjected. "And looked after, just in case whoever came after you has other ideas. They'll be safe. Guaranteed."

Thorne studied Ross's reaction: Playing hard-nosed to cover up that he was scared shitless? Or was he really that tough?

"I don't need nobody watching out for my family," Ross growled. He shifted his eyes back to Corrigan.

"Who's this long drink of water anyway?"

"You're the one who wanted to see the feds," Corrigan replied. "You get what you want, Johnny. This is Agent Frank Thorne, FBI's organized crime unit. He'll be your main man from here on."

Ross's smirk was exaggerated by the bandages.

"I'm terribly fucking impressed," he said. "But what do I know from this organized crime stuff? Some jag-off trying for an easy stick-up takes a shot at me, and you guys want to turn it into the *Valachi Papers*."

"I'm not here to lean on you," Thorne said. "We thought you wanted some help."

"You'd be smart to talk with the man," Corrigan said.

"Yeah? What can he do for me I can't do myself when I walk out of here?"

"Cut out the Little Caesar number," Corrigan said,

losing patience. "You're not walking anywhere unless you want your head ventilated again."

"We can help you, Johnny," Thorne repeated. "All I need back from you is enough to make it worthwhile."

Ross didn't hesitate.

"How'd you like the two creeps who tried offing me? That make you feel better about getting me a telephone?"

"So now it's two guys," Corrigan said.

"Yeah, two."

"That's a start," Thorne said. "But I didn't get up before dawn to talk to you about street crime. For that you don't need the Bureau or what it can offer you.

"Which is what, Stretch?"

"Protection for openers. Maybe a spot in the witness program—new identity, nice place to live, whatever else you need to make a fresh start. It can be done."

"This guy beautiful or what?" Ross yelled at Jack Corrigan. "Witness protection program! Big fucking deal! Those guys got a life expectancy of three, maybe four years. I know a dozen bookmakers who'll lay you eight-to-five on the under."

"Better odds than you'll get if you turn me down," Thorne said. "Unless you consider three to the head a minor reprimand."

"This didn't come out of the family," Ross said with less than conviction. "These two scumbags were working on their own. Nobody upstairs gave the order. It wasn't voted on."

"You telling me there has to be a referendum before somebody gets taken out? That's garbage, Johnny. Stop trying to peddle it for jewels."

"Listen up, Thorne. What I'm telling you is, you give me a clean phone and ten minutes alone to check out some things, I give you two hoods on a platter. And I'm talking big people here. People worth your goddamn while."

"That's a start," Thorne said again. "But I've got to aim a little higher. I understand your wanting me to help settle the score with the guys who shot you. But I want more than their names for the effort."

"Ha!" Ross laughed. "You want the old man too?"

"Exactly."

"Get bent!"

"No joke," Thorne said. "We know where you sit inside the family, and how much you know about operations, gambling in particular. These people have written you off, Johnny. Not just the triggermen. The old man and the nephews too. You can go to the window on that."

"Not a chance!" Ross hollered again.

"I'm trying to help you," Thorne repeated.

Ross wouldn't budge.

"You do two things for me," he said, "I give you a name for each one. First, I go to the pay phone and nobody listens in. Two, you keep an eye on my family until I say pull back."

"They're covered now," Jack Corrigan said.

"Hey, lieutenant, I'm talking with the Gee here. I want only federal guys on the job. No disrespect intended, but I know too many of your people who'd suck a joint for an extra hundred a week."

"You little bas—!"

"Easy," Thorne said, cutting in front of Corrigan, staring him into silence. "Johnny's got a right to be worried. Used to be nobody ever went after the wives and kids. Not like the Colombians and that Israeli mafia on the coast. Right, Johnny? But anybody who'd set you up like they did doesn't play by the old rules."

"I want a nice discreet lookout," Ross said. "All clean-cut types so my family don't get embarrassed. That and a phone call, you get a good package in return."

"I'm still waiting," Thorne said.

"How does Sid Paris sound to you? Sid Paris and Chuckie Franco, to be exact."

"You saying Paris gave the order?" Corrigan asked anxiously.

"Gave the order? He set me up like a duck and Franco pulled the trigger from the back seat. That fuckhead's so stupid he couldn't get the silencer on right, so the medics tell me."

Thorne said, "I don't know this Franco or what he's worth to the Bureau."

"A juice loan operator mostly," Corrigan recalled. "Plus he runs a few businesses either for the family or with their blessing. Candy, gum, stuff like that."

"He works directly for Sid Paris and nobody else," Ross said. "The old man won't touch him any more."

"An old time enforcer," Corrigan added. "Lots of muscle, short on brains."

"You got that right," Ross said.

"Keep talking," Thorne said, figuring he had Johnny Ross ready to roll.

"Franco's important because of how he's tied in with Sid Paris. He's the collector, the factor. He knows all Sid's accounts, all his businesses. Now, I give you Sid Paris all tied up for a racketeering bust, you know you're getting somebody worthwhile."

Thorne dragged a chair to the side of the bed. Johnny Ross, worried about his family, hating Paris and Franco, was ready for the counterpunch.

"Johnny, I appreciate what you're offering me here," Thorne said. "But we've got a little problem with timing."

"Yeah, what's that?" Ross asked guardedly.

Jack Corrigan almost spoke, but the old pro in him won out. He nodded at Ross like he knew what was coming next.

"It goes like this," Thorne said. "Our people have been putting a major case together for some time now. It includes you, Tony Scarpo, Sandy Lowenstein, the whole outfit that handles the sports book. Even Dan Bagley up in Rockford, which tells you we aren't missing much. This kind of complicates my being able to help you out when all you're offering in return are two people. I'm going to need more than that to do anything special for you."

Ross slumped back into his cushion of pillows.

"It's like that, huh?"

"It's like that."

"You're a rotten motherfucker, you know that?" Ross snarled.

"I'm being straight with you, damn it." Thorne leaned closer, spoke in a softer voice.

"You're looking at hard time, Johnny. Interstate gambling, conspiracy, racketeering, whatever else the bright boys in Justice can come up with. The heat's been on a long time now. You, Scarpo, Lowenstein— all your asses are on the grill."

"You got nothin' tying me to any of them," Ross said. "You want to try a gambling rap on for size, then you go ahead. Even if it fits, I walk in two, three years tops."

"If you live."

"What's that mean?"

"It means that if the family thinks we wrapped up this case with your help, getting through a year at Terre Haute won't be easy. Not to mention getting sent to Marion, where you got no shot whatsoever."

"You *are* rotten," Ross fumed.

Ross pulled at the snarl of white linen wrapped around his waist. He grubbed a cigarette from Corrigan, smoked it slowly. A sense of calm swept over his face that baffled Thorne.

"So where do we go from here?" asked Thorne.

Ross gave him a sinister smile.

"You go straight to hell," he said. "You say you got a case on me like you got on Scarpo and Lowenstein. Well maybe you do, maybe you don't. Either way you can shove your witness program and save your time pushing me to play ball. Matter of fact, you get nothing from me until I get to a phone."

"You at least have to tell us about the hit," Corrigan stepped in, saving Thorne from his own temper. "If the family didn't give Sid Paris the nod, that means he's going after the old man's chair. Any way you slice that, it sounds like war."

Ross shook his head painfully.

"Just a power play," he said. "Sid Paris is trying to get everyone in his corner for when the old man's gone. He's thinking political."

"You call trying to air out your head baby-kissing?" Corrigan said. "You all that important?"

"When you figure all the money I cost him."

Thorne walked to the window, stared out at a rough, green Lake Michigan. He had his answer about Johnny Ross. He *was* as tough as he came on, wasn't about to give away anything on the family no matter what Thorne threatened or promised.

Thorne watched a twelve-meter sloop tacking northward toward Belmont Harbor, wished he were on it and didn't have to think where everything was pointing for Sonny Greco.

"Sid Paris, that rotten cocksucker," Ross went on fuming. "The other night I'm drinking with him out northwest. Then in the car, he's asking after my family, talking about getting together for a round of golf. When I came to, I figured Franco had took both of us out. You hear that, Thorne? I was worried Paris got hit too. Last time I ever worry about anything."

"I'll take whatever you can give me on Paris," Thorne conceded. "And do the best for you I can when the indictment comes down."

"You're a prince," Ross sneered.

"A sucker for a friendly face," Thorne countered.

"Hey, faces are what I know," Ross said. "Yours,

for instance. I can't help wondering why yours is so familiar. Like I know you from someplace."

"Never had the pleasure," Thorne said, inwardly cursing AAG James Jonathan Bidwell, wondering why he was so insistent Thorne sacrifice his cover when he was getting so close.

"Tag along with me," Jack Corrigan said as he and Thorne slipped out the nurses' exit.

"We going to have our talk now?" Thorne asked.

Corrigan didn't pick up the glove, or didn't want to. "There's this place down by the newspapers," he said. "Stays open all night for printers, reporters, cops, drunks. We can get eggs, booze, whatever."

"Skip the eggs and I'm with you."

They walked down Fairbanks Court, cut west on Ontario, ducked under Michigan Avenue to the dark, cement-pillared lower level. Thorne bought the first pair of drinks, followed Corrigan to a small, wobbly table in the rear of the empty tavern.

"I'll have to team up with Violent Crimes to follow this," Corrigan announced halfway through his drink. "We can get the warrants for Paris and Franco out this morning. A VC detail will haul them downtown, if they haven't split already."

"They're going nowhere," Thorne said. "The old man may be chair-bound and breathing his last, but they know better than to try running from him."

"You really think they'd pull this without his go-ahead?"

"The way things are going in the family these days, all the nephews jockeying for position, nothing's certain."

"So how do we handle Johnny Ross? It doesn't sound like he's ready to give us squat."

"He has to stay on ice for a few days," Thorne said. "I'll have federal marshals relieve your people at noon. All the phones will be shut down too, so Ross can't talk to anyone until we see how it shakes out with Paris and Franco."

"He wants a lawyer, what do we do?"

"We lie," Thorne said. "Screw him, he's delirious. Three head wounds can do that to a man."

"Might cost you a case, Frank. You think about that?"

"What case? Johnny Ross said it first. He's only the victim."

Corrigan said, "So you were bullshitting about those indictments."

"Firing for effect. Scarpo and Lowenstein we've got. Johnny Ross will be a hard sell. That's why we've got to keep him out of circulation—material witness, injured reserve, whatever. Between CPD and FBI moving the papers around, it should work."

"You're playing hardball," Corrigan said.

"The only game in town."

Thorne drained his glass, bought another round. "I think you should concentrate your fire on Chuckie Franco," he said. "We've got him placed behind the gun. Make sure he'll give us Paris for ordering the hit."

"You want to be around when we grill Paris, just say the word," Corrigan offered.

Thorne said, "He'll tell us nothing we don't know already. And he sure as hell isn't going to lead us upstairs. Not when he's more scared of what will happen with the old man than of doing the laundry in Terre Haute. Let's put the stress test on Franco."

Lieutenant Jack Corrigan determined there was another way.

"Say we turn both of them loose on a low bond. Put them back on the street after the arraignment so it looks like they're cooperating with us. The state's attorney will go along. That should either scare them into talking, or maybe shake the old man's tree hard enough that he'll make a mistake."

"Now who's playing hardball?" asked Thorne.

"How many choices we got?"

"I don't know how City Hall's going to feel when the bodies start popping up."

"It's their bodies, my ass."

"It's your round," said Thorne.

Corrigan brought back another pair, this time doubles. He played with his wrinkled tie for a minute, looked at Thorne with knowing eyes.

"Johnny Ross made you, you know that? He covered it up pretty good, but he placed you from somewhere. So you going to explain how that fits into your La Salle Street operation? Or maybe you're finally going to talk about Sonny Greco?"

Thorne said, "You're a smart cop, Jack. Nobody ever says different. Not even Tom Massey."

"So you spotted him," Corrigan said without emotion, embarrassment. "You're not bad yourself for an ex-swabbie."

"How smart is it for an old Marine gunny sergeant to put a tail on a federal agent who's working undercover? That's no way to advance a career, Jack, get those captain's rails. Especially when you use an asshole like Tom Massey, who's been telling you nothing the last two weeks."

Corrigan slammed his glass into shrapnel.

"You bastard, Thorne! You bought my man!"

"Massey sold himself to me for five hundred a week."

"That prick," Corrigan hissed. "No wonder the narcs were laughing at me for taking him. Jesus, I hate bad cops."

"Enough to bust him?" asked Thorne. "You know it makes the Department look bad. And I know your loyalties are all there. So, you want to handle Massey internally, slap his bent hand a little? Or do I hand over his fully corrupt ass for compensation?"

"Compensation for what? For screwing me out of what you've got going with Greco, Catania, whoever the hell else you're playing footsie with?"

"Answer the question," Thorne said. "If I give you Tom Massey with his hand in the cookie jar, will you take him down hard? Even if it means egg on the Department's face?"

"I hate thinking about it," Corrigan said. "I can give you tons of reasons why cops go on the take. Not just the pay, the frustration, the way our whole justice system sucks. Sure, you know this too. But if you don't know I'll take down any crooked cop I get my hands on, then you don't know Jack Corrigan worth shit."

"I know you," Thorne said. "Which is why I'm asking for some slack. You'll be there when this comes together, for a full share of the action. But until then, do nothing to go after Sonny Greco or anyone else in the family until you check with me first."

"You asking me? Like I have a choice?"

"I'm asking," Thorne said.

"But you've got some clout to back it up."

"Right into Washington, and from there, all the way to the top."

"So I play it your way," Corrigan conceded. "Anything I get from you and the Bureau will help make up for the black eye the Department's going to take over Tom Massey."

"I'll need a week or so to play out the hand, see where it ends up," Thorne said.

"You don't know?"

"If I did, you'd get the whole package here and now." Thorne looked up from his glass, made his point in slow, halting syllables.

"I'm nobody to you but Frank Becker. Money-mover type who likes a little betting action on the side, and has a few players in his book to roll with."

"You're keying everything on Greco," Corrigan realized. "Using him to get something going with the family."

"I was trying to," Thorne said. "The move against

Johnny Ross may have changed all that. Probably has."

"I must be losing it not to have seen where you're going," Corrigan said.

"You're a long way from losing it," Thorne said. "Now, do we climb into bed together for a week?"

Jack Corrigan came up with a rare smile.

"Just tell me one thing, Frank. Am I the fucker or the fuckee?"

14

THE MERCEDES limo arrived in front of the house three minutes early. Greco grabbed a tan windbreaker and hurried outside. It was the first warm, windless day of spring.

The front window came down in a slow electric whine. Vinny motioned him to ride shotgun.

"You okay, Sonny?"

"Maybe you can tell me."

"Relax," Vinny said. "We're just going over to the house. He wants to talk to you, is all."

Greco took a deep breath as they eased away from the curb, but tension still tightened his gut. The old man wasn't one to waste time reassuring people that things were fine. Not with the little time he had left.

"How's he feeling?" Greco asked.

"Good as can be expected. You know, physically. But it's been a tough three days for him. All this going on has to hurt a lot. You work a whole lifetime to build something that lasts, a good organization. Then it starts falling apart for no reason. It hurt him a lot."

"Didn't do much for Johnny Roses either," Greco said.

"He's looking forward to seeing you. Kept asking

me all morning, 'When's Sonny coming? Ain't it time
to pick up Sonny?' You've always been special to him.
You know that?"

Greco said he did.

But he knew the rage would be there too: Johnny
Roses locked up somewhere with the feds; Sid Paris
walking the streets with Chuckie Franco on his arm.
He hadn't seen the old man pissed off in years, and
wasn't looking forward to it this mellow afternoon.

Vinny kept talking like he was the only one who
knew him.

"Just because he likes you, Sonny, don't even think
about handing him any bullshit. Whatever questions
he's got for you, better make the answers straight. The
body's breaking down, but the noggin is right there.
Nothing gets past him."

"Nothing ever did."

Vinny paused at the next corner, whipped a U-turn
back past Greco's house, cut through an alley. If there
was a tail, neither of them could spot it.

"You've been smart, done what you were told and
haven't moved out of the house."

"When I knew it was you on the phone at Bella
Sicilia, you think I'm going to go out for pizza, maybe
head up to the Cairo Club and have a few pops on Sid
Paris' tab? The old man wants me home, I stay home."

"It's been appreciated. I know how tough it's gotta
be to hang in there alone, just waiting."

Greco figured Vinny knew anyway, probably had
one of the back-up drivers watching his house. "My
friend Sal Catania came over when the news hit. He
hung around a while, we had some drinks."

"I don't understand you and that powderhead. Everybody knows he's not worth shit."

"He is to me."

"I guess that's your business."

"You guess right," Greco said. "So lay off."

Vinny tried to sound like he was changing course,

but Greco knew the press was still on. The question nagging him was, who was Vinny asking for?

"That broad you've been running with, the one used to work at the Cairo? How's she doing these days?"

"If your watchdogs did their job right, you know I haven't seen Diane in ten days. I told her I was heading down to Lauderdale. It looks like she decided to take off herself, for wherever."

"That's right, your family's down in Florida. I guess your wife's uptight about what's been going on here."

"With Diane and me?"

"Naw," Vinny laughed. "I mean with Johnny Roses and all. The television and newspapers are making this sound like World War III. She's got to be worried."

"We both are," Greco said. "But what can I tell her about anything? I've been stuck in the house, remember?"

"For your own good."

"Maybe. I was heading down to see her the night they tried to ice Johnny Roses. Going to spend some time with her and the twins."

"I think you should tell *him* that," Vinny said. "You know how he feels about families, kids. He might call down there himself, let Camille know everything's fine."

"You telling me it is?"

"Far as I know. Then again, I ain't the boss."

"So cut out the twenty questions," Greco said. "Or is there something else you want to hear about my private life?"

Vinny put his right arm on the seat back and stretched behind the wheel.

"Only other thing you can tell me is what you think of our new Chicago Cubs. We gonna find a lefty reliever?"

They finished their critique of the Cubs roster as Vinny reached the high gates that secured the old man's property. He punched some numbers into the electronic gate-guard and climbed up the oval drive.

The early spring flowers running along the base of the gabled brick mansion were just coming into bloom. Too bad the old man couldn't get outside and tend them like he used to, Greco thought. Next to sinking a birdie putt and seeing his horse win, flowers were what he loved most.

Vinny pulled up by the white front door.

"I'll wait here. This time you get a round trip."

Greco had had it.

"Either you've gotten a big promotion I don't know about, or you got balls too big for your own good. Want me to ask inside which it is?"

Vinny started to say he was only kidding, but the slamming car door cut him off.

Greco found the old man in his library, sitting alone, thoughtfully staring at the stacks of leather-bound art books, a thick unlit cigar dangling between his bent arthritic fingers. Greco leaned over and hugged him gently. The once hard-muscled body felt as bony as a chicken wing, just as frail and ineffectual.

"You look good, Sonny. Like you've been working out."

"A little," Greco lied. "But with the wife away . . ."

"I know. Bad hours, bad food. Makes you appreciate it more when she comes back."

He pointed to the bar setup that filled a waist-high shelf of bookcase.

"Fix yourself something to drink. You don't see what you want, I probably have it down the basement."

"Looks like everything is here."

"That decanter on the left. Pour me a small glass of that."

"Are you sure?"

He made a feeble beckoning motion with his twisted hand.

"Just a little sweet wine. Some kind of imported muscatel. Twenty-five years old, supposed to be good for the heart."

"Maybe I'd better try some," Greco said.

"You crazy? That stuff's for old men," he said, wishing he could take something stronger, urging Greco to it vicariously. "There's good brandy, whiskey. Go on, it's after lunch."

Greco poured their drinks into stemmed Waterford glasses etched deeply with a pineapple design and heavy enough to feel like grenades in his hand.

"Come sit close to me. Right here."

Greco pulled a leather ottoman near his chair. They toasted each other's life and health, the old man shaking his head sadly at the thought.

"Tell me what I can do for you. How I can help."

"I want you to listen," the old man said.

He wiped a dribble of wine from his lower lip. "Just listen to me, Sonny."

"To whatever you say."

"I thought I'd outlived the bad times," he began. "Now, when I'm supposed to take it easy, when I thought everything and everybody was taken care of, something like this thing with Johnny Roses happens. It sickens my heart."

Greco was surprised to hear the deep level of sorrow in his voice. Especially when he was expecting rage. All he could reply was, "I understand."

"I know you do. You're a good kid. That's why I wanted you out of the way until I got things settled down. You were okay, nobody's got problems with you. Still, I didn't want to take chances."

Greco nodded gratefully. The old man sipped his wine. When he spoke again, the sorrow was gone. His trembling voice rose as close to anger as age allowed.

"I put Johnny Roses into that job. Sidney Paris had the responsibility of running things day to day, but Johnny Roses worked for *me*. Whatever he might have done, any mistakes he made, he still worked for me. And I swear before God Almighty, nothing like that happens to anybody who works for me!"

"Then why?" Greco asked. "Just because we were taking a beating on football. . ."

The old man signaled him to be quiet.

"Sidney started thinking for himself. He figured, with all Johnny cost us the way he handled the book, Sidney would make himself look like a hero for taking Johnny out. He also figured the other nephews would all back him up when they heard about it. This way, he's got a head start to take over things when I'm not around any more."

"A long time to come," Greco said.

"Not so long now. But death is a part of life, Sonny. Except when some greedy pig like Sid Paris makes the decision. I blame myself for a lot of what's happened. I should have taken steps with him years ago. He always wanted to take the hard road. I think he likes getting blood on his hands."

Greco watched the wine slosh in the old man's shaking glass.

"I still don't get it," he said. "Why Paris thought the rest of the family would open up their arms if he hit Johnny Roses."

"You don't understand because you got honor. Just like your father, God rest his soul. But Sidney doesn't see things like we do," the old man sighed, shaking his head. "He starts thinking—with Johnny dead, we don't have to pay off all his customers. Their man gets killed, who's going to complain? We save ourselves another half million bucks."

"People have been hit for a lot less than that," Greco said.

"Not by me!" the old man raged. "Not by my people and never because we owe. Now, somebody steals from us, strongarms people we care about, rats to the cops"—that's something different. We got a right to protect ourselves, our interests. But never because we lost!"

Greco took the glass from his trembling hand. The

old man demanded a refill, drank half the measure quickly. The wine took immediate effect, relaxing him into retrospection.

"You know how I started out, Sonny? Not like everybody thinks. I never worked as a muscle for the big shots, never pushed any buttons to work my way up. That's all PR stuff, what the newspapers like to write. I admit, it's kept some competition from trying things they shouldn't try. But let me tell you the truth.

"I started out running numbers in the Loop. It was good business in those days. The Depression. Nobody had nothing. So, for a quarter, a half-dollar, you got a shot at a dream. Get some money in your pocket, pay off the landlord, feed the kids a steak. It was the lottery of that time. I picked up the bets and . . ."

"Paid the winners," Greco said.

"Always," the old man nodded, trying to smile. Greco watched him look longingly at the unlit cigar.

"Later on, I ran a horse parlor from this basement on South Halsted. Went from an old hand-crank telephone to the first wire in town. Used to have fifty, a hundred people a day come in to play. I worked hard, got all the blessings I needed, paid everybody with a right to get paid, fought off anybody who didn't. There were lots of reasons I moved up, expanded my territory. The most important one, Sonny—nobody ever had to come looking for me. In the early days, even if I had to take the streetcar home and eat beans out of a can, my customers got paid off. This is something Sidney Paris could never understand. You do, I can see it. You know it's the real legacy for me to leave you. Honor."

"Thank you."

"So now, you pull together all your paperwork. Then we sit down again, see where the house stands with everybody we owe from Johnny Roses' bank. They all get what's coming to them."

The old man paused, then hit Greco with the hammer.

"After that, I'm shutting down every bookmaking operation we run. *Tutto finito!*"

"For how long?"

"Until I say different. I got no timetable in mind, except maybe longer than shorter."

"That's going to hurt," Greco said. "Me, at least."

"If it does, it's because of what *you* did, Sonny. You went and took side action after Johnny Roses warned you not to. You put yourself in the hole. Nobody did it to you. And then, getting into Franco for twenty thousand more. I can't understand what you were thinking. You know what it's like owing that much to a man like Chuckie Franco."

"I was helping out a friend," Greco explained. "If I didn't step between him and Franco, he was going to get hurt."

The old man nodded, his eyes on the floor.

"You always step in," he said. "Too much for your own good. A blessing and a curse, but not for me to criticize."

He began to cough and seemed to be in pain. He spoke again as if wanting to conclude matters quickly.

"As of now, you owe Franco nothing. That's a small part of what he has to pay back for what he's done. But you're off the hook with him. You and your friend Salvatore Catania."

Greco recalled Vinny's words: "The noggin is right there. Nothing gets past him."

"So you know about that too," he said.

"I never thought he was much, this Pizza Sal. He wouldn't get another job from me if he washed my feet in St. Peter's Square. But if he did something for you, enough so you put yourself between him and Franco, that's enough for me to let him off."

Greco thought about Pizza Sal in Miami, wondered if he should get him back before he made the move with Delgado, wondered about the twenty-five thousand he'd shorted the house and whether that was history too.

"I'm very grateful," Greco said. "Sal will tell you he is too."

The old man waved and said he wanted to hear nothing from Pizza Sal.

"You look worried about something," he said. "Tell me."

"I was thinking about Johnny being on ice with the feds, how pissed off he must be."

"Nobody has to worry about Johnny Roses," the old man said.

"But if he thinks Sid Paris was acting for the family, that he had a blessing . . ."

"Johnny knows what's going on. The cops thought they were smart, hiding him in some women's hospital. But they forgot about the window cleaning service we run. Johnny got the truth written out for him in soap, just like the price of tomatoes at the market. Sidney didn't spill anything to the cops either. They just want it to look that way, turning him and Franco loose for a few thousand bail. But he said nothing about our business. All he wants from me is another chance. Still, after what he did . . ."

The old man's voice trailed off. What Greco said next sounded just like it came from Johnny Roses' mouth.

"I still think we can recover a lot of what we lost if the house stays open, if we keep our customers playing."

The old man's stare had turned stone-like while he thought about Sid Paris. When he shifted it to Greco, it cut like a laser.

"The worst mistake you can make in this business is thinking you know what you don't know." He pulled a piece of folded white paper from his sweater pocket, handed it to Greco. "You read this, then forget you ever saw it."

Greco read down the column of negative numbers. Not only the major losses from Chicago, but from St. Louis, Milwaukee, Kansas City, even Rockford . . .

"Holy Christ!" he blurted.

Greco heard a dying man's loathing of blasphemy.

"Watch your mouth! You don't take His name in vain inside my house!"

Greco apologized twice.

"Read!" the old man ordered.

"These numbers are astronomical. Everybody's been getting crushed."

"I've talked to all the other families," the old man said. "There are these rumors coming out of Vegas about an operation the Justice Department has going. Some people think they have someone inside moving the lines around so we lose. I've even heard that they've set up a team of FBI agents to bet against us when the lines are soft. That's some rumor, Sonny. But the figures in your hand support it pretty good."

"It's possible," Greco realized. "All the new players we took on have been winning big, hitting all the moves."

"That sound right to you?"

"I'm not sure," Greco replied, telling himself it couldn't be, not when Frank Becker was losing right along with him.

"Last week things started to turn around. We got back a little of what we'd lost. I took on this one guy . . . but Johnny and I had him checked out all the way. Unless . . ."

The old man shook his head.

"Don't go looking for cops under your bed. People we know for years have been hurting us too."

"What do we do about the feds?"

"We do nothing," the old man said. "If the government has been working us over, we pay them off and call it a day. Then it's finished. We got other businesses to worry about, other places to grow."

"We could be more selective and still keep open," Greco said.

"Do you really like it that much? You need action all the time, Sonny?"

"It's what I do," Greco said. "What I've done for you and the family all along."

"You're still a kid." The old man tried laughing. "You'll find out there's more to life than running a book."

"It's my living. I've got my wife, the twins, a mortgage—"

"It used to be," the old man interrupted. "Back when I started out, you could make a living doing what you want to do—run an honest book out of your wallet, people who bet a few dollars on the big games, take a few horses in the spring. No more, Sonny. Not today. Now everybody's got a computer in the basement keeping stats, predicting winners. And you win, so what? First you get the feds coming over, asking you to fill out Form II-C or you're in trouble with the IRS. Then you have to go chasing people to collect. No, Sonny. It's not good business any more. Not for us, not for you. Maybe later, in the fall, we open up a little to keep our bar owners happy, give some guy who got laid off a little side job on the phones. But as a line of business that's worth the time, worth the risk, it's finished. We're going to close down. So are you."

"You're not leaving me with much," Greco said.

"You're wrong. I'm *giving* you a lot," the old man countered. "I'm giving you a chance to do something with your life. You got the brains, you got the education I never had. Use them and get out on your own. Do something good for yourself."

Greco went to the bar and poured himself a refill.

"You saying there's no room for me in the family business?"

"If I had enough time left to me, if God willed that, there'd be all the room in the world," the old man said broodingly. "But I don't think you'll like how it's going to be when I'm gone. You know what will happen? One faction fighting another, family against family. This thing Sid Paris did to Johnny Roses was just a warning of what's down the road. I'm almost glad I won't be here to see it. Now I'm making sure you won't have to either. Whether you want it or not, I owe it to your father to cut you loose."

Greco knew his mind was made up, unchangeable.

"I've been considering some other things," he admitted. "Maybe starting up some kind of business, getting myself a seat on the Exchange."

"A business is good, maybe a nice restaurant. You decide to get something started, you come back and see me. Anything you need comes from me personally. Nothing to do with the family, no strings attached. Let's hope I'll be alive to see your opening."

"Please God."

"I know I've got a lot to answer for," the old man said softly. "But if I was half as bad as people say, God would never have given me as much as He has. I'd never even *be* my age."

Greco, uncomfortable with the old man's melancholy, got back to business.

"It will take me a week to wind things down," he said. "I'll have to go through all Johnny's papers, get a final figure for you. And there's some collecting to do."

"Then no more. Find yourself a nice tavern where the bartender takes action on the side. Enjoy yourself like that. Get a hot tip, you can put a sawbuck down for me."

He took another sip of wine and the coughing resumed. Greco stepped forward and took back his glass.

"Whatever you need to pay off," the old man wheezed, "you let me know and Vinny will deliver it. Now go home. I'm getting too tired to talk."

Greco leaned over and hugged him good-bye.

"One more thing," the old man whispered. "You get your wife back home and make things right again. That's what I really want you to do."

"That's just what I'm going to do," Greco said. But his mind wasn't on Camille and the twins at all. He was thinking about Pizza Sal in Miami, and how he was going to handle Frank Becker.

15

THE EASTERN 727 roared out of the ground fog at Miami International, banked hard in its noise abatement pattern, and finally leveled off over the Everglades. Pizza Sal settled back in his seat and, feeling so good, decided to spring for a round.

"Do the whole plane," he told the stewardess. "Anybody wants a drink gets one on me."

She froze in her tracks and gave Sal a toothy smile. The way he was looking back, she started to believe him.

"Say again."

Sal made a circling motion with his right index finger.

"Get drinks for the plane," he said. "Champagne for me. Whatever they want."

The stewardess bent over as if whispering a secret.

"That's very generous of you, sir. Except cocktails are complimentary in the first-class cabin."

"Champagne too?"

The stewardess nodded. "It's California. Korbel, I think."

"Yeah, well, if that's it."

"Champagne it is."

Some bullshit flight, Pizza Sal thought. Can't even

enjoy yourself, party a little, meet some people. Hell with it. Everything else had gone great. Camille had told him Johnny Roses was going to pull through, even though the feds had him. And Sonny had gotten them a nod from the old man himself. The debt to Chuckie Franco was history. Camille seemed almost happy handing over the safety deposit key, asking him to tell Sonny she'd come back as soon as he wanted her, needed her.

As for the rest of it, it was perfect. Sweet.

They were heading north over Big Cypress Swamp when the stew brought his split and told her blond colleague from coach, "This is the one."

"Hi there," Sal beamed.

"I've been flying eleven years," the blond said. "Nobody has ever tried to buy a round for the entire plane. Nobody *once.*"

"Hey," said Pizza Sal, in a manner usually reserved for the baccarat table, "I closed up a little business deal in Miami, and made a few pennies. You go around once, right? So enjoy it, spread it arond. Why not?"

"That's the way we feel, Sharon and me," the blond said. "I'm Colleen."

"I'm S. J."

"You from Chicago, S. J.?" Sharon asked.

"Chicago. All over."

"We're based in Chicago. I'm surprised we haven't met before, in town or if you fly south a lot."

"Me too," Sal replied.

Sharon flashed her overbite again and pushed the bar cart forward.

"Nice girl," Sal remarked.

"We room together," Colleen said. She, too, leaned over as if whispering, only to scribble the seven digits of a SUperior phone exchange on his in-flight menu.

"Give us a call the next time you're Near North. Maybe we'll take you up on the drink offer."

"Hey, whatever else you want."

"What else did you get in Miami besides lucky?"

"Ha!"

Pizza Sal folded the menu and stuck it in his wallet, in with the five thousand he had left of Greco's advance money—five dimes he'd put to good use as soon as he could get back out to Sportsman's Park.

Colleen patted his shoulder and returned to her duties in coach. Sonny ain't gonna believe this, Sal laughed. Never in a million years. But some night, maybe before Camille got home, the four of them . . . Jeez!

He took a sip of champagne: tasty enough, but too warm to enjoy. He'd order something else when Sharon passed by again, something to celebrate the way he'd handled the deal with Kerry Delgado.

They had met at a private club out near Coconut Grove, sat on an empty veranda overlooking Sailboat Bay. Sal had worn a plaid sports coat and all his chains. Delgado, medium height, thin, sandy-haired and fair-skinned, looked like a goddamn lawyer in a khaki gabardine suit with narrow lapels and *cuffs,* for Christ's sake.

Sal relished the way Delgado reacted when he heard the size of the deal.

"Ten kilos is a lot of merchandise," Delgado said.

"More than enough to earn me a volume discount."

Delgado agreed, but said the exact amount would be up to their contact in Chicago. His fee, however, would stay fixed—an even ten percent, the price of one full key, to broker the deal, make all the contacts with the importers and see that the goods were transported safely north from Gulfport.

"I'll require twenty-five thousand up front," Delgado said. "The other ten on delivery. As for any discount, cut the best deal you can with the lady up there."

"I'd better be able to cut more than that," Pizza Sal said. "When you're getting thirty-five dimes a key."

"What you're buying is so pure you could go fifty-fifty on it with vitamin powder or baby laxative and your customers would still kiss you for getting it. We refine the paste here in the States, so you're not getting strange chemicals, anything less than medical quality. This is top-shelf merchandise, S. J. I mean that sincerely."

"I hope so, for your sake. The people backing me in Chicago are well connected. Right to the top, understand? Anything but primo quality, delivered on time . . ."

Delgado put up his hands. He'd heard it all before, Sal figured, everybody claiming they were connected to the outfit. But it was still a good move to make.

"Right to the top," he repeated.

Delgado said, "I'll take charge of the delivery personally. Forget the old ladies and pralines. I'll get it there myself, assuming you have the earnest money ready for me."

Pizza Sal discreetly slipped him the twenty thousand.

"I get a percentage from everybody involved," he announced. "I can't make any exceptions in your case. Wouldn't be fair."

"I don't discount," Delgado said flatly. "I want the full twenty-five up front."

"Hey, who's discounting? I'm not talking any discount here. But I got expenses to handle—airplane, hotel, dog track. I say it's only kosher you make an investment too. What's five dimes in all this? We got a good future together."

Delgado pocketed the twenty thousand.

"The first and last time you try this," he said. "I'll write it off as seed money. But never again."

"This is no one-shot deal," Sal insisted. "You'll make a lot more than that on what I'll be bringing you. Now," he said, pulling a hundred from his pocket, "let's get somebody out here for a drink order. My pop."

Sweet! he thought again, as they nipped over the Gulf and cut across the Florida panhandle. Did it ever go smooth.

Sharon had donned a serving smock and was asking for his meal order. He decided to skip the beef *à la Borman* and, after downing a double vodka-Seven, sample the quarter-ounce Delgado had given him. When he returned, sniffling, from the lavatory, Sharon flashed another smile.

"Feeling better?"

"Just fine."

He was back in his seat before realizing he'd sprung a leak in his right nostril. He tried wiping away the mucus as surreptitiously as he could. Sharon, still watching him, laughed openly as she handed out trays.

Damn, Pizza Sal saw in a flash, it was too fucking simple. Didn't it ever cross your mind the Gee might be working stews undercover on the Miami run? Don't that make sense? I mean, I'm no dog to look at, but the only broads who ever volunteered me their phone numbers were hookers, or that one in Vegas thought I was Frankie Valli. All this could be a setup, he concluded, using these girls as narcs. Good thing the tickets were in Airlines Al's name.

He was wondering how much of the quarter he could do before landing at O'Hare, just in case they had those dogs sniffing around the place, when Sharon made another pass.

"How about a newspaper to keep you company? We have the *Tribune*, *Sun-Times*, Miami *Herald*."

"*Sun-Times*," he said.

"You trying to win the Wingo?"

"Me? I don't gamble."

He checked the sports log for final scores, but with nothing down on anything, got bored fast and flipped to the front page. The tabloid had gone all the way with the story—120-point banner, photo across four columns.

Pizza Sal's heart went from its rushing cadence to a dead stop.

EXECUTION KILLING!
Gangland boss slain,
dumped in car trunk

He had to read the lead paragraph twice before his eyes focused properly. Jesus, first Johnny Roses. Now, he squinted to make sure he was right, now it was Chuckie Franco.

Franco, the story said, had been released on bond for the alleged murder attempt on gambling kingpin John Ross. Sidney Paris, a co-defendant in the case and also free on bond, was reported missing by the Chicago police. It was suspected that he, too, had been silenced by syndicate bosses. Because kidnapping was a possibility, the Federal Bureau of Investigation was preparing to enter the case.

Pizza Sal followed the story as carefully as he could, what with the paper shaking in his hands.

John Ross remained in protective custody, it said, although the U.S. attorney hinted an indictment against him would be forthcoming.

He studied the photo of Franco's contorted body resting in the trunk of his Buick. No wonder the old man had given Sonny a pass on the marker. Maybe I should tell Sonny about the five dimes I saved with Delgado, Sal thought. At least split it with him fifty-fifty.

Fuck no! he decided. What's a few crummy thousand when he'd just put together a *million dollar deal*! They'd all get rich on him and who he knew. What's five thousand?

He hit the john three times more, doing at least another gram before dumping the rest into the swirling blue waters of the toilet, breaking his heart.

When they reached O'Hare, Pizza Sal was the first one off the plane. The chest pains started up as he scurried through the terminal. By the time he climbed into a taxi, he was doubled up with a full-blown attack of angina and barely able to give the driver Diane's address.

Lieutenant Jack Corrigan stormed into the office of Assets Management Partners, Ltd. and stood smoldering at Frank Thorne's desk.

"I should have my head examined!"

Thorne, ready for what was coming, didn't flinch.

"Take a seat before you pop an aneurysm."

"I ought to pop *you*, you son-of-a-bitch. 'We'll play out the hand together, Jack. I'll keep you posted on everything.' Why you goddamn . . ."

Corrigan looked over at MaryAgnes McCaskey, who was silently calling up the Bureau's five-star football picks from the central computer bank at 935 Pennsylvania Avenue.

"Lookit, lady, you better relocate yourself for a while. I've got some things to tell your boyfriend here."

"If you wish."

Thorne's grin enraged Corrigan further.

"What's so damn funny?"

"She'd better stay and referee. She's quite good at it," Thorne said. "I think it's about time you two were introduced. This is MaryAgnes McCaskey. Special Agent McCaskey, Jack. She's running this operation right alongside me."

"A pleasure, lieutenant," McCaskey smiled.

"Oh, Christ," Corrigan moaned. "Sorry."

"Take a seat and tell me what's on your mind," Thorne said.

Corrigan picked up the tempo again.

"On my mind? How about I find Chuckie Franco stinking up his car trunk in some shopping center. And who the hell knows where we'll find Sid Paris, if we ever do. My guess is he's gone the Jimmy Hoffa route—probably holding up some new bridge on the tollway extension, cement in his ears."

"I never saw it happening that way," Thorne admitted. "It sounded right when you said it—putting them back on the street."

"We're about the only ones who think so," Corrigan said. "I've been taking heat all day for pushing the low bond. Even the state's attorney is copping out on me."

"You'll bounce back when you nail the triggerman who did Franco," Thorne said.

"You know better than that, Frank. The guy's back on some beach right now, sucking down piña coladas and grabbing ass."

"Probably true," Thorne shrugged.

"To top off my day, I find out this morning you had Johnny Ross moved out of Northwestern. I get some bullshit apology from Doc Hermann's newest flunky about protective custody, material government witness. I got nothing about where he's stashed."

"I didn't have time for a conference call," Thorne shot back. "We had to move Ross fast, before he could get word about the Franco hit. If he finds out the family is settling his score, he's got no reason to give us anything about Sid Paris' business. Which leaves both of us with baby shit."

"The fact that Ross recognized you has nothing to do with the move?" Corrigan asked. "That if he managed to get in touch with his people, there goes your action with Greco and the rest of your new pals?"

"It's crossed my mind," Thorne said.

"Well I won't stand still for it, Frank. Playing ball with you is all one-sided. I want my turn at the plate."

"You can see Johnny Ross whenever you want," Thorne said. "Agent McCaskey will get you there and back, just say the word. Now take a seat and keep quiet for five minutes, you'll get your time at bat."

Thorne asked for the file folder he and McCaskey had put together in anticipation of Corrigan's visit.

"This is for you, lieutenant."

"Thanks, lady."

"Agent McCaskey."

Corrigan winked at Thorne but got no sympathetic response.

"The cover page is a quick summary of the operation we've been running," Thorne said. "It's code-named Clothesline."

"You guys just love making up shit like that."

"A legacy from J. Edgar," McCaskey said. "If they can do it at Langley, he figured we could too."

Corrigan ran through the brief, mumbling to himself as he read.

"This is impressive stuff, but I see a lot of holes in here, Frank. Like nothing about Tom Massey. He supposed to be my tit for sitting around while you fly solo?"

"I told you, he's yours if you want him."

"Terrific. A cop who goes on the take with a federal agent when he *knows* he's a federal agent. That would get Massey a damn promotion for initiative."

"Not the way it's playing out," Thorne said. "I give you Massey wrapped up tight for bribery and conspiracy. You also get all the local action I can throw you on the Scarpo and Lowenstein busts—their phone men, runners, drop points, like that. Mostly you get Scarpo," Thorne reminded him. "Lowenstein's strong in the north suburbs, and I need something to keep the county bulls happy too."

"Sure you're not cutting your pie too thin?"

"Plenty to go around, Jack. Read on."

Corrigan went back to the folder.

"The other big hole here is Sonny Greco. You want to give me something, that's what I want."

"No way," Thorne said absolutely. "Greco draws a bye on this round."

MaryAgnes looked at Thorne in disbelief, as if everything she'd told him had been lost, forgotten. Corrigan just slammed the folder shut.

"How come Greco gets all this special handling?" he asked.

Thorne knew he had to lay it out for both of them, as best he could anyway.

"All Sonny Greco will get from me is the alternative of doing double-digit time for narcotics trafficking or working for us and the old man at the same time."

"So that's the play you're making," Corrigan said. "To run him as a snitch."

"It is now," Thorne replied. "The timing is going to be critical when we make our move. We'll need a close, consolidated effort to pull it together. Other words, Jack, I need your help bad. Are you in?"

Corrigan took a micro-second to decide.

"For a chance to have Sonny Greco working for us inside the family? Bet your ass I'm in."

Jack Corrigan was back at Eleventh and State an hour later. Thorne poured himself a straight Scotch. McCaskey, declining to join him, sat stiffly in her chair.

"I can understand your wanting to keep Corrigan at arm's length," she said. "But not why you've held back on me."

"I might be jumping the gun by telling you *now*," Thorne said. "I still have to meet with Greco and Catania. There's a good chance Sonny will back down."

"Why?"

"I honestly don't think he wants to do the deal. The only reason he'd consider it is because we're squeezing him so hard for cash."

"Are you hoping Greco does or *doesn't* make the buy? I'm not sure which, Frank. I'm still not sure how you feel, or even if you know yourself."

"I want more out of this than Sal Catania," Thorne said. "If Sonny decides to step into the coke trade, he's got nobody but himself to blame. Either I screw his ass to the wall, or I run him as a special source inside the family. That's his call."

"Still the Lone Ranger, Frank. Running a one-man show."

"You forgetting about Tonto?" Thorne protested. "The only reason I haven't told you everything is I'm not sure myself how it will go down. I haven't even tried it out on Bidwell."

"To hell with Bidwell," McCaskey said. "He's got his computers to play with. Like you said, he knows nothing about the street."

"You're beginning to sound like a cop."

"I'm learning from one. A pretty good one, I'll give you that much. Only I'm not sure I have the stomach for it. Not when it gets this rough."

"Another two weeks you'll be back in Rockford checking out tax returns."

"I think that frightens me more."

Thorne understood and told her so.

"You'll be right there with me," he said. "I'll know how after I see Greco tonight. Want me to give you a call?"

McCaskey opened her desk and retrieved a small ring of house keys.

"Better take these," she said. "I might be asleep when you get back."

Sonny Greco heard the noises coming from Diane's bedroom.

"What's going on?" he asked. "I thought Stacy was at your mother's tonight."

"She is."

Diane followed through with her warm, welcoming kiss before pulling Greco inside.

"Pizza Sal's here washing up," she said. "He just got off the plane from Florida."

"Why here?"

"Ask him."

Sal came out of the bedroom and half-collapsed onto the couch. His face was flushed, his breathing hard and irregular.

Greco said, "If I didn't know better, I'd think you just got laid."

"Aw, c'mon," Sal wheezed.

Diane closed the front door. Greco noticed she wore a thin summer blouse and had picked up a little tan.

"What are you doing here?" he asked Sal.

"I didn't want to go by your place. All this shit going on, Franco in one trunk and Sid Paris probably in another. How do I know who's waiting around? And the phones—hey, forget it."

"You were scared," Greco realized. "So you had Diane call and drag me over here."

"Drag?" Diane snapped. "I thought it was welcome home."

Greco started to answer, but Pizza Sal saved him the trouble.

"Okay, a little worried," he said. "I thought you'd be heading over here anyway."

"So did I," Diane said angrily.

Pizza Sal pulled himself into a sitting position and wiped the sweat from his forehead, behind his ears.

"Besides, I'm not feeling so good."

"What you get for sampling every pharmaceutical in south Florida," Greco said.

"Hell, no," Sal insisted. "It's just I get airsick on those damn planes."

"Not when you're going to Vegas."

"He does look pretty punk," Diane agreed.

Sal found the safety deposit key in his pocket, offered it up to Greco. His eyes kept darting over to Diane as he spoke.

"I picked this up from your old lady, just like you asked. She says she's ready to come back whenever you say so. She says . . . some other stuff."

"I'll make some coffee," Diane volunteered.

"You have any gin?" Greco asked.

"Since when did you start drinking gin?"

"Since you've been gone and the sun came out," Greco said. "Suppose you go get some while I talk to Sally. No rush getting back."

He dug into his pocket and tried handing Diane a twenty.

"Stick it!" she barked. "I don't need your damn money."

Greco sat down next to Sal as Diane stormed out. Sal spoke first.

"You never used to treat Diane like that. She don't deserve it."

"I'm supposed to win a personality contest when people are getting offed all around me?"

"What's your problem? I hear the old man himself gave you a clean bill of health."

"Sure. He wants me to open up a pasta palace and lead the quiet life. Five years selling spaghetti and I can pay back what I owe the house, all my players. Not to mention what you cost me in Florida. Which is what I want to hear about."

Pizza Sal summarized his meeting with Delgado, skipping the part about his five-thousand-dollar rake-off.

"Delgado's our insurance policy," he said. "It's worth the price of a kilo to make sure we get what we're paying for. Besides, your buddy Frank has to hold up his end. Let him pay Delgado the balance."

It sounded better to Sal just saying it, like the extra cash in his pocket was really coming out of Frank Becker's.

"You let me worry about Frank," Greco said. "There's something with him I'm not sure about."

"So we cut him out," Sal said. "Why spread the wealth around three ways?"

"You got the quarter-million to pick up his end?"

"Yeah, well . . . maybe we could . . ."

"I'll handle the financing," Greco said. "What I need from you is the bottom line."

"I got us good news there. The people I'm in touch with here say they'll discount two dimes off each kilo. So, lookit . . ."

He grabbed a copy of *Vogue* from the coffee table and started scribbling numbers in the white space around Carol Alt's swimsuit layout. Greco saw he had the math down pat. Whatever else he was, when it came to cash and dry measures, Pizza Sal was the best.

"We got thirty-five ounces per key," he wrote. "The stuffs so good, we'll push it to sixty with the cut. Two dimes an ounce retail, right?" he totaled.

"Sonny, we got ourselves a *million dollar deal* here!"

"We move nothing smaller than an ounce," Greco said.

"Hey, I'm not talking playground sales," Pizza Sal said. "The people I deal with are movers and shakers. They do a lot, share it around for friends, for business. They're not buying for profit. They get a free ride on what they use, and look like mavens for getting such quality stuff. So relax, will you? This is better than gold."

"The last guy who said that was on video tape with a bunch of DEA agents in his room," Greco said.

"I *know* these people," Sal assured him. "You'll see for yourself when we wind up the deal."

"You know them. I don't."

"Their rules, Sonny. Nobody meets nobody else until the sale is closed. You gotta understand their position."

"*You* got to understand I'm laying my life on the line. The old man finds out, I'm a ghost."

"Then go make marinara sauce the rest of your life."

Greco was too busy thinking about Frank Becker to get pissed off. Any chance the guy's a cop . . .

"I'll talk to Frank," he said automatically.

"He puts up the quarter-mil and doubles his money pronto," Sal said. "Less my commission, of course. Now us, we put up a hundred grand and make back five times the investment. And don't forget, we don't have to tell Frank nothing about the two dimes per key discount I got us."

"You work everybody over, don't you Sally? Every angle bends your way."

"Hey, I never did it to you," Sal replied. "Not after the way you went to the mat for me with Chuckie Franco. I'll never forget that, Sonny."

Greco read the numbers again. One shot and he'd be back on his feet, out of the deepest goddamn hole he could ever imagine being in. Afterwards, the old man might change his mind, open up again . . .

Pizza Sal said, "It's a cinch. I got a place up on Lincoln Avenue all set up for the buy. I can test the merchandise right on the spot. Anything less than what's been promised, we take a pass."

Diane appeared in the doorway, dangling a fifth of Beefeater.

"What are you two passing on?"

"I hope nothin'," Sal told her.

Greco studied the contour of Alt's buttocks and shredded the page of computations.

"Do we go?" Sal asked. "Or just eat the cash I paid out to Delgado?"

Greco knew it was the only door still open.

"If it works out with Frank, we make the move," he said.

Pizza Sal took a deep, painful breath and struggled to get off the couch.

"Damn," he said. "I just get so fucking airsick."

Diane straddled Greco's back and began to massage his shoulders.

"You're tense. I can feel it."

"Do business with Pizza Sal, you'd be tense too."

"Everything will go fine. Sally knows what he's doing."

"How do *you* know?"

"We talked a little before you got here," Diane said. "You know how he is."

"That's why I'm tense."

"Look on the bright side," Diane said. "A while from now, you'll be in a position to do whatever you want. I still think getting on the Exchange makes sense."

"Puts and calls, points and odds. It's all the same crap."

"Sonny, if you don't want to make the deal, then forget about it. Just stop giving me a song and dance about wanting out of the business and being on your own."

"I'm out no matter what," Greco said. "The old man has seen to that."

"Good. Then there's nothing anyone can say about how you live your life—who you see, what you do. Consider yourself lucky, a free man at last."

Diane worked her thumb between each vertebra of Greco's spine, kneaded the muscles of his lower back expertly. Greco again forced the image of the Cairo Club from his mind.

"I missed you a lot," she said. "Even if you think Sally dragged you over, I'm glad you're here."

"Why didn't you tell me you were going out of town?" Greco asked. "Nobody even knew where you went. I still don't."

"Where's not important," Diane said. "I was angry with you. Hurt, too, I guess. When you said you were going to Florida to see Camille, I didn't know it was only to get your safety deposit key."

"Sally again," Greco knew.

Diane rubbed a spurt of skin cream into his flanks.

"He also said Camille is hoping to work things out

between you two. Is that what you want? All one happy family again?"

"The only thing I'm sure I want is being with you," Greco said. "Until I sort out this mess I'm in, that will have to be good enough."

"I told you when I cut things off with Donny that I'd thrown away the rules. Too late to change back now. I'm here whenever you want me to be."

"I want you," Greco said.

"Then suppose you roll yourself over. You'll be surprised what I can do with this cream."

16

GRECO got to the Friendly Northside Tap between the time the after-work crowd had split for dinner and the night-timers started coming in. Dead Dom's son was alone at the bar, eyes fixed on the projection TV as some black broad and a wimpy lottery official mixed up a Lucite cylinder full of numbered Ping-Pong balls. He made a plaintive, moaning sound as the final number was drawn.

"You're a loser," Greco called out.

"Two of four ain't worth shit," Dom agreed.

Greco asked for a short bottle of Bud. Dom got up and flipped a rug on the bar. There was an ominous tone in his voice.

"We got to talk."

Greco foresaw the problem.

"Tell your people we'll settle up next week. Stall them for a while."

"That's all I've been doing," Dom said. "What I'm talking about is, when I cleared out with Berwyn Bobby last night, he tells me you're closing everything down. This weekend and that's it."

"Football's off as of now," Greco said. "I'll finish up the NBA playoffs myself. That could be July, the way they're going. But at least we're not getting killed taking it."

"Except I got people here who want to keep playing. What do I tell them? Take your business elsewhere? Go find another gin mill and leave your money there?"

"Tell them you'll have a new number by next week," Greco said. "I know a couple independents who'll take small action, nickel a game limit. Let them throw the party for a while."

"That ain't small action for my guys," Dom said.

"So maybe Berwyn Bobby will handle it himself, now he's getting laid off."

Dom reached back blindly and found the square bottle of Jack.

"I know the outfit's been getting beat bad," he said. "But to just shut down, call it quits."

"I got my orders," Greco said.

"Enough said," Dom understood. "I figured with all the lead flying around, something like that had to happen." He downed his shot in one gulp, poured a back-up.

"I wonder where they planted Sid Paris."

"I don't want to think about it," Greco said. "Neither do you."

Dom looked at him with concern. "What about you, Sonny? What are you gonna do?"

"Take the summer off, catch a few Cubs games while they're still playing day ball, nothing special."

"You could always come in here with me," Dom said. "Buy a piece of the place so you have something to show the IRS."

"I'm thinking about a restaurant," Greco lied.

"That's always good."

"You sound like somebody else I know."

Greco checked out the clock that told everyone it was Miller Time. Backing off the fifteen minutes Dom ran fast, he had a half-hour before Frank was due.

"You got a bar gun?" he asked.

"One at each end," Dom said. "Syrup cans and CO_2 tanks are down the basement."

"You catching an early case of brain death? I'm not talking about mixers. I want to know if you keep a piece here. Something clean."

"What's with you, Sonny? You never fool around . . ."

"You got something or not?"

"I don't like this at all," Dom bitched. He walked to far ends of the bar, took a pistol from each.

"Take your pick. The Colt's a nice number. Or do you want the automatic?"

Greco picked up the nickel-finished Colt. For a snub-nose, it felt surprisingly heavy in his hand.

"There's no hammer."

"I had it bobbed. This way it don't catch on anything. Here, look." Dom emptied the cylinder and showed Greco its firing action.

"No safety either?"

"It's a revolver, for Christ's sake. If you're worried, keep the drop chamber empty. And maybe get your ass over to the range, practice up a little before you hurt yourself."

"I'll take the automatic," Greco said.

"You ever fire one?"

"What do I need, an engineering degree? Just show me how it loads."

"Look, Sonny, automatics can be tricky."

"It's got a safety. Show me."

Dom gave in and took him through the mechanics of handling the Walther.

"Single or double action, see. When the hammer's back, the trigger's real sensitive. Get nervous, there go three, four rounds in a hurry."

Greco got a quick feel for the slide and hammer sequence, slid the magazine carefully back into the grip.

"I'll get it back to you in a week or so."

"Just be careful, will ya?"

"Why the hell do you think I want it?" Greco stuffed the PPK in his belt, pulled the V-neck over it.

"A little farther back," Dom directed him. "Good. It's easier to reach, harder to spot."

Greco said, "I'm going in the back and run your figures. You remember Frank, guy from downtown who plays with me?"

"Tall guy, red hair?"

"He'll be around later. Send him back."

Dom looked at Greco and took the Colt off the bar. "You need any support back there, call me."

"Just don't ask any questions if I do," Greco said. "And let's both hope I'm wrong."

Thorne felt confused.

On the drive north, heading toward Dead Dom's, he began scolding himself, as if he were talking to Sonny Greco: It's your own damn fault, he'd say. You let it happen. Even if Pizza Sal handled the dirty end, you knew what you were doing. This wasn't just some commodities trade; it's a long way from making book to backing a drug buy. You got what you deserve.

So what was wrong?

Getting someone inside the family was a cop's dream. And he was saving Greco from hard time in Terre Haute by turning him as an informant. Play it right, the family would never find out and Sonny could walk away clean.

Thorne went through it again. It still didn't feel right.

Entrapment? he wondered.

Sure, but not the way a jury would see it, not how some flaky judge would define it. Besides, the way Thorne had it planned, Greco would never see the inside of a courtroom.

But it was entrapment.

Thorne had created the pressure, shoved Greco into doing the deal with Pizza Sal: he'd bled him dry and

kept pressing for more. He'd do it again tonight—
squeeze him for the hundred thousand he owed the
Bureau's players, knowing all the time that Sonny *had*
to square up with everybody he owed, knowing that's
the way he was put together, especially when it came
to his good friends, people like Frank Becker.

Entrapment? Thorne wondered again.

Or betrayal?

He swung back into the lot behind the bar and
walked halfway around the block to Dom's front door:
Mister La Salle Street in a light gray suit, carrying a
cordovan briefcase.

"He's in the office," Dom said. "Go on back."

"Diane's off tonight?"

"She quit."

"Too bad."

"Why, you looking for work?"

Guess everybody's wound tight, looking over their
shoulders, Thorne figured. Take it as a portent of how
it would be putting the final screws to Sonny Greco.

Thorne found him sitting at the small dusty desk,
nervously rolling a pencil between his fingers, looking
tense and tired. When Thorne shook his hand, it was
limp and sweaty.

"I haven't heard a peep out of you since we left the
restaurant," Thorne said. "I was wondering where to
send the flowers."

"I had to lay low," Greco said. "Nobody knew
what'd happen next. You were in my shoes, you'd
duck too."

"At least a phone call," Thorne said. "All I get is a
midnight message from Pizza Sal saying he's going
ahead with the deal, saying you're in it with him and
there's plenty of room for me. That any way to do
business?"

"Could be," Greco said vaguely.

Thorne dropped his case on the desk and decided to
keep up the pressure.

"I'm under the gun with my clients," he said. "Nobody knows enough to put you and Johnny Ross together, but they know enough to worry about getting paid. Since I'm the man in the middle, so am I."

Greco stared at him, icy, silent.

"Tell me where we stand," Thorne said.

"We stand down," Greco said at last. "The house is closing up for a while. Your people get the news tomorrow night, when they call in."

"Just like that! You're leaving me holding a six-figure bag."

"I told you up front this isn't investment banking," Greco said, equally steamed. "We both took our chances. We lost."

"You also told me you always paid up. Since when did the rules change?"

"My boss says everybody we owe gets what's coming to them," Greco answered with restraint. "I'll run the final figures this week. Then it's history."

"Your boss is locked up somewhere with cops for nurses," Thorne said, wondering if the family could have gotten to Johnny Ross before the move from Northwestern. "How did you talk to him?"

"I'm talking about the big boss," Greco said.

"The old man?"

"What are you digging for, Frank? I said all your people get paid. No need you should worry about how, or from who."

"Look, I'm pressed for cash too," Thorne said, trying to align himself with Sonny. "I don't give a damn where it comes from, just so it comes."

"If that's all you're worried about . . ."

"That's enough."

"Then here's something to tide you over."

Greco slid open the desk drawer. When his hand came out, Thorne found himself staring into the teeth of a Walther automatic. He started to yell but Greco flipped the thumb safety for effect, exposing the red-dot firing indicator, shutting Thorne up.

"Don't even breathe till I tell you," Greco said.

He got up and and opened the door, the PPK fixed all the while at Thorne's belly. Dom came inside a second after Greco's call.

"Pat him down good," Greco said. "See if he's carrying a piece or wearing any wires."

"You're crazy," Thorne barked.

"You think so. Then you don't know shit. Go on," he ordered Dom again.

Thorne stood motionless as Dom ran his oversized hands across his chest and back, up and down his legs, into his groin. Greco wouldn't do this on his own, Thorne knew. Somebody had to order it. Question was, where would Sonny take it from there?

"He's clean," Dom said, rising from Thorne's ankles.

"Check the briefcase."

Dom went through the case as Thorne emptied his pockets on the desk top.

"We got a *Wall Street Journal* in here, some magazines, a pamphlet."

"It's called a prospectus," Thorne snapped impatiently.

"The calculator's legit, nothing in the lining." Dom picked up Thorne's wallet and dumped its contents. "License, bunch of credit cards, pass for the Exchange, all of them say Frank Becker."

"What'd you expect, Efrem Zimbalist, Jr.?"

Dom grabbed Thorne's thumb and bent it back painfully. "Shut your damn mouth."

"I'll take it from here," Greco said. "You get back to work and forget you ever saw this guy."

Dom looked as if he missed having a chance to break Thorne's fingers one by one.

"Call if you need me."

Thorne straightened his thumb into joint and stared at Greco.

"You always treat your partners this way?"

"People've been partners for years are zapping each other all over town," he replied. "I'm supposed to be the only one around who plays by Hoyle?"

"I never screwed you," Thorne said.

"I had to make sure who *you* are," Greco explained. "There are rumors flying around about the feds moving in on the family book. If you're as straight as you say, then be glad I'm covering all the bases. For both of us."

Thorne put on a worried look. It came easily.

"What are the feds after?"

"Word has it they've been fixing the lines, betting against the house. Not bad, when you can call all the moves."

"Look at all the money I've been winning," Thorne reminded him.

"Not you maybe. But what about your customers?"

"You think that, I say we call it quits here and now. For everything," Thorne said, hating to take the chance, knowing he had to.

Greco looked at his pistol in dismay and stuck it back inside the desk.

"I've always been a hunch player," he said. "No sense changing your bet at halftime. Take it as an apology."

"Any chance that's for real about the feds moving in?"

"It looks real possible every time I check the numbers," Greco said.

Thorne rubbed his chin contemplatively and noticed his hand was shaking.

"Then I could be the one looking at an indictment," he said. "I told you my clients are judges, politicians, all that. Some of them could be using me, maybe figuring I could give them names, connections. Or, with the judges, maybe they're buying their way out of their own indictments."

"You said you knew these people for years," Greco recalled.

"How long did Sid Paris know Johnny Ross?"

Greco nodded and fell back into his chair.

"No one can tie me to you," Thorne said. "No one ever will. I just got a phone number off the street, is all. Then some guy I don't know from Adam comes around once a week with an envelope."

"You're not the one they're after," Greco said. "Besides, my boss told me not to look for cops under my bed. People we know for sure have been winning too."

"I'd think about changing your phone men around," Thorne said. "That might help."

"Another week it won't matter. We came up craps."

Thorne started putting his wallet back together. So the outfit had gotten wind of Clothesline. It'd only been a few hours since he'd told Jack Corrigan. No worry there. Let AAG James Jonathan Bidwell start getting his own house in order. Within the week they had left.

Greco said, "With all this going on, I think we'd better pass on the deal with Pizza Sal. Everybody's on edge, looking over their shoulder. I get caught doing that, cops or family don't matter. I'm dead."

Thorne wished he *could* tell Greco to drop it, could walk out and head for McCaskey's, forget the whole thing. Instead, the cop inside him said, "Any other time I'd go along with you. But these cash problems . . . some money I've been playing with wasn't exactly mine . . . all I lost to you . . ."

"You saying you still want to do it?"

"I'm saying I don't have many choices left. But I don't play unless you come in too. Not with Pizza Sal."

Greco hovered on the brink of an answer. Finally, the words snagging in his throat, he said, "Let's go talk with him."

"One question first," Thorne said. "If you'd found out I was working for the cops, you would've pulled that trigger?"

"I kept asking myself the same thing," Greco said. "Tell you the truth, I never came up with an answer."

They met Pizza Sal at the Italian beef stand on West Taylor Street, the one behind Circle Campus, across from the lemon-ice place. He sat in the last of a row of redwood picnic tables that ran alongside the parking lot. So no one would bug him he'd bought six sandwiches, each wrapped in a double layer of wax paper but still leaking greasy juices, plus a couple of sodas and two paper plates mounded with French fries.

"Better we talk out here," Sal said. "You never know which walls got ears."

"Looks like everybody's going wire-happy," Thorne said. Greco kept quiet.

"All them satellites they got spying on people, why take any chances," Pizza Sal said, only half-kidding. "Here, eat something. I think this one's got sweet-and-hot."

Thorne turned him down; Greco munched nervously on some fries. Under the vapor lamps that lighted the parking lot, Pizza Sal looked older, more tired and strung out than he had the first night Thorne met him at the Cairo Club. In contrast with the Dodger-blue warm-up jacket he wore, his usually flushed face looked beet-red.

"So, we gonna do business?" he asked.

"We went through the money end on the way down here," Greco began. "Frank says he can come up with the two-fifty."

"Great," Sal chirped.

"Only if I double it inside ninety days," Thorne said.

"No problem."

"Maybe one," Thorne said, trying to get more to go

on. "I figure if I'm banking you for two-fifty large, I have a right to know more about the people I'm dealing with."

Pizza Sal wouldn't bite.

"Hey, you want to be a banker, maybe you should go loan out some mortgages. Or, you want to make a quarter million fast, you go along with me, no questions."

Greco bounced a handful of fries off Sal's forehead.

"Don't pull that number on us," he growled.

"I don't want to know all your secrets," Thorne said. "But I don't like walking in the dark either. So let's hear what kind of arrangements you've made."

"There's nothing to it," Sal insisted. "I make my call tonight and the stuff gets here next Tuesday. My man from Florida, this guy Delgado who's brokering the deal, brings up the goods himself. We meet him and his local partner, I test the stuff, we pay them off if we're satisfied. It's as simple as I'm making it, like buying a pair of shoes."

"Who holds the merchandise?" Thorne asked.

Pizza Sal shook his head disgruntledly.

"I've set that up myself," Greco said. "Someplace safe, out of the way. Nothing goes out until the cash is in from the last sale. You get paid first, less Sal's commission."

"Gonna slow me down a lot," Sal bitched. "Making all those trips to wherever."

"Tough," Greco said. "We move the goods in fifty-dime increments only. You try and unload it too fast, you're asking for problems."

Thorne decided to give it one more try.

"I still say we should meet these people before we do any business. All I got's you, some Latin hustler from Miami, and a mystery man you won't talk about. That makes me nervous."

"You're nervous, they're nervous," Sal replied. "That's why I'm here, making everybody calm. This way, nobody has to know where, when, or who until the deal comes down."

"I can see it from their side," Greco conceded. "Lots of people get ripped off or walk into a trap."

"Two of them, two of us," Sal added. "And we got Sonny outside keeping his eyes open, covering our tail. It's simple."

"Like buying shoes," Thorne said.

"You're looking for ninety days, I'll guarantee you're paid in thirty," Pizza Sal said. "It's a seller's market out there. I got nothing but triple-A customers lining up, all of them waiting with cash in hand. It's a cinch."

"Nothing's ever a cinch," Greco said. "You oughta know that by now."

Sal shrugged in disdain and turned back to Thorne.

"Let me ask you something," he said. "You're so uptight about this, why you coming in at all? Big broker like you has lots of ways to make a fee, with or without paying taxes."

Thorne had been anticipating the question.

"Corn," he said.

"What's corn?"

"I took a position on some corn contracts that went south. I'm in a jam unless I make up my losses fast."

It worked. For the first time Pizza Sal seemed to relate to him: kindred spirits.

"Some shit," he said. "You guys down the Exchange ain't nothing but bookies wearing suits."

"You got it," Thorne said. He turned to Greco when Pizza Sal ceased chortling.

"I'm satisfied. Let's do it."

"Go on and make your call," Greco told Sal. "We'll have everything ready for Tuesday night. But anything doesn't look perfect, don't go off highrolling on your own. Talk to us."

Pizza Sal said, "Hey, what's say we get together this weekend? I'll see what I can do about getting some samples. We'll party a little to seal the deal."

"That's why I like you so much," Greco sneered. "You're nothing but heart."

Driving back north, Thorne noticed that Greco still hadn't unwound.

"You worried about Pizza Sal?" he asked.

"We go with him or we have nothing," Greco said.

"That's not what I asked."

"Sally's fine. A deal like this, he's one hundred percent. It's the small shit you have to worry about, the nickels he beats you for."

"Then what's on your mind?"

"It's a high stakes roll," Greco said.

"So we step back from the table and pass the dice."

"No," Greco decided as they pulled alongside Thorne's car. "You and me make a good team. We might as well hit the line together."

Thorne checked his watch before pulling the car door closed: almost eleven-thirty, plenty of time to get over to MaryAgnes' apartment, maybe find her awake. He reached for the fresh pack of Luckies stuck in the sun visor.

The next thing he knew, he was about to die.

The muzzle dug hard behind his right ear, freezing his arm in mid-reach. Who could have set him up? Why did it have to end now, forever? He heard a voice snarl:

"How do you think it'll feel going in?"

Thorne waited for the blast, wondering if there really were warmth and bright lights on the other side.

Click!

The hammer fell with a heavy metallic rap on an empty chamber. Thorne recognized Detective Tom Massey's sadistic snicker.

"How do you like it, Thorne? Just sitting in your car like I was."

"You ever try this again," Thorne barked, "you'd fucking well better have a round in place."

"If I have to, believe me I will," Massey said, pulling the gun away from Thorne's mastoid. "Just because you carry federal papers don't mean shit out here. Not on my streets."

Thorne's fear had turned to rage. Looking down two gun barrels the same night was too much. Time for his turn to come around. Bringing Tom Massey down would be the best part of it all. He'll love it in Stateville, playing dodge-ball all the junkies and pushers he'd shaken down, beaten up, busted.

"What's your problem, Massey? Why the hard line?"

"You owe me money."

"I've got a thousand in my pocket," Thorne said. "That should bring us back in line."

"Hit the lights and show me."

Thorne pulled out the fresh C-notes. Massey ripped them from his hand.

"It hurt to think you might try to screw me," Massey said. "I keep up my end of the deal, set the picks for you downtown, and all you do is disappear on me. No more Fairweather's, nothing. Good thing I remembered this place. Your puss's apartment was the next stop, and you wouldn't want me to catch you in the saddle."

"You got your cash. Take off."

"Yeah, you had me worried," Massey went on. "I figured the deal you're working was over. You got what you want and I'm stuck the two dimes you owe me. Then, next thing I know, you're out eating sausage with Greco and Sal Catania. I know about Catania, remember? I wonder how he's making out now, not working the phones since he got cracked."

"I'm paying you to stay *off* my ass," Thorne said. "The way you're talking, I think I deserve a refund."

"Just looking after my investment."

"Or getting greedy."

"A terrible affliction," Massey said, leaning over the front seat. "But not when I smell something big going on."

"The only thing big was my sandwich. And your feet."

"Funny, I ask after Catania at the Cairo Club and they say he's down in Florida. I see he's got no tan, so what would you think? He went to watch the grey-hounds, some *jai alai;* maybe play a pony or two?"

"I think you're dreaming."

"Could be. But all those years I spent in Narcotics, all I know about Sal Catania, that can cause a man nightmares. I say it's worth more than another thousand to get me back to sleep."

"You know nothing," Thorne said.

"I know you, pal. You got a shit-paying job as a legman for the J. Department. You're getting yourself a divorce and you got a sweet little puss on the side. Probably costing you plenty, putting her up Near North. I also know your own people pulled you off the street, stuck you in some office chasing stock swindlers. Maybe they got wise, found out you've been dabbling in what you're supposed to turn in. Like the book, for instance. Or that stuff people put up their nose."

It's getting better all the time, Thorne told himself. Tom Massey is so fucking warped he sees himself in everybody. He knew exactly where to take it.

"You said you did pretty well for yourself back in Narcotics."

"That I did," Massey said. "Freedom's an expensive buy. Fact is, the price is going up every day."

"How much now?"

"Say another five thousand. In one lump."

"You're out of your mind!"

Massey reached over and grabbed a clump of Thorn's hair, yanking it hard enough to force his head over the seat-back.

"I don't want to hear that," he hissed. "I say the

three of you are putting a buy together. To anyone's got half a brain, it's worth five dimes to make sure you get no hassles. Which you'll have for sure if I talk to Jack Corrigan."

"Do that and you cut yourself out of everything," Thorne said through his pain-clenched teeth.

"Might be worth it," Massey said. "Kind of an insurance policy to get me in good with the boss. Then, once Corrigan's a believer, I got myself room to navigate, turn up some other action."

"I can do better than that," Thorne said. When Massey released his grip, Thorne knew he'd won.

"I'm not asking a fortune," Massey said. "What's five dimes to the people you're playing with? Greco's watch probably cost more than that."

"Not a bad guess. But everything else you're saying is."

"I don't think so," Massey said. "I got one out-of-work bookie who's known to be real free with the blow. I got another guy Jack Corrigan tells me captains the North Side action for the family, but who's lost so much his boss gets three slugs bounced off his head. And I got you. The Bureau yanks you off the strike force, cuts off your side action just when you need cash the most. Tell me, Thorne, in my shoes, how would you see it? You, Greco, Catania—all trying to pick up the slack with an investment in Peruvian powder."

"If you were a straight cop, you'd make commander in a year," Thorne said.

"Yeah, and maybe earn enough to buy a new Jap compact. I'll go my own way, thanks."

"What's to keep you from moving in on us after I pay the five grand?" asked Thorne. "You might want a double dip, first the cash, then a cut."

"I told you, greed is a terrible affliction. I'm not looking for any troubles. I get the cash, I get lost. That's my secret to longevity."

Thorne finally got around to lighting his cigarette, and it was all as clear as the flaming match in his hand. McCaskey wanted to be a cop, she'd get her chance.

"I'll have your cash next Tuesday night," Thorne said. "Give me a number where I can reach you."

"Screw off," Massey flared. "No telephones, Thorne. I wasn't born yesterday."

"Then come by my girlfriend's place. I'm not going to mess around there, take a chance on something going wrong. Consider it a neutral field."

"Astor Street. First floor."

"You followed me there enough times," Thorne said.

"Yeah, sweet little puss, that one. Maybe on Tuesday she gets a friend over and we have ourselves a party. No use always being at each other's throats."

"Don't push it," Thorne said. "You don't get to walk erect for five dimes."

"You got some attitude, Thorne. You're doing a deal with scumbag wops like Greco and Catania, and you treat *me* like a creep."

"Think what you want, as long as I don't have to look at you until next Tuesday night."

"You're making a mistake," Massey said. "I know the trade, pal. You'd be smart to keep that in mind for the future."

Thorne knew the pump was primed, the well full.

"Could be you're right," he said. "We're looking at some things where your background could help us, where there's room . . ."

"Finally I get a truthful answer," Massey said. "So now we understand each other, what say we take off the gloves? Like in that movie, the beginning of a profitable friendship."

"I'll settle for absence making the heart grow fonder."

Massey opened the door and stepped out on the driver's side.

"You're not the first fed cop to go this route," he

said. "Look at it this way—what the fuck has Uncle Sam done for us lately?"

It wasn't much of a weekend.

Thorne spent a long lonely Saturday at home going through the details again and again. He even drew up an operational flow chart on some large pieces of graph paper that Patsie once had used to plan a management presentation. The timing, he knew, was critical: bringing it all together at once—Jack Corrigan, Doc Hermann, the guys from Tech Services who held his life in their hands, MaryAgnes McCaskey. He wouldn't be wearing an assault jacket this time, nothing with FBI emblazoned on it in large fluorescent letters. One screwup and the crossfire was sure to nail him.

He was slapping together a sandwich of Kraft singles when Patsie phoned. She'd set up a conference with her attorney and wanted to know if Thorne would make it, if he'd even bothered getting counsel for himself.

"Next week is out," Thorne said. "It will have to wait."

"Waiting won't change anything," Patsie said. "I hope you understand that and accept it."

"I just don't have the time."

"What else is new?" Patsie carped. She hung up before Thorne could respond.

Sunday morning, after a few fitful hours of sleep, Thorne dug out his sweatsuit and decided to jog along the lakefront. Get the smoke out of his lungs; maybe quit when all of this was over. He was halfway out the door when McCaskey called from Rockford, where she'd gone to pick up some summer clothes and, what she called, take care of business.

"If you'd like a late breakfast, I could come back to Chicago early," she said.

"I'm here alone," Thorne said, without knowing why he had.

"I know, Frank. I'm not checking up on you."

"I guess we should meet," he said. "There are some things I have to go over with you."

"How romantic. Should we invite Sonny Greco too?"

"Look, I have a lot on my mind. But that doesn't mean we have to spend all day on the operation. Or all night."

"Words of love, soft and tender," McCaskey said bitterly. "No thanks."

"Satisfaction guaranteed or your emotions cheerfully refunded," Thorne tried joking.

"I'll settle for returned intact."

"You're angry," Thorne realized.

"Just thinking what will happen after Tuesday, after it's over."

"If we play Greco right, it might not be over for years," Thorne said.

A long and chilly pause.

"Frank Thorne," McCaskey said. "Fella I thought I was falling in love with. If you run into him anywhere, tell him I called to say hello."

17

TUESDAY. The six strike force agents who'd attended the final briefing left Assets Management Partners the same way they'd arrived: one at a time, three minutes apart, using the service stairs and rear corridor leading to an alley on the Wells Street side of the Exchange Building. The assistant U.S. attorney in charge of the operation took his role as Bidwell's surrogate to heart and asked another half-dozen questions, in Thorne's eyes all of them redundant.

"For giving away half the store, you'd better make damn sure we get enough in return," he said.

"You got it," Thorne replied.

The attorney finally collected his notes and walked out of Thorne's office listing to starboard under the weight of his briefcase.

The section chiefs from Tech Services and Communications went through their drill another time, assuring Thorne that everything he'd asked for would be accomplished "no sweat."

The TS chief asked Thorne to demonstrate the Clothesline program by giving him a real line on Sunday's Blaze game at Soldier Field.

"I'll have that on Friday," Thorne said. "Get your job done right, I'll make sure you have a winner."

"Damn," the TS chief said, still staring at the computer screen. "I'd have saved a lot of money if you'd briefed me on this sooner."

"Keep us in mind for the NFL," said the Commo chief. "This is beautiful."

They checked their watches in tandem and headed out the door. Only Doc Hermann remained, his black-suited bulk filling McCaskey's chair.

"I wish I was as sold as they are," Hermann said. "We had a lot more margin for error jumping into Normandy. I think you're shooting for too much here."

"Give me a better idea," Thorne argued. "If the family knows enough about Clothesline to make them shut down, I have to go with all we've got. Your people wrap up Scarpo and Lowenstein, I do my thing with Jack Corrigan, and like Greco says, we all go to the window."

"You're only thinking tactics," Hermann countered. "I have strategic problems to worry about. A lot of people have their noses out of joint, especially the way Bidwell's kept them in the dark. Either they're jealous or they're wondering why they haven't been put on-line. And you think it's easy walking over to Justice with what we have here? Those guys believe six months is short-time for getting indictments drawn up."

"You retire next year, so screw 'em. Go out with a bang."

"Not to mention that DEA is going to be hotter than hell," Hermann worried on.

Thorne went over to the flow chart that McCaskey had transferred from his graph-paper scribble to a neat, multi-colored illustration board.

"Look, the drug bust goes down as a local operation. It's the only way I can isolate Sonny Greco for us and still give CPD and the county boys a fair cut. If you're worried about making DEA's golf outing this summer, offer them the Florida connection."

"Linking a narcotics deal to someone inside the Chicago family would make them happier."

"Because they've never done it," Thorne knew. "And they're not going to start with Greco."

Doc Hermann lifted himself wearily and walked to Thorne's chart.

"Here's my worry," he said, jabbing his index finger inside the central circle. "You're hanging too much on Jack Corrigan. I'll give you the fact he's a good cop. I see why we've cut him a deal for Tom Massey. But with everything else involved, I say I should head down to Eleventh and State and bring the brass up to speed."

"Doc, please," Thorne pleaded. "They'll go nuts with all this. The place will be crawling with Tac cops and SWAT teams and God knows what else. Maybe a couple of reporters thrown in so some deputy chief gets his picture in the *Trib*."

"You're asking a lot," Hermann said, jabbing Thorne's chart again.

"I owe Corrigan this one. At least with him, I know there's no chance of a leak."

"Talk like that can get you in trouble."

"Yeah? Then wait till you meet Detective Tom Massey."

Doc Hermann tugged nervously at his tie, checked his watch.

"Okay, Frank. You get to call the shots tonight. Maybe I've been sitting behind a desk so long I've forgotten what goes on when you're undercover. Since this may be my last chance to find out, I'm going along with the Red team and take Mister Anthony 'Tony Shoes' Scarpo myself."

"Have a ball, Doc," Thorne said. "We're going to get it all."

"We'd better, for everybody's sake. That includes your job's."

Thorne phoned Jack Corrigan as soon as Doc Hermann was out the door.

"Set on this end," he said.

"The car's ready," Corrigan said. "Dry run went perfectly. Ditto for Astor Street."

"Watch out for her, Jack," Thorne said. "She's liable to make rookie mistakes, try too hard, let it go too far."

"You got my word," Corrigan said. "If I have to take him on the spot, I'll settle for that."

"Deal," Thorne agreed. "How much time do you think I'll have with Greco?"

"Three, five minutes max. Get him out of there as fast as you can."

"Wherever that is," Thorne said.

"Yeah, be nice if we knew."

Thorne held the phone until a dial tone came on. No sense planning it any farther, he told himself as he broke down the easel and locked away his chart. Here on in, it's guts-ball.

He took the Model 19 from his desk, flipped open the cylinder, and exchanged the first two hard-ball rounds for the 125-grain + P soft points that Jack Corrigan had given him the night Thorne sat in his kitchen and told him Tom Massey had taken the lure.

Greco was outside in a flash. He jumped into Thorne's car and hit the door locks.

"We go collect Pizza Sal and we're on the way," he said, looking down at the seat between them. "That what I think it is?"

Thorne reached for the case and flipped open the latches.

"That's what a quarter million looks like."

"Awful pretty," Greco said, staring at the neat stacks of Ben Franklin faces. "So's what it will buy."

Thorne closed the case and spun the lock.

"How about we play I've shown you mine, now you show me yours," he said.

"You get mine when we pick up Sally and his chemistry set."

"You left your cash with Pizza Sal?"

Greco seemed surprised by Thorne's concern.

"Listen, why do you think I asked you to get a rented car and do the driving? I'm a known associate of some people getting shot at or winding up in car trunks. Good chance the feds are keeping tabs on me, maybe pay a house call any time. They find that kind of cash and what happens? I got no way to prove it's income, so they lift it for taxes, evidence, whatever they feel like. It wouldn't be the first time."

No it wouldn't, Thorne remembered. The only time the Bureau ever dented the old man's ego was when they raided his mansion and pulled out ninety grand of undocumented and untraceable cash.

"Like you say," Thorne shrugged. "We trust Pizza Sal or we have nothing. Where to?"

Greco checked the time.

"Eisenhower's all torn up again," he said. "Thing's like an obstacle course with all the shines knocking over the lane markers for kicks. Head over and we take Lake Street."

Thorne hit the ignition and, in the same movement, activated the transmitter and tape drive that were wired into the flasher switch. It was time for the kickoff: Thorne figured he'd better let his team know whom they were facing.

"You bring that automatic you pulled on me the other night?"

Greco opened his camel's hair blazer just enough to reveal the black checkered grips that stuck out of his waistband.

"Sal's word is good enough for me," he said. "Only we don't know for sure who *he's* believing."

"There's another piece in the glove compartment,"

Thorne said. "I'm telling you now, in case you two decide to shake down my car."

"Lookit, what happened at Dom's is history. You gonna blame me for getting spooked when the old man tells me the Gee is everywhere? Forget it, okay? Let's just hope this goes as smooth as Sally says."

"You listen to me instead of him," Thorne said dryly, "it probably will."

It took forty minutes to weave through the traffic and make it to Sally's bungalow. Thorne pulled into the driveway and followed Greco up the steps. He recognized the girl standing behind the storm door as one of Pizza Sal's friends from the Cairo Club—Marci or Carol, he couldn't recall which.

"Sally's taking it right down to the wire," Greco whispered. "Probably has six more broads waiting to party when he brings home the good stuff."

"Jesus, thank God you're here! Jesus!" the girl babbled frantically. "It was *terrible*!"

"Slow down," Greco yelled back, pushing her inside. "What are you talking about?"

"Sally. It was terrible," the girl said, her voice still quivering. "He was just sitting there, counting this money. Then, God, he fell right on the floor. He was choking, kicking, we didn't know what to do."

"He gagged on some food?" asked Thorne.

Greco knew better.

"Caught his heart attack at last," he said.

"It was terrible," the girl nodded. "One minute he's sitting there . . ."

"Shut up!" Greco barked. "Tell me when it happened, where he is."

Thorne watched the girl tremble under Greco's glower and silently began reciting the principle of Murphy's Law: *Whatever can go wrong will* . . .

"About two hours ago," the girl said.

"Were you alone with him?"

"Marci was here. She went and called the paramedics. They got Sal wired up to those machines and took him to the hospital. Marci went along too. I think Sal wanted her to, or maybe she was hysterical. I couldn't watch any more, him kicking and throwing up."

"So you're Carol," Thorne said.

"I remember you," she nodded. "That night at the club."

Thorne reintroduced himself as Greco paced the room like a frenzied bull.

"Calm down," Thorne told Carol. "Everything will be fine."

"Jesus, it was scary," she said.

"Tell me about Marci. Did she come back? Have you heard from her?"

"Nothing," Carol replied. "She ran to her car so fast. Maybe she thinks I went home or something. But Sal told me to wait here for Sonny. 'Don't move till Sonny comes,' he told me. Then they gave him some kinda shot and stuck a bottle in his arm."

"They should have used this," Greco said, picking up a liter of Smirnoff.

"If you're pouring, I'll take a double," Carol said.

Greco handed her a warm one.

"What about that cash Sal was showing off?"

"It's all here. Honest," Carol said, her voice fright-filled. "I'm not dumb enough to mess with money like that."

"Then be a good girl and get it for us," Greco said, patting Carol lightly on the ass. She scurried off to Sal's TV room and came back with a thick, olive-drab money pouch.

"I didn't touch a cent," she swore again. "Nothing. Honest."

"Open up your case," Greco told Thorne. He made a quick count of the cash and married it with the Bureau's.

"So you don't even know if Pizza Sal's still alive," said Thorne.

"He was when they took him away. The two paramedics—they were really nice guys and all, good looking . . ."

"Cut the crap!" Greco raged.

"They said he'd probably be all right," Carol resumed. "They were taking him over to Gottlieb Memorial. It's the closest."

Greco locked the case and gave Thorne a nod.

"Come on. We're outta here."

"Right behind you," Thorne said.

"Hey, what about me?" Carol asked. "I'm not hanging around here any more."

"So go home," Greco said.

"I got no car. Marci took it to the hospital."

"Then walk."

"Oh Jeez," Carol whined.

Thorne reached for his wallet. "Here's a hundred. Call yourself a taxi. You and Marci both get a nice bonus when we straighten things out. You've been good girls."

"I couldn't hang here another minute," Carol said, thanking him with body language and rolling eyes. "I mean, I get the creeps just thinking about it, like somebody almost dying right in front of me."

"That's why it's good you forget all about it," Thorne said, knowing what a rotten witness she'd make anyway. "Go home, relax. I'll be in touch."

"Hey, thanks," Carol said. "I hope so."

Greco climbed into the car and held Thorne's briefcase on his lap. Thorne slumped behind the wheel, lighted a fresh Lucky. He was generally pissed off.

"You believe this?" Greco said. "Sally catching the big one?"

"Whatever can go wrong will go wrong," Thorne said. "Murphy's Law."

"What were we supposed to do, get him a stress test up front? It's un-fucking-believable."

Thorne's next words were for transmission.

"He should have told us where the meeting was set. Now he's locked up at Gottlieb Memorial and we don't have the foggiest idea where Delgado's waiting. That's how *we* screwed up."

"I should have pushed him harder," Greco agreed, shaking his head. "Too late now. It's a dead horse."

Thorne wasn't ready to let go, not with the entire strike force moving, not if Corrigan's people could read him correctly and were ready to move faster than planned.

"We've got one shot left," he said. "I think we have to pay Sally a sick call at Gottlieb."

"I don't," Greco said.

"You want to pull out?"

"Maybe I've been a gambler too long," Greco said. "But something tells me this whole deal is nothing but bad luck. I'm not going to push it and go against the flow."

"That's how you make money," Thorne said.

"Yeah? Well this ain't the Super Bowl."

"It's worth a try," Thorne insisted. "We get to see Pizza Sal and he'll tell us where the meeting is set. You and I can handle Delgado and whoever else is there."

"I told you I'm a hunch player. And this move doesn't feel right to me. Not a bit."

Thorne rolled down his window and sucked in the fresh spring air.

"Look, Sonny, I need this deal bad," he said. "We walk away now and there'll be some serious consequences for me."

"You in that much trouble?"

Thorne, hating himself, said yes.

"Okay, we give it a try," Greco decided. "No sense letting all this cash get cold. If Sally can talk to us, if he has somebody lined up to handle the distribution, then maybe we can still bail our asses out of the hot seat."

"We're on the way," Thorne said, dropping into drive.

"I sure hope he pulls through," Greco thought out loud, "so I can personally break both his legs."

Thorne wove slowly through the suburban side streets, angling obliquely toward the hospital, hoping it would be arranged when they got there. Greco was growing more tense and shaky by the block.

"Doesn't this thing have a high gear?"

"You want to get stopped with all this cash and two pieces in the car?"

"We get stopped, it'll be for driving too slow," Greco shot back. "Let's move it."

Thorne punched the gas but still managed to turn the ten-minute drive into twenty. He bought even more time because the parking lot was nearly full and he had to take a space in the row farthest from the entrance.

"Leave it out front," Greco insisted.

"That's towaway country," Thorne said. "Besides, the emergency room is back over there."

As Thorne pointed out the entrance, he slammed his rear fender hard into a low cement retaining wall that was invisible through the rearview mirror. He bounced off the steering column painfully, the briefcase on Greco's lap flew hard into the dash.

"That's five hundred at least," Thorne said, inspecting the damage, stretching the ache from his bruised ribs.

"Another week you can buy two," Greco said. "Let's go see Pizza Sal."

Thorne looked around the waiting area for a familiar face, saw none. Greco said how much he hated hospitals and always gagged on the raw smell of disinfectant.

"We'd like to see Salvatore Catania," Thorne told

the ER receptionist, a large black woman with a soft and compassionate manner.

"Might you be members of the family?" she asked in a lilting Jamaican accent.

"I'm his brother," Greco said. "Him too."

"And surely the young woman who came in with Mister Catania was your sister," the receptionist smiled. "The family resemblance is astonishing."

"My sister Marci," Greco said.

"Certainly yes," the receptionist shook her head. "Well then, since she has gone, I can allow one of you to visit for five minutes only. Even that . . . well, five minutes and no longer."

"How is he?" asked Thorne.

"The attending physician will have to tell you," she replied. "But I think your brother is a very lucky man. For now he is under observation in the cardiac care unit. If it were intensive care, then no one . . ."

"We'll be brief," Thorne said.

The receptionist found a green visitor's pass in her desk.

"Bring this back in five minutes."

"You go on," Thorne told Greco, hoping he could get to a telephone fast.

Greco grabbed his arm forcefully as they backed away from the desk.

"We're going up there together," he said, leaving no room for argument. "They want to throw us out and start a brawl in a heart ward, then let 'em."

"You think I'd split with your cash?"

"I think you and me stick close together from here on in," Greco said. "Come on, up the stairs."

Thorne followed silently, wondering about Greco's sudden caution, hoping he wasn't listening to his hunches again. They both were breathing hard when they got to Sal's room. No one had stopped them or asked for their passes.

"Almost too easy," Greco said.

"The lady said it wasn't that serious," Thorne reminded him. "Let's hope he's not too doped up to talk."

"With him, who could tell?"

Pizza Sal was flat on his back, but awake. Thorne and Greco approached him slowly, as if not to interfere with the clicking and beeping sounds of his monitors. Sal gave them a bleary-eyed grin and tried pointing to the IV bag that dangled over his bed.

"Is that ever mellow," he said weakly. "They got some kind of downers in there. Wow."

"So what happened?" asked Greco, impatient but concerned.

"I been getting these chest pains again," Sal told him. "Then today . . . they don't think it was a bad attack, but they got to check out the damage. One doc says I might need some new plumbing, like a bypass or something."

"Better have them do your sinuses while they're at it," Greco said. "That's half your problem."

"Hey, doing a little stuff don't mean you catch a heart attack," Sal insisted. "If it did, Sonny . . ."

"Okay, relax," Greco said softly as he held Sal's hand. "You got to rest, do what they tell you. You don't and maybe you won't walk out of here."

Sal gave him a weak, smiling nod.

"Jeez, I'm blasted," he said, eyeing the IV. He let his head fall back and appeared to be asleep.

"Let's go," Greco said to Thorne. "He's in no shape to talk."

"We need five words from him," Thorne said, shaking Sal gently. "I'm going to get them."

Greco reached out to stop him. Pizza Sal opened his eyes.

"Words? What words?" Sal asked.

"The meeting with Delgado," Thorne said. "Sonny and I want to go ahead with it, make the buy."

"No chance."

"We have to," Thorne pressed on. "Now tell us where it is."

Pizza Sal stared up at Greco.

"You're still in," Greco assured him. "This changes nothing."

"You get the cash?" asked Sal.

Thorne held up the case. "All of it. Carol didn't run out on you."

"She's fine. Marci too."

"Yeah, lovely," Greco said. "So tell us where we go for the meet and you can get some sleep."

Pizza Sal whispered the Lincoln Avenue address and room number.

"You gotta be there ten sharp," he said. "And don't go looking for problems. Everything's set right. I get out of here in a week, I can still handle my end for you."

"We've got no way to test it," Greco realized suddenly. "We can't trust this guy Delgado without your chemistry set."

"Maybe we'll have to," Thorne said, not wanting to give Sonny another out. "Or Sally can tell us how."

"No need," Sal said softly.

"Why not?"

"Diane."

"Diane? What about Diane?" Greco asked.

"She's been my source for six, eight months now," Sal explained. "Nothing as big as this before, but she's the one put me in touch with Delgado. It's her deal."

"You're tripping out on me," Greco said. *"Diane?"*

"She kept working at Dead Dom's so nobody would know," Sal went on. "But she's got the contacts in Miami, Gulfport, wherever else. That's where she went to, Sonny. Make sure everything was straight. I think it goes back to that guy she married, the biker. He set her up in business, kind of a settlement."

"She went to set up this deal?" Greco asked, still incredulous.

"To make sure it was all right, so you won't get screwed on the merchandise." Pizza Sal reached up and took hold of Greco's sleeve. "Listen to me," he said. "Don't get upset with her. Diane's got a right to get ahead. She has a nice pile already stashed away. A deal this size, she can take care of her kid the right way. No more Cairo Club. No more pouring shots at Dead Dom's. Fuck, Sonny, you want to blame her for that?"

"Blame her? She could have gotten both of us killed if the family found out."

"Nobody's finding out nothing," Sal insisted. "That's why I couldn't tell you. She wanted me to handle everything so you'd be covered, off the hook."

"Well all bets are off," Greco raged.

"She'll be right there for you, Sonny. Top-shelf merchandise, no hassles."

"He's right," Thorne said. "It makes better sense to go, now that we know our supplier."

"I still don't like it," Greco said.

"Go on," Sal told him.

"We're on the way," Thorne said.

Sal nodded and let his head roll back. Thorne pulled Greco toward the door, but Sonny stopped cold when Sal called his name.

"Sonny, come here."

"Right here, Sally."

"You gotta know this," Pizza Sal said. "In case something goes wrong and I don't walk outta here."

"You will," Greco assured him. "Like you have from everything else."

"Delgado only got twenty dimes from me," Sal said. "I held back five on you to take care of some people I owe. I figured, since I got the discount on each key . . ."

Greco had no option but laughter.

"You're the best. The absolute best," he said.

"Put it on my figure," Sal demanded. "I'll make it up to you on my commission. That and everything else

I owe. No more screwing around, Sonny. I swear to God!"

"Take care of yourself," Greco said.

"Come back tomorrow. Tell me how smooth it went."

Agent MaryAgnes McCaskey opened her blouse one more button and took a deep, calming breath before opening the door to face Detective Tom Massey.

"You're even prettier up close," Massey said, stepping inside the apartment.

Though Massey was no taller than Thorne, McCaskey felt somehow dwarfed by him. Was it the thick barrel chest that stretched out his tweed jacket? Or simply the way he leered at her?

She introduced herself as Mary.

"Frank had to step out for a few minutes. My orders are to fix you a stiff drink and keep you entertained until he gets back. I hope you won't mind."

"You kidding? It's a pleasure."

McCaskey forced herself to smile into his hard eyes. Massey sat in what had become Thorne's favorite chair.

"A drink then?"

"Bourbon, if you got it. Over one ice cube."

"Any way you want it."

She fixed two drinks, taking Massey up on the invitation to join him. He eyed the apartment carefully, scrutinizing it as he had her bust line. When he spoke again he seemed satisfied.

"So where'd Frank go?"

"He didn't say," McCaskey replied. "He's always running in and out like that. I don't understand why he's in such a hurry all the time."

"Pressures of business," Massey said.

"I can put some music on if you'd like."

"Skip it," Massey leered again. "Drinking good booze and looking at you will do me fine."

"I'm not sure I like the order of that."

"Nothing else I can do in a few minutes time. Or is there?"

McCaskey knew she was blushing and scolded herself silently.

"I don't think Frank had *that* kind of entertainment in mind," she said.

"I wasn't about to ask him."

"I didn't think you would."

"So tell me," Massey asked, "you two been together long?"

"A few months now, since Frank's been separated."

"You the reason?"

God, he won't let up, McCaskey thought. The man has some way with women.

"That it, or you just filling in?" he pressed on.

The question was real enough.

"Sometimes I think so. People get back together. It's happened before."

"To you."

"Sure. And every girl over twenty, I'll bet."

Massey took a long pull of his whiskey.

"Me, I've been divorced ten years. No strings attached. Nothing. So anything ever happens between you and Thorne, you let me know."

"Don't make it more than it is," she teased. "We're not engaged or anything."

"But Thorne pays the rent. That counts for something."

"Nine-fifty a month," she said. "I'd say he gets his money's worth."

"You're something else," Massey laughed. "So why we wasting time talking about Thorne. Let's hear about you, sweet thing."

McCaskey went through her routine about working at O'Hare, meeting Thorne at Fairweather's; about how he'd rescued her from this married pilot who enjoyed slapping her around after each time he got stuck in a holding pattern. She kept it up for fifteen minutes to Massey's half-hearted interest. Only when she shifted gears and told him about a weekend with Thorne in Miami did Massey appear to listen well.

"Boy, he has some strange friends down there," she said. "All these Latin types right out of *Dance Fever*."

"Lots of strange people down there," Massey said. "But when you've got business . . ."

"I don't even know what Frank does," she persisted. "But it sure eats him up inside. It's like he can never relax—phone calls all night, always running around."

"That so?"

Come on, McCaskey prayed. You should have put it together by now. Make your play.

"I think Frank wants to move down to Florida," she said. "Him and his friend Sal, who's *really* strange."

"He can move wherever the fuck he wants," Massey barked, his patience ebbing. "As long as he gets back here fast. I don't have all night to waste."

"I'd no idea my company was that boring." McCaskey leaned over to refill Massey's glass and threw him some more cleavage.

He looked like he was hit with a jolt of electricity; his body tensed, his eyes went wild as he reached out and grabbed McCaskey by the wrist.

"You rotten bitch!" he roared. "You've been stalling me here."

"Let go," she winced. "Stop it!"

"I'm supposed to sit here happily looking at your tits while Thorne's out putting his deal together," Massey raged. "That's it, isn't it?"

"What do you mean? Ow!"

"I fell for it like a schmuck," Massey said.

"You're hurting me," McCaskey cried.

"I'll do worse than that," Massey roared as he came out of his chair and covered McCaskey with his stale whiskey breath. "A lot worse, you don't tell me exactly what's going on tonight. I want to know where

Thorne is, who he's meeting, or I'll break your pretty little arm."

"Don't, please," she pleaded, the pain from Massey's wrist lock bringing tears to her eyes.

"So where is he?"

"All I know is he left an envelope for you," she said. "In case you started getting nervous, Frank said I was to give it to you."

"Now that's better." Massey easily flung her halfway across the room. "Get it!"

She found the white envelope in the table drawer.

"Take it and get out," she hollered.

Massey tore off the end of the envelope and rifled through the stack of bills, holding up several to check for counterfeit or markings.

"There's only a thousand here. He's light another four."

"That's all he left me," McCaskey said. "He told me, 'Give this to Massey, tell him to sit still and wait for the rest.'"

"Sit still. Sure I'll sit still."

He appeared to calm down as he stuck the cash inside his coat. Then, more quickly than McCaskey could see, he slammed his open right hand across her unguarded face.

She made a gasping noise that could have become a scream if Massey hadn't struck her again, harder this time, the force of his blow propelling her against the wall. As she began to slide down to the floor, Massey grasped her shoulders, bruising them instantly as he pulled her erect.

"Please, don't hit me."

"Tell me where Thorne is," Massey yelled. "You know. I can see it in your eyes. Tell me!"

"He never says where he's . . ."

"Don't play dumb with me, puss. I'm not going to sit here and settle for a lousy thousand while he's out making a score."

When McCaskey denied knowing anything, Massey smiled at her. The bastard was enjoying it, she knew.

"Talk to me, puss!"

His next blow landed just below her sternum, forcing her to exhale a stifled cry of pain. She again started to fall on her knees; Massey again pulled her erect, this time ripping open her blouse and exposing her breasts.

"For the last time," he said.

"No more! Please!" McCaskey caved in. "I'm not getting paid enough to take a beating."

Massey pushed his thick body against hers.

"So where do I find Frankie boy?"

"A motel," McCaskey began as her breath regulated itself. "Up on North Lincoln somewhere. Frank said he had to meet some people there and didn't want you hanging around. That's all I know, I swear."

"Which motel? There's a string of them on Lincoln."

"Star-something," she said. "Starlight. Starbright. Something like that. I just overheard him talking on the phone, talking to these people in from Florida. Star-something was all I could make out."

"Stardust Courts," Massey guessed. "I busted some dust merchants up there once."

"I think that's what he said," she admitted. "The Stardust Courts."

"When? When's his meeting?"

"Now. Ten o'clock."

Massey finally released his grip. McCaskey struggled to the nearest chair and gathered her torn blouse over her breasts.

"You bastard! You didn't have to do that!"

"Would you have told me if I didn't?"

"Maybe. I was really starting to like you."

"You'll like me a lot less if I find out you're lying," Massey sneered.

"I'm telling you all I know," McCaskey insisted. "I was supposed to keep you here while Frank made his meeting. He said you wouldn't move without the rest of the money you had coming. He didn't say I was going to get beaten up."

"The fucker set us both up," Massey realized.

McCaskey's pained voice had turned to rage.

"Go find him. Kick the hell out of each other for all I care. You're both nothing but shits."

"That wasn't so bad," Massey said. "You might even think of it as foreplay."

"Get out of here, you prick!"

Massey pulled out his Bulldog revolver and spun the cylinder ominously. McCaskey thought for a second it would be all over before Jack Corrigan could even get there.

"One more thing, sweet tits," Massey threatened. "Keep your mouth shut about my ever being here. You know nothing, understand?"

"Nothing's all I want to know. Nothing's what you are."

"You're a real tough lady," Massey laughed sadistically. "It all goes like it should tonight, I'll give you a call, make amends for this. You might like the other side of Tom Massey."

"Stay the hell out of my sight," McCaskey warned him. "Just because you're a cop . . ."

Massey shrugged and walked out the door before she could launch her assault on his ancestry.

18

AT NINE-FORTY Thorne pulled into the Stardust Courts Motel, a cut-rate cheaters paradise six miles northwest of the Loop on a strip of Lincoln Avenue dotted with Korean groceries and restaurants. He swung past the A-frame office building, cut his lights entering the interior courtyard. The only car parked near Room 112 was a blue Caprice wagon piled high with camping gear and wearing Mississippi plates.

"Ever see those wheels before?" asked Thorne.

"No, none of them," Greco replied as he scanned the four other cars in the lot. "But anybody dumb enough to leave all that gear outside wouldn't make it from Mississippi with a canteen left."

"Still a good way to mule the stuff cross country."

"Yeah, throw a few bicycles on top and maybe rent a kid for good measure. Smart."

Thorne pulled into a slot that gave them a clear view of both the room and the Chevy. The courtyard was bounded on three sides by connecting rows of dingy, stucco-faced units. On the open end, a one-time swimming pool had been filled in with gravel and planted with a cluster of pines that looked limp and desultory under the blue and white floodlights spilling over them in a shabby simulation of stardust.

Greco kept up a nervous lookout as Thorne lit a smoke and checked the time.

"We've got twenty minutes," Thorne said.

"Stick to the schedule," Greco advised. "Show up too soon, we're liable to spook this guy Delgado."

It sounded good to Thorne: give Jack Corrigan and his team time to catch up with the play. He saw Greco tense as an incoming pair of headlights flashed across the windshield. An old Trans Am parked two slots away; a couple of kids darted into a downstairs room carrying only a brown bag for luggage.

"Just going to get his wick wet," Greco sighed.

Thorne said, "Nothing looks more like a bottle than a bottle in a bag."

Greco's eyes kept traversing the courtyard, entrance, roof-line. Finally he said, "I'm going to scout around some, make sure everything is kosher."

"Pizza Sal swore it's all up-and-up," Thorne said, trying to keep Greco in line. "And Diane wouldn't try to screw you."

"Glad you're so sure of the bitch. I thought I was the one who knew her."

"You're really pissed off."

"In shock," Greco said.

"Because she's dealing, or because she didn't tell you about it?"

"I can see her sticking it out in that three-room crib, working Dead Dom's nights so nobody gets wise. What I didn't see was any of that cash Pizza Sal says she stuck away. All the trouble I was in, and not even offering a few dimes plus interest."

"Maybe Sal got it wrong and Diane's just fronting for someone else," Thorne guessed, thinking like Greco that Diane was an unlikely source for a million dollars worth of blow. "Could be her ex-husband's pulling the strings."

Greco shook his head sullenly.

"Sally's a flake, and we both know he'd cheat his own mother at bingo," he said. "But mistakes like that he just doesn't make."

"So listen to what he says." Thorne spoke softly, not wanting Greco to overreact and pull something stupid with the Walther when it came together. "Diane kept her mouth shut because she knows how your bosses feel about dealing. She didn't want to get *you* in trouble."

"Yeah, maybe that's it."

"So she puts together a few nice deals and heads off to Florida like some rich widow. Joins the PTA and all. Hookers do it all the time."

"She wasn't no hooker," Greco snapped.

Stupid move, Thorne told himself. Let Sonny deal with it on his own.

"Whatever she is—mother of the year, for all I care—she wouldn't set you up for a ripoff."

"That's not all I'm worried about," Greco said.

"What now?"

"It ain't crossed your mind that the cops might be watching Pizza Sal since he walked out of court?" Greco said. "Especially with all the heat on?"

"We're ready to make our buy and *now* you start worrying about Pizza Sal?"

"I'm starting to think straight," Greco said. "It happens when you're fighting for your life."

"You're getting paranoid."

"I'm telling you, Frank, there's too much spin on the ball. And you're too anxious to swing at it."

"The last thing Pizza Sal would do is throw you a curve," Thorne said, sounding as confident as he could. "He even 'fessed up about the money he held back. Heart attacks can give anybody religion."

"So can a stretch in prison," Greco said.

"You see any cops? Anything saying we shouldn't go in there and take care of business?"

"You go," Greco said flatly. "Tell Diane what happened, cut the best deal you can. With your money."

"We go together or not at all," Thorne insisted.

"That makes sense. Let's both take a pass."

Thorne knew what he had to do, and how it would sound on the tape. Okay, Sonny, you're smart enough to make your own breaks, he decided. But I'm not going to give the rest of it away. Not now, not this close.

"I can't drive out of here even if I wanted to," he said. "I'm the one's got problems with the law. Ever hear of the SEC, CFTC, like that?"

"Bullshit," Greco barked, his stare unrelenting as he grabbed the money case and shoved it onto Thorne's lap, freezing him against the wheel.

"Unlock that thing," he demanded. "I'm taking my cash out. You want the deal so bad, you go meet the lady and the spic."

"And do what with the merchandise?"

"Give it to your friends in the FBI!"

Before Thorne could move, Greco had the PPK drawn and aimed straight at his forehead. This time Thorne knew he could use it.

"We've been down this road before, Sonny. It goes nowhere."

"Too much spin on the ball," Greco repeated. "Too much spit."

Thorne tried to keep cool, hold the line between calling Jack Corrigan to the rescue and folding his hand forever. But in Greco's shaking grasp, the muzzle of the Walther looked larger than .38 inches.

"It was so slick I almost bought it," Greco snarled. "But something happened today you don't know about. I had to see the big boss again, help straighten out some business. You want to hear what he told me?"

"What the hell do I care?" Thorne shot back, thinking that if Clothesline had been blown apart and Bidwell hadn't warned him, he'd kick his damn . . .

"He told me a story he heard from Milwaukee," Greco went on. "About this executive type who tells the number one bookmaker up there he's got a lot of people in his company looking for action. Wants to know if this book can handle the big numbers, maybe work him in for a commission. That sound familiar, Frank?"

Thorne started his denial but Greco waved him quiet with the automatic.

"People up there were all making the big moves, always coming up winners. The old man is still pretty smart. So he checks with the Milwaukee family and gets a copy of their action. And guess what? Their sheets look like carbon copies of what your players have been doing to me and the other offices in town. Same games, same moves, day in and day out."

"Look, if there's been a setup, I'm the one who's been had. Maybe some judge figured he could buy his way out of a scandal by giving the feds . . ."

"I hoped for that too," Greco said. "Hoped like hell. Only this guy in Milwaukee gets himself recognized by one of the boys. Turns out he's an FBI agent named Olson. I bet you know him real good, Frank. See, I know you're playing for the same team."

"You *are* paranoid," Thorne said, feeling the sweat bead on his forehead, swearing to himself that if he lived through the night he'd get Bidwell in some alley and break his goddamn face.

"It was *sooo* smooth," Greco said. "Only tonight I got my brain jump-started. You know how I finally figured out who you're working for? Back at the hospital, Frank. I remember how it was when my old man had his heart attack. I remember my mother trying to fight her way in to see him. No chance, they tell her. Not when he's in cardiac care and not for twenty-four hours, until he's stabilized. But with Pizza Sal, we waltz right in his room like he's there for a checkup. The shine broad even hands me a pass card."

"She said it wasn't serious," Thorne tried to remind him.

"This is Sally's third trip," Greco said. "Two shots of angina, then a heart attack bad enough they're talking about a bypass. That's not serious?"

"So we caught a break," Thorne said.

"Somebody gave us the break. Because if we don't get to see him, you don't find out where this meeting's set. Which means you can't tip the cops."

"I never left your side," Thorne countered. "Who could I tip?"

"You're too smart to wear a wire, so it must be the car. Got a beeper on it, Frank? Something to call in the cavalry?"

Thorne saw Greco's hand shaking again and put his own on the steering wheel. What else was there? Greco had him cold and right in his sights.

"Even if I'm working with the feds," he said, "you're not dumb enough to blast me just to beat a gambling rap. All that'll buy you is a cell next to John Wayne Gacy's on death row."

"Only you wanted to trade me up for a narcotics bust," Greco said. "What was that going to buy *you*?"

"A little cooperation," Thorne admitted.

"You rat bastard!" Greco raged. "You *pushed* me into this deal. You and Pizza Sal started the ball rolling that night at the Cairo Club. I only came along to help my good buddy Frank Becker out of a hole. If that's even your name."

Thorne was surprised at how easy it was to tell Greco the truth.

"Frank Thorne," he said, knowing exactly where Greco was heading, willing to give him the out and take whatever else he could.

"Well, *Thorne*, I didn't want to get involved with this deal," Greco said. "Admit it!"

"I knew that all along," Thorne conceded. "I'm just surprised it took you this long to back down."

"So bust me right now if you're going to," Greco said. "But no way am I going in that room. My action's just taking phone calls. That's all you get."

Thorne saw Greco break into a weak grin as he lowered the automatic. Thorne let go of the wheel and took the gun from his outstretched hand.

"Everything's okay here," Thorne said loudly, hoping Corrigan hadn't decided to move too fast trying to bail him out. "I have weapons control and will go ahead on schedule. Stay with the plan. Repeat, stay with plan."

Greco exuded a deep sigh and slumped back against the door. Thorne placed an index finger across his lips; he had to keep Greco quiet until he hit the flasher button and broke off radio contact. Call it Plan B, call it whatever-the-fuck-will-work, but he had to cut the deck one more time.

"We're off the air," he said. "No ears, no tapes."

"Why? You want to say how sorry you are for nailing me to a cross?"

"That's part of it. And we have some business to talk over, things I don't want the Bureau to hear."

"You turned out to be one rotten cocksucker," Greco hissed. "I got to give you credit for big balls, but I'm not about to do any business with you."

"Lookit, Sonny, I'm a federal investigator, not some jerk vice cop looking for an easy bust to make quota. I've run the whole undercover operation against the Chicago family. I'm the one who has Johnny Ross locked away. All of which means I have a little latitude on how to handle this. You ought to know you're not the only book in trouble. The Bureau's dropping in on Tony Scarpo and Sandy Lowenstein right now. The locals are in for a piece too, rounding up your phone men, runners, anybody that's got a scrap of flash paper in his pocket."

"Sleep well, America," Greco sneered. "Your country's safe from the evil menace of betting on football games. Great job, Thorne. But I bet you'll still find some scumbag to take your rotten twenty-dollar-a-game action."

"I don't make the laws, Sonny."

"But you fuck your friends to make your salary."

"I didn't want it that way," Thorne said.

"But that's how it is. So me and Shoes and Sandy will have to serve a few years. What the hell, doing federal time, we get to polish up our short game."

"Listen to me—"

"Go fuck yourself!"

"I'm offering you a break," Thorne yelled back.

"For what? Wire me and send me over to talk business with the old man? Give me immunity if I put a hood over my head and testify? No thanks, pal. I'll take my chances with what I'm facing now. Which maybe ain't as much as you think."

"I know what I've got," Thorne said. "So I know you're making a mistake."

"I don't think so," Greco said smugly. "Entrapment's a real good defense, especially when it's on your own damn tape machine. You admitted dragging me into this, and Pizza Sal can tell the judge how you leaned on him when he's drugged out in the hospital, when I wanted to call it quits. I'll walk just like that car-man did, only in one-tenth the time."

"You've got a quick mind," Thorne said. "Only I knew what you were doing, spouting all that crap about *never* wanting to do this deal. I opened the door and *gave* you the out. That's going to cost me, Sonny. I'm supposed to know better."

"Tell me you did it for old time's sake. Because we're pals."

"I did it because I don't want to see you dead," Thorne said calmly. "You told me what happens if the family puts you within a mile of a drug deal. You'll end up in a trunk like Chuckie Franco, whether the old man likes you or not."

"You're all heart, worrying about me like that," Greco sneered. "But you can still go screw. I'd end up the same way playing ball with the feds."

"I'm not asking you to," Thorne said. "That went south the minute you backed out of the buy."

"Then what?"

"I need your help," Thorne said. "Here and now."

"So you can bust Diane and grab a few keys of blow? You've got to be hard up, Thorne. Even though you'll make it sound like a hundred-million dollars when it hits the papers."

"I don't give a rat's ass about the drugs, or Diane and her playmate. I've got other business to settle— somebody I'm expecting to crash our party, a crooked cop I want real bad. Now, I try walking in there alone, chances are Diane and Delgado will walk away. No Sonny Greco, no Pizza Sal, who'd blame them? Their merchandise is good anywhere. But I can't let them walk until . . ."

"Jesus, you *do* have balls," Greco said in amazement. "How many other scams you got going tonight?"

"With you on the record turning down the buy, one less than I thought," Thorne said. "But I still need you to help me."

"To keep the game going until your friend shows up?"

"It's a tight timetable," Thorne said. "Without you along, it probably won't hold up. And the odds will be three-to-one against me."

"If I say no?"

"I go in anyway and do the best I can."

"You're saying I can walk out of here," Greco said.

"Sure, go over to Dead Dom's and wait to be arrested by someone else. Because I'm still going inside and try to hold it together."

"Three-to-one's long odds."

"It's the only line in town," Thorne said.

Greco said, "Problem is, something goes wrong and

you get yourself bumped off, I got more than a book-making rap to worry about. No entrapment defense will work if a fed gets wasted."

"You make me feel real confident."

"I'm just thinking that we need each other."

"I won't ask you to snitch on the family," Thorne promised. "The drug charge is dead and I'll do the best I can for you with the rest of it. My management has to be satisfied since we got Scarpo and Lowenstein and Johnny Ross."

"No guarantees," Greco knew.

"Just my word I'll do all I can for you."

"What about Pizza Sal?"

"You really do look out for your friends."

"Try it sometime."

"I'll wash Sally out on a 4F," Thorne said. "No sense having Uncle Sam pick up the tab for his bypass. But Diane and her pal take the full fall. No way out of that one."

"Too bad," Greco said. "But maybe her kid's got a better shot if Diane's not around. The grandmother's an okay lady."

"Sonny we have to move" Thorne said. "Go or no-go?"

Greco reached over and took back the automatic.

"I'll cover your scheming ass," he grinned. "Only some day you're gonna cut one deal too many and get yourself in real trouble."

MaryAgnes McCaskey clutched at her stomach as the nausea overpowered her. She lunged into the bathroom and heaved a rank mixture of bile and blood into the toilet. Lieutenant Jack Corrigan's voice sounded miles away.

"You all right?"

"I'll make it," she said, splashing cold water on her face and accepting the towel from Corrigan's hand.

"We should have moved in and taken Massey right here," he said. "You ran one helluva risk."

"Worth it," McCaskey said as the pain welled in her abdomen. "As long as you got all of it."

"Every word. I can't wait to bust the prick with his pockets full of dope."

"*You* can't."

She dried her face and felt the cut flesh inside her cheek. Corrigan took her arm, helped her back into the living room. A detective named Carl was removing the mikes and concealed cameras.

"Take Agent McCaskey over to Northwestern emergency," Corrigan instructed him. "Get her checked out. I'm going to start this show moving."

"I'm fine," McCaskey insisted. She suddenly pulled away from Corrigan as if just realizing who he was.

"Why the hell are you still here, lieutenant? You should be covering Frank at the motel."

"Damn right I should," Corrigan said, knowing he had to tell her. "Only Thorne's radio went dead when he and Greco got to the hospital. We haven't picked up a peep since then. So I had to hang around here and hope he'd figure out a way to get in touch with you."

"You mean he's out there alone?"

"We're rolling now," Corrigan said. "Don't worry, he knows how to stay afloat."

"Dead radio," McCaskey moaned in disbelief. "The whole operation riding on . . ."

"I can't figure it either," Corrigan said. "We checked and doublechecked everything. He was pulling into the car-park at Gottlieb, everything was fine. Then we heard this *pop* and nothing but dead air."

"It's ten o'clock now," McCaskey saw. "Get moving, Jack. Please."

Corrigan directed his people to get the Massey tapes downtown and put under lock-and-key with the state's attorney. On his way to the door, he stopped and put a warm hand on McCaskey's shoulder.

"Good thing Thorne got word to you," he said, "or we still wouldn't know where Catania had set the meeting."

"He *didn't* get word to me," McCaskey said tensely. "Frank still thinks you're monitoring his transmissions from the car."

"Then how?"

"As soon as I heard that Catania was in the hospital, I sent an agent over to wire his room. The only chance we had to tie Catania into the deal was to get it on tape. But that was only supposed to be backup."

"So you weren't stringing Massey out with that Starbright, Starlight stuff."

"Catania's voice was weak, barely audible when I heard the tape played back. But I never thought you'd lost contact with Frank."

"Jesus H.," Corrigan sighed. "Some operation."

"Get moving!" McCaskey yelled again.

"You got a lot of guts, lady," Corrigan said as he took the arrest team with him, leaving behind only the cop who was ordered to get MaryAgnes McCaskey to the hospital no matter how much she protested.

19

THORNE could hear nervous chattering inside the motel room after Greco knocked and identified himself. The man who called himself Kerry Delgado unfastened the safety chain and opened the door. Thorne saw he was a tall, light-complexioned Hispanic, nattily dressed in navy blue trousers and pastel-striped shirt. He also had a Beretta .25-caliber Jetfire palmed snugly in his left hand.

"Where's Catania?" Delgado asked.

"Change of plan," Thorne said, stepping in first. "You've got a new banker tonight."

Thorne held up the briefcase to catch Delgado's attention, Greco walked straight toward Diane. She sat tensely at the foot of the rumpled bed, her usually tight blond curls wilted, as if she'd just climbed out of the shower or, more likely, Thorne figured, out of Delgado's embrace. He could only hope Greco had too much else on his mind to notice as well.

"Sal swore to me he'd come alone," Diane said. "I didn't want you to know."

"We'll do business as usual," Greco said. "As long as your friend here brought the goods."

"Where's Pizza Sal?" Diane persisted. "What happened?"

"On sick leave at Gottlieb Memorial," Greco said. "Those chest pains of his went from *agita* to angina to a first-class heart attack. He caught it this afternoon. Good thing he had some playmates from the club around to call the medics."

"God, poor Sally," Diane sighed.

"He'll pull through. Like always," Greco said.

"I don't like it," Delgado bitched. "We're supposed to do business with S.J."

Greco spun around and faced him squarely, staring him down hard, either not seeing or not caring about the Beretta.

"Call the hospital, you don't believe me," he shouted.

"It's the truth," Thorne said, stepping between them. "Sal only told us to come here when we went to see him at Gottlieb. He said there's no reason we shouldn't do business without him.

Diane stood and took Delgado's arm. She spoke softly, telling him it was fine.

"Sonny's the one I told you about," she said. "The one Sal used to work for."

"You remember Frank," Greco said.

"Haven't seen you around for a while," Diane said. "How's your friend Mary?"

"Fine," Thorne lied, trying to force the thought of her with Tom Massey from his mind. "We should get together sometime, celebrate a successful venture."

"Sure," Diane said, but seemed uncomfortable with the idea.

"If you're through with your class reunion, maybe we can get on with business," Delgado spoke up.

"As soon as you put that belly gun away," Thorne said.

"For God's sake, Kerry. They're friends of mine," Diane agreed.

Delgado begrudgingly stuck the baby automatic in

his back pocket. Thorne extended his hand; Delgado's was cool and dry, which meant he had all the nerve it took to use the Beretta.

"Fix us a drink," he told Diane.

"Sounds good to me," Thorne said, still buying time.

Diane began unwrapping the plastic glasses that sat on the pine dresser. Greco filled them with ice from a grimy plastic bucket.

"I would have told you about this when the time was right," Diane whispered. "As soon as it was safe for you."

"No sweat," Greco said. "A girl's got to live."

"It'll all be fine," she assured him.

Diane handed Thorne a Scotch rocks, then brought Delgado a bourbon and Coke. The look she gave him underscored that there was more to their relationship than business.

"To everybody doing well," Thorne said, bumping glasses with Diane.

"Believe it," she said.

Delgado pressed ahead.

"Before we start any party, I'd like to see the color of your money."

"You see the green when we see the white," Greco broke in. "That's the way it works."

"The man has a right," Thorne said, trying to keep everyone cool. He placed the briefcase on the bed, opened the lid.

"This should make you more comfortable. All used bills, only a few thousand in sequence."

Thorne saw that Delgado was used to cash: seeing it, counting it, making certain it wasn't queer or wearing any marks. Behind his back Diane took Greco's hand and squeezed it gently. She was keeping her balance perfectly, playing both sides in a masterful performance of trust. But Thorne still wondered how she could wind it up without turning into Lady Macbeth.

"The money's right," Delgado announced.

"We'll break it down later," Diane said as she looked longingly at the stacks of bills. "What's yours and what's mine."

"Your turn for show and tell," Greco said.

"The stuff is terrific," said Diane. "You'll be real happy."

"I will be when Pizza Sal's back on his feet."

"Don't worry about that," Diane said. "I have some names for you, people who'll handle the merchandise at a good price."

"I was worried about him getting well," Greco said coolly.

"Sure, so am I."

As they talked, Delgado went into the bathroom and began unscrewing a vent cover. Thorne moved to the door and slipped the bolt. With any luck at all, it would be Massey first, Corrigan second. It had better be.

Delgado emerged from the john carrying two orange nylon rucksacks. Diane took one from him; they sat together on the bed unfastening the pack laces.

"We just sit still?" Greco whispered to Thorne.

"That's it."

"I don't like people talking behind my back," Delgado snapped. "It makes me nervous."

"We didn't take no vow of silence," Greco shot back. "Worry about your own end."

Diane again defused the confrontation.

"Take a look at this, gentlemen," she said, pointing to the rectangular packages spread over the bed. "Ten kilos, all broken down in twenty-three one-pound bags. The extra pound was Pizza Sal's special commission. Even if he's out of it, a bargain's a bargain, right?"

"I told you he's the best," Greco nodded at Thorne.

Delgado took out a penknife and carefully slit open a wax-sealed package.

"Try it out," he said. "Use a kit, use your nose,

whatever you want. It's top-quality Peruvian, refined in the good old U.S.A. so you don't have to worry about bad chemicals."

"So we heard," Greco said.

He took the bag and rubbed some powder across the tip of his tongue.

"You don't mind if we make our own draw," said Thorne, grabbing two other bags at random.

"Do what you want," Delgado replied casually. "Lay out some lines, you'll see how good it is."

"We'll test it our way," Thorne said, "so nobody ends up with a nose full of ketamine."

"You think I'd pull shit like that?" Delgado fumed. "You think I'm some goddamn bandit from—"

"They don't know who you are," Diane intervened. "Don't blame him for being careful."

She took Delgado's knife and opened one of the bags in Thorne's hand. She said, "For someone who works on La Salle Street, you know all the tricks of the trade."

"Where do you think most of this stuff ends up?" Thorne smiled back.

Diane dipped the tip of the knife into the bag and took a large hit. "Terrific," she sighed, dipping in again and bringing the blade up to Thorne's nose.

Delgado had finished checking the cash and started transferring it to the rucksacks.

"We got no time to throw a party," he said. "Let them get high. We're hitting the bricks."

"You're leaving with him?" Greco asked Diane.

"Sonny, listen to me for a minute," she began. "There's something you have to understand . . ."

Thorne, still guessing at how she'd handle the kiss-off, was almost sorry she didn't have the chance to play it out. But Tom Massey kicking his way through the door made her apologies futile.

Massey came in fast and low, his right hand steady on the thick combat grips of the Police Bulldog that stuck out in front of him like a jouster's lance. Delgado made a dumb move for the automatic in his back pocket. Thorne tried to grab his wrist, but Massey was quicker.

"Reach back there, you lose an arm," Massey yelled. "Now everybody stand real still. Don't get nervous in the service here."

"Listen to the man," Thorne said, throwing Greco a reassuring nod. "Do what he says."

"That's the first smart thing I've heard out of you, Frank."

Massey scanned the room carefully. Satisfied everyone was covered, he kicked the door closed behind him. The shattered links of the safety chain fell jingling to the floor amidst the shards of the door jamb that had held it.

"Well, how about this," Massey said as he fingered the bags and money-filled rucksacks that were still scattered across the bed. "When you say you're making a move, Frank, you're not just whistling through your teeth."

"You'll get your money," Thorne said. "Just like I told you."

"That a fact?" Massey hissed. "I thought all I got was some free time with that puss of yours, and maybe a few measly thousand."

"You guys are working partners," Delgado guessed. "Well let me tell you what happens to people who try ripping—"

"Shut up, Pedro," Massey barked back. "Don't you know first-class police work when you see it?"

He reached into his coat and flipped open the wallet that held his police star. Diane let out a mournful moan, Delgado's eyes flashed at her with unconcealed rage. Massey was thoroughly enjoying his moment, Thorne knew.

"I pick up this phone, and everybody here pulls hard time," Massey said. "Just like this."

Delgado saw Massey's eyes drop as he feigned dialing. He rolled forward on the balls of his feet and made a tennis-serve grunt as he lunged toward Massey's revolver.

He was halfway there when Thorne planted the rabbit punch on the back of his neck.

"Hold it!" Thorne hollered at Massey, who had his sights lined on the fallen Delgado.

"You dumb fuck!" Massey screamed. "Try that again, you buy yourself a harp."

Thorne reached down, pulled the Beretta from Delgado's pocket and threw it on the bed.

"Nobody's going to screw with you," he said. "Get that hammer back down."

"It would cost me a lot to ace any of you," Massey growled. "But Frank here will tell you I got no problems doing it."

"Okay, please," Diane said. "It's not worth dying for."

"I've gotta like all your sweet ladies," Massey leered at Thorne.

Delgado pulled himself to his knees and started bitching about warrants, about Massey not knowing who owned the goods or the money, about how his case was full of holes.

"Detective Massey isn't here to bust anybody," Thorne said. "He wants a piece of our action, not a departmental citation."

"I told you he's a smart man," Massey said.

"A fucking shakedown," Delgado fumed.

"Shakedown my ass," Massey said. "I'm here to protect your interests, to keep the bad guys away. I want all you people to make a nice profit. This way you'll come back to town and we'll do business again. Chicago's the commodities center of the world, right? And you've got the greatest commodity I know of."

"I'm not looking for partners, or protection," Delgado said. He started pulling himself upright, but Massey's thick oxford brogue landed hard in his ribcage.

"You got one now, asshole!"

Delgado coughed in pain and sank down again to his hands and knees.

"Stop it!" Diane cried out. She went to Delgado, tried helping him up. Her teary eyes flashed at Greco, who stood paralyzed against the dresser.

"You did this to us," she yelled. "You did it."

"Take it easy," Thorne said. "It's nobody's fault."

"You got too much pussy involved in your business," Massey said. "Who's this one?"

"She's just along for the ride."

"I got it. A little blow for a little head."

"Drop dead, you creep," Diane spit at him.

"A real toughie," Massey laughed, poking the Bulldog in her direction. "Pretty too."

Delgado, back on his feet, made a growling noise. Thorne knew he couldn't keep it together much longer and wondered what the hell Jack Corrigan was waiting for.

"How much will it take for you to get lost?" he asked.

"The fucker wants all of it," Delgado said.

"You think I'm that greedy? Or that stupid?" Massey said. "I rip off the whole deal, I got nothing but crazy spics from Miami, Colombia, God knows where else, coming after my ass. So let's see here," he said, making a quick inventory of the goods. "About ten kilos in one-pounders, figure three hundred dimes, more or less, in those bags. I make it a ten percent shot. Thirty thousand's only fair."

"A nice round number," Thorne said.

Massey picked up three stacks of one-hundred hundreds each and stuffed them in his jacket.

"Plus a little something to pick me up, keep the party going."

"Only one bag," Thorne insisted, wondering how

long he could keep Massey in the room. "More than that and people who don't give a damn about your star will get real unhappy."

"I'm petrified," Massey said. "But a pound should hold me until you want to do business again."

"Next time you'd better hire yourself an army," Delgado snarled.

Massey's gun hand wavered slightly as he picked up the cocaine. Delgado looked like he was going to try another move, but before he could set his feet, Massey had the Bulldog's front sight stuck under his nose.

"Why do you keep trying to fuck with me, Pedro? Be happy with what you're making here. Walk away a winner or you go back to Cuba in a box. *Comprende?*"

Delgado backed off.

"I don't understand you people," Massey said. "Down south you pay big money to keep the cops happy. But you want to come up here, the depressed industrial north, and you want to walk away scot-free. That's dumb, Pedro. So remember this: Next time you want to do business in Chicago, you make sure Frank lets me know in advance and I'll guarantee you safe conduct for a fraction of what it costs down south. See, the mayor's got this big campaign going to bring new business to town. I got to do my part, right?"

"You mick asshole," Delgado growled.

Massey held the revolver steady and opened the door behind him. "We'll do this again sometime," he sneered back at Delgado.

Thorne watched helplessly as Massey stepped into the corridor and left nothing behind but the sound of disappearing footsteps. Jack Corrigan? What the hell was going on?

A second later, Delgado was in his face.

"You set this up," he yelled.

"Sure, so I could cost myself fifteen thousand."

"Thirty," Delgado said. "You know the man, so you pay him."

"Bullshit, we split the loss," Greco said.

Thorne didn't see it happen, but sensed Delgado had given Diane some kind of prearranged signal. Her scream froze Thorne and Greco as it shook the room. Delgado never hesitated as he dove for the bed and came up with the Beretta.

"Nobody rips me off. Never."

Thorne saw him flip the safety and bring the gun into firing position. This time he believed he'd see the final flash. Only Greco came in from the left, stepping in front of Thorne to make his parry.

When the gun went off it was pressed into Greco's right pectoral muscle; his flesh suppressed the explosion but before the resonating stopped, Greco's shoulder was spurting blood.

"No!" Diane screamed again, this time imploring Delgado not to shoot.

"These fucks," Delgado swore. "I should off them both."

"Come on," Diane said, tugging on Delgado's empty hand. "We've got it all. Don't mess up by killing anybody."

It took Delgado several seconds to stop shaking and regain his cool. Thorne stood motionless, hoping the shot would finally bring Corrigan inside. Greco was sprawled across the bed, moaning softly, blood seeping through the fingers he pressed over his wound.

"Grab the cash and take a key of soda with it," Delgado said at last. "That'll make up our loss."

"That the way you want it?" Thorne asked Diane, hoping to keep a discussion alive.

"I kept my part of the bargain," she said icily. "The cop's your headache. Sorry about Sonny, but it was a stupid thing to try."

She gathered the cash and two bags of coke, and stuffed it all into the rucksacks. Delgado couldn't resist the temptation to settle his score with Thorne. He planted a solid left on the jaw; Thorne fell backward into the dresser, taking the booze bottles down with him. He waited for Delgado's follow-up kick to the groin, but Diane saved him.

"Let's go, Kerry. Please."

"Behind you," he replied.

Diane stopped to check Greco's shoulder. "You'll be all right," she said.

"Just great," Greco winced.

"You'll still make out on the deal. Sal will have to cut it back some more, but the stuff is strong enough to take it. You'll be fine."

Greco rolled his head sideways and looked at his bleeding shoulder. "See you around," he said.

"I don't think so," Diane said, trying to sound dejected. "I've dreaded telling you this, but I'm through with this town."

"You and Delgado are a team."

"Take care of Camille and the twins," Diane said. "Just remember how much fun we had."

"Yeah, great party," Greco snickered.

"This way!" Delgado ordered as he pulled back the black-out curtain and motioned Diane out the patio door. "Get the car started. I'm right behind you."

"Leave them alone," Diane pleaded.

"Take her advice," Thorne said. "Don't go super-macho over a bum deal, especially when it cost you nothing."

"Come through this curtain before we're out of here," Delgado said, "I'll give you back the one your pal took for you."

"You've got the cards," Thorne said, hearing the Caprice kick over. "The pot's yours."

"Adios, motherfucker."

When Delgado pulled the curtain closed, Thorne went to the bed and checked Greco's wound. The slug had angled upwards, penetrating the flesh beneath the collar bone but, luckily, missing it and coming out of Greco's armpit with little damage. Thorne ripped Sonny's shirt-sleeve apart and put a pressure bandage over the entry wound.

"I'm sure glad Pizza Sal told us Delgado was a class guy," Greco said.

"Hold this tight. It'll stop the bleeding."

"Great operation you run," Greco winced again. "I'm still trying to figure out if you're really a cop or working with that scumbag Massey. And what the hell happened to the cavalry?"

"Shut up and listen to me," Thorne commanded. "Is that Walther traceable?"

"I got it from Dom. He said it was clean."

"Then wipe it down good and stick it under the mattress. You've never seen it before."

Greco struggled to dust the piece over the sheets as Thorne parted the curtain. All he could make out were a few more cars in the courtyard.

"Where the hell are you?" he muttered. "Where? Where? Where?"

"What now?" Greco said.

Before Thorne could answer, the sound of a bull-horn roared in the courtyard.

This is the police! Drop your weapon and stop where you are! This is the police!

"Stay right here," Thorne said. "Don't talk to any-one until I get back."

Greco tried to smile.

"This has to be the biggest fuck-up I've ever seen," he said. "I think Pizza Sal's the luckiest one of all."

"I've got a feeling you're right," Thorne said as he ducked through the curtain.

Three unmarked Chicago police cars formed a barri-cade at the entrance of the Stardust Courts, their headlights now on high beam and blinding Thorne as he stepped from the room with hands high. Finally he heard Jack Corrigan's amplified voice telling his men to let go of their triggers: The man in their sights was a federal agent.

Thorne moved out of the headlights' throw, saw Diane and Delgado spread-eagled across the front fenders of the station wagon. Delgado cursed out the policeman searching him until a firm hand on his genitals turned the profanity to a whimpering groan. Diane had hit her tear button, but no one was buying her act, least of all Lieutenant Corrigan, who stood next to her stoically and used the car hood as a table to spill out the contents of the orange rucksacks.

"Nice haul," he said as Thorne approached. "You got the rest of the soda inside?"

"Where the hell have you been?" Thorne asked back angrily. "You forget we had a timetable?"

"We had problems."

You had problems? I almost took one in the gut."

"You look fine to me."

"Don't play cute, Jack. I came within an inch of walking a beat in St. Peter's precinct."

Corrigan refilled the sacks and looked at Thorne calmly.

"Beats hell out of me. Your damn radio went dead halfway through the show. We had you on line as far as the hospital, then nothing."

"The tape recorder too?"

"I checked your trunk," Corrigan nodded. "The whole system was power-out—transmitter, backup recorder, everything. If Agent McCaskey didn't have the smarts to put a mike inside Catania's hospital room, we wouldn't be here at all."

Thorne slumped against the car and looked into the night sky. Greco had called it right: a complete fuck-up.

"You can't blame the tech boys if you back into a wall," Corrigan said. "I think that's what knocked you off the air."

"What'd you expect me to do? Ask Greco to fix it?"

"Where is my friend Sonny Greco?"

"In there," Thorne said. "He took a slug with my name on it through his shoulder."

"I'll call an ambulance."

"An aid-man can handle it for now. I'll take Greco downtown myself and get him looked after."

Corrigan stopped a plainclothesman and told him to check out the man still in the room.

"You'll also find a briefcase full of cocaine," Thorne told him.

"I should have iced your ass," Delgado spit at Thorne. This time Corrigan silenced him with a 180-degree twist of his ear lobe.

"Those two make a nice-looking couple," Corrigan said. "Like a yearbook picture. Class Felons."

"I've got a few things to say to Tom Massey. Where do you have him?"

"Massey?" Corrigan asked in surprise. "We never even *saw* him."

"You what?"

"I figured he grew some brains and decided to keep his nose clean," Corrigan said. "We never saw a sign of him."

"Dammit, he ducked out five minutes ahead of these two with a pile of cash and a pound of blow."

Before Corrigan could speak, Thorne got to his car and pulled the Model 19 from the glove compartment. He sprinted into the gangway that connected the main wings of the motel. Corrigan was beside him quickly. Thorne checked the east corridor, Corrigan the north.

"Nothing," the lieutenant said.

"If his car wasn't out front," Thorne started thinking, "where could he drop it?"

"There's a gin-joint behind this place," Corrigan said.

They raced behind the filled-in swimming pool and found the gate in the chain-link fence surrounding the Stardust Courts.

"Unlocked," Thorne said.

They moved through the field behind the motel like advancing infantry, coming out of the mud and weeds in the parking lot of a go-go joint named Mickey's Mouse House. Tom Massey's department car sat on the far side of the bar between a Jeep Renegade and an ancient Buick. Corrigan moved up to it with his snub-nose drawn; Thorne covered him from behind the Buick.

"Empty," Corrigan confirmed.

Thorne lowered his weapon. Even with five minutes' head start, where could Massey . . . ?

It hit him in a flash.

"Back!" he yelled at Corrigan. "Back inside the motel."

Corrigan gave him a confirming nod before kneeling out of Thorne's view.

"That'll keep him here," Corrigan said as he folded up Delgado's pocket knife and listened to the rush of air emanating from the slit he'd opened in Massey's front tire.

Thorne was back in the gangway first. He stood with his chest heaving until Corrigan caught up.

"Have your people cover the exits at the end of each wing," Thorne said. "And get somebody inside the office."

"You know where he is?"

"I'll bet you a dozen steak dinners Massey flashed his star to the manager and picked up a pass key. I didn't think about it because I unlocked the room door and he just had to bust the safety chain. But that's how he opened the gate."

"Then he's gone," Corrigan guessed.

"I say he's waiting it out inside, figuring he can slip out the back when we're not looking."

"Watch yourself," Corrigan said.

He hit the parking lot in sprinter's form and began directing the arrest team to seal off the hallways. Thorne

took a deep breath and slowly opened the glass door
that led into the longest wing of the motel.

He eased his way past the soda and ice machines in
a small pantry. The first door he put his ear against
vibrated with the beat of Salsa music: somebody was
throwing a party and didn't give a damn about bright
lights and bullhorns. Farther down the hall he heard a
young woman's voice nervously asking about the arrests.

"They got some guy and a girl in cuffs," a man
answered.

"Whew, thank God," the girl sighed. "I thought my
father might have sent them."

"Your father?"

"Yeah," said the girl, who Thorne placed as the one
carrying the bottle in a bag. "He's deputy chief of
patrol, or something."

"Son-of-a-bitch!"

Thorne kept moving.

All he heard as he passed the next rooms was the
whirr of the ventilation system rattling loose duct plates.
He was almost to the end of the wing when a door
creaked open behind him.

Thorne spun around and dropped to one knee.

Detective Tom Massey stepped halfway out into the
corridor. Thorne caught his break when Massey looked
the other way first and brought his right, flannel-
trousered leg fully out of the room. All the rules said
Thorne had to issue a warning. Even Tom Massey was
entitled to that much, a chance to drop his weapon
and go in peacefully.

Thorne mouthed the words in a whisper his heart-
beat overpowered.

Then he fired.

The + P soft point hit Massey squarely in the knee.
The patella seemed to pop through the shredded pants
leg like an exploding bottle cap. It sailed against the
off-side corridor wall in a mass of gore and bony
shrapnel.

Massey went down in a twisting, screaming ball of pain. Thorne was over him instantly, tearing the Bulldog from his quivering hand. It didn't matter much: Massey went into shock and stared sightlessly at the ceiling.

Thorne bent over and took twenty thousand from Massey's pockets, making sure he had the other ten and the cocaine still on him. Then he found the wallet holding Massey's star and Miranda card.

"Here," Thorne said as he stuck the card between Massey's teeth.

"Sufferin' Jesus, what happened?" Jack Corrigan asked as he kneeled next to Thorne.

"I was reading Massey his rights," Thorne said. "I got as far as silent."

Thorne watched the ambulance carrying Tom Massey and a pair of special cops from Internal Affairs roll out of the Stardust Courts parking lot.

"We could of made a fortune off those jerks," Massey had said when the morphine kicked in, before he realized it was Thorne who'd blown apart his knee.

"I had enough partners already," Thorne replied.

"Like who?"

"Jack Corrigan for one. And Agent McCaskey of the Bureau. She's the one you call sweet puss."

Massey growled a hard consonant as Thorne slammed the ambulance door and signaled the driver to get him the hell out of there.

The arrest team began climbing into their cars and heading home. When the coast looked clear, the young couple who'd arrived in the Trans Am dashed bottleless from their room and skidded off into the night. Thorne finished his cigarette and went back to Room 112.

Sonny Greco sat on the bed wearing half a shirt. A white taped bandage wrapped his shoulder just above the sling cradling his arm to his chest. Greco's eyes moved from Corrigan to Thorne and down to his manacled wrists.

"Take those cuffs off him," Thorne commanded.

"Wish I could," Corrigan replied. "But it's gone too far for that. I'm afraid all bets are off."

"Another screwing," Greco said, biting his lip.

"We had a bargain," Thorne insisted. "Nothing changes that. Greco walks out of here with me."

"A matter of jurisdiction now," Corrigan said. "I've got a shooting team and half of IAD outside. The watch commander is yelling like hell about us moving in his district without prior notification, and a deputy chief's on his way here thinking Tom Massey's some kind of hero. No way I can let you skip with Greco."

"Greco came in here on my side," Thorne said. "Not only did he stop a bullet, but he helped me keep things going until you finally turned up. If my radio hadn't blown, you'd have that on tape."

"Only it did and we don't," Corrigan said. "There's nothing I can do about that."

"I trusted you, Jack," Thorne said bitterly. "I figured if anyone would keep their word, you were it."

"What do you want from me?" Corrigan complained. "Greco's girlfriend is telling everybody that he set up the whole buy. She just came along for the ride and the party, she says. It was all Greco and that guy Querino Delgado."

"That's Diane," Greco snickered. "She'd turn Flipper into tuna salad to save her ass."

"Sure, Greco set up the deal," Thorne said. "But by that time he was working with me. I'll testify to that if you want, Jack. All that'll get Greco is a terminal spanking from the family."

"I think you're lying through your teeth," Corrigan snapped. "But if you take full responsibility here, I won't fight you on it."

"Take off the cuffs. Greco's a protected federal

witness. Tell that to your watch commander or whoever the hell else wants to know."

"They won't like it," Corrigan said as he carefully
slipped the handcuffs from Greco's wrists. "But what
do they know about undercover cops."

"How about another favor?" Thorne asked as he
grabbed Corrigan warmly by the neck. "Get on the
horn and find out from the Bureau's dispatcher if it's
wrapped up with Scarpo and Lowenstein. We're not
going to get any second chances after tonight. I want
to make sure we got it all."

"Will do," Corrigan said. He started for the door,
then turned back to Thorne as if suddenly remembering something. "By the way, Agent McCaskey did one
helluva job tonight. She went all the way with Massey,
right to the mat. Wait until you see the instant replay."

"She's okay?"

"Will be. Massey roughed her up a little, but she
held on tight. I had her delivered to Northwestern for
a look-see. Just some bruises, a shiner and a cut cheek."

"God damn him!" Thorne raged.

"I'd say losing a kneecap settles the score," Corrigan
grinned. "What do you think, Sonny? Can you see
Massey limping his way around Stateville for ten years?"

"I thought the outfit played rough," Greco said.
"But you guys are unbelievable."

"Spread that around to your pals," Corrigan said.
"We could use a tougher reputation on the street."

"After tonight, who do you think's gonna listen to
me?"

Corrigan chuckled as he flipped the handcuffs into
his coat pocket.

"I still got a lot of paper to push," he said. "I'll
clear things for you and Greco on the way out. Let's
talk soon, Frank."

"Let me know if the brass gives you a hard time,"
Thorne said. "I'm not sure now where my stock is

with the Bureau, but I think Doc Hermann will keep the lid on for us."

"I've been there before," Corrigan said. "And Sonny, consider yourself lucky. If you're gonna have somebody stand up for you, this guy's as good as there is."

"Yeah, he's a prince," Greco said.

Thorne found the knocked-over bottle of Scotch and drained the remaining few ounces into a glass. He took a quick shot and handed the rest to Greco.

"I'm loaded up with pain killers," Greco said. "But give me one of your smokes. I'm not going to be around long enough to catch cancer."

"You'll be all right," Thorne said, handing him a lit cigarette. "We'll head down to the Bureau tonight and work up a statement. Corrigan will keep things quiet until I can wash this out with my bosses."

"What am I looking at?"

"Violation of federal wagering laws, maybe some tax problems," Thorne said. "It's the lowest I can go, the lowest you'd want me to go. Anything less and the family's liable to think you were saying something you shouldn't."

"You know," Greco ruminated, "when we first got together, I really thought my luck was going to change. Only I never guessed which way. First you break my bank and start a war inside the family. Now I end up getting a federal bust and a slug in the shoulder that cost me a hundred grand to buy."

"The money's evidence," Thorne said. "Nothing I can do about that. For the rest, I think it's better you take your chances in court so your friendly nephews don't ask too many questions."

"Then what? You got a special place to send bookmakers you used to be friends with? Something with a view?"

"I promised I'd do what I can," Thorne said. "Be happy you're walking way from a narcotics charge."

"I did that for myself. And you guys have my bank-roll on top of it."

Thorne hoped he could deliver on the next words he spoke.

"I don't think there's hard time in front of you," he said. "As long as you understand you're out of the business for good."

"I was thinking about a career change," Greco said. "The old man himself recommended it."

"Listen to him."

Thorne picked up Greco's jacket and wrapped it around his shoulders.

"We'd better get moving. I'll try to get you processed before the press moves in and starts taking pictures."

Greco stood up and adjusted the makeshift sling.

"I'd better get hold of my lawyer," he said.

"It wouldn't hurt," Thorne said. "I'll call in some favors with the U.S. attorney and try for a low bond."

"I wonder if J. J. O'Connor will take my marker," Greco said. "That's about all I got left for a retainer."

"You that busted?"

"Tap City. Plus."

Thorne reached into his coat and pulled out the twenty thousand dollars he'd taken from Tom Massey.

"I saved this for you," he said. "Stick it in that sling of yours. The Bureau has enough cash in evidence to take care of Diane and her Latin lover."

"This for real?"

"It was yours to begin with," Thorne said.

Greco stood dumbstruck as Thorne tucked the two bundles of hundreds under his forearm.

"I'll make sure nobody peeks in there until your lawyer shows up," he said. "Consider yourself already searched."

"If I told the old man about this, he'd think I was the one going senile," Greco said in amazement. "A federal cop who blows off kneecaps hands me twenty dimes to make bail . . ."

"Maybe your luck *is* changing," Thorne said.

He steered Greco toward the door and out into the parking lot. A pair of uniformed cops were headed back into Room 112 for a final look. Thorne told them about the automatic hidden under the mattress, said he saw the girl put it there, only she had gloves on.

"Can't leave any loose ends," he told Greco. "So in case anyone asks, 'You have the right to remain silent. Anything you say can be used against you in a court of law.' All that bullshit."

20

IT WAS the fourth night in a row Thorne had endured with only fitful moments of sleep.

In McCaskey's dark, alley-side bedroom it was impossible to pinpoint when the street lamps died and sunrise began. Thorne guessed it was dawn when she awoke and reached out for him. He held her as carefully and gently as he had the night before, still mindful of the marks Tom Massey had left on her. Only this time she intensified her movements, urged him to stop babying her. She came with a sudden contralto cry when Thorne was high above her breasts, bending her knees over his shoulders. Had he been with Patsie, Thorne would have called it a grudge fuck. With MaryAgnes, he couldn't be sure what it was.

Afterward they were silent.

At seven o'clock MaryAgnes wrapped herself in a blue satin robe and announced she'd fix Sunday breakfast. Country style, she said, the way God intended breakfast to be before everyone got so hung up on cholesterol and fiber.

Thorne downed two giant mugs of coffee and a couple of Luckies while MaryAgnes worked in the tiny kitchen, moving almost frantically, as if racing an invisible timeclock. Patsie always behaved like that when a confrontation was imminent. Thorne guessed MaryAgnes was heading that way too: Now that the operation that threw them together was finished, she'd naturally want to know what came next.

Thorne wondered just when and how the questioning would start. All MaryAgnes asked was how he wanted his eggs.

"Over easy."

"I'll baste them. They're cooked the same, only you get the taste of bacon."

"Any way's fine," he said.

Thorne was on his third smoke when she delivered their plates. The satin robe seemed to reflect shimmers of blue light into her black hair. Somehow it reminded Thorne of the floodlit trees at the Stardust Courts.

"You didn't sleep again last night," she said.

Thorne hesitated before shaking his head.

"A little bit. It's a lot to come down from."

"I could understand if you were still up," she said. "Only you seem more depressed than wired. Sad, actually."

"Could be," Thorne admitted. "A natural let-down."

"I know you have problems with Bidwell. No matter how he thinks it should have gone, you did a great job. I think so, anyway."

"If I did, how come you got that?" Thorne asked, pointing to her cheek.

MaryAgnes touched the welt gingerly.

"Not my first black eye," she said. "Hopefully it's the last."

"You want to tell me about the others?"

"No, I don't."

"That ballplayer used to throw you the knuckleball whenever he got drunk?"

"Stop it, Frank! Whatever's bothering you, don't take it out on me. Please!"

Thorne apologized, claiming he didn't mean it the way it sounded.

"I keep sticking my finger in light sockets," he said.

"Give yourself some time to sort things out. You haven't had the luxury for a long while."

Thorne prodded an egg with his fork. The yolk was cooked on the outside, still liquid at the center, just the way he liked it. Patsie, he recalled as if it were decades ago, hated eggs in any form. In fact, the list of things she hated would take Thorne hours to compile. So why was he still thinking about her?

"I talked with my wife on Friday," he said. "A long talk."

"Don't feel you have to tell me about it."

"I want to. We're signing the final papers this week. The house in Evanston goes up for sale along with everything in it Patsie doesn't want."

"What do you keep?"

"I don't want anything," Thorne replied. "We split all we have right down the middle. After that, no alimony, no payments, nothing."

"You sound like Sonny Greco covering his bets," MaryAgnes said. "Or is that called laying off?"

"It's called a hedge against future liability," Thorne said. "Anyway, I thought you'd like to know it's over and done with. I don't even have to walk into a courtroom. *Nolo contendere.*"

"That's passive," MaryAgnes said. "What you plead when you know you can't win."

"Exactly."

She poured refills of coffee and watched Thorne eat half the food she'd cooked for him.

"I guess you'll start looking for someplace to live," she said.

"I thought after we wrap up the details and shut down the office, you'd be heading back to Rockford."

"So you'd like to move in here."

"Your name's still on the lease," Thorne said. "Don't make it sound like I'm asking you to leave."

"Thanks for that."

"I was only thinking out loud," Thorne backed off.

"At least have the courtesy to check with me first," MaryAgnes said. "Then you'd know that I applied to Doc Hermann for a transfer here. I've had it with ledgers and tax returns, I want to do more field work. Doc says my chances are good."

"The way you handled Tom Massey, I'd say so too. Which means I'd better start hunting up an apartment."

"Frank, it's not that I don't want to be with you," MaryAgnes said. "But I think it's just too easy to slide from one relationship into another. Some time alone will do you good."

"Look, I know I'm burned out," Thorne said. "But my getting a divorce has nothing to do with it."

"You may think that—even believe it. But no one walks away from a marriage feeling whole. You wouldn't be much of a man if you could."

"That's not it," Thorne insisted.

"If it's the way Bidwell has been leaning on you, stop worrying. He's gotten enough from Clothesline to look like a hero with the Director. As soon as the indictments come down, they'll all forget about your deal with Sonny Greco. Unless there's more to it."

Thorne felt he should tell her about the money, about a lot of other things he'd held back. But that would mean more talking and, on a fresh, sunny Sunday morning, it was the last thing he wanted.

"I'm not worried about Bidwell," he said. "I'm just thinking over the whole thing, my sticking it out with the Bureau or looking for something else. Maybe some kind of job where a guy who stops a bullet for me gets more than losing every cent he had to his name."

MaryAgnes grew impatient with his logic.

"You're doing it again, Frank, defining the law as *you* see it. It doesn't work that way. No cop can make the law fit his own private sense of what's right and what's wrong. Sonny Greco brought his bankroll along to buy drugs. Even though he smartened up at the last minute, it was still his call."

"So was going for Delgado's automatic."

"That's what's eating you? You stay awake nights because you think you betrayed your pal Sonny."

"Could be."

"I always thought you'd come up with a way to save his backside," MaryAgnes said. "And damn if you didn't. What's a bookmaking charge to him? Barely a wrist slap."

"I still think he deserves better."

"Like what?"

"A chance to get even," Thorne said.

"And you want to give it to him."

"I'll need your help."

"How?"

"Bidwell is keeping Operation Clothesline alive, thinking he can pull it off on the East Coast. I want you to go down to the office and access his data bank one more time."

"God," MaryAgnes erupted. "Are you serious?"

Their prearranged meeting place was the chess pavilion on North Avenue beach, at the foot of the long, question-mark breakwater that juts a quarter-mile out into Lake Michigan.

Thorne walked around the cluster of concrete tables, watched groups of elderly, Eastern-bloc refugees argue the subtleties of varying ploys and traps, all the players and kibitzers still wrapped in their long winter coats to guard against the warm but stiff lake breeze.

Greco arrived at eleven.

"Why all the mystery? You working as a spook now?" he asked, looking askance at the chessplayers. "Checking on all these Commies?"

"Let's walk," Thorne said.

Greco followed him silently onto the breakwater. Thorne sat on the stone retaining wall and looked south toward the Drake Hotel, the Hancock Building, the other towers of the glistening Michigan Avenue skyline.

"What's going on?" Greco asked nervously.

"Just wanted to check in with you," Thorne said. "See how your wing was feeling."

Greco said it was fine; even the throbbing had stopped.

"I figured you wanted to meet here because my phone is tapped," he said.

"Your phone *is* tapped," Thorne said. "Mine too, probably."

Greco thought he was joking and began to laugh.

"Because of the bad company you keep," he said.

"Is everything cool with the family?"

"So far," Greco said. "Funny thing, the word I'm getting is nobody knows who hit Sid Paris. He disappeared before the boys could find him. Maybe somebody from the outside took care of business for them? Or Paris went underground somewhere? Either way, it's like they're waiting for the other shoe to drop."

"So nobody's asking you a lot of questions."

"Naw," Greco shook his head. "Between that, the busts on Scarpo and Lowenstein, and Johnny Roses stashed at one of your hideouts, my problems with the law don't seem to matter much."

"They'll matter a lot less after Tuesday."

"What's Tuesday?"

"That's when Assistant Attorney General James Jonathan Bidwell comes to town and tells a press conference that Sid Paris has become a protected government witness and is going to spill everything he knows about the Chicago family."

"You're joking."

"For real," Thorne said.

"Jesus, I figured if Paris wasn't dead he'd probably

split for Costa Rica or someplace. But going to the feds . . ."

"Sid Paris didn't become one of the nephews by being stupid," Thorne said. "When he and Chuckie Franco made bail for the Ross hit, Paris knew to watch out for number one. He put a tail on Franco to make sure he wasn't doubling back and spilling to the cops. When he heard that the muscle had grabbed Franco, Paris knew he had to be next on the trunk roster."

"So he goes to the cops himself," Greco guessed.

"He's smarter than that," Thorne continued. "He figures there are too many leaks inside the CPD, and that maybe the family's keeping an eye on the Federal Building. So Sidney jumps on an Amtrak for Milwaukee and walks into the FBI office up there looking for immunity and witness relocation. Friend of mine named Vic Olson called me on it, the same Olson the old man told you was running a string of phony players. Olson's laughing his ass off on the phone, wondering what the hell's going on in Chicago that we can't even get the mob to trust us."

"Paris talks, the whole pot's gonna boil over."

"One reason I wanted to see you," Thorne said. "So far, only a handful of people know about Paris rolling over. I didn't even tell my partner. But I thought you had a right to get a head start."

"You mean out of town?"

"I mean as far away from the family and the old man as you can get. If that's out of town, then hit the road ASAP."

"In case you forgot," Greco said grimly, "I got a federal gambling rap hanging over my head."

"With all that Justice has to work on now, I can pretty much guarantee you're going to the bottom of their list. Besides, I got a few favors left to call in. One of them can be a tag on your release papers saying you're not confined to barracks. Who knows, by the time they get around to you, the evidence might be contaminated—too many spoons in the soup."

"Camille and me have been talking about making a break," Greco said, almost daydreaming. "Maybe head southwest. She's a little scared about leaving all the relatives. But for a fresh start, without all the ghosts, where the twins won't be pegged as outfit brats . . . I figure a good dago restaurant would go over big down there."

"Down where, exactly?"

"Wherever," Greco said. "Where nobody knows how to make good *marinara* sauce."

"Restaurants take cash up front," Thorne said. "You come into a recent inheritance?"

"I still got a line of credit," Greco said. "Somebody else who thinks restaurants are the way to go."

"You don't want that kind of backing. Not if you really want to shake loose from the family."

"Look, I appreciate what you did for me back at the motel," Greco said. "The twenty dimes will help a lot. But unless you want to see Sonny Greco delivering cheese again, I got to take advantage of every option I got. So if my father's best friend wants to loan me some start-up funds with no hooks in them, you expect me to say no?"

"Maybe I have something else for you."

"That why I'm here, Thorne? You still want to put me on your payroll?"

"Not a chance," Thorne grinned. "We're full up."

"So what, then?"

"So you know any books around who are still open for big action? People you trust to pay off if they lose?"

"Come on, ain't you got enough off me?" Greco moaned. "You guys got conspiracy charges floating around that make Watergate look like a candy store heist."

"I thought maybe in another state. Vegas, for instance?"

"I don't know what you're talking about," said Greco, confused.

"I'm asking one more time if you can get down a large bet," Thorne said.

"I guess so. I know some bookies back east, Jersey mostly, who used to help me lay off. They're not mainstream mob guys, 'cause back there, the big families are all into importing smack from the Sicilians. So, yeah, these people I know would take my action."

Thorne checked his watch. It was noon sharp. McCaskey was nothing if not punctual. Time to move.

"Come with me," he said.

Thorne saw his car in the lot behind the bathhouse, MaryAgnes McCaskey waiting inside. Greco stood on the wet grass as Thorne approached her and watched the window roll down slowly.

"Could you get it?" he asked.

"Right here," she said, handing him the envelope. "Our access clearance ran through the end of the week."

Thorne ripped open the envelope.

"Selections for the weekend and Monday night," he read.

"The Justice Department was two-for-two yesterday," McCaskey said. "I checked."

"Thanks. I know this wasn't easy for you."

"Maybe you'll start sleeping now," she said dryly. "Maybe you'll understand I care about you after all."

Thorne watched her pull away and head for Lake Shore Drive. He and Greco walked to the beach.

"I'm still in the dark," Greco said. "What the hell you got there?"

"What somebody once called a billion bytes of government computer muscle," Thorne said. "The picks we've been using to beat the pants off you. I'm going to see if there's a five-star winner left for us."

"I knew there had to be more to it than just moving the spreads around," Greco said. "You fucking guys had your own *service* going."

"The spreads were backup," Thorne said. "The computer's where the real action was."

He ran through the print-out of games scheduled for Sunday, Monday night.

"I hope your friends in Jersey still handle the USe-FuL," Thorne said.

"You mean the *Useless*," Greco replied. "Just ask Johnny Roses about that. But, yeah, I can get down on it."

"Your thinking southwest looks like a good omen. The Bureau's cinch-of-the-week is Arizona getting three points at home. Based on their best-play versus the opponent's best-defense matrix, your own government forecasts Arizona to win straight up."

"You know what you're letting me do?" Greco said.

"This ends it," Thorne said absolutely. "It squares everything between us, and you can make a clean break from the family."

"One last shot."

"Your biggest, lastest move," Thorne said. "Go to the window."

"Arizona," Greco repeated. "Well, I've always been a hunch player and Arizona sounds good. Besides, like Pizza Sal says, anybody's stupid they don't bet the dog at home."

"How's he doing anyway?" Thorne asked. "I haven't had time to check with the hospital."

"He escaped the hospital," Greco said.

"He what?"

"Sally calls me the other night from some pad Near North where he's partying with these two Eastern stews he met coming back from Florida—Colleen and somebody else I forget. He told me when the docs got serious about opening up his chest, he decided to say *adios.* 'I escaped right outta there,' he says. 'They took away my clothes and all, but I still got out.'

"Don't ask me how he did it," Greco went on, "but two hours after he walks out of a hospital in Melrose Park wearing nothing but a gown and paper slippers, Pizza Sal's got himself two broads, an ounce of blow, and is having himself a major league party on Clark Street."

"Doing things like that, he'll end up dead," Thorne said.

"I say he'll be doing lines at *our* funerals."

Greco picked up a handful of wet beach sand and let it filter slowly through his fingers.

"So it's Arizona. Underdog at home."

"The Department was two-for-two yesterday," Thorne said. "Their five-star plays have been twenty-two and one on the right side."

"What about you, Thorne? You want me to put you in for a piece?"

"I've got enough problems," Thorne said. "Leaking a winner is one thing. But my bosses decide to stick me on a polygraph and it reads out I've been making private placements, I might wind up in the same dorm with Scarpo and Lowenstein."

"What kind of noise you making about lie detectors?"

Greco might as well hear it now, Thorne decided.

"Seems like that twenty thousand I stuck in your sling wasn't yours after all. Literally, not figuratively," he explained. "The piles of cash got all mixed up on the bed when Massey was making his move. What you got was the Bureau's cash, all recorded serial numbers, so they know it's missing."

"You telling me it's dirty?" Greco was stunned.

"They also know it's hopeless to trace it now. None of it was in sequence," Thorne said. "Just be careful about dropping a bundle in one place."

"*Madonna mia!* You gotta be in trouble."

"I can ride it out," Thorne said. "I've got them

thinking that Massey had a partner at the Stardust Courts who took his cut pronto. Anyway, the Bureau's not going to risk the credibility of my testimony by putting the screws on for twenty dimes, which we stole from you anyway."

"It's still not going to do your career much good," Greco knew.

"I'll probably jump ship as soon as this is over," Thorne said, realizing for the first time it wasn't small talk.

Greco looked out over the lake as Thorne lit a match and put it to AAG Bidwell's print-out. It turned black in seconds and disintegrated into the green surf.

"What's a guy like you going to do without his badge?" Greco asked.

"Soon as I know I'll tell you," Thorne said. "I'm an old sailor, you know. I've always had this idea about running a charter service down in the islands. Maybe now that the Marines are out of Grenada and they're looking for new blood . . ."

"What about your partner? I thought you two had something going besides being cops."

"Soon as I know I'll tell you," Thorne said again.

"Ah, broads," Greco sighed. "I'm gonna lay low myself. Too many Dianes out there."

"She gave me a message for you," Thorne said. "Stopped me on the way out of her arraignment, when the judge wanted fifty-thousand cash bond because of the Walther the cops found in the motel room."

"What'd Diane say?"

"She said for you to get fucked, to rot in hell forever, I forget the rest."

"Yeah, that sounds about right."

Thorne looked down at his watch.

"You'd better take off for a phone if you're going to catch the Arizona game."

Greco faced Thorne squarely, stammered for a second and held out his left hand.

"To Italians the left hand's an insult," he said. "It's *sinistra*. Sinister. But with this sling, it's the best I can do. Thanks."

"Bring home a winner," Thorne said.

"You too, pal. Call me when you find work."

Thorne threw his shaving gear into the suitcase, gathered his half-dozen shirts from MaryAgnes McCaskey's closet and packed them inexpertly in a crumpled ball.

"There's a little Scotch left," MaryAgnes said as he came out of the bedroom. "Suppose we have one for the road."

Thorne sat down and rolled the frosty glass in his hand. When MaryAgnes went into the icebox for her bottle of chablis, he turned on the television without volume.

"Have you ever considered quitting the Bureau?" Thorne asked. "Trying something else?"

"Not really," she replied, quickly enough to let Thorne know it hadn't entered her mind at all. "Why do you ask?"

"No reason."

"Are *you* thinking about it?"

"I've never stopped," he said, "from the day I signed on."

"Only more so now," MaryAgnes guessed. She stood in front of him, her glass extended for a toast. "If you ever opened up to me, I wonder if I'd still recognize you? Or like you?"

"Maybe some day you'll find out. Cheers."

"Cheers," she said back. "To us both finding what we want, even if it ends up being each other. God help us."

MaryAgnes sat down beside him and gave him a long erotic kiss that was out of context with all she'd said since Thorne had asked her to open up Bidwell's magic prognostication machine.

"I'll miss you."

"I'll miss you too," Thorne answered automatically.

Before he knew quite what was happening, Thorne found himself back in MaryAgnes' bed.

Unlike their morning lovemaking, this time Thorne knew exactly what her frenzied movements meant: It was good-bye. One for old time's sake. Let's both make it good.

She mounted him determinedly, sliding down over him, moving her hips in circular rhythms; her head bent back, her eyes closed.

Thorne lifted his body to meet hers, slid a bit to the right as he brought down his hips. He could barely make out the TV screen: the clock frozen at two minutes, the scoreboard saying Arizona was deadlocked with Jacksonville, 28-all.

He slid over another inch, trying to see who had possession. It was just enough to make MaryAgnes straighten her head and look down at him. She also knew enough to peer over her left shoulder.

"You rotten son-of-a-bitch!" she screamed. "You're watching a football game!"

"Me?" Thorne said, pulling her face into the crease between his neck and shoulder, rubbing her spine with his fingertips.

"Me? Not a chance!"

MaryAgnes McCaskey made a strange noise burrowing against Thorne's flesh.

It sounded almost like laughter.

ABOUT THE AUTHOR

Richard Martins was born in New Jersey and is a 1963 graduate of Rutgers University. He has worked as a journalist, public relations executive, and corporate speech writer. An inveterate city dweller, Martins currently lives in Chicago with his wife, Ellen Soeteber, and three cats too many. *The Cinch* is his first novel.